There had never been any doubt about who killed Christine. Her killer had left a message on the wall beside the bed, two words sketched in Christine's blood: LOOK JOE.

The room was thick with flying insects, in the air, on Christine, on the bloodsoak. They were a black swarm spelling out Joe's name on the wall. His instinct was to move, but he wanted to know what the Caller wanted him to see; what he was supposed to find when he looked at Christine.

\*

*Christ, I feel good, Joe. I feel so good I could kick down walls, I could tear up trees. It's remembering Christine, Joe, that's what's making me feel this way. I looked at her, Joe, I looked at her so closely, and I watched her go, I watched her all the way. I watched her change.*

*Change.*

*Oh, I want to talk to you, Joe. We really need to talk. This is alive, Joe; this is what alive feels like.*

\*

*Joe said, 'We'll get him, Paddy,' and heard the hollowness in it.* LOOK JOE.

Jack Curtis is the author of five previous thrillers which have been translated into fourteen languages. Born in Devonshire, he now divides his time between London and a remote valley in the West Country.

*Jack Curtis*

# THE CONFESSOR

**ORION**

An Orion paperback

First published in Great Britain by Orion in 1997
This paperback edition published in 1997 by Orion Books Ltd,
Orion House, 5 Upper St Martin's Lane, London WC2H 9EA

A CIP catalogue record for this book
is available from the British Library.

ISBN: 0 75280 870 2

Typeset by Deltatype Ltd, Birkenhead, Merseyside

Printed and bound in Great Britain by
Clays Ltd, St Ives plc

*To Victor Thorne*

# *Acknowledgements*

I called on the help of a number of people while writing this book, and my thanks go to all of them, but most particularly to Dave Cook, David Protheroe and Ian West.

# One

The call came in on a Wednesday. It was only the third day of the heatwave and people were wondering if it would hold up through the weekend. A big rotating fan stood on the floor close to the women taking the police and emergency calls. They sat in a row to answer the calls, and the false breeze lifted strands of their hair in turn; in turn it cooled one side of their faces.

Janice Colby picked him up. She crooked her finger to clear a blown hank of hair from her mouth and asked which police station he was calling.

'It doesn't matter.'

'What is the nature of your enquiry?'

'To report a crime.'

'Is this a serious crime?'

'Yes.'

'Do you wish to speak to an officer in CID?'

'It doesn't matter.'

'What is your name and address?'

'Put me through to someone.'

'Could I have your name and –'

'Put me through. Put me through to someone. Put me through now.'

Janice connected the call to the CID office at Fellgate Cross where it was picked up by Detective Inspector Joseph Morgan who was still suffering the stomach-head combination of a bad hangover. He sat with his face in his hands as a rod of pain went from his gut, lapped in acid, then up through his gullet to rattle his teeth before it climbed like a bolt to his brain. Joe had done everything you have to do to feel that way, but even so he didn't believe he deserved it. He was scheduled to make a follow-up visit to a break-in report on the Hartsmede Estate but the heat and the hangover made him shaky on his feet and he was stealing some recovery time. That's why it was Joe who lifted the phone and gave his name. It was chance, or it was bad luck, or it was written in the stars.

He heard someone say: 'I want to report a murder.'

Joe's eyes had remained closed; now they opened. He said, 'Your name –?'

'I don't want to say it.'

'You have to say it.'

The Caller chided him. 'No I don't.'

'I need your name.' Joe looked round as if for backup. He was on his own in the room. Other phones on other desks looked innocent and dormant.

'Do you want to hear about this or not?'

'Go on …'

'Someone was murdered. An old man.'

The Caller's voice was light and unhurried; it bore the trace of an accent, something musical that might have been West Country or Welsh.

'Okay. What was *his* name?'

'I'll tell you that another time.'

Behind the Caller's voice was a low rush of noise, like surf, that Joe knew to be the sound of traffic. He laughed. 'Sorry. This is a joke, am I right?'

'It's not a joke.'

'I'll need some more details.'

'Another time.'

'Why are you talking to me? You say you've called in to report a murder. You won't say who you are, you won't tell me the identity of the victim –'

2

'Another time.'

'How do you come to know about this murder?'

'How do you think?' There was a little pause, as if between people who knew each other well and spoke often and had run out of things to say. 'DI Morgan.'

'Yes?'

'Detective Inspector Morgan.'

'Yes?'

'What's your name?'

'You've already –'

'Your given name ...'

A fan ticked over on another desk. It was standing close to a computer screen carrying columns of data, and the lines appeared to shift and waver as if stirred by the whirring blades. The screen on Joe's desk was blank apart from Joe's own shadowy reflection. A narrow face, the angles not as taut as they had once been now Joe was in his late thirties. Broad brow, thin nose, mouth a little too wide to be in proportion, though it made the nose seem less severe. His hair was brown and worn long, cut to the nape of his neck, and he'd developed a habit of sweeping it back with stiff fingers. The reflection was monochrome and lacking in detail, but you could see lines of stress in it.

'What?'

'You know. First name, Christian name.'

'Joseph.'

'Do your friends call you Joe?'

'You're wasting my time.'

'Okay, Joe.'

Hartsmede, deer meadow, the pasture of the deer.

'Look at this fucking place.' Gerry Tobin stirred in his seat as they drove onto the estate. He was peeling the legs of his trousers off damp thighs. Detective Sergeant Tobin was six feet four and carrying too much weight, like a ring-rusty

3

boxer. His sandy hair was cut aggressively short. 'Jesus Christ, look at it.'

It was a long time since Hartsmede had seen a deer, or pasture, or even a blade of grass. Five slab-built towers each twelve storeys high, concrete walkways reeking of piss, tongues of rust scarring the frontage, broken windows everywhere. A wooden carousel and a rope climbing frame were set in a fenced-off patch of dry dust thick with dogshit and broken syringes. Whoever named the place had possessed a grim sense of humour.

They drove past an arcade of shops, some boarded up, some open for trade; those still doing business carried mesh grilles over their windows. Concrete arches formed a colonnade lurid with graffiti. At night, the arches, the walkways, the fouled spaces, were no man's land. Someone from Fellgate Cross made a visit here pretty much every day; it was crime-rich, as if ley-lines of violence and greed and madness crossed and recrossed the place to make a black cat's-cradle of statistics.

Joe got out of the car, watching a group of young men who sat on a low wall and watched back. Gerry slammed his door with a great sweeping gesture, like someone hitting a tennis forehand. 'Look at them. Pockets crammed with crack and other people's money.'

'You're right. Let's stroll over and arrest the bastards.'

Gerry laughed. 'You do that. I'll go and see the old lady.'

They entered the third block and didn't even bother to check the lift. The graffiti artist here was called Zac; he'd tagged every wall, every door, every ceiling, every step of the stairway.

'Fuck's that?' Gerry asked.

'What?'

Gerry sniffed like a pointer. A miasma rose in the stairwell, rich and noxious.

'Bad bowels and bad intentions,' Joe told him. 'What floor are we on?'

'Christ knows. Feels like fifty-eight.'

Heels came clatter-clatter down towards them and a girl of about eighteen rounded the corner. It was just past eleven in the morning and she was dressed for a party. She went between them and showed her teeth and said, 'Fucking filth', as she reached the lower landing. Gerry Tobin paused in his stride, but Joe took his arm.

'You've heard that before.'

Gerry stopped for a breather. He was feeling the climb. 'Yeah. I never liked it though.'

Joe laughed at the wryness. 'Is this eight? Are we on eight?'

They found the flat, its door graffitied with *HEDS* in pink and mauve. Raw new planking was nailed onto the fore-edge where the lock had been kicked off.

There were three armies on Hartsmede: North End, The Brokers and Hed Bangers Inc. Nesta Burbage lived in the heart of Hed territory. She moved around the shabby interior of her apartment like someone on patrol, her small, wrinkled features intent, a little frown clouding her brow. She was seventy-five and weighed eight stone. *A punch would break her bones*, Joe thought. He walked with her, while Gerry took notes. Joe and the old lady could be heard all over the flat; it was very small.

'I was here when he come in,' she said, 'but he never touched me. I were in bed. He took my rings. I didn't have them on. He broke some stuff, but there wasn't nothing to take except my rings. He never touched me.'

There was a heavy smell in the place that Joe was trying hard to identify. It reminded him of something in his own past.

'I don't know what time it was, perhaps two o'clock, I don't know. I woke up and he were in the room with me,

5

but he never touched me. Middle of the night ... I were shaking. It still makes me shake just to think of it. There's no one I can go to.'

They went from room to room as Joe took descriptions of the rings and a description of the man which added up to medium everything wearing a ski mask. The whole place was fiercely neat: nothing left out that ought to have been put away; fussy, cheap ornaments arranged precisely on shelves or tables. The bathroom carpet bore a film of white and the same smell thickened the air.

Joe told Nesta to expect someone who would dust for fingerprints. She nodded her neat little crab-apple face. He asked her if she felt that counselling would help, but she didn't want to hear.

Gerry opened the window of the car and lodged his arm outside to get a breeze into his shirt. 'Just another one,' he said. 'Just another SOC.'

'That's right.' But Joe wanted to say: *Is that right? Just another one to add to the list? Is that the best we can do?*

'Torch the whole fucking issue,' Gerry suggested. 'Nuke Hartsmede, that's my offer.'

The wind circling the interior of the car was hot and had a meaty smell.

'Round the bastards up, ship them out, napalm the whole fucking estate. Bring it to the ground. Ash and bits of scrap metal. Definitely.' Suddenly Gerry sounded genuinely angry, a bite of ill temper to his voice.

'What about Nesta?'

'Weed out some of them, the few decent ones, yeah ...'

'And the rest?'

'Fuck, I dunno. Nuke them too if you like.'

'That's your plan, is it?'

Gerry looked at Joe for a moment, as if he were seeing a new face in the car, then his tone turned boisterous; he let out a series of great, bounding laughs and punched Joe on the upper arm.

'You fucking a social worker, or what?' Joe smiled. The punch had hurt. Gerry liked taking risks with rank. His promotion had been a long time coming and he was sour about it.

'Clear them out: it's the only way. Things have gone too far, you know? Half-measures won't do it.' He glared out at the bleak view. They were driving out of the estate through North End territory – a fact proclaimed by massive graffiti painted in black and red on the blind end of one of the tower blocks.

They passed a row of slab-built garages, their rollover doors battered and bent; three gutted cars; a clump of plane trees, ragged and dusty, their roots pushing up tarmac. Joe drove in silence. He was thinking of his wife, Connie, who that morning had wondered aloud whether a divorce might be the best solution.

There were two messages on Joe's desk, both taken by DC Frank Potter. He had a florid handwriting style, loops tangling with loops. The first said: *A guy called, said you'd spoken this morning, he'd call back. No name.* The second said: *Same guy as before. Will call again.*

Joe wrote a report on Nesta saying no progress and showed it to Gerry Tobin, who said: 'Yeah. That's what happened. Nothing.'

A sudden rush of recollection swamped Joe's senses. He asked, 'Did you notice that smell in her place?'

'Smell?' Tobin grimaced. 'The whole fucking estate smells. It smells like a lavatory where someone's been cooking fish.'

'On her,' Joe said. 'Coming off her.'

'Perfume,' Gerry agreed. 'Yeah. Heavy smell, like flowers.'

'No,' Joe told him. 'It was talcum powder. The bathroom carpet was covered in it.'

'She'd taken a bath.'

'It was so strong. She must have been coated in the stuff.'

'What?' Gerry was trying to read Joe's thought.

'She was caked in it.'

A pause while they both backtracked to the crapulous estate, the dowdy flat, Nesta walking from room to room like someone marking boundaries, the cloying odour of 'lilies of the valley'.

'You think she was raped?'

'Yes, I do.'

*He never touched me. He took my rings, but he never touched me. I woke up and he were in the room, but he never touched me.*

'Send a counsellor,' Gerry said.

'Sure,' Joe nodded. 'I'll send a counsellor.' Then: 'She'll never tell anyone. She would never press charges.'

Gerry walked away from Joe's desk, laughing as he went. 'That's okay then – because we'll never find the shitehawk who did her.' He sat in his own chair and lifted the phone on its first ring. 'As you know.'

The call wasn't for Tobin, it was for Joe.

The Caller's voice was soft, scarcely above a whisper. 'I could tell you where. Where to find the body.'

'There's no body,' Joe said. 'You haven't murdered anyone ...' Tobin glanced up. Joe offered him a shrug and he looked away again. '... but you obviously want to have fun, so listen – there are hundreds of police stations in the Greater London area so why don't you make a list and start from the top? Just remember you've already done this one. Okay?'

As before, that steady roar like an undertow – lines of traffic pouring into the city, pouring out.

'An old man. I cut his throat. There was a lot of blood. I wouldn't expect old people to have that much blood in them, would you, Joe?'

8

'Hadn't thought about it.'

'And he kept breathing. He kept breathing for an incredibly long time.' Something about that knowledge made Joe hesitate. The voice said, 'It makes you think, Joe. Doesn't it make you think?'

Joe kept quiet. He waited for more. After a moment he heard a soft click and then he listened to the dialling tone for a few seconds. Tobin went past on his way to fetch a coffee. He asked, 'What body? Who hasn't murdered who?'

Joe shook his head. 'Someone having fun.'

The calls continued for three days. Joe applied to SO11 for permission to record them. The Caller introduced a little variety, twice telling Joe to go to a certain location at a certain time to collect vital evidence. Joe went, the first time with Tobin, the second time alone, but no one approached him and there was no evidence to be found. After that, the calls stopped. After a week, Joe no longer thought about them. One of the things that helped him to forget was a sudden blip in the black statistics in his area. Hot weather, hot tempers. A waiter took a bottle to an impatient customer; a husband threw his wife out of a bedroom window; one driver used his bull bars to ram another, going back and forth a dozen times or more, so that the victim had to be cut from his car.

Then there was Connie's unhappiness: another thing on Joe's mind. Sometimes it irritated him, sometimes made him afraid. He'd tried to talk to her about it, but her method of avoiding that was to blame herself. 'I don't know what it is. It's nothing you've done. Leave me to work it out.'

Joe was beginning to hear the missing phrase in that remark: 'Leave me to work it out *on my own.*'

Joe would have liked someone else to talk to, but the people in his life were few. He was the only child of a late marriage and his parents had died within a few months of

9

each other when Joe was in his early twenties. Joe's father had owned a small electrical goods shop; his mother had been the book-keeper. They worked hard, passed the time of day with customers, and kept their own company; in Joe's recollection, it was a relationship that seemed distantly polite. They met up with relatives only at weddings and funerals. It was as if simple fondness had been bred out of them.

Other people might have called a friend – someone to get drunk with; someone whose ear you could bend; someone who'd offer good advice and not mind when it was ignored. Most policemen have policemen friends. Joe had colleagues. His parents' guarded life had taught him to travel light.

Just before noon on the twelfth day Joe emptied half a cup of coffee over a sheaf of reports; in the same moment the phone rang. He mopped with one hand and lifted the phone with the other.

The Caller said, 'I will tell you, Joe, I promise. I will tell you where to find him.'

# *Two*

Connie Morgan walked twice round the gallery, travel-ling clockwise with the sun, the direction of good fortune. She wasn't thinking of that, not really, but instinct might have led her; instinct, and the fact that the paintings on exhibition were all Italian landscapes, energetic, near-abstract canvases carrying great planes of hard-edged sky and burnt earth, with deep-green verticals that were the cypresses of the south. It was mid-afternoon and Connie was the only person there apart from an emaciated girl with sashcord hair who handed out catalogues and took calls from her friends.

Heat in the canvases, heat outside in the streets, but air-conditioning chilled the gallery so that Connie felt goose-pimples lifting the hairs on her forearms. She was hoping against hope that he wouldn't come. She was hoping he'd forgotten, or thought better of it, or never meant it in the first place.

*I'd like to see you again. Is that possible? Is there a reason to say no?*

She didn't want to see him, she couldn't run the risk of seeing him, and she turned to leave as he arrived, smiling at her and standing just inside the door, as if waiting for permission to come further. The skinny girl handed him a catalogue without breaking her murmured phone conversa-tion. He stood alongside Connie; together they looked at a canvas that showed a hillside and a distant farmhouse and acres of sky. He touched her arm briefly, then turned to look at her while she continued to look at the picture. Her face was just short of beautiful, but so striking that it made classic lines seem wasteful. Pale skin, dark hair curling loosely over her collar, nose slightly out of true, a tiny, sickle-shaped scar at the corner of her mouth – little, intriguing imperfections. She acknowledged his scrutiny with a half-smile, then moved away towards the far end of the gallery.

'Are you going to buy anything?'

Connie laughed. 'No money.' She had laughed because it was the remark he'd used to pick her up in the same gallery three days earlier; same remark, same response.

'No ... No, I don't think so either. I've seen this sort of work before. It looks new, but it's not.'

'How can you tell?' Connie asked.

He smiled at her wryness. 'Let's get a drink. Let's go somewhere.'

They found a pub on the river and sat at a table on the terrace where they could just catch the outside edge of a breeze. Connie knew that his name was Michael Bianchi, that he knew something about painting, that he drove an old, battered, well preserved Mercedes. She knew nothing else, least of all why she was having a drink with him and watching the early evening light skip and skitter on the full tide. As if in answer to a question she said, 'I'm not free. You ought to know that.'

He picked up her glass and his own, both empty, and said. 'White wine again, or –?'

'Yes,' she said. 'White wine,' and watched him disappear into the pub, knowing that he would simply put the glasses down on the bar and keep going across the crowded pub and through the door and out into the street.

After ten minutes, she got up to leave. In the same moment, he emerged with their drinks, smiling, telling her about the scrum at the bar. After that they sat in silence for a while, until he said: 'I thought it was something like that.'

'I don't know if I can see you again. I don't know why I'm seeing you now.'

He smiled and shook his head. 'No ideas at all?'

'I went to an exhibition of paintings, I don't know why I did that either, it was ... I was passing by and I saw the one that was just splodges but it looked like a field of sunflowers –'

'Was that the one called *Field of Sunflowers*?'

'– and I walked in as if that was where I'd been going all along.'

'You were on the run.'

'Yes. Was it obvious?'

'Only to those who've been on the run themselves.'

'Just about everyone, then.'

Michael laughed. 'I suppose so.'

'The question is: Am I still on the run? Will I stay on the run?'

'Questions, plural.' Martins were screaming and wheeling in close formation over the rooftops then swooping like Stukas towards the water. 'Got any answers?'

'There are lots of women,' she told him. 'And many available.' The sudden hardness in her voice accentuated the flat vowels of a faint south London accent.

*Let him know where I come from*, she thought. *Let him see the difference between us – him with his county drawl and his family money*.

She was guessing, making a stereotype of him, trying to whip up a little aggression, a little dislike, but it wouldn't work.

'I'll bet there are,' he grinned. It was no use. She wanted him and she was on the point of letting him see it. 'So what is it about me?' she asked.

He thought it was her off-centre beauty and her air of restlessness and risk; it was her sexuality, pungent, like

13

something in the air; it was something sad about her, something needful.

To play safe, he said: 'I don't know yet.'

They had one more drink, then walked beside the river for a while, but didn't talk about themselves. When they parted, he touched her arm again, just as he had in the gallery. She looked down and found he was holding a piece of paper with his phone number on it. 'Commit this to memory,' he said, 'then burn it and eat the ashes. If you can still recall it after a week, destiny is on our side. If you can't –' he shrugged '– I'm in the phone book.'

Connie could hear the message machine as she went through the door, a man's voice just finishing his piece: 'Okay, Joe ... Okay?'

The place had been closed up all day. Connie went from room to room opening windows. The evening air was still hot, but stirred a little and was easier to breathe.

She stripped and walked naked to the bathroom and stood under a cool shower. She thought of Michael and there came into her mind a remark she'd overheard at her office – two men talking who imagined she was out of earshot: 'I wonder what Connie's like on her back.' It had angered her at the time, but now she wondered whether Michael might have had the same thought and the phrase took on a sudden crude erotic charge that made her shiver.

In the kitchen, wearing a light robe, she poured another glass of wine, sipped, and with that sip realised that she was beginning to get drunk. She walked through into a tiny conservatory and opened a sliding door onto a patio that measured about ten feet by eight. She turned a canvas chair to take the evening sun and sat down to finish her drink.

*Yes*, she thought, *I wonder* ... She closed her eyes, booze-weary, and watched the sun swim up behind the lids in pinpoint explosions of black and red, sunspots and flares. *I wonder what Connie's like on her back. Well, how would I ever know?*

When Joe returned he found her asleep in the chair, face to the setting sun. He returned to the kitchen, called a pizza delivery outfit, found the wine she'd opened and gave himself a glass. She woke when the doorbell rang, looking round dozily then giving a little leap of surprise to find Joe there.

'Pizza,' he said, 'American hot, extra pepperoni, extra chilies, extra anchovies.'

Connie remembered they'd had a row that morning – or was it last night? – but couldn't remember why. She thought it might have been her fault, but knew it didn't really matter; fault wasn't the issue.

As she stepped into the kitchen the phone began. She lifted it and said hello. The voice that replied was light and conversational. 'Is Joe there?'

'Sure.' Connie held the phone away from her mouth as she yelled: 'Joe!'

'Okay.' He was paying for the pizza.

'He's on his way,' she told the Caller.

'Fine. Is that ... you're his wife.'

'Yes.'

'And he told me your name but now I've forgotten. Elizabeth, is it? No, no, I know who Elizabeth is; no, you're –'

'Constance. Connie.'

'Connie, of course. Connie.'

There was a silence on the line that made her feel oddly uncomfortable, as if she were visible to the Caller, standing in her own kitchen, her robe open from the waist. When Joe took the phone from her she rearranged the robe, overlapping right to left, and pulled the belt tight.

'Joe ... You didn't get my message.'

The voice brought a fizz of recognition and alarm that jolted Joe's wrists like electricity. He glanced at Connie. She was fetching plates down from a rack, paying no attention.

'Message. No, I didn't.' As if it were anyone's business he said, 'I just got in.'

'Sorry ...' Connie looked up from opening the pizza. 'There was a message.' She would often join a telephone conversation as if it were three-way, commenting on what she could hear and guessing at the rest. Joe used to find it funny. 'I didn't really have time to tell you.'

'Connie forgot to tell you,' the Caller observed. 'I'll make you a bet, though. I bet she hasn't actually played it back.' He laughed. 'I'm pretty sure of that.'

Joe said, 'Wait a minute,' and put the phone down. To Connie he said, 'Business.'

She nodded like someone who'd heard that before. 'Sure; okay.' She loaded the pizza and the wine bottle onto a tray and took it out to the patio.

Joe went to the bedroom and picked up. 'I'm going to find you,' he said, 'and before I charge you with wasting police time, I'm going to give you one hell of a fucking smack.'

'What are your movements tomorrow, Joe? Busy day?'

'Look, what is it you –?'

'I might give you a call tomorrow, Joe. Tell you where to look. Remember the old man?' A pause, then: 'Did I mention that his name was Daniel?' Another pause. 'Perhaps I'll tell you tomorrow. Tell you where to find him, tell you where to dig him up. Then you'll believe me. Won't you, Joe?'

Neither man spoke for a while. Finally Joe said, 'Okay. You killed a man and you want to tell me where to find his body.'

'Think I want to, Joe. *Think* I want to.'

'Why don't we go there together?'

The Caller laughed. 'Why not? That's an idea. Maybe we should go there together.' His laughter grew, as if acknowledging it as a ludicrous idea.

'You need help,' Joe said. The laughter continued, continued and swelled as Joe's anger swelled. 'You'd be better off dead, wouldn't you?' Joe asked. 'Don't you think you'd be better off dead?'

Now the Caller was laughing as if he didn't know how to stop. He put the phone down on his own laughter. Joe went through to the garden, drank half a glass of wine and cut a slice from the untouched pizza. He looked at Connie.

'I'm not really hungry,' she said.

'Did you pick up a message? That guy's message?'

'No. Heard the tail end of it as I came in. Who is he?'

'Mystery caller. He phoned me earlier; now again.'

'Ah …' She could hear him asking her to be more curious, but the wine was making her heavy and dull. She slipped into a doze and when she woke it was dark.

Dark in the tiny garden, dark as she walked through the kitchen, dark in the hallway, dark as she lay down beside him knowing his eyes were open, like hers, and focused on blackness. She covered his body with hers and lay still, letting him bear her weight.

'I'm sorry,' she said.

'Good start.' His voice was level and low, but she felt the tension in his limbs. He reached round and stroked her back, taking his hands down over her ass then trailing upwards with snaky fingers. 'What is it?'

'I don't know what it is. If I knew, I'd take a pill.'

'Is there a pill for it?'

'I don't think so.'

His fingers walked along her flanks, up over her ribs and shoulder blades, then down her spine, making her shiver.

'Like I got out of bed the wrong side,' she said, 'and parted my hair differently and couldn't fit into my skin.'

'Can I do anything about it?'

'You're doing fine,' she said, 'I love you.'

He said the same thing to her. Neither of them knew quite how true it was.

He ran a finger between her legs and she opened, letting her thighs fall either side of his. After a moment she asked, 'Am I good on my back?'

'What?' She had taken him by surprise and he let out a little hoot.

'Don't laugh. Am I good on my back?'

'Women don't use terms like that.'

'I'm not using a term, I'm asking a question.'

'Terrific.'

'Am I?'

As if to reassure, he wrapped his arms round her waist and turned over, turning her too. All he could see was the moistness of her eyes taking a gleam from the window. Their love-making was slow and familiar. At one point, Connie thought of Michael, wondering how he might be different, his moves surprising, his rhythm strange. Joe was featureless in the dark. She muttered something to him in order to hear his voice and other thoughts vanished. Almost vanished.

He cried out, then he kissed her and she held his head, hard, to kiss him back, their faces damp with sweat, or tears perhaps, or both.


She said, 'Mystery caller ...'

'Yeah, mystery,' his words slow and soft with sleep.

'He knew my name.'

'What?'

'He called me by my name.'

'Yes ...' Suddenly, Joe's senses came back to him on an

indrawn breath, as if someone had brought a needle close to his eye. 'Did you give it?'

'Give my name?'

'Yes.'

'I might have done. I can't be sure. I just seem to remember him calling me Connie.'

'What else did he say?'

'Nothing. Asked for you. No, he did – I did tell him. He thought my name was Elizabeth.' Joe lay still, but it wasn't the stillness of sleep. She could tell he was thinking it through. 'Who is he, Joe?'

'He wants to hand over some information. He's a grass.'

'Is he?'

'I think so. He's got something to sell.'

'Oh …' Believing him, she lost interest and turned on her side in the hope of finding a cool patch on the cotton sheet.

Through the darkness, she heard him say, 'I love you.'

'I know,' she said. 'I know that, Joe. We'll be fine.'

'Will we? This morning you wanted a divorce.'

'This morning I was angry.'

'I could tell.' He gave a laugh that died. 'Angry about what?' She was silent, so he prompted her. 'Exactly what?'

'I don't know.'

'It's your anger. You must know.'

'Yes. But I don't.'

'Is it me?'

'No. No, it's not. Absolutely not. I don't know what it –' She shook her head invisibly. 'I feel black – you know – black moods. I feel itchy and out of sorts.'

'There's nothing I can do, then,' he said.

'I don't know. Honestly, Joe. Hang on?'

'I'll try.'

After Connie was asleep, Joe lay in the darkness with questions still to answer.

*Connie's name. What use to the Caller was that?*

*All policemen are ex-D. How did he get my number? Why me?*

# Three

When the call came through at just after ten the next morning, Joe had Gerry Tobin on one extension and DI Mark Proctor on another. The room bore a smell of stale tobacco, tinny and sour, that would soon be displaced by today's smoke, today's ash, today's scree of butts. Policemen are the last of the really dedicated smokers. Joe was a rarity, but he still inhaled the equivalent of two packs a day. While they were listening, Proctor and Tobin held their cigarettes delicately, as if anxious for the next pull.

The Caller said nothing new. After he rang off, Tobin said, 'The streets are full of crazies. Here's one of them. Painless injections, yeah? They're as good as dead already.'

Proctor drew the coal on his cigarette down half an inch, screwing up his eyes against the smoke. He said, 'Log it. Ignore it. Gerry's right, he's nuts.'

'I know,' Joe said. 'Maybe I should tape it.'

Proctor laughed. 'Tell him to call Gipsy Hill. The guys there haven't got a hell of a lot to do.'

At eleven, the Caller was back on the line. 'You had someone with you, Joe. Am I right?'

'With me?'

'Don't be stupid. Why be stupid?'

'It was just me.'

'Listen, Joe. I only want to speak to you, okay? One person – one – and it's you.'

'Why?'

'Because that's how I feel about it. What I'm telling you is

21

pretty personal, isn't it? Killing people? I don't want an audience, you know? This isn't a show. This isn't a fucking TV show. I'm telling you about important things in my life.'

'Why?'

'Because you picked up the phone.' Joe was trying to read the accent — a lilt to it, so that *phone* sounded a little like *fawn*.

'Anyone could have done that.'

'But it was you.'

Killing people. Killing *people*, was that what he'd said?

'What do you want to tell me?

'Many things. Many things, Joe.'

'You killed someone. You cut his throat. You've told me, now why don't you find someone else to tell? I can give you a list of numbers to call. I'm sure that people will want to hear from you.'

'Joe, listen to me, Joe. Don't be impatient. I'm just outside. I'm calling from a phone booth, it's almost opposite. Come and find me, Joe. Come and find me and I'll tell you the rest. Don't be angry, Joe. Why be angry with me?'

'Because I think you're full of shit.'

Joe could see Tobin at his desk, laughing as he got through some paperwork. His shoulders shook and his head wagged from side to side in a knowing way. Joe hung up the phone. To Tobin he said, 'I think you're full of shit, too,' which made Tobin laugh harder.

Joe shouldered his way out of the room and bought a can of Lilt from a dispenser in the corridor. He punched a code into a wall-mounted security lock and walked past the desk to the door. The uniformed sergeant on the desk was trying to solve a problem for two middle-aged women who were working up to a fine hysteria. They spoke no English. They shouted at the sergeant, then they shouted at each other. The sergeant looked about in desperation.

'What language are they speaking?' He was asking a WPC who was going through carrying a cup of coffee.

'Spanish, isn't it?' she offered. 'Or Greek?'

The sergeant was a friend of Joe's from back when. He turned this way and that while the women mouthed off.

'Joe …' he asked. 'Joe?'

'It's not French,' Joe said. 'Does that help?'

The light in the street was white; the heat was inescapable. Joe went down the short flight of stone steps and started to walk.

Fellgate Cross was a concrete and glass warren, an inner city fortress among streets of poor housing, but also streets of almost-fashionable housing; of glass tower blocks that housed banks and shipping brokers and lawyers' offices and shady import-export firms; of underpasses, arterial roads, shabby back streets, timber yards, good schools, terrifying schools, pubs where you could get a cocktail and pubs where you could get killed. The area ought to have moved up, forcing the poor out as more streets were taken over by those who worked in the tower blocks, but that hadn't happened. The recession had soured things: the poor became poorer and the middle-classes bedded down in what they'd got. Now the bad streets were pretty cleanly divided from the good streets by the Hartsmede Estate.

Joe walked past a display of radios and TVs, a hardware shop, a slot machine arcade, each window giving him back to himself: a man of medium height in chinos and a light green polo shirt, hair a little long, features a little out of proportion, eyes slitted against the city glare. He paused and peered, as if he couldn't quite recognise himself, then leaned against the wall of a print shop to watch four guys working the other side of the main road. One of them was holding a leash out of reach while his dog leaped to grab it, squat body squirming with effort, blunt muzzle snapping at the leather. Finally the dog got a hold. The owner kept the leash high, his bicep popping up to stretch the sleeve of his T-shirt. The dog swung to and fro, jaws locked.

The men laughed, but there was no delight in the sound and their eyes were covering the street. A kid of about fourteen on roller blades came out of an alley to their left. He skated over and made a quick score, then floated off, effortless and smooth on the small wheels. Joe watched while the men made another half-dozen sales. Two were selling, two watching the street. Joe thought he recognised the party-girl who'd said 'Filth' on the stairs leading to Nesta Burbage's apartment.

Joe lobbed his Lilt can at a garbage bin fixed to a lamp-post. It missed by an inch and bounced off the rim into the road. The guy with the dog looked across and saw Joe and held his eyes. Even at that distance Joe could read the message: *It's a war. Cross the road and you're dead meat. So cross the road.*

The other men caught their friend's stillness and followed his gaze as Joe pushed off from the wall and walked to the very edge of the pavement. The men did the same. A truck went past, masking the men from Joe's sight. When it cleared they were still there; they hadn't shifted their gaze.

One of them lifted a hand and pointed at Joe. It meant: *You. I'll remember. Marked man.*

Joe passed the desk. He said, 'There are four guys dealing on Chandler Street, just by the alley that leads through to Hartsmede.'

The sergeant looked up. 'Okay.'

'They saw me.' Joe wasn't sure whether the lob-and-miss he'd made with the soda can was a mistake or a challenge.

'Okay.' A weariness in the response. 'It doesn't make that much of a difference. They'll be gone.' The sergeant's hand went out for the phone, unhurried.

'Was it Spanish or Greek?'

'What?'

'The women.'

'Jesus ...' The sergeant shook his head, as if to say more would be a burden.

Joe went back to the CID office which was full of smoke, just like the air in the street.

'You think he's genuine,' Proctor said.

'I think he may be.'

'Why? He's just pulling your wire, isn't he? How many of these have you had before? How many hundred?'

'I know that.'

'When he gives us a body — that'll be different.' Proctor shrugged. 'Why not tape him if it makes you feel better?'

'It's the way he speaks; the things he says.'

'Something in the way he smiles,' Proctor suggested. 'Don't tell me: it's a hunch.'

'Fuck you,' Joe said.

Proctor laughed. 'It's the weather, Joe. We always get some crazies when it's like this. Heats the blood. How many times has he called?'

'Six. But I only spoke to him three times.'

'Who took the other calls?'

'Frank Potter took two — just messages to say the guy had called. One was on my answerphone at home. Connie took the other.'

Proctor looked surprised. 'At home?'

'Yes.'

'You didn't tell me that.'

'No.'

'How did he —'

Joe's response overlapped the question. 'I've asked myself that.'

'What was on the answerphone?'

'The same stuff.'

'He's targeted you? What? How would he do that?'

25

Suddenly Proctor was interested. 'Someone you nicked ... someone who owes you a bad turn.'

'It's possible. I don't recognise the voice.'

Proctor gave a little grimace that meant, Would you expect to? He asked, 'If so, who?'

'Well, I don't think it's that.'

'No? Okay.' Proctor lit a cigarette, thickening the blue. 'So let me know when you find the body.'

Gerry Tobin came over and stood by Joe's desk. There were fans turning in the room, but Tobin's shirt was wet to the collar with sweat; he was carrying a spare on a wire hanger – making his way to the men's room for a sluice and change.

'I'm gonna die in this heat.' He handed Joe a page torn from a phone pad. 'A follow-up. General store in North Street. Two kids walked in with a sawn-off, took the money and some booze. The manager died.'

'They shot the manager?'

'Heart attack.'

Joe nodded. 'Okay.'

'Give me five minutes,' Tobin said.

During that five minutes, Joe's phone rang. The Caller said, 'Write this down, Joe. Have you got a pen?'

'I'm getting tired of you,' Joe said.

'Write this down.'

The Caller was precise about directions, precise about the location, precise about the name of the dead man: Danny McMahon.

'Know the place, Joe? Think you can find it?'

'Find what? What's there to find?'

'Joe ...' The voice was chiding, amused. 'Come on, come on, Joe...' and he ended the call on a dry little laugh that became the dialling tone.

Tobin called to him from the door. Joe noticed that the

26

man's fresh shirt was already showing dark half-moons under each arm.

In the car, he handed Joe the details he'd taken down in the office. The sheet of paper fluttered madly in the slipstream from the open windows. 'I know these kids,' he said. 'Positive ID. I know this fucking redhead.'

They drove half a mile to North Street and ducked under the tape. Seven eye-witnesses were gathered in the manager's office. Joe and Tobin divided them three and four. Their descriptions were variations on a theme.

Joe told a uniformed officer to arrange a photofit session, then he and Tobin started back to Fellgate Cross. Tobin drove one-handed, smoking greedily with the other. Joe had taken a map of the city out of the door pocket.

'What's that?' Tobin asked, meaning: What are you looking for?

Joe shook his head. 'Nothing,' he said. 'My guess is it's nothing.'

# *Four*

Nothing as bleak as urban wasteland. Nothing as unnatural as this five-acre plot of scrub and bramble and rubble and dusty hawthorn. On one side lay the main line for trains out of London to the west: beyond the line, a little scree of shingle; then a wire and stake fence that went all the way round the waste plot; then a long, broad strip of oil-soaked grass. On the other side, a dual carriageway led out towards the airport. Built alongside it were access roads to car repair workshops, lock-up garages, a derelict pumping station. It was part of the city's hinterland, occupied by the city's scroungers: rats, foxes, kestrels.

The morning had started with a dappled sky, thin veils of cloud drifting across the sun, and the faintest of breezes. By eight o'clock, the breeze had dropped and the cloud had burned off. Members of the Search Team, carrying spades and sweating heavily in overalls and boots, were taking a diagonal course from the lock-ups towards the railway line. They had clambered over a five-bar metal-rung gate and were now waist deep in fern and bramble. Joe watched as they converged on a line of three telegraph poles that had once carried phone wires to the pumping station.

Ted Simpson, the Team Sergeant, sat on the gate and smoked a cigarette like a farm worker taking a break. He said, 'You don't have to be here, Boss.'

Joe nodded. 'I'm curious.'

'We'll call you if we find anything.'

'Give it an hour,' Joe said. 'It's good to get a lungful of this country air.' You could almost hear the haze of pollution crackling above their heads.

An Intercity train rocked by at full speed on the embankment, bringing a foul wind with it, leaving a dead stillness.

'Let's take a look, then.' Simpson ground out his cigarette on the top bar of the gate, hopped down, then started towards the line of poles. Joe followed as if Simpson were blazing him a trail.

Four men in the team. They had covered the ground for about twenty feet in all directions from the middle pole, but the focus of the attention was a tangle of green scrub and a sudden crop of wild lupins.

Simpson picked a small bunch of the flowers and handed it to Joe. He kicked at the tangle of fern and bramble. 'If anything's buried here, it happened a while ago. He didn't give you anything more precise?'

'By the pole,' Joe said. 'Alongside the central pole.'

They taped the area and started to clear the ground.


Connie drove past the address four times. At one end of the street, a low wall, then the river; at the other, a roundabout. She went back and forth like someone on rails. Eventually she parked at the river end and sat in the car for twenty minutes, as if to think things through. In fact, the idea was to not think at all, but that wasn't working. She thought of Joe, which gave her the perfect reason to drive away, and she was glad of it. She turned the ignition key but, after a moment, switched off again. She was surprised by the strength of the impulse that held her there: surprised and impressed and worried. Finally, she got out of the car and walked half-way up the street to Michael's door.

'I'll give you the address,' he'd said on the phone, 'but we could meet anywhere.'

Connie rang the bell. He took a while to come to the door, but he'd told her that would happen.

His apartment was above a boat-house, two rooms both enormous; at least fifty feet by thirty, Connie reckoned. One room was where he lived, the other was where he painted. He guided her into the living area. A glass roof steepled high above their heads, part of it shrouded by blinds, the rest giving a view of wharves, tall chimneys, cranes, endless sky, gulls. Where it was struck by the sun, the glass seemed to dissolve to a white glare. Beyond that was a folding door, open onto his studio. The wall on the river side had four vast windows, making it seem all glass, all light. Twenty or so large canvases were ranged round the studio: abstracts, it seemed, though there might have been human forms and animal forms among the shapes.

Connie turned round twice, then turned again, as if she were playing blind-man's buff. 'You didn't tell me you were a painter.'

'We didn't tell each other anything, did we? What should I know about you?'

'I work in media research.'

'Which means …?'

'It's to do with advertising – the effects of advertising. I'm not …' Connie paused, as if she were thinking about her job for the first time. 'It's not an important job. I make a lot of phone calls; they're all the same – questions, follow-up …' Her voice trailed off. 'It's a job.' She looked at him, suddenly surprised. 'You could be anyone.'

'I suppose I could.'

'I ought to go now,' Connie said. 'I'd better go now.'

'Sure, okay.' Michael walked towards her and touched her arm just as he'd done at the gallery. 'Stay for a drink.'

She nodded, as if the gesture meant less than speech. Michael said, 'White wine, yes?'

He crossed the room to a big galley kitchen ranged against

the far wall; the trip seemed to take him miles away. Connie sat on a chair, looking round the whole time like a cat in a new home. She glanced up and saw gulls drifting against hard, flat planes of blue, their wings like knives.

The Caller sat on the low wall by the river and watched the same birds against the same sky.

Joe, he thought. Joe, oh, Joe, my friend, what is going on in your life? What in hell is happening here? Joe, you ought to know this — I called Connie's office and they told me that she had phoned to say she was ill. A touch of 'flu. Don't you love that? A touch. A *touch* of illness: as if from a dirty finger. But it's not true, Joe. There might be some *touching* going on, might be some *fingering*, but I don't think anyone's ill, Joe. I think everyone's fine. Except you, that is. Except you.

The city was parched. Even here by the river, a dry dust seemed to fall along with the sunlight. The Caller walked back along the street to Connie's blue Fiat and wrote *CALL HOME* in the dust on the rear window. He wrote it in reverse.

Things brought to light, he thought, and gave a chuckle. Danny McMahon emerging piecemeal from the good earth. Connie's little flutter exposed, her timid risk. Some buried impulse …

The Caller went to the boat-house and read the name on the bellpush. *Bianchi*. He continued up the slight hill towards the web of backstreets that would take him to an Underground station, singing softly as he went, a breathy falsetto, each note a true one.

*Oh Danny boy, the pipes, the pipes are calling …*

Ted Simpson pointed to the plot where he'd picked the wild lupins. The scrub had been ripped back, leaving a bare patch about ten feet square. 'There you go,' he said. The ground bore the faintest depression, almost a shadow. 'They don't want it to look like someone's buried there, so they level the earth out – bang it flat with the back of a spade. After a while, it sinks a little: starts to cave in.'

'That's a grave?' Joe asked.

'Yeah, that's a grave. The flowers were the first indicator. Most of the nutrients leached out of this soil a long time ago. There are lupins and poppies scattered here and there, but these were doing particularly well. The undergrowth grass was greener. Did you notice that?'

Two of the search team went back to the equipment van and fetched a tent. The others started to dig, working wide of the lips of the depression, like archaeologists anxious to preserve something fragile, something unique.

Joe watched as Danny McMahon came to light, his face grey and folded, like clay that had collapsed under the potter's hand; his knees drawn up to his chest; his arms folded across in a final gesture of piety.

The search team were laying the soil aside carefully; later it would be sifted for evidence. They worked in silence; experts with a job to do, they looked confident and capable, as if decaying human remains were an everyday find. When they'd gone as far as they could go, they put up the tent.

Joe said, 'Photographer, exhibitions officer, video operator, doctor, forensic ME if one can be found.'

Simpson said, 'Already in hand, Boss.'

A foul miasma rose, filling the tent. Joe got down on his haunches and looked at the husk of Danny McMahon.

# Five

The Caller was excited. Joe would have found the body by now. Poor old Danny, old Danny Boy. And what would he look like now? A worm farm. A bag of blubber. He wondered what Joe had thought as the grave opened up, as old Danny came clear. What a sight. What a stench. What a sudden burden of belief as Joe witnessed the immense truth of what the Caller had told him.

Sceptic! Doubting Thomas! Put your hand into old Danny's wounds. Give that old sack of slime a kick and shout down your unbelief.

It felt strange, to have brought Danny back. Back into the light. It had started with a walk, the day unnaturally hot, unnaturally bright, and noise coming in off the street. The Caller had woken late, the heaviness of a skinful of whisky still on him. He had drunk a lot of water, then shaved with extravagant care and left the house without any real understanding of whether he would turn left or right when he stepped onto the street, or whether he would get much further than the end of the block, or whether he would ever return.

Random walking had brought him to a park, the same park he was sitting in now, the park with a bank of public phones close to the entrance gate. Danny had been on his mind for a while. The Caller didn't feel bad about Danny; didn't feel *guilty*, for Christ's sake. He felt like someone who possessed something rare, something startling, but couldn't show it around or have people admire it.

He had lifted the phone and made the triple nine call without knowing what would come next. The park was full of rollerbladers, cyclists, kids playing ball, lovers lying full length on the grass, eyes closed, touching each other as if no one else were there. The Caller marvelled at it. He could look at their world, just look, but never enter.

The woman who'd answered his call had angered him with her tartness. Another time, he might have hung up, but that day her tone sharpened his purpose.

*Put me through to someone. Put me through now.*

Then Joe Morgan had picked up the phone and the Caller had felt good. Something in the voice of weariness and regret had made him smile. He'd wanted to say, Hey: are things that bad? He'd felt, Here's someone I can talk to, someone I'd like to get to know.

Beside him on the bench was a two-litre bottle of Evian. He brought the neck to his lips and sunlight washed down with the water; it tasted warm and salty, sour in his stomach. Drunk was dangerous, he knew that. Last night, he'd gone cruising. The realisation made him shudder. Driving drunk. Attracting too much attention, maybe, in a couple of late-night clubs. Finally, he'd got past drunkenness, or seemed to, and arrived at a condition where everything was clear, everything had purpose and pattern. He left the last club, shaking off some fairweather friends, and drove the early morning streets with quiet deliberation, as if he were steering from the back seat.

In Queensway he'd picked up a baby blonde who seemed to have been waiting for him all night. They had driven to a quiet square behind a church – chestnut trees in their summer plush stirred by a night wind; innocents sleeping behind open windows; the bright top-floor lights of the city's bruised insomniacs. She'd ducked her head to him and he'd held back the screen of her hair, the better to watch.

How close you are, he'd thought, with the tips of my

fingers brushing your neck, brushing your cheek, brushing your throat. The very tips of my fingers. How close, how close, how *close*.

Joe put in a call to missing persons and found that Danny McMahon wasn't on file. He flipped through the London phone book and found there were eight entries for McMahon, D. Phoning a man to ask whether he's dead is a good way to foul up his day. After making the calls, Joe was left with three uncertainties to be checked later. Without that distinguishing first initial, however, there were better than two hundred entries in the name of McMahon: all possible connections to the dead man. Someone else's job, thought Joe. Someone on the AMIP team.

Almost all murders are investigated by the Area Major Investigation Pool: they move in and take over. A Detective Superintendent who divides his time between the local incident room and AMIP HQ; a Detective Inspector, who runs the show; two or three Detective Sergeants – one of them the Super's bagman; an exhibits officer; a scene of crime officer; some Detective Constables; and some Trainee Investigators – kids on the job who are gaining experience and catch most of the crappy jobs.

Unless the team were lucky enough to be assigned one of the city's five computer suites, then they would also come with a basic card-indexing system. Computers and card-indexes alike would be organised by a team of civilian filing and data clerks, usually young women. Wherever the murder happens, that's where they set up shop.

Danny McMahon's body was found at nine-fifteen that morning; by noon the AMIP team was in place. They took over a space at Fellgate Cross that had once been a storage and records room. It was a semi-basement, with barred windows and hanging neon strips behind frosted glass that must have been in place for twenty-five years. The DI running the team was called Steve Tranter. He and Joe Morgan looked at one another and laughed because they had met in a previous life.

Tranter said, 'Was it you who took the calls?'

'Yes.'

'Notes?'

'There are notes, yes.'

'Good,' Tranter said. He was still wearing a smile. 'Hand them over and stay the fuck out of my face. Get my extension from one of the team. When this joker comes through again, transfer him to me.'

They were standing in the corridor outside the CID room. Tranter shouldered past, making his way towards the underground incident room. Without looking back he added, 'I might need a couple of your DCs.'

Joe let Tranter get almost to the end of the corridor, then followed. They went down two flights of stone stairs, Tranter reading a report, Joe one flight behind. As Tranter got to the bottom, Joe jumped half the final flight; when Tranter turned to the sound, Joe grabbed his man, then turned him and shoved him into a little cul-de-sac between steel filing cabinets and the men's room.

Tranter laughed. His eyes were locked on Joe's, looking for the first narrowing that telegraphs a punch.

'Not on my patch,' Joe told him. 'You don't talk to me like that on my own patch.' Joe raised a finger and pointed at Tranter. 'Remember I told you.'

An even match, you'd have thought: Joe crowned out at five feet ten, a light frame that carried very little extra weight. Tranter was about the same height, but bulkier; there was a slight sag in the jowls and the heaviness of his gut filled his white, short-sleeved shirt so that it bagged down to hide his belt buckle. You'd bet that Tranter could punch his weight, that he could absorb some punishment too, but the smart money would be taking into account the look on Joe's face.

Tranter's laugh faded to a thin smile. 'Notes,' he said. 'Give them to DC Harker.' As he eased past Joe, Tranter ran a gob of saliva back and forth through his front teeth, like a man getting ready to spit.

One painting was blocks of yellow, some the colour of corn, some deeper like old gold, some red-and-ochre like the setting sun. Another was done in degrees of silver, bright columns framing a hollow square that was tarnished and modulating to grey. You could find seven shades between the edge of the canvas and the centre.

Most of the paintings were like that – different shades and tones of a single colour produced in bold slabs using big, positive brushstrokes, with certain areas of the canvas left untouched.

Connie looked at the arrangement of yellows and saw totemic shapes that held the eye, though she couldn't have said at first why they compelled her. She looked harder and deeper at the first canvas, getting past the notion of 'squares or rectangles or strips', and saw a woman sitting naked, arms lifted to tie her yellow hair back; morning sunlight was pouring through the open window.

She looked at the seven different silvers and saw the steel and glass tower blocks of the city, saw a low, sullen sky and a pale curtain of rain drifting across a broad bend of the river.

Michael Bianchi watched her as she scrutinised his work. Tennis shoes, blue jeans, a white T-shirt: she looked beautiful dressed like that; she looked just perfect. He looked away and looked back, sneaking glances as if she were with someone else; a slim profile, dark hair falling in a double wave to her shoulders, the nose very slightly off-centre, the little crescent scar. He could see her puzzling out the paintings and the innocence in her gaze moved him.

He took her wine glass from her and set it down, then tilted her face to the sun and kissed her on the lips. The kiss was so light, and she so dazzled, that it could have been his breath and nothing more that she felt. He put a fingertip to the point of her chin, to the base of her throat; he traced the underside of her breast and held its fullness just fleetingly, so that the memory was stronger than the touch. She was mysterious to him: her off-centre beauty, her quick laughter and sudden, secret, anxieties. He could sense the changes in her, the risks she was taking. There was a desperate energy about her, sometimes, both threatening and erotic.

She said, 'I have to go now.'

'Yes, I know. When will I see you again, Connie?'

'Never. You'll never see me again.'

AMIP had made a formal application to SO-11 for a tape facility on a specific line in the incident room. In addition to that, the line was connected to a trace at BT's Malicious Calls Bureau.

DC George Harker was briefing Joe. He sat in a chair alongside Joe's desk, a fleshy young man in a suit that would have looked classier if he'd filled it less well. His blond hair was centre-parted and a little too long for the effect he wanted. Harker didn't know why he'd been given the job, though he'd been on the receiving end of Tranter's ill-temper and had decided to tread carefully. Some old war between his boss and this DI; some wound that still gave trouble.

'The idea is to give him a number to ring – direct line – so that he doesn't always route through emergency or the station switchboard. You make it sound as if you're providing him with special access. If he comes through direct, we press a designated number on the keyboard and the trace is on automatically. The MCB will have it in a few seconds.' Harker wrote the number of the incident room phone on Joe's pad. 'If you're not here, whoever catches the call will route it through to the incident room and we'll give him the same story.'

Joe smiled at Harker. He said, 'Tell DI Tranter, lots of luck.'

Harker half-returned the smile, then proceeded to read out loud Joe's written profile of the Caller: 'I would place the subject at between twenty and fifty, softly spoken, though this might not be a genuine characteristic. He has a slight accent which could be West Country or Welsh. If West Country, the subject is probably white, though this is based on statistical evidence only.'

'That's right,' Joe confirmed. 'Tell DI Tranter that's about right. Not much, is it?'

'And I've got transcripts of the conversations you've had with him so far.'

'No you haven't,' Joe said. 'You've got rough versions of what I remember.'

'We've sent copies for profiling.'

'Lots of luck to them, too.'

'And I gather that you're writing a report on –'

Joe waved a hand towards the VDU on his desk. 'Daniel McMahon. If that's who he is.'

'There's a doubt?'

'He wasn't carrying ID. Someone phoned and told me there was a body buried in a certain place and that the corpse – in life – was called Danny McMahon. Well, there was a body, and at that exact location, so the assumption I'm making is that the rest of the information was genuine. But who knows? I expect that's what DI Tranter would've said, too.'

Joe's phone rang and Harker waited as if a piece of luck had just come on the line, but walked away when Joe glanced up and shook his head. Tobin was on the far side of the room, sandwiched between two rotating fans, trying to keep his paperwork from becoming airborne. Joe got off the phone and strolled over to him, a man bringing a gift.

'Two kids just caused some havoc at a filling station out beyond the Westway. One of them had red hair.'

'Oh, good.' Tobin trapped his reports under an ashtray the size of a bucket. 'Did the description go any further?'

'Better than that.'

'They're on video.'

'Lovely little performances – lots of shouting, sawn-off waving about like a wind-sock. The tape's on its way, but I don't think we need to bother. One of the uniformed men saw it at the SOC and identified both of them. Richard Lyall and John Decker.'

'Decker's the redhead,' Tobin said. 'Who's going?'

Joe smiled. 'About twenty heavily armed guys and us. We're late.'


The Caller watched as a rollerblade rider banked into a corner, hanging low, arms spread for balance. He watched kids chasing in a circle. He watched the girls in their summer dresses.

What next, Joe? What's our next move? Here's another question: What's *Connie's* next move? It's all so intriguing, Joe. I didn't know I was going to get this involved. I didn't know I was going to become *family*.

Do you have any suspicions, Joe? About Connie? Any intuition, any moments of pause, any *inkling*? Does she make love to you in a different way? Does she suddenly have new friends, friends you've never met? Does she have new interests that keep her out a couple of nights a week? Is there a bracelet she says she bought for herself – just on impulse? In her drawer, silk underwear that she claims to have had 'for ever'? In her pocket a theatre ticket. In her eyes a look you've never seen before?

Women are a problem, Joe. Women can be bitches. I've known a few. Sometime, I'll tell you.

Listen, Joe, here's what I'm going to do. I'm going to keep an eye on Connie for you. Just like a detective, Joe, just like a *sleuth*. Because you're going to be busy. Oh, *shit*, are you going to be busy. I expect Danny is already taking up a good deal of your time – would I be right? Right. But Danny's just a part of it; and Danny's history. I mean, I'd pretty much forgotten about Danny until I decided to give you a call, and one thing led to another, and that old corpse seemed useful, a bit of an offering, a bit of what you might term *evidence*.

No, no, no … Danny isn't as fresh in my mind as someone like Serena.

# Six

You walk into a bar, just looking for a drink, and you know at once that it's the wrong place to be. One guy has just thrown a punch at another guy. You walked in during the space between that first blow and the one that's about to happen: a loaded pause.

Or else you're about to round a corner of the street and you get a sense of heavy air, something thunderous on the other side. What you see is an accident that's just happened. You never heard the sounds of the accident; they were drawn off into a terrible vacuum that hangs just above street level, waiting to be filled by the screams and the bellowed instructions and the blind anger of horns.

When Joe Morgan and Gerry Tobin drove onto the Hartsmede Estate, that pause was what they found. It lay in the stillness of groups of young men sitting on walls or standing by the foul patches of dying grass and garbage that separated the tower blocks. It lay in the arcade of shuttered shops.

Tobin stopped the car close to a marked police vehicle. A uniformed man was standing alongside, his shoulder-radio rasping. Two others sat in the car. Tobin asked, 'What's the story so far?'

The uniformed man looked tense; his eyes were everywhere. 'We came on to the estate about half an hour ago. Decker and Lyall weren't at home. They're here though. The officer in charge decided we ought to have a look round. The natives aren't friendly.'

42

'Your name?'

'Hobbs.'

'I'm DS Tobin. What have you been told to do?'

'Sit tight. Offer no provocation.'

'You're a provocation just being here.'

'I know that, Boss.'

Joe came up on the other side; he was watching five guys stringing themselves out along a high walkway – footsoldiers from the estate's three gangs. The uniform was cut-offs, T-shirts, baseball caps reversed.

Joe asked, 'The officer in charge – who would that be?'

'Inspector Colby.'

'Does he know he's got a problem?'

'He's called up an ARU.'

Joe calculated the odds on one armed response unit holding things down on the Hartsmede Estate that evening and decided they were piss poor. When he looked up again, the five men had become eight.

'What happened to the suspects?' Joe wanted to know.

'They're in there somewhere. We've got men on a house to house.'

Tobin wandered a little way off, as if getting the closest tower block into perspective, then returned. He looked at Joe. 'Guess what?'

Joe nodded. 'I know.' Looking at Hobbs he said, 'You know, too, don't you?'

Hobbs said, 'We're not alone,' and tried for a little laugh.

'That's right.'

Tobin said, 'I expect your boss knows what he's doing, doesn't he?' The wryness was heavy as stone.

It started with a word. The police were on the way out, having decided that Decker and Lyall would keep for another day. A couple of workers from the estate community centre were there, trying to be all things to all men while twenty footsoldiers followed the police towards the street. Ahead of them, twenty more.

After the word came laughter.

After the laughter, a few voices, shouting.

After the shouting, a bottle that curved low out of the crowd, spinning a glitter as it flew; it took a policeman full in the face as he turned to look back.

After the bottle, a howl of delight and fury mixed.

Already, more footsoldiers were crowding the concrete walkways, running along the bleak shopping colonnade, going to vantage points and exit points.

Already, three buses of policemen in full riot gear were converging on Hartsmede along with four TV news units, newspapermen, photographers, rubberneckers, thrill-seekers, troublemakers.

Joe and Gerry Tobin were standing on the street as the riot squad went in. Three petrol bombs went up from somewhere inside the estate, each towing a flicker of flame. Crowds were running between the tower blocks, switching direction like a herd of antelope being coursed by lions. Another busload of policemen crowded the sliproad that branched out to become the estate's road system. Their visors were down and their shields made a carapace.

Tobin said, 'No quarter. I hope someone told them that.'

'That would be your policy, would it?'

'Decker and Lyall are in there somewhere. They saunter into a filling station and shove a gun in some poor bastard's face. We come down here to arrest them and we're treated like the fucking Gestapo.'

'Simple minds,' Joe told him, 'simple solutions.'

'Yeah …' Tobin's response meant: Fuck you. It sounded that way, too.

Joe decided to pull rank. He said, 'You write the report. I'm going home.' Which is what might have happened if

John Decker hadn't come over a side wall and hit the street running.

Entire streets had been taped off on both sides of the estate, holding back traffic and pedestrians. Between the tapes were police vehicles and personnel, fire engines, ambulances. Decker crossed the street at a sprint, splitting a group of firefighters who were offloading equipment. None of the men made any real attempt to stop him because he was holding the sawn-off shotgun he'd used in the filling station robbery.

Tobin gave a yell. He was in action before Decker had gained the far side of the street, but was following his man from a thirty-yard handicap. Joe started after Tobin, paused as if there might be a better idea, then kept running. The three of them went in line down a side street, terraced houses on one side, a wall just above head height on the other. Decker swerved and leapt at the wall, getting a fingertip hold on the top and kicking his way up the brickwork until he could get astride and drop on the other side.

Joe saw Tobin follow, but had no idea how that could have happened. In theory the man was too heavy to throw a leg over a bike, let alone a seven-foot wall. He sat for a moment atop the wall looking to see which direction Decker had taken, then dropped out of sight. Joe increased his stride, jumped, and got a handhold. When he lifted himself over, he could see a play area with swings and a slide and a wooden menagerie on rocker-springs. Further off was a pitch for basketball and five-a-side. The games area was surrounded by a chain-link fence, the gates fixed with a padlock. Decker was running back and forth looking for somewhere to go but it was a lost cause.

Tobin was walking towards Decker, unhurried. Eventually, he stopped, some thirty feet away, and stood still. Joe dropped down from the wall, but didn't catch Decker's eye. Tobin heard him, though, and extended an arm backwards, fingers spread, meaning: Stay back. Joe looked beyond him to Decker; he was seventeen, perhaps younger, and you might have expected to see fear on his face, but there was no trace of that. Just hatred and hard defiance. He was holding the gun so that it pointed at Tobin's gut.

From the direction of the Hartsmede Estate came the sounds of sirens and yells and engines and the small detonations of petrol bombs; but when Decker's back rattled the chain-link fence the noise seemed to ring in the air for a long time.

Tobin said, 'Put down the shooter, sunbeam.' He took a step forward. 'Okay? Let's put it down. Nothing bad's happened yet. Put the safety on, lay the gun on the ground and kick it away.'

Another step forward – not to gain ground by stealth so much as to make a statement: I'm coming forward, you're going nowhere, resign yourself to that. The boy lifted the barrels of the gun slightly, so that they lined up with Tobin's chest.

Joe was thinking, *Don't stand off too far; don't get too close too soon.*

Tobin was thinking, *As soon as that gun's on the other side of me, I'm gonna kick the living shit out of this little bastard.*

What the boy was thinking was anyone's guess until he brought the gun up to his shoulder like someone on a duck shoot and let go with both barrels, taking Tobin in the chest and throat and throwing him back like a bale off a truck.

When Joe fell on him, Decker's hand was in his pocket feeling for a reload. He swung the gun at Joe's head, managing a glancing blow that was enough to knock Joe sideways. One cartridge went home, but Joe was upright before Decker could close the breech. He half turned and took Decker in the throat with his bent elbow, not finding quite the right spot but getting close enough to disable his man. Decker's shoulders hit the fence. His hands were wrapped round his own throat and he was choking like someone with a fishbone across the gullet.

Joe turned him and cuffed him through the mesh fence and went over to Tobin. What he saw was a red mess with Tobin's eyes somewhere in the middle of it. The blast had taken out a large area of flesh from the man's jaw to his sternum. His throat was laid open and working wetly.

Tobin's eyes watched as Joe made a call on his mobile phone. They watched as Joe knelt beside him, his face blank, because blankness was the only alternative to revulsion. Tobin's body was utterly still apart from the grisly movement of his throat, red bubbles welling and bursting with each exhaled breath.

Joe said, 'They're on their way, Gerry.' He said, 'You'll be fine. Don't worry. It's okay, it's okay, they'll be here soon, you'll be fine.' He kept saying things like that as the light slowly drained from Tobin's eyes, until they seemed oddly opaque and brittle and took on a yellow tinge like shellac.

Tobin didn't move when he died, or make a sound, but his body seemed to grow more still. A short way off, the sounds of the riot on Hartsmede swelled and thinned like blown smoke. Decker was leaning on the cuffs in order to gaze at Tobin's body.

He said, 'He's dead, yeah? I killed him.'

'Shut up,' Joe said.

'Jesus, I really killed him.' Decker's voice was moving towards laughter.

'Shut the *fuck* up,' Joe told him. He got up and stood a little way off, guarding both the living and the dead, as the row of sirens grew louder.

He was asleep in the tiny garden when Connie found him. His breathing, long and heavy, was like that of someone drugged. The last of daylight had gone from the sky, and there was only the contrast of blues that followed the setting sun: deep and fathomless to the east, a brittle aquamarine to the west; that, and the false light of the city like a distant fire.

The moon was up, a clear three-quarter, and Connie could count nine stars. A childhood rhyme came into her mind, and the rhyme brought a tear, and the tear brought an angry shake of the head and a silent sneer. She wanted to cry, but she wanted a better reason than that.

She sat with him for an hour or so, then went into the kitchen when she felt the strong need of a drink. She took vodka from the freezer and poured a big splash over ice and filled the glass with orange juice. It was like a sudden hunger; she took a large sip before putting the bottle back, then had second thoughts and topped her glass up again. When she turned, Joe was with her in the kitchen.

He said, 'That's what I meant to do.'

Connie found another glass and made him a drink. 'What happened?' she asked. It was plain in his face.

'Gerry Tobin got shot.'

'Jesus. Is he hurt? I mean —'

'He's dead.'

'Dead.' She said the word as if trying to puzzle out what it might mean in the case of Gerry Tobin.

'There was a riot on Hartsmede —'

'There ... what?'

'The locals went in after a couple of boys who'd done a filling station. Silly, but that's what they did. One thing led to another. Gerry and I were chasing one of the holdup artists. He had a shotgun.'

'Joe ...' Connie stepped towards him, then paused. Just as there was no right thing to say, so there was no right thing to do. She asked, 'Are you all right?'

'I was with him. I caught the kid, then I waited with Gerry while he died. I didn't really like him that much, you know? Where have you been?'

48

He asked the question suddenly, seamlessly, as if it were something he'd been saving.

'To a movie with Marianne.'

'Any good?'

'A comedy. English.'

'Bad luck.' He took a long pull on his drink, then puckered his face and shuddered. 'Fuck of a lot of vodka.'

'Have some more.'

'I think I will.'

They were playing a game called 'light banter in the face of life's blacker moments', and they were playing it because it had worked before. They had used it when Connie miscarried because the loss had threatened to overwhelm them. They had used it when Connie's father died and her grief was so great and so complicated that it seemed to call for a language she hadn't learned. It worked, but it was heartless.

They went to bed and lay like statues, not sleeping, not touching, listening to the sounds of the city: cars in the street, the drone of a night-flight coming in illegally late, a songbird duped by the streetlights; and somewhere, far off, a low hum, like a dynamo that never shut down.

Much later, more than an hour later, Connie drank down the tumbler of water she'd taken to bed and went through to the kitchen to fetch another. She thought she had seen Joe's eyes watching her as she moved, naked, through the bedroom's near-dark – the glisten of his eyes – though his head didn't move.

She squinted as she put the light on in the kitchen. She opened the door of the refrigerator and the desire to cry was suddenly on her, stronger than ever. She stood holding the fridge door as if for support, head bowed, and wept silently, heavy tears falling straight from her eyes onto her naked breasts. She wanted to howl and the effort of not doing that made her body shake. The fridge's man-made winter flowed out and chilled her where she stood.

She went back to bed and Joe hadn't shifted his position. It was too dark to be sure, but she imagined his eyes tracking her as she moved round the bed and put her water down. She wondered how much he'd heard of her grief.

Connie lay down as if trying not to disturb the dust. 'I'm sorry about Gerry,' she said. 'I'm sorry it happened,' but she was saying it to a sleeping man.

Like Connie, the Caller lay awake. The woman beside him slept like a child: deeply, and caught up in her dreams. She was lying on her side, her back to him and one leg drawn up, so that her haunch was a full globe from hip to cleft. The night was so hot that her skin carried a film of sweat, soft as the bloom of dew on unpicked fruit.

The Caller dipped his head and put out his tongue, taking a line of moisture from her rump and wetting his lips with it like some thirsty night insect. He watched the rise and fall of her waist as she breathed, and thought: *How strange the difference ... this slight motion, or else utter stillness. This flicker, this almost imperceptible rise and fall, means 'alive'. Stillness means 'dead'. Just that. The only change.*

Later, there are other changes, of course. He knew about decay. But in that moment, in that instant, the only difference was this tiny movement that he could measure with the flat of his hand as he held it just a tad, just a lick above her body, the swell of breath bringing her flesh up to his touch, the loss of breath making it fall away.

An inch; perhaps, less than an inch. All life was in that fraction.

Joe, he thought, ah, Joe. You couldn't find it in Danny, could you? Find the difference? No. Not in that jumble of hair and old leather.

But Serena ...

# Seven

Joe was on the Hartsmede Estate taking follow-up statements. The Caller was told that DI Morgan wasn't available and maybe he'd like to leave a message. He hung up.

Hartsmede was like a battlefield that had been cleared of its dead and wounded; there was a terrible silence in the air, the silence of shock. Half the apartments on the ground floors of the tower blocks had been burned out: the battle had left refugees along with its other casualties.

There was a heavy police presence on the estate, but Joe knew that he was walking through the calm that follows conflict. *And precedes it*, he thought. Throughout the day, reinforcements would appear: armoured vehicles carrying riot police, members of SO-19, the tactical firearms unit, traffic units, tactical analysts, siege experts, all parking in nearby streets and waiting for darkness to fall.

If they got through the night, fine. If they got through the following night, well, maybe they could relax a little. A week would make them feel secure – a week without incident. Until the next time.

The list of battle looked like this: one policeman dead, killed by a double blast from a sawn-off shotgun. Sixty officers injured, many suffering concussion or cuts caused by bottles. Three of these were badly burned, and ten less severely, when a petrol bomb had fallen flush into an advancing line of men. Twelve were suffering the effects of beatings; one of them was still in a local ITC unit. He had been part of a rout, men running back full tilt along one of the upper landings, when he'd fallen. The estate's footsoldiers had swarmed on him like predators. By the time some of his colleagues had got back to him, using batons and tear gas, he'd been beaten with staves and baseball bats and iron rods and taken more kicks than anyone could count. In time, he was likely to be the second police fatality.

From the estate, five were dead: three heart attacks, one suicide, and a guy who had fallen from a high walkway, dying on impact. The suicide was Nesta Burbage, who had shut herself into a cupboard at the back of her apartment. The cupboard held brooms, tins of polish, carefully folded plastic grocery bags, Nesta's winter raincoat, a bucket and floor mop, and piles of free newspapers. There was just enough room for Nesta.

It had seemed to her that she'd stayed there all night in the dark, in the musty, stifling heat, but still the noises hadn't stopped – the shouts and screams, the cursing and crashing. Bodies had slammed into her front door and she'd heard the glass go. Eventually, Nesta had drawn one of the plastic store bags over her head to hide her face, to block her ears, and she'd rocked back and forth and sung a little song to herself until she'd fainted, toppling forward against the cupboard door. She had stopped being able to breathe about three minutes after that.

Joe was doing some legwork with DC Potter; they had seen lots of nice, frightened people who had nowhere else to go.

'Look at this place,' Potter said, and Joe remembered Tobin saying the same thing just a few days back. *Nuke it* had been Tobin's solution, but that wasn't in Potter's voice. 'Look at it: no one stands a chance.'

They went from walkway to walkway, from door to door. Everywhere was rubble, charred wood, articles of clothing, discarded weapons, splashes of darkening blood.

'Isn't that right?' Potter asked.

'No one,' Joe confirmed.

The Caller had hung up eight times now, and he was growing angry. He walked back to his bench in the park and looked at his watch.

Half an hour, Joe. You get half an hour. If we don't speak in that time, then you don't get Serena. Sorry, Joe, but that's the way of it. I don't intend to be fucked around, you know?

He was edgy: needing to talk but having no one to talk to. Wanting to share but having no one to share with. He got up and started to walk round the park.

Once round, Joe. That's all you get.

It was lunch time and the park was crowded with sunbathers and office workers sitting in groups, each with a picnic. The lovers seemed never to change: they lolled against one another all over the park; a girl was giving her boyfriend butterfly kisses; a boy had slipped his hand into his girl's blouse and was holding her breast as they talked.

All these lives, Joe. Isn't it strange? All these people living in the instant and never thinking about the Old Man – about death. And he's only a fraction away, isn't he Joe? You turn a corner, expecting – what? Expecting nothing in particular. Expecting the usual. And there he is.

There I am.

He had come full circle; now he lifted the phone and dialled.

Joe said, 'Fellgate CID.'

'Joe ... You found him, did you Joe? Found Danny?'

Joe pressed the '1' button on his phone. He said, 'You want to talk about that?'

'I want to talk to you, Joe.'

'This is a busy line; everyone uses this. I'm going to give you a number where you can always get me. Or else leave a message. It's my direct line.'

'What?' Joe could hear the wariness in the Caller's voice.

'It's a direct line.' He gave the number, then he said, 'Just a minute', and put the call on hold. Then he paged Tranter's phone in the incident room.

'DI Tranter.' He sounded like a man with a mission.

Joe said, 'He's on the line.'

'Give him to me,' Tranter said, and Joe patched the call through.

Tranter paused for a count of five, then he said, 'We found Danny, like you hoped we would.'

There was a matching pause. 'Who are you?' the Caller asked.

'Steve Tranter. Steve. I'm a detective inspector. I'm one of the people who found Danny McMahon.' Tranter had already pressed '1'.

'No,' the Caller said. 'No, I speak to Joe Morgan. I don't speak to you.'

'It's okay,' Tranter said. 'It's okay to talk to me. I know you want –' He stopped talking, but not in order to listen. When he turned in his chair, there were four people in the room, all looking at him. 'Hung up,' Tranter said.

There was a radio up on a shelf close to the box files named for each officer on the case; it was tuned to City Country Music on the Classic Hour and playing *Jolene* so softly that in the usual buzz and bustle of the office it was barely audible. For a few seconds you could hear every word of the song.

Tranter got up and hurried towards the door. 'Hung up, the son of a bitch.' He went upstairs at a run and entered the CID room barely lessening his stride. 'You pegged him?'

'I did,' Joe replied.

'Me too. Let's hope he was calling from home.'

Joe smiled. 'I'm sure he was.'

Tranter cast Joe a look and said, 'Bastard', under his breath.

54

Joe wasn't going to ask so Tranter had to tell him. 'He hung up because he wasn't talking to you.'

'Well, listen,' Joe said, 'I don't want him.'

'No.'

'I don't want the sick fucker.'

'I'm going –'

'I mean, he's yours. He's your problem.'

' – to call in someone from the negotiating team. A shrink.'

'Good idea. That's what I'd do,' Joe agreed, 'if he won't talk to you.'

'Fuck you, Morgan.' It was loud enough to turn a couple of heads. 'What did he say?'

Joe handed Tranter the tape. 'Not much. What did he say to you?'

Tranter left, closing a door that had been left open since the heatwave began. Potter got up to open it. He asked, 'Met DI Tranter before, Boss?'

'West Eleven,' Joe said.

All Potter said was, 'Never mind.'


The MCB trace gave a street phone close to Kensington Gardens. Tranter took a photographer and drove down there. They parked at the neck of a sidestreet and watched for a while. About thirty people used the phone while they were there, nineteen of them men. They all fitted Joe's description of twenty to fifty and probably white.

After an hour, a photographic unit took over, scouting apartments across the street until they found someone who was in and would allow them to make use of a room opposite the park. They shot every man who used the phone between their set-up time, 2.30 p.m., until nine that evening, when they were replaced by a second crew who snapped away until three a.m. A third crew took the shift until ten a.m. and the original crew came back for the rest of the morning.

Throughout the entire period, the Caller was silent. His next call came at midday. He dialled the number Joe had given him – a dedicated line that would be used for no other call. He got a negotiator called Nick Ramsden. He said, 'I'll talk to Joe. You understand? I'll only talk to Joe Morgan. There's more to tell, but you're not going to hear it. Morgan can hear it. Just Morgan.'

Ramsden did everything he knew and he did everything right, but it was like telling the wind which way to blow. The call had come in from a street phone in Camden. In the incident room, someone drew a line on a map from the Camden street to Kensington Gardens. The idea was that it might be the first strand of a web.

After that, six more calls, six more lines on the map, but everyone could see that the call pattern was random. Each time, the same message. Ramsden put the phone down on the seventh message and turned to Steve Tranter.

He said, 'Want my advice? Let him talk to Morgan.'

Detective Superintendent Harry Fisher was a career copper with a talent for politics. He liked to put in as much time as possible at AMIP HQ and leave the running of the incident room to a good DI, and Steve Tranter had been his first choice. Tranter was hard and he got results.

What Fisher didn't like was any notion of things coming off the rails: especially the rails that ran in a clear straight line from Superintendent to Commissioner. He reached across his desk to where Tranter had put his cigarettes down and took one from the pack without looking up from the notes he was reading. He put the cigarette in his mouth, held a Cricket lighter up to the tip, but didn't immediately stroke out a flame.

He asked, 'What was it between you?'

Tranter sat in a chair on the left corner of Fisher's desk, Joe in a chair at the right corner, so that Fisher had to look from one to the other like a man watching a tennis match.

'What was it?' His voice was soft and carried a note of amusement; Joe thought that Fisher wasn't expecting an answer; that, in all probability, he didn't want one.

Fisher finally thumbed the lighter, took a quarter of an inch off the cigarette and let the smoke eddy out of his mouth a little way before pulling it back on a heavy indrawn breath. Joe thought Fisher's smoking was as flashy and mannered as the matt blue signet ring on his right little finger.

Fisher's head wagged to and fro. 'Don't fuck me about,' he said. 'Please.'

Tranter shrugged. 'Different working methods, Boss. Different ways of looking at police work.'

'Clash of personalities,' Fisher said.

'That's right, Boss.'

Fisher nodded. 'Bollocks,' he said. It was almost genial. He remained silent for a full minute, smoking, occasionally glancing from Joe to Tranter and back again.

Joe thought, *This guy's done an SAFL course*: the way he maintained his silence, the way he challenged Joe and Tranter with looks. Other aspects of the Self Assertion for Life week would have dealt with how to function and win in corporate structures, how to make the other man's strengths work for you, how to locate your centred self, problem solving through positive thinking, and status control. The course had been fashionable among high-ranking careerist coppers for a few years. The less well advertised aspects, in Joe's view, were looking like a prick and behaving like an asshole.

Fisher continued the slow smoking technique for a while, then rapped the cigarette into an ashtray, all brisk and sudden movement, as if he'd just received a pure blue flash of insight into the meaning of life.

'You don't want to say, I don't want to know. Perhaps that's best. If there comes a stage where I decide I have to know, then you'll tell me, okay? You'll tell me. But for now, I'm not interested. For now, my principal concern is to find this guy, okay? I want him found. We've got a body and not much more. It seems possible that there might be more bodies to come. The press are going to like this, but I'm not. Okay?'

Joe decided that a statement followed by a question must be an SAFL assertion technique. He shifted in his chair, moving as far as he could to his right, making it necessary for Fisher's gaze to travel even wider as it switched between him and Tranter.

'What have we got on the presumed Daniel McMahon?'

'PM tomorrow, Boss,' Tranter said

'That aside?'

'Not much.' A beat, then Tranter added, 'Nothing.'

'I've read the shrink's report — what's his name?'

'Ramsden.' Joe was letting Tranter do the talking.

'Ramsden, yes.' Fisher picked up the report as if to verify what Tranter had said, then tossed it down again — a moment of emphasis, a little power-play. 'You'll work together, okay? That's the way it's going to be.'

'Boss, can I say —'

'No, Steve, you can't fucking say.' Fisher pointed at Joe. 'You're working with him. Why? He's the key. You don't have to French kiss him, but you do have to work with him, okay? He's on the team.'

Joe put a hand to his mouth as if thinking something through, though in fact he was wiping a smile. In order to make Fisher's life a little more difficult, he said, 'I don't really want it. I never looked for OCU work. The Hartsmede Estate's still smouldering. Chances are the lid'll come off again before the end of the week. I'd sooner be where I'm needed.'

Fisher's shoulders dropped an inch or two, which probably wasn't a characteristic smiled on by SAFL tutors. 'Did you hear me provide you with the option, Morgan?'

'Well, isn't that something –'

'– I should have discussed with several ranking officers directly and indirectly responsible for you and your activities, yes, and of course I have, and of course they agreed to have you seconded to the AMIP team here, and that's exactly what's going to happen. Has already happened, okay? You're needed. The shrink says so, I say so, and the Assistant Commissioner says so.'

'I take the phone calls ...'

'You take the phone calls and you talk to this guy because he seems to have fallen in love with you from a distance. Difficult to know why, but there it is; and the idea is to make him love you even more. You know what we want from you and from him. That's one aspect. The other is that you make yourself a useful functioning member of the Fellgate Cross AMIP team, working in concert with DI Tranter.'

'And reporting to?'

'Me. In effect, you and DI Tranter will run the investigation two-handed. If you need backup, ask for someone from your own CID room. I've cleared that.' He glanced at Tranter to let him know that he was included in the next remark. 'You can act independently, but you are not to keep one another in ignorance, understood? No secrets.' A pause, then: 'Steve?'

Tranter nodded. His mouth was stretched, not a grin so much as the shape made by a ventriloquist saying the word 'grin' over and over.

'Bring any problems to me,' Fisher told them, 'except I don't want to hear about any problems.'

A threat wrapped up as a joke, Joe thought. SAFL handbook of advanced techniques, page three, paragraph five.

'I want to know about the PM soonest. Who's attending?' Tranter said, 'I'd like to be there.'

'Morgan?'

'Fine,' Joe said, 'just fine.'

Fisher stretched to take another of Tranter's cigarettes, lit it, tossed the pack down again. He looked down at his notes. When neither Tranter nor Joe moved, he looked up as if surprised to find them there.

'So?' he asked.

SAFL wrap-up device, designed to put the interviewee on the back foot. Tranter gathered his cigarettes and lighter and left, imagining that Joe was close behind. It was only after he'd walked halfway down the corridor and turned to speak that he realised he was alone.

Fisher pushed his chair back and lifted a foot, lodging it on the corner of his desk. Joe looked up from under his eyebrows: not an SAFL technique perhaps, but pretty effective when it came to unspoken sarcasm.

The little Mexican stand-off was broken by Fisher. He said, 'There's something you think I should know … ?'

'There's something I think you already know.'

'Sir,' Fisher reminded him. 'What's that?'

'You asked why there's a war between me and DI Tranter. I expected you to ask. We ducked the issue. You expected us to. Part of the game. But you know why.'

Fisher sighed deeply and lit the cigarette he'd taken from Tranter, letting smoke belly out like a spinnaker before snatching it back. 'I don't know, Morgan. I've decided not to know.'

'Fine,' Joe said, and got up as if a point had been settled. 'I don't care. Just so long as you know I know you know.'

Connie was treating Joe with a delicacy and care that had as much to do with Gerry Tobin's death as anything else. She let him stretch out on a cane sofa in their kitchen area while she cooked. She opened a bottle of Sauvignon Blanc, cold from the fridge, and took a glass to Joe where he sat. She asked him questions that she thought he might want to answer.

'I worked with him in West Eleven,' Joe said, 'about six years ago, or seven. No, it was six.'

'Just after we met.' Connie was making a sweet dill marinade. She mixed oil and wine vinegar and spread the herb on a chopping board.

'I suppose it must have been.'

'I don't remember hearing about any Steve Tranter.'

'No? Maybe I didn't know you well enough for that sort of confidence.'

'You knew me well enough to fuck me.'

'Different thing.'

'You're right, it is.' Connie chopped the dill, making the board rattle. As she scraped it into the oil and vinegar she asked, 'What happened?'

They had opened the doors through to the little back garden in the hope of finding a breeze, but the air was heavy and motionless. The sweat-mark on the back of Connie's T-shirt was a ragged triangle.

'He found an ounce of coke in someone's pocket: much to the surprise and indignation of the someone in question.'

'Who was the someone?'

'A guy called Flitney Green. Definitely a bad man, definitely deserving of a jail sentence. Sadly, Tranter wasn't able to find the evidence necessary to send Flitney away.'

'Except on the occasion of the lucky ounce.'

'Unlucky for Flitney; at least, it would have been.' Joe finished his wine and went to the fridge for more, glancing over at Connie as he poured. 'For you?' he asked.

'A touch.' She nudged her glass towards him, using the back of her hand because she had reversed the cutting board and was laying out strips of fish.

'What is it?'

'Monkfish. About to be monkfish brochettes in a dill marinade with baby new potatoes and artichoke hearts vinaigrette.'

'Why?'

'To let myself know that I hadn't forgotten how to switch on the stove. The guy at the pizza place knows my voice. I say, "Hi, it's –" He says, "One American hot, one *quattro stagione*, extra tomato, extra olives." Don't fret. It's simple and fast and the artichoke hearts are canned.'

'It'll be nice to eat together.'

'It'll be rare. What happened then?'

'He asked me to agree that we'd found a substantial amount of a proscribed recreational drug in Flitney's pocket. I said I wasn't prepared to go quite that far, though I was more than willing to say that I'd seen him plant it there. He was miffed. Want some help?' As he asked, he was lowering himself onto the sofa.

Connie smiled. She almost felt good. It wasn't like old times, but it was like a version of old times. She cut the monkfish into chunks and cored a cucumber. As Joe watched, she gave a little hop, a shudder.

'What's wrong?'

'Goose stepping on my grave.'

A black imp, a little tufty-eared djinn, had come to sit on her shoulder; it had asked, *'What would it be like to make this for Michael? Are you practising for that?'*

In order to crowd out the thought she said, 'Miffed … How miffed?'

'Miffed as in blood-feud that will span the generations causing our seven-times great-grandchildren to swear undying hatred. Miffed as in I spit on your old grey-haired mother's grave, defile your daughters and hamstring your cattle.'

Connie laughed. The imp laughed back. She said, 'How come Tranter didn't know he'd picked the wrong copper?'

'He'd been four years at West Eleven; I'd just arrived. Anyway, in Tranter's book there's only one sort of copper – the sort that obeys the rules. And the rules are: get a result the best way you can. I broke the rules. I also put Tranter in shit up to his armpits. I think he'd've killed me if he could.'

'Real hatred,' Connie remarked.

'Oh, sure. Having to work with me must be driving him nuts.' Joe took a large sip of wine and rolled it round his mouth before swallowing. 'Of course, he did it for the best of reasons.'

'Protecting an innocent public.'

'Ambition. A flawless motive.'

Connie had skewered alternating chunks of monkfish and cucumber; now she switched on the grill, placed the brochettes over a long fish plate and poured on the marinade, then picked up her glass of wine from the counter and turned to face him.

'And the outcome?'

'About a week later, Flitney was caught in an orchestrated drugs bust at an address in one of those classy roads off the south end of Ladbroke Grove. Flitney and about five other guys. They were holding enough stash to keep west London glassy-eyed and smiling for a month or more.'

'There's a moral to the story.'

'You're right. Made no difference to Tranter, though. His version of events made me a ... Judas asswipe, I think it was.'

Connie turned back to the stove and slid the brochettes under the grill. She took knives and forks and a couple of place-mats out to the conservatory and set a small table that was hemmed in by house plants. When she came back for candles, Joe reached out and snagged her skirt between finger and thumb. She smiled at him, but twitched free.

Joe thought she looked more beautiful than the day he'd

met her, her hair tumbling damply into her nape, the minute scar set in the corner of her mouth, white and shaped like the new moon. She wore a glaze of sweat from working at the stove.

He could feel the effort she was putting in and it made him jumpy. To begin with there had been disaffection and irritability between them; then blinding rows, bitter rows, rows when things were said that should never have been uttered; and now, on Connie's part, a sort of desperate need to pretend, or to avoid, or maybe to try again: he wasn't sure which. He could detect a change in Connie, a certain restlessness, and knew it was dangerous, but wasn't sure what had brought it about. He wondered whether it might be boredom, or regret; or both.

They ate among the plants, a four-branch wooden candelabrum shedding a haze of yellow light against the blue of evening. The scent of night-blooming lilies mingled with the pungency of dill and the sharp, gooseberry odour of the Sauvignon. Joe talked about Tobin's death and Connie knew that he was really rehearsing his own, thinking about the where and when, but most of all the how. He spoke without looking up, taking a bite of food now and then, his eyes dark beneath the broad brow, shadows filling the angles of his narrow face.

'When the kid shot him … he just let go with both. He wasn't even thinking far enough ahead to save a barrel for me. When I got the cuffs on him, I went over to Gerry and he was all chewed up by the spread of the shot. The kid was near to laughter, you know? He said, "I killed him. I really killed him". Gerry was looking at me, but I don't think he could see me. I don't know what he knew. I mean whether he was dying.' Joe seemed a little drunk, but Connie thought it was really fatigue. 'I wonder what he knew.'

A big beige moth slammed against the window, then hovered there, wings whirring. Connie could see its eyes, bright white like diamante chips, and its long antennae stroking the glass.

'What is it?' Joe asked. 'With you. Between us.'

'Sometimes I think I know, other times I don't.'

'That's helpful.'

'Yes ... sorry.'

'Still want a divorce?'

'Joe ... it isn't ... I didn't say that to threaten you or score points. Just ... I'm not sure what I can give you any more.'

'Oh, *fuck*!' Joe gave a hot, plosive laugh. 'Oh, well, fuck *that*.'

'It doesn't make sense to you because it doesn't make sense to me.'

'Sure. Well, that's okay then. That's great.'

But Connie knew that some of it did make sense. She thought of terms like *waste* and *weary* and *missed chances*. She thought she loved Joe – that she'd always loved him – but in another life perhaps. And now *a new life* was the idea that seemed to haunt her; she thought about it every day; and if she searched for reasons, in truth they came to her readily enough. Her father's death setting her free – the sense of elation inseparable from sorrow; the child she had lost two years earlier – the way she and Joe closed off from one another, grieving privately. But there was something else, something unconnected with those events that break into our lives bringing the possibility – or the danger – of change. It had to do with a sadness in Joe, like a shadow that no sun would disperse. More and more, Connie felt that she lived in the shadow.

The phone rang and Joe got up to answer it. He came back to the conservatory door and said, 'A problem, Connie. I'll take it upstairs,' but in a voice so low that she barely heard him.

'I told them, Joe. I told them I'd only speak to you.'

Joe pressed '1' on his dial pad and the Caller's phone patched in to the Malicious Calls Bureau. Every incoming call was now automatically taped. He said, 'Why me?'

'I like you, Joe.'

'You don't know me.'

'Yes I do, Joe. Yes I do.'

'How? How do you know me?'

There was a long pause. Joe could hear the slow sound of ruffled air – the Caller's lips close to the mouthpiece.

'You found Danny, then. You found old Danny Boy.'

'We found him, yes. But where did *you* find him?'

'He just wandered into my life, Joe. Tottered into my life.'

The MCB operative was called Susan Klinman. She dialled a direct line at Fellgate Cross at the same time as sending a back-up fax.

'Why did you kill him?'

'He was there.'

'Sorry?'

'He was there, Joe. He was there. Available.'

'Do you have a name?'

'A name, Joe. Yes, I have a name. You don't expect me to tell you what it is, do you?'

There came a sharp rasp of laughter. Joe thought, *Stay there, pal. Stay there and keep talking.* He said, 'Tell me about it. Tell me about killing Danny.'

'Joe, Joe, come on Joe, what are you after? This isn't you talking, is it? No … it's some profiler. Some shrink. Some old shit-eater who wants my cerebral matter on a slide, some old turd-muncher just dying to get a probe into my brainbox.'

'It's me. I want to know.'

'I have to go now, Joe, before your lads come beetling up the street. But I do want to share, Joe. I do want us to be able to swap notes. I'd love to know about poor old Danny. What he looked like. How he *seemed* to you after all that time underground.'

'I'll tell you.'

'No time, Joe,' the raspy laugh again, 'no time at all. But here's something you ought to know. Serena's waiting for you. I'll tell you where to find her. She's in a sorry state, Joe. Past help, I'm afraid. Past all help.'

Joe wrote an address on the bedside pad. He said, 'Who is Serena? Tell me about –' but he was talking to empty air.

Connie made coffee and took the cafetière back to the table. She sat down opposite Joe's empty chair and poured two cups. The djinn hopped up from the broad green leaves of a rubber plant and dug its shiny black claws into her shoulder.

*How would it feel if that were Michael's chair? Suppose Michael were the person about to come back into the room, wearing that little smile of his that seems as much a question as a smile. Wouldn't you like to cook monkfish and dill brochettes for Michael, share a bottle of Sauvignon Blanc with Michael, and then, a little scared, a little tipsy, go into the bedroom with Michael, along your nerve endings a thin fizz of anticipation, of curiosity, of lust?*

A column of winged insects swam above the candle flame, whirling and dipping, being dragged down and consumed lick by lick. They crackled and hissed liked singeing hair. Connie hadn't been to bed with Michael, but she had felt his mouth on hers, his hand covering her breast.

When Joe came into the room she was leaning forward, her face close to the candles, watching the thin black scribble of insects shrivelling in the yellow blur.

He said, 'I have to go out. I'm really sorry, Connie. It's my shout – no option.'

She leaned back and shadows half masked her face. 'I won't wait up.'

It was an old joke but Joe couldn't muster a smile. He walked to the door and paused a moment, searching Connie's expression for a clue. She smiled and raised a hand to wave him off: *Your shout; no option.* The drift of her thoughts had made her restless, and now she realised that the restlessness was really desire and she wanted someone to make love to her.

'It's not this, is it?' he asked, meaning late shifts and dirty work.

'Neither of us got the right life, Joe. You're too clever and funny and thoughtful for what you do; and me ... I never really *found* anything to do, did I?' The faint twang of south London in her voice had broadened defiantly.

'You feel as if you're wasting your life ... something like that?'

Connie smiled and shook her head, hoping she was making a good job of the denial because, in truth, it *was* something like that. Something a lot like that.

After he'd gone she sat still and watched the reflection of candle-flame in the glass; it lulled her, seeming to hop and flutter somewhere way off in the dark; her eyes glazed and she let her thoughts run.

She slipped her hand under her short skirt and eased aside the leg of her briefs, then stroked herself gently, tentatively, staring at the window, the hypnotised moth, the darkness beyond.

A few seconds later, she paused, glancing round at the table, the remnants of their meal, the plants and hanging baskets, her multiple reflection in the dark glass panels of the conservatory; it seemed she might reach for her wine, get up, start to clear the table perhaps. Then her eyes closed as her fingers began to move again; she slipped down a little in the chair as her legs parted; she let her head tilt back.

Images swam up at her. The moth battered the glass, its eyes glowing.

# Eight

The house was a in a grimy terrace south of Olympia; the street ended in a cul-de-sac and police vehicles were drawn up in a little circle like a threatened wagon train. Joe and Steve Tranter arrived almost simultaneously. As they walked towards the house Joe said, 'I kept him on for as long as I could. He knew what was happening.'

'Sure.' There was no recrimination in Tranter's voice; in times of need, a little truce could be called for the sake of convenience.

'Where was the call box?'

'Tooting Bec.'

'He gets around.' Joe ducked under a line of SOC tape and held it up for Tranter.

'He's no fool,' Tranter said, 'is he?'

'Doesn't sound like one.' Joe was the only person who knew that; the only person who'd had the chance to judge. 'I'm talking to a profiler.'

'When?'

'After the PM, if you want to be there.'

'I'll look at the report.' The night was dark and close and Tranter was sweating freely. 'He called you at home.'

'For the second time.'

'How did he get the number?'

'Good question. A communications officer is trying to solve the puzzle – Pearson; so far he's drawn blanks.'

'Usual checks on anyone who –'

'Friends and relatives: yes, of course. Plus anyone else I can

69

think of. A couple of uniformed men have been round to look at the obvious ones. Guy from the local pizzeria, Connie's hairdresser, a store where we ordered a fridge; also anyone who's been to the house to do repairs and read meters – but they'd have to know how to self-dial: the number isn't posted on the phone.'

They got to the open front door of the house and peered in, but didn't enter. George Collins was standing just inside: the lab sergeant whose task it was to clear a path to the body.

'Have the photographer and the video operative been in?' Joe asked.

'Just finishing, Boss.' Collins was looking away along the dark downstairs corridor.

There would be a complete record – stills and moving pictures of the body, where it lay and how it lay; of the immediate area, fixing the position of objects and recording them; of blood splashes; of the position of any weapon; of exactly the way things were when the body was found. As soon as investigating officers moved in, the scene was likely to be contaminated. Someone can't resist the temptation to peer under that fallen newspaper; someone else stubs a cigarette or forgets to take away his Coke can.

'Virgin ground,' Collins commented, 'what with the killer giving us the location. No one to find the body and jump around the place in panic, offloading fingerprints and fibres and hanks of hair. I had someone faint on the body last week. Hopeless.'

'What's this like?'

'Messy. White female, late twenties or early thirties, throat cut. The rest's for you to say.'

The photographer was coming downstairs, followed by the video man. They both stood in the small front garden, amid waist-high weeds and blown trash, and lit cigarettes.

Joe and Paddy Godwin had worked together before. The Forensic Medical Examiner was a tall man, and thin, a slight stoop in his shoulders as if he'd spent half his life ducking lintels. He followed Joe and Steve Tranter upstairs, three pairs of feet beating a loud irregular rhythm on the uncarpeted treads. Twenty years ago, someone had papered the walls with vines and cabbage roses. You could still see green and pink under the grime. A door was hanging off its hinges, but it was old damage and, in any case, there wasn't any doubt about which room contained the body: the temperature had been in the upper eighties at noon and there was a heavy smell hanging in foul layers, like smoke.

Joe could hear a noise that sounded like distant conversation – a radio, perhaps, almost out of earshot. He opened the door and the noise came clear: the sound of a hundred, maybe two hundred flies, the air thick with them as they banged about the room or made a black, shifting curtain over the closed window.

She was naked, lying sideways on a low bed, one knee drawn up, her arms outstretched as if she were reaching for something with both hands. The odd tilt of her head showed how deeply the Caller had carved her throat. Flies were moving on her in dark rivers; others were grazing in crowds on the enormous patch of congealed blood that stood out like a shout against the bed-linen.

Her back was turned to Joe and he went round to confront her, as if there were something left to say. She was wide-eyed and grinning. For a moment, Joe couldn't quite grasp what it was that made her stare so furious and her smile so broad; then he saw that her eyelids had gone, and most of her lips.

Paddy Godwin formally pronounced her dead. 'Not long,' he said. 'A day, or maybe two.' He made a cursory routine examination. 'At a rough guess, I'd say she died as a result of a knife wound to the throat and I'm prepared to rule out notions of suicide.' He laughed but the laugh died quickly. He said, 'Jesus Christ, Joe,' then he sighed.

Tranter walked once round the room, as if fulfilling some

obscure duty, then said, 'I've seen enough', and made for the door, waving his arms like someone trying to be seen from a hilltop; flies eddied around him as he left.

Godwin smiled but without humour. 'Vegetarian is he?'

'Her name's Serena.' Joe was staring down at the body without moving. Flies settled on his face, on his bare arms.

'How do you know?'

'Someone told me.'

It was strange, Joe thought, how some things about her seemed so normal, much as they must have been in life. Clear varnish on her fingernails, a splash of freckles over her breasts, her long hair, thick and bright blonde, glossy as if she had brushed it only a few minutes ago.

Godwin had been kneeling beside her; now he got to his feet cautiously, as if expecting to bump his head. Joe didn't move. After a long moment Godwin asked, 'Do you need me for anything?'

'Nothing.'

'I'll tell them they can have the body.'

'Fine.'

'Joe?' Godwin held the door open like an usher.

'Yes,' Joe said, 'yes, okay,' and he nodded, but his gaze didn't shift.


The Caller was on a spree. He had been drinking all night, but he wasn't drunk. The booze seemed to fuel his energy, though: a high-octane fix that fizzed in his sinews and made his mind blaze. He was sitting in a members-only Soho club, though most of the people there had become members that very evening.

*How did she seem to you, Joe? How did she look, the serene Serena? Did you notice the quality of stillness in her, Joe, so profound, so deep? Something had left her, hadn't it? Something had abandoned her forever. Listen, Joe – I saw it leave. It shook her. It made her body quake. It felled her as I watched and her heels*

72

*drummed the bed and her legs and arms worked like a runner's. Then she calmed down, she grew quieter, just a little flip from time to time, a little leap, like someone tripping on the edge of sleep. Then that stillness; that instant when she was suddenly only Serena by name. Well, Joe ... what a mystery. What a conundrum.*

A girl wearing only a gold G-string brought a drink to his table and the Caller laughed as if the very sight of her caused him delight. There had been a dozen opportunities for a pick up, but he'd let them all pass. This mood left him just in control – just – like a man on a cliff edge, his toes over the drop, using his judgment and the strength of the wind off the sea to keep from falling.

A comedian came on and ran through a series of obscene jokes in a dreary monotone. The Caller laughed at every joke, laughed fit to bust. The barman glanced towards the disturbance; he saw a tall man in his mid-thirties who looked lean and fit, and marked him down as trouble-in-the-bud.

After the comedian, a stripper. She had been stripping all that evening, working her way up and down clubs in a network of eight streets, and she was weary to the bone and beyond, her hair damp, sweat-tracks scoring her belly and shoulders. Half a beat behind the music, she climbed out of her clothes, turned this way to show them this, turned that way to show them that, then struck a pose until someone killed the light. The Caller sat through it all, his eyes wide with wonder.

*Have you noticed, Joe, the way that sometimes things seem bigger and brighter and easier to come by? The jokes were so funny I got a pain in my gut. The stripper was so sexy I got a pain in my balls. Bigger than life, Joe. Have you ever thought about that phrase? What's bigger than life?*

He went to another club, then another after that, wired up on vodka and a sort of furious rapture. He howled at all the comedians; he fell in love with all the strippers.

*

At dawn, lying on his bed as the room slowly saturated with pale light, he sensed that great energy beginning to ebb. He was tired; and he could detect the first touch of a deep anger like an itch behind the eyeballs. If things got really bad, the anger would sour into depression. He had to fight that.

He slept for nine hours, then woke feeling shaky but clear minded. The room throbbed with heat. He took a lukewarm shower and pulled on a T-shirt and a pair of shorts, then went out.

Just past one o'clock. The dedicated phone rang and everyone in the room turned to look at Joe as he answered it.

'How did she look, Joe? How did she seem? What did you think of her?'

Joe pressed '1' but the call had already ended.

# Nine

'In the first daylight after death, bluebottles and green-bottles lay eggs in the moist, dark places – eyelids, nose, mouth, rectum, vagina. Flies tell us a lot. Some like fresh meat, some like it with a touch of rot. A few days at the sort of temperatures we've been having – I'd expect to find maggots and beetles and flies all over the body. We sometimes use an on-call entomologist to help us fix times of death. You get waves of insects, waves of attack, you might say, at different stages of putrefaction. The entomologist would take pupae from the body. The length of pupation might determine when infestation first took place. It's useful science.'

Jim Dutch was stocky and moved with a crouch, like a boxer. He was fifty, but his hair hadn't begun to turn grey, so maybe daily confrontations with death acted like a grim antidote to his own mortality. He crouched over Serena's body, delicate with swabs and tweezers now; soon the greater violence would begin. Joe had often wondered how pathologists ever touched a body in passion.

'I'd say she'd been dead a couple of days. We'll know more soon.'

'What about the eyelids,' Joe asked, 'and the lips?'

Dutch nodded. 'Yeah ... What's your guess? A psycho who likes to take souvenirs?'

'He didn't use the knife,' Joe observed.

'That's right.'

The flaps of flesh where eyelids and lips ended were ragged and carried a rich, ruby colour.

'They look torn off – or bitten.'

'So they were,' Dutch agreed. 'Cats, most probably.'

'Not our man?'

Dutch shook his head slowly. 'For one thing, I've seen it before. For another ... you weren't here for the McMahon PM, were you?'

'Tranter.'

'Who?'

'DI Steve Tranter.'

'Ah, yes, I remember. He stood in a corner looking pale as death. Well, paler. Anyway, you seem satisfied that McMahon is down to the joker who killed Serena here.'

'He told us where to find them and he clearly wants to lay claim to them. Not conclusive, I grant you, but, yes, I'd be bloody surprised to find that someone else had done the killings and this guy knew about them and was anxious to take the blame. We're assuming he did both.'

'That's what makes me sure this was the work of the cat next door. We'll know soon enough, anyway – swab evidence. But there was nothing like this about the McMahon cadaver – no sign of sadism or frenzy. You've seen my report?'

'Not yet,' Joe told him. Tranter had done a good job of delaying documentation; a pettiness that was about all Tranter could officially manage.

'Tough to be conclusive about McMahon,' Dutch said. 'London has a high water table, so putrefaction is helped along quite considerably. By the time I got him, he looked like Tollund Man: covered in adipocere and everything folding up like a landslip.'

Joe had seen examples of adipocere before: a result of the changes that decay brings. After a while, body fats convert to long-chain fatty acids and large areas of the body are covered with a crumbly, waxy surface, almost like candle tallow, that shows the body outline, but masks it. On one occasion, Joe had seen Dutch scrape away the adipocere on the corpse of a woman to reveal a tattoo. The tattoo had been a man's name through a winged heart – the name of the man who'd killed her.

'McMahon suffered stab wounds – you could see nicks on the rib cage clear as day, and defence wounds that lay across the phalanges; some went deep enough in the palms to have scored the metacarpals. I'm pretty sure, though, that the fatal wound was to the throat – just as your telephone voice told you. Now, if you care to look, you'll see the same thing in Serena. Cuts to the forearms, the fingers, the palms of the hands, and like McMahon only the one killing wound – the throat again.'

Joe nodded; he'd looked for the defence cuts before Serena had been moved from the scene of crime.

'Nothing fancy, though,' Dutch continued.

'No loony tunes? You're sure?'

Dutch pursed his lips. 'Okay … Definitely not with the girl. With the man? – Not as far as I could see.'

'How far was that?'

'It you want the complete truth, at that level of mummification it's tough to be certain about anything. Wounds can be made after death by animals, or just be the effect of decomposition.'

'How long had McMahon been dead?' Joe asked.

'Months. A year or more, I expect. We're trying to get a more precise fix by calculating the degree of root growth through his rib cage and pelvic region.'

Joe's mind went back to Serena, to walking into that room, the numbing stillness that lay in her, the business of the flies.

'I didn't see a cat.'

'Open window somewhere,' Dutch said. 'Betcha. That's

how the flies got in. Okay.' He had finished, now, with swabs and tweezers. He took a scalpel and made the great Y-incision on Serena, clavicle to pubis, the cut that would allow him to fillet her. He smiled at Joe.

'Sugar and spice and all things nice,' he said, 'that's what little girls are made of.'

Later, Jim Dutch gave Joe a verbal sketch of his report. The victim had been killed by a deep transverse incision that had severed the carotid artery and the trachea. Death would almost certainly have followed within a minute. She had probably been dead for three or four days, though further tests would fix the time lapse more precisely. Stomach contents indicated that she had eaten four or five hours before death. Tests would be made for alcohol and drugs. There was no sign of sexual assault, though swabs had been taken, and from what he could tell Dutch would expect to hear that tests showed seminal positives indicating that sexual activity had taken place a few hours before she died.

Joe said thanks. He said, 'Do you ever think of what's missing?'

Dutch's mind was already elsewhere. He had a queue in storage: a street accident, a long-term undiagnosed illness and two classified as 'in suspicious circumstances'. 'Missing?' he repeated.

'When you look inside. Not the organs; not the guts. Just ... whatever's gone that makes them dead.'

Dutch peered at Joe. 'How many of these have you seen?' He meant post-mortems: stiffs on a slab.

Joe shrugged. 'My share.'

'So it's a silly question.'

'I know.'

'Then why ask it?'

'Something,' Joe thought back, 'something about the stillness when I went into the room. I'd never noticed it

78

before. It went deeper than stillness. It was … something had changed.'

'Heart stopped, breathing stopped, no vital signs – equals dead,' Dutch said, but he wasn't trying to be helpful. 'Ask a priest; ask a philosopher.'

'You never think about it?'

'With her?' Dutch pointed to Serena's cobbled-together corpse on its steel slab.

'Her for example.'

Dutch shrugged. 'It's what we all come to.' He paused a moment. 'When it's my turn … maybe I'll know then.'

Jim Dutch didn't have a theory; Leonard Ackerman had plenty. Joe sometimes thought that profilers were a little like astrologers.

*Some sort of change is about to come into your life, something to do with houses. Are you shortly moving house? You're not. Then someone close to you is about to move. No? Oh, but there's some sort of movement, something connected to travel – a holiday, perhaps. Not a holiday … right … but movement, financial movement, perhaps. I wonder whether you've just come into a little money … No? Quite the reverse. Ah, yes, that's it then – the movement of money but away from you, an unwelcome change of fortune, yes, this brings us back to change, doesn't it, which is what I said to begin with …*

Ackerman offered the same sort of options, though in this case he had little enough to go on. Joe had gone to Ackerman's home, a tall pastel-coloured mews house off Holland Park: Joe's old pitch. The hall was narrow, crowded with framed paintings and drawings; Afghan rugs covered polished oxblood tiles; there were fresh flowers on a half-moon walnut table along with that morning's mail, still unopened. Ackerman led Joe into a small sitting room and went away to get some drinks. Ceiling-high shelves held books and records, though it was clear that these were an overspill from other rooms.

It was two in the afternoon and the temperature was pushing ninety. Ackerman's windows were open onto the cobbled streets of the mews and a thin stench of car exhaust from Holland Park Avenue eddied in to hang in the still air of the room.

Ackerman brought beer and iced water; his bare feet left damp prints that faded almost at once to a smudge on the stripped pine floorboards. He set his laden tray down on an Indian wheel-and-glass coffee table.

'There's not a hell of a lot to help me, is there?'

He was short and slight and had the sort of baldness that cuts a swathe down the centre of the pate from front to back, leaving bushy strips on either side. In his St Laurent glasses, linen shorts and polo shirt he might have been bringing drinks to the poolside in a Tuscan villa.

'I've read your notes on the calls. There's more meat on them than on the bodies, if you see what I mean. Beer?'

Joe said he would and was immediately chastened when Ackerman poured water for himself; he felt as if he'd been tricked into running to type.

'How much more meat?' he asked.

'Not much. A little. We're assuming he killed them both …'

'In the absence of any other —'

'Sure, sure; right …'

Joe felt a lick of annoyance at Ackerman's curtness. You work for me, he thought, despite appearances, so get your face out of my face. As if to confirm any prejudice Ackerman might have, Joe ignored the glass the other man had set down and drank a long swallow of beer from the bottle.

'Okay, so both, he did both, well …' Ackerman paused as if collecting his thoughts, then spoke seamlessly, looking beyond Joe as if towards the back of a lecture hall.

'What's interesting about the victims is that there appears to be no common factor apart, perhaps, from the method of killing. If this guy turns out to be serial in any serious sense – and maybe he will, given one or two remarks in your notes – and the choice of victims remains as unpredictable, then we've got a real oddity on our hands. No sexual motive so far as we can tell, though if there were, that would be bizarre in itself – one male probably in his late sixties, one female in her mid-twenties. No obvious motive like robbery ...?'

It was a question. 'No,' Joe confirmed.

'No – nothing to link the victims in any way, no other crime-related issue that can be found. Two people dead, different sexes, vastly different ages, seemingly motiveless crimes.' Ackerman paused as a thought struck him. 'It's occurred to you that you'll probably never find him?'

Joe shrugged. 'Some we find, some we don't. Why?'

'The sheer randomness of it. No clear motive is bad enough. No clear *preference* is something else again.' Ackerman poured more water for himself. He said, 'That second beer's for you.'

Joe didn't reach for either the bottle or the opener. 'You don't drink beer?'

'Yes, I do – mostly Labatt's Ice and I could murder one right now. I've run out. My girlfriend brought this in for me: she wouldn't know. It's wheat beer; I can't touch it – fierce allergy.'

Joe felt silly and hoped it didn't show. He opened the beer and took a pull. 'Doesn't that tell you something? The fact that the two victims *are* so unalike?'

'Not really. Though there are moments from his phone calls that are interesting.' There were some file index cards on the table; Ackerman picked them up and flipped through, looking at his notes on Joe's notes. ' "He just wandered into my life ... He was available." ' Ackerman fanned the cards like an illusionist looking for the knave. 'Then somewhere else ... Yes: here where he talks about the amount of blood and the fact that his victim kept breathing for a time. Then he says, "It makes you think, doesn't it?" '

'Something like that,' Joe agreed. 'I don't remember it word for word.'

'Then again –' Ackerman dealt a hand, rejected it, dealt another. 'Yes, here, he asks you how she looked and then, "What did you think of her?" '

'I remember. What does that say to you?'

'He's showing you something he's proud of, perhaps. He's a collector giving you sight of his treasures, sharing them with you. That would make some sense. I mean, the choice of victims might not matter so much if the most important thing about them is that they're dead – and by his hand. It would make sense if he'd wanted them to be prime specimens – if he'd made his selections because of sexual or physical type. Beautiful women, for example; angelic children; then preserved them – perfected them – by killing them. He'd be a recognisable type. But maybe that's not so important to this guy, and his reasons for collecting are different.'

'Meaning what?'

'Not sure, sorry. This is all chaff in the wind, really.'

'You said "recognisable type". What type?'

'Collector? If he *is* a collector ...'

Ackerman took off his glasses and set them on the table. Without them he looked oddly boyish despite the baldness. Joe noticed for the first time that the man had slightly prominent teeth.

'Possibly lives alone, though not necessarily. A loner, at any rate. Possibly has a reputation for being a bit withdrawn – for being quiet. Obsessive, fastidious ... Possibly abused as a child.'

'Lots of possibly.'

'Show me more of a pattern and we might shade into probably.'

'If he's collecting ... what? There'll be more?'

'Bound to be.'

'More eventually ...'

'That's right. But also more already. I think he'll have wanted to collect more in the time between McMahon and Serena. McMahon might well not be the first, of course. And Serena won't be the last, that's for sure; unless you catch him of course.'

'How does he collect them?'

'You mean, because he seems not to have tried to keep the bodies?'

'Yes.'

'Well, that's one of the reasons for doubting he's a collector. Keeping the entire body – or having it buried nearby – is an extreme form of collecting. More often there's a kind of tokenism involved: a bit like train spotting or bird watching. You don't take the train home, or cage the bird, you log it. And having logged it you effectively possess it.'

'Notches on a gun.'

'Exactly. The tokenism can often involve a minor amputation: a finger, an ear, an organ, part of the genitalia. In one case, I remember, an eye. There wasn't anything like that in this –'

'No,' Joe said, 'nothing. And if he's not a collector, but there are more victims – either yet to be found or yet to be murdered?'

'I'm interested in this business of his wanting to know how Serena's body looked.'

'I thought he was either gloating – you know, rubbing it in that he'd killed her; or else hoping that I'd thrown up at the sight of her.'

'Provoking reactions in others ... yes, it's possible. Killing for the publicity, for the attention: a version of Munchausen's-by-proxy. There's another possibility, which is that he was genuinely curious; that he really wanted your opinion about the way the body looked. Except he said "seemed", didn't he?' Ackerman switched a couple of cards to the back of the handful in order to find the note. ' "How did she seem? What did you think of her?" Yes, perhaps he was genuinely seeking an opinion.'

'On what?'

'Not sure. I'm not sure quite what he would have wanted you to see.'

A big chocolate tabby cat ambled into the room and began to make figures of eight round Ackerman's ankles, then hopped onto the window sill, sniffed the air and put its ears back.

'I listened to the little that was on tape. I think I'd put him between late twenties and early forties, which might improve on your estimate but doesn't make a jot of difference, of course. I agree he's probably white but, like you, I'm working off demographics based on what seems a regional accent. I suppose it's just possible that he's adopted the accent to fudge his real speaking voice, but I don't think it's likely. Mummerset isn't a favourite for that. Most disguised voices are northern or Scottish.'

'Why?'

'Christ knows. Easy to do? The only other thing I know about him is something you already know yourself.'

By now Joe liked Ackerman enough to say, 'You're being coy.'

'Me? No. You.'

'He won't speak to anyone else.'

'That's right.'

'Meaning he's focused on me.'

'Meaning he's decided he likes you. In fact his feelings about you are probably a lot stronger than the word "likes" can adequately suggest.'

'Sorry?'

'It's stronger than liking.'

84

'So what is it?'

'Love ... of a sort.'

Joe felt a little jolt of emotion: a cocktail of repulsion and embarrassment. He looked away towards the window, then his eye skated off to roam the books behind Ackerman's head, then he looked down at his hands.

Ackerman's laugh was friendly. 'This guy's an obsessive, we know that. He's in the grip of some twisted *idée fixe*. He's chosen someone to share that with. It's you. Who knows why? Most likely because you were the guy who lifted the phone – simple as that. He's invested you with whatever he needs to feel: you're a confidant, you understand him in a way others won't, your voice sounds sympathetic, he likes your name. He's on a journey, and he's chosen you to be the other passenger.'

Joe was still looking uncomfortable.

'No one's suggesting that any of this is rational. But he's convinced himself, now; you're his man. What he feels for you isn't rational either – but it's more than liking, more than simple friendship. You're part of the process.'

'What process?' Joe asked.

'Confession. He wants to confess, can't you see that?'

'Then why doesn't he walk into a police station and unload?'

'I didn't say he wants to be captured, or go to jail. He wants to tell someone, wants to share the experience, wants to boast. More than any of those, he wants to *examine* his actions along with another person – a conspiracy is what he's really after. A conspiracy to understand.'

'Understand what?'

'That's what I don't quite understand.'

Joe picked up his beer bottle and shook it to raise some foam. 'This is still conjecture is it?'

'Some of it.'

'If you're right – what's his next move?'

'He wants your attention. He wants to get closer to you. He'll take more risks. I'm guessing.'

'More risks?'

'Coming closer to you means coming closer to capture.'

'What else?'

'To catch your eye, as it were? Well, you know the answer to that. It's perfectly possible that he'll decide to kill again. Then he'd be sure of having your attention – wouldn't he?'

# Ten

The city was cracking up and so were the people. Days started warm and clear and were weakeningly hot by mid-morning. The figures for ozone pollution were off the scale and you could practically see exhaust particles swimming in front of your eyes. The air lay in strata, heavy as London clay, unstirred by any breeze.

Fellgate Cross was feeling the heat. Overnight, there were twelve different disturbances at pubs on the manor. At one an arresting officer was clubbed with a baseball bat; he was currently in ITC surrounded by relatives who had been told that he might wake up soon or never.

At another, a young black man had been the subject of a bottle attack by five white men with swastika tattoos; he hadn't died, but in years to come no one meeting him for the first time would know what he had really looked like.

The reports stacked up through the morning.

Two flights of stone steps with steel-section bannisters went down to the incident room. Joe walked through the open door into a little cloud of perfume and sweat carried on the false breeze from a small battery of rotating fans. Both scents came from Carol Mitchie, one of the civilian clerks operating the incident room log-and-file system. Carol was bottle-blonde, legs and cleavage, barmaid's make-up, tart's earrings and fuck-me shoes. Her method for card indexing was idiosyncratic but brilliant and she never missed a trick. The Metropolitan Police had five investigation suites that were computerised. Just five. All other incident rooms relied on people like Carol and a lazy Susan indexing system.

Carol said, 'There was a call for you, Joe. Not on the dedicated line. DS Cooper took it. There's a Post-it note.' She spoke without looking up from her work, turning the cards with long, cerise fingernails. Two cigarettes were burning in an ashtray on her desk – one almost a stub, the other just begun. The smoke rose in a dead straight column, until it was scrambled by a rotating fan. 'Also DI Tranter's called a progress meeting in fifteen minutes.'

Joe looked at the note. The call was from Ackerman. He called back and got Ackerman fading in and out behind the whine and buzz of a cordless phone.

'I'm in the garden,' he said, 'trying not to breathe deeply. There's something I forgot. You asked what his next move is likely to be. Here's another question: what's yours?'

'Investigate what I've got; wait for his call.'

'Yes, I know that. I mean when he *does* call.'

'Go on,' Joe invited.

'You must give him more of what he wants. Well, that's my suggestion. I'm not telling you what to do.'

'Aren't you?'

Ackerman's laugh was an acknowledgement. 'Put it this way – I know what I'd do in your place.'

'Okay – what?'

'Join the game. Talk to him about the things he seems interested in. Try to figure out what's important, what he wants to know. Do everything you can to become the confidant he seems to need. The confessor. The more you know about him the better, obviously.'

'Obviously.'

'Has anyone talked to you about this?'

'Not really. Well, not at all. They tried to put a negotiator on to him. He wouldn't have it.'

'No, of course not. He wants you. Okay, I will if you

88

want me to – talk you through, I mean. Analyse the calls; try to see where he's going, what he's up to – guess the rules of the game, really.'

'Okay, yes. Thanks.'

'Let him talk is the secret. Make a friend of him. Whatever's inside his head – that's what you're after.'

Steve Tranter stood close to the information boards that were posted with the basic breakdown on any murder: victim's name, the name of the senior investigating officer, of the pathologist, of the crime management officer; then the name and telephone number of the coroner and the civilian lab liaison officer, the Fellgate Cross front office number and address, laboratory reference numbers and crime report reference numbers. It was topped and tailed by details of the place where the body was found and the place where the victim was last seen alive. Both Tranter and Joe were listed as 'Dep. SIO', though Tranter had top billing. The AMIP team lounged on chairs and desks.

'Her name was Serena Matthews. She was twenty-seven. She rented the place but other people often stayed there for a short time; it's thought that she was sub-letting rooms for cash – almost certainly to itinerants, some maybe just arrived in the city, others beggars and rough-sleepers who fancied getting a roof over their heads for a night or two. We're still doing a house-to-house in the area and I want that to continue – in fact I want it to broaden. She was known by sight in local shops, but no one seems to remember if she had a boyfriend, or whether anyone was seen with her on a regular basis. We've traced her mother; the father left ten years ago and hasn't been seen since. We need to talk to him for elimination purposes. Anyone who ever stayed in the house is high priority. We're searching the house and garden for the murder weapon, but I wouldn't hold out any hopes. The scrubland where Danny McMahon was found was clean, too. We've made an appeal to the public for any information that might be relevant – anyone seen leaving the building that night and so on. The Super might be doing a spot on the local news. We're still not linking the murders of Danny and Serena; that way we'll stand a better chance of screening the sick bastards who want to make false confessions.'

Tranter looked at Joe as if to say: Any problems? Joe shrugged. Tranter turned to DC Harker. 'Lettings agencies? Private landlords?'

'On the case, Boss. Anyone who's moved away from the area within a week either side of the murder. It's a long list, but it can't be near complete. We're checking neighbours and shops and clubs and pubs for the same sort of information.'

'DI Morgan's been to see a shrink,' Tranter said.

'There'll be a report,' Joe said, 'by tomorrow and a brief profile for all of you. It doesn't add up to much, really. We don't really know why he killed Danny McMahon and Serena Matthews. We're not even completely certain he killed both, though it's a working assumption. I think he did, for what it's worth. I think he's psychotic, that he's killed others we don't know about, and that he'll kill more if we don't catch him.'

Tranter said, 'So far we've drawn a blank on Danny McMahon. Register of births and deaths, missing persons, possible relatives of the same name, hostels, criminal records – nothing. Serena Matthews is a fresher trail. We know things about her; we know people who knew her. There's a fair chance that someone who knew Serena knew her killer. It's a chain. Find the links.'

Everyone had a job to do. Before he left, Tranter said, 'The mother has asked to see a senior officer. She's got a boyfriend who lives in. They both want an interview.'

Joe was sitting at his desk, running through some fresh AMIP team reports. 'Okay,' he said. 'When – tomorrow?'

'I'll get Harker to set it up.' Tranter paused. 'I'll be doing some legwork. I like to spend time on the basics.' It sounded defensive when it was supposed to seem virtuous.

Joe nodded, his face expressionless. 'I'm a senior officer. I don't mind seeing them. It's fine. Don't worry.'

The reassurance irritated Tranter, as it was meant to. 'Anything from the PM?'

'I'm tempted to say I'll let you have my notes. Where are yours on Danny McMahon, by the way?'

They were speaking in low voices. Carol Mitchie was still in the room along with DC Potter who had been seconded to act as Joe's bagman. Tranter turned his back to them and leaned over slightly, bringing his face down towards Joe's. His lips barely moved when he spoke and his teeth were clenched. 'Walk carefully, Morgan. Are you hearing me?'

Joe glanced up, a winning smile on his face. A flush had spread into Tranter's cheeks and dappled his forehead.

'Have you had a medical recently?' Joe asked. His voice was friendly and soft. 'You look like shit.'

Tranter washed his face with his hand, like someone trying to wipe away tiredness; his index finger and thumb stayed at his temples and squeezed for a moment. He might have been trying to destroy an errant thought. What he said next was barely audible. 'You want to settle it?'

Joe laughed. 'Any Sicilian blood in your family, Steve?'

Tranter walked to the door, then walked back again. Carol and Potter were deep in what they were doing; trying to go deeper. Tranter's finger was an inch from Joe's face but he couldn't think of a word to say.

Much later, Joe sat in an almost empty incident room, the phone at his elbow. Carol was going home. She said, 'Same old story. Saturday night, you in your party frock and no one calls.'

Joe smiled. He said, 'I'd sooner stay at home with a glass of warm milk and a good book.'

'She came from Liverpool didn't she – Serena?'

'That's right.'

'Looking for a job in the prosperous south, living off social security, letting rooms for cash to other no-hopers.'

'That's the way it looks, yes.'

'Picking up waifs and strays.'

'What?'

'Your man. The phone-call man. He picks up waifs and strays.'

Carol looked into her make-up mirror and seemed to lose her train of thought. She repaired her lipstick with a grimace and a steady hand, flicked on some mascara, then threw the equipment into her handbag like a magician packing his props and waved a hand at Joe.

You could be right, Joe thought. The faint burr of the incident-room radio playing *Stand by Me* seemed to point up the quietness. I bet you're right.


When Connie stepped out of the air conditioning of her office building, the early evening heat was like a sudden shove. There was a hot wind, like a wind off the desert, trailing scarves of pollution. Each street had its static lines of traffic and every car had its sound system working, as if the *whack-whack-whack* of the bass line could swamp the senses, helping the drivers to forget that they were trapped in a motionless tunnel of toxic waste. Bike riders in heavy masks and goggles slalomed their way to the front of each line.

She turned into the backstreets close to Bloomsbury Square and found the pub they'd agreed on. Drinkers were crowding the pavement: office workers, their attaché cases stacked by the wall with their jackets draped over them.

Connie found Michael inside the pub, almost alone, sitting under a ticking plantation fan, reading the evening paper and drinking beer. They kissed, briefly, and he smiled; she covered his hand with her own; it was as if they had met this way a thousand times before.

Connie asked for a spritzer and Michael went to the bar to fetch it, then they sat in silence for a while.

'Well?' He said it with a smile and a little shrug.

'I met you ... you picked me up at the gallery. I wasn't looking for something like that to happen –'

'Yes, you were.'

' – but I let it happen. And I did want to see you again –'

'Yes, I knew that.'

' – and when I came to see you at your place, I didn't know what to expect –'

'Nothing in point of fact.'

' – stop it, Michael, let me ... ' Connie was silent a moment. 'I didn't know what to expect of myself. I still don't, not really. More importantly, I don't know what to expect of you.'

Michael waved a hand as if trying to clear the air. 'How do people meet?' he asked.

'Sorry?'

'How do people meet, how do they get together, become attracted, become lovers?'

'Oh ... ' Connie shrugged and stirred the ice in her glass. 'Dinner parties, introduced by friends, at work ... '

'Eyes across a crowded gallery. I mean, how we met doesn't make much difference, does it? I saw you, I was attracted to you, I spoke to you, you responded, it all sounds pretty standard to me.'

'Standard except for the fact that I'm married.'

'Not unheard of. The question is: why did you come for a drink with me that day? Here are some other questions: why

93

did you come to the studio? Why are you here?' He paused. 'And what happens next?'

The plantation fan gave a little groan on each circuit, orchestrating oddly with the electronic blast from a fruit machine on the other side of the bar.

'Isn't it difficult for you?' Connie asked. 'It must be difficult.'

'You see, Connie, I'm not thinking about that. I'm thinking about you and me.' He finished his beer. 'I bought a chicken and some corn on the cob and I made a salad. I've got a barbecue out on the balcony. No deals involved. Or we could have another drink here, then you could go away and think some more. That's okay too.'

'Or just go away.'

'Or that.' His voice carried nothing of challenge or anger.

The rooms were even bigger than she remembered them. Michael opened a sliding door that let onto a small balcony. The sky was pure unbroken blue and the river carried long lines of sunlight. He started the barbecue, then went back for their wine glasses. The smoke went straight up. Connie leaned against the wrought ironwork at the far end of the balcony and looked upriver, into the glare, until the brightness filled her vision and she became dazed.

When Michael turned her, his face was lost in the afterglare. He kissed her, taking her breath away. Their hands were everywhere.

His bed was under one of the great windows.

Connie lifted her arms to him. As he went inside her she gave a little howl and kissed him and shifted to get him deeper.

They made love for a long time, but not long enough. She

rolled on top to hold him inside her. Michael saw gulls drifting in dry air.

He shifted his gaze and Connie was watching him. Her look broke into him like someone picking locks.

'What Joe? Who — ?' Connie muddled the words, coming awake, suddenly, at the sound of Michael's voice. He was standing nearby, fully dressed, and reading the newspaper he'd taken to the pub.

'I asked, "Is this your Joe Morgan?" '

He walked to the bed and showed her the report of Serena's murder.

'Yes. That's my Joe Morgan.'

She would have said more but Michael leaned and kissed her, very softly as if to quieten her, and cupped his hand between her legs.

The balcony was just big enough for a table and two chairs and a striped umbrella canted towards the sun. Connie ate greedily. Her wine glass bore a dew of condensation and there were brilliants skittering on the surface. The wine was very cold. She held it on her palate till her teeth hurt. She felt it would be terrific to get drunk.

'Where are you supposed to be?'

'I don't have to lie. I just have to be home by eleven.'

'If you're not?'

'Then I have to lie.'

'Does it make a difference?'

'I don't know. I'll have to lie eventually, I suppose.'

'Will you?'

'I don't know, Michael.'

'Would you lie to me?'

'What is there to lie about?'

'How you feel. What you're going to do.'

'I could ask you the same question.'

'So you could. But I asked first.'

'Would you, Michael?'

'No.'

'Just like that.'

'Just like that.'

The whole western sky was a deep, dusky red except where a broad line of aquamarine scored the horizon. A thin shelf of cloud, red like the sky, hung just above the edge of the world.

'I left school and got a job. Maybe I could have gone to university – I mean, maybe I was good enough. I don't know. There simply wasn't the chance of it. My parents … we didn't live in that sort of a world. I met Joe when I was nineteen. We saw each other for a while – two or three months? – then stopped. We met each other again eight years later and got married.'

'What sort of a world *did* you live in?'

'The sort you try to leave behind. My brother lives in Toronto. New country, new life. He's rich.'

'Your parents?' He was greedy for knowledge of her, as if it were barter.

'Mother somewhere,' Connie said, 'father nowhere.' She laughed, then fell silent. After a moment, she added: 'He killed himself.'

'That's dreadful.' Michael felt a blush run into his face. 'I'm sorry.'

'Everyone was sorry.'

'Why did he …?'

'Depressions,' Connie said lightly. 'He got depressions. I'm going to need a taxi. I'm a bit drunk.'

'I know.'

Another silence fell between them; then, as if the conversation had never shifted, she said, 'He's a great guy,

96

Joe. I can't … It was such an odd thing, you know? Meeting again after all that time. Joe had lived with someone for a while, so had I – came close to getting married. It seemed meant. He wasn't a policeman when we first met; so many things had changed. We got married and it was fine. For a long time, it was really okay. There's still nothing wrong that you can see. He's so puzzled and hurt by what's going on.'

'What do you want, Connie? What do you want to happen?'

She looked upriver to where the colour of the sky was deepening to plum. 'I can't remember the past. Okay – some things – Joe getting hurt once, a miscarriage … my father dying; those moments, of course. But if I look back, I can't really tell one day from another and it's my life, all a bit vague, all a bit of a blur, and one day, not long ago, I told myself things had to change.'

'And I'm the change … part of the change.'

Connie laughed. 'Well, you're a bit of a surprise, that's for sure.'

'So it's no promises.'

'If I make any promises, I'll keep them.'

'Okay,' he said, 'good.' Then, 'Did you make any promises to Joe?'

The taxi company said ten minutes.

Connie led Michael to the bed and unzipped him and laid him down. She hiked up her skirt and straddled him. There was a heat coming off her as if the sun had got into her bones.

No one said 'Call me', or 'When will I see you again?' Light from the street door was buttery and held their shadows, almost a single shadow.

Connie put a hand on Michael's shoulder. He brushed her with a kiss and she shifted her hold, gripping his arm hard as if in fear or anger, then got into the cab.

The Caller strolled by in time to see Michael shut the door; in time to wave Connie off.

'Joe ... We haven't had a proper chance to speak. What happened? Who's been taking your calls? I can't speak to those people, you know that.'

Joe pressed '1'.

'Other officers. Other officers investigating Serena's death. And Danny's.'

The Caller asked, 'Is that still a problem?'

'No it's not.'

'I'll only speak to you, Joe. If they keep at me, I'll stop calling.'

'Don't worry.'

'That's why I'm calling you at home, Joe.'

'Sure. I understand. But you can call me any time on the number I gave you. It's just me, okay? Only me.'

Connie sat up as if waking from a nightmare. She looked at Joe and read his expression then slipped out of bed and went into the kitchen.

'Is Connie with you now?'

Joe gave a start and looked round foolishly. 'What?'

'Is Connie with you?'

'Why?'

'Trying to get a picture of it, Joe. Trying to see it in my mind's eye.'

Joe wanted to turn the conversation, but didn't dare try. He thought perhaps a minute had gone by; two maybe. The MCB would make a trace, call it in and send a fax backup. Fellgate Cross would contact the nearest police station to the phone box. Someone there would alert a mobile patrol. He looked at the LCD display on the clock radio; it read two twenty-eight.

Leonard Ackerman had given Joe a list of questions not to be asked: *How did you get my number? How do you know*

*Connie's name? Why did you kill them? Are there more victims? Why don't you give yourself up?* Other things not to say included *Let's meet – I'll come alone, I understand, at least tell me your first name* and *you're a sick shithead.*

'I'm listening,' Joe said. 'What do you want to tell me?'

'Tell you? Nothing, Joe. I want to ask you some questions.'

'Fine.'

'Danny … Tell me about Danny.'

'Okay. What do you want to know?'

'What did he look like?'

Connie appeared in the doorway holding a glass of whisky, ice to the brim. Joe motioned to her to go away. She sat on the edge of the bed.

'Like old leather,' Joe said. 'Like something tanned.'

'His face. What did that look like?'

Joe paused, which he knew was a bad thing. The Caller said, 'Joe?' sharply.

'Yes, I know, I'm trying to a find a way.'

'Could you see what it was?'

'Yes, you could.'

'Tell me.'

'It was like a face buried inside another face.'

Joe heard a little hiss, almost a sigh. The red digits on the clock gave two thirty-two.

'And Serena?'

'Not the same.'

'No … When I killed her, Joe, she was so light under my hands. She was so –'

It was a second or two before Joe realised he was listening to the dialling tone. He thumbed the reset button and dialled 'Memo-1'. The station sergeant at Fellgate Cross picked up.

'DI Morgan,' he said. 'Did you get a number from MCB?'

'They're on their way, Boss.'

'How long ago?'

'Two minutes? Bit less?'

Joe sighed and put down the phone. Connie hadn't moved from the door. Her glass was empty apart from ice. She said, 'Hadn't you better tell me?'

'I don't know how he got the number, Connie.'

'No, okay. Let's go a step further. Does he have the address?'

'No, of course not.'

'Of course not? How did he get the number?'

Joe shrugged. 'I don't know, but he –'

'*Does he have the fucking address?*'

'Connie – no. How would he –'

'That's my point, Joe. That's the point I'm making. How would he? Get the number? Get the address?'

'He hasn't got the address.'

'You don't know that.' She drank the ice-melt in her glass and left to get another whisky. As she went from the bedroom into the hallway she said, 'Do you?'

He followed her into the kitchen and she poured him a drink without bothering to ask then leaned against the kitchen worktop, arms loosely folded.

'There's no way to get an ex-D number, is there?'

Joe sniffed the drink; lots of scotch with a finger or two of water, which meant her own drink was the same strength.

'Not really. But there are times when you might give it to someone –'

'You meaning me.'

Joe shrugged. 'Or me, I suppose. Have you?'

'Why would I?'

'You order pizza, they ask for your number.'

'You don't think the guy at the pizzeria –'

'No. We've had a look at him, along with some others. I'm just making the point.'

'Who?' Connie asked. 'You said others. Who?'

'Meter men. The order department at John Lewis. The

guy who came to glaze the kitchen window. Everyone I could think of.'

'You didn't ask me. Maybe I'd've remembered someone you'd forgotten. Or someone you didn't know about.'

'Can you?'

'I don't think so, no.' Connie was wearing a peacock-blue raw-silk robe. Jots of condensation from her glass had made a stutter from waist to knee. She said, 'You didn't tell me because you didn't want to scare me.'

'Connie, you're making too much of it, believe me. Having the number isn't the same thing as having the address. It's a piece of electronic trickery that we haven't worked out yet.'

'Okay.'

'But if you want to feel completely safe, then I guess you'll have to move out.'

'Okay.'

It wasn't what Joe had expected her to say. He took a drink, then sighed and sat down.

'Where would you go?'

'Marianne would put me up for a while.'

'You're over-reacting.'

'I haven't said I'm going. You said I could, I said okay.'

She knew what she was flirting with; she knew that she had lucked-in to a good excuse.

'There's a guy called Pearson who's looking at this stuff. I'll talk to him in the morning.'

'What does he say?'

'Pearson?'

Connie smiled. 'Joe ...'

'He just asks how they looked. The people he claims to have killed.'

'What does he mean?'

'I'm not sure.' Joe got up and opened the patio doors. The

air in the garden was warm and thick like black flock; no hint of any breeze.

Connie followed him out. They sat in canvas chairs listening to the drone of traffic on an arterial road almost a mile away. Although the sky was clear, there was no sign of a moon. Joe and Connie were almost invisible to one another.

Joe said, 'He'll only talk to me. If anyone else answers, he hangs up.' Connie looked at him sharply but didn't speak. 'I spoke to a shrink called Ackerman. We use him for profiling. He says the guy is fixated on me. Luck of the draw – just that. I was the first copper he spoke to. The theory is he liked my voice.'

'He hasn't heard you singing in the shower.'

Joe smiled. 'It's been quiet lately. Is that a good sign?' By quiet he meant 'no rows'.

'I suppose I'm not so angry about …' She shrugged. 'I don't know what made me angry.' It was a necessary lie. *Waste*, she thought. *Your sadness dragging me down.*

'But no happier?'

'I don't think so,' she said, a voice out of darkness. 'No, I don't think so.'


They sat together for twenty minutes without passing a word. Joe heard a whisper of silk on silk as Connie's arm slipped from her lap to hang beside the chair. When he looked closer, he saw that her head had rolled sideways and her cheek was resting on her shoulder.

The phone rang and kept ringing until he picked it up. He pressed '1' in the same moment that the Caller's voice began.

'– so light, so unsubstantial, not like Danny, not at all like Danny, but what I could feel under my hands, Joe, the thing I was taking from them, the thing I was stealing, it was the same. The same. I burgled the house, Joe; I opened the safe. But what was it I took away with me?'

'What?' Joe asked.

'No, I'm asking you.'

'I never saw them alive,' Joe said.

'She was lovely. Serena was lovely.'

Naked, her body seething with insects, the great wound in her throat gaping purple and gristly white.

'I didn't see her like that.'

'No …' The Caller seemed thoughtful. 'I've heard it said, Joe, that even though you're a lover, or a parent, or a brother, or a lifelong friend, you might not recognise a loved-one in death. Isn't that mysterious, Joe? Or a husband, of course. Or wife.'

'Did you love her?'

'Serena?'

'Yes.' Joe seemed to remember the question as being on Ackerman's forbidden list.

'Oh, no. I didn't really know her that well.'

'What about Danny? Was he a friend?'

The Caller gave a laugh, like paper being rustled. 'I told you before — he just popped into my life for a while. I wasn't expecting him. Serendipity, Joe. It was serendipity.'

'What is it that you want to tell me?'

'Nothing, Joe. What is it that you want to tell me?'

Joe was lost. He didn't reply, and the pause grew to a silence, the silence to an absence.


He went back to the garden and sat down. Connie hadn't stirred. He worked back through the conversation, trying to find something that would help, some giveaway, but it wasn't there.

*What is it that you want to tell me?*

The night was lighter, suddenly, a false dawn. A tiny rag of cloud shifted to reveal a single star high and clear above the orange stain of city lights.

Connie said, 'I might move out, just for a while. Until you catch him.' She seemed to sink back into a doze for a while, then got up and went through into the house, moving slowly.

Joe heard her say, 'I'm not sure.'

# Eleven

Philip Pearson went down to the incident room to give Joe his report. Joe went to a fridge the crime management officer had stolen from an upper office and took out a bottle of mineral water. Pearson was a dapper man with trim hair and a neat beard. He slid a folder onto Joe's desk and gave a slight shrug. 'It's virtually impossible to know.'

'Thanks.'

'Sorry. I can think of only two ways to get an unlisted number. Well, the same way, really. You get someone who's unlisted to call you, then tap in the 1471 code after they've hung up. The number's then read back unless –'

'The code has been blocked, in which case the number registers as not recorded.'

'Which is the case with police phones. And the same applies with caller display on an LCD readout. It's entirely confidential – I mean, if someone calls directories and asks for an ex-D number, it doesn't register on the operator's screen along with instructions that the number's not to be given out. All the operator gets is "unlisted". I checked to make sure, and the block is still on your phone. My best guess is that it's someone who has been given your number for some reason or another – the way you give it to a theatre when you book tickets for a show.'

'Hacking into the computer records?'

'Here at this nick? Not easy. Possible of course. But I didn't really think too long about that sort of thing, because it doesn't sound much like your man, does it?'

'No, you're right.' Pearson got up to leave. 'Having the phone number,' Joe asked, 'how much of a lead does that give him on the address?'

'He can work out which area of London; that's about all.'

Frank Potter came in as Pearson was leaving. He handed Joe a list of names.

'Who are they?'

'The only people we've been able to trace as having recently left accommodation close to the address where Serena Matthews was killed. Forty-three altogether.'

'They've been seen?'

'All except six – three are old women, two others women in their thirties – so we'll call back but there's no real point except the possibility that they knew Serena, or saw something on the night of the murder. One man moved out of the city – back to Scotland. He hitched rides all the way from Hanger Lane to Fife, so it looks as though he's pretty well alibied. The locals are having a look at him to be on the safe side. The fact is that there's no one who's really likely, but there are five that might stand a second look. I've asterisked the names. Hopeless task, really. It's a shifting population in that area. Christ knows how many people came and went about that time. People sharing rooms, people in squats, people paying their rent in cash.'

'We looked at hostels and hotels?'

'Sure. You could register as Mickey Mouse.'

'I know.'

'The mother's here, Boss. In three.'

'Upset?'

'Difficult to say. She's got her boyfriend with her.'

'Okay.'

'Another last night,' Potter said, as if it might come as a surprise to Joe.

'Two last night.' Joe pointed at a marked map mounted on

the far wall. Two new pins showed where the Caller had phoned from.

'That's interesting.' Potter pointed to a second pin alongside the one that marked the street phone by the park. 'A repeat. What about the other call?'

Joe pointed. 'A couple of streets away.'

'He's getting cheeky.'

'He's taking risks.'

'Why would he do that?'

Joe shook his head as if to say: Anyone's guess. But he thought: *Impatient... Why do I feel that you're getting impatient?*

Serena's mother was called Patsy. She was forty doing her best to look twenty: pelmet skirt, blouse open to the fourth button, wired bra. She wanted to know whether Serena had left anything. Anything at the house. Anything that might have belonged to her. Anything that her closest relative ought to have. Maybe someone had found it at the house and had brought it to the police station. Maybe it was evidence and could only be released later. Was there anything? Anything at all?

Her boyfriend sat next to her. He was wearing a Fat Willy's T-shirt and a butterfly tattoo on his earlobe.

'What?' Joe asked.

'Money,' Patsy said. 'Anything. Anything like that.'

Serena's past checked out near-blank: a few friends, a few old lovers, a family thin on the ground and sour with indifference.

Same with Danny. It was as if that old corpse had never lived.

*Waifs and strays*, Joe remembered.

That morning, Connie had left for work at the usual time, but she had been dressed for something else. Joe wondered how he knew this. He considered that it wasn't so much the clothes she was wearing as the way she wore them. She had been quiet and preoccupied, moving about the flat with a sense of purpose, though she was doing nothing more than making coffee and toast, glancing at the paper. Shedding her robe and getting dressed as if no one were there.

*Neither of us got the right life, Joe.*

When the phone rang it was a moment or two before he registered the fact. Carol looked up from her work and said, 'Joe.'

He lifted the phone and set the trace, then said: 'Joe Morgan' – a reassurance – me; me, not someone else.

It was like being touched with a live wire. Joe hopped in his seat. He looked round the room, eyes wide, as if someone there might provide an easy answer to an impossible question.

A woman's voice had said, 'I was told I could get you on this number.'

'Who are you?'

There were three people in the room beside Joe. They stopped their work and looked towards him, an audience trying to fathom the plot.

'This is DI Joe Morgan?'

'How did you get this number?'

'I'm trying to confirm that I'm speaking to DI Morgan.'

'I need to know who you are and how you got this number.'

'I'd like to talk to you about the murder of Serena Matthews.'

'Give me a name.'

'And the murder of Daniel McMahon.'

'Sorry?'

'Because they're related, aren't they?' Joe said nothing. 'They were committed by the same man.'

Frank Potter took a call on the incident room general number. He scribbled a message and passed it to Joe.

'And this is a man who will speak only to you.'

Joe looked at the MCB trace that Potter had given him. He said, 'Are you going to tell me your name? Or should I ask your editor?'

'Very good,' she said, 'I'm impressed. That'll be the Malicious Calls Bureau in action. It's Lynda Lomas. I thought we might meet – would that be a good idea?'

'You know how to get here.'

'I do, yes, but I'm not coming there. Police stations and hospitals – both make me uneasy.'

'I could send a car with a couple of officers, some handcuffs and a charge sheet already made out.'

'Lynda Lomas in a police cell. My readers would love that.'

Joe said, 'Where?' She gave him the name of a pub on the river. 'If I see a photographer anywhere near the place,' Joe told her, 'I'll arrest you. If you think I'm kidding, try me out.'

'An hour from now?'

'An hour,' Joe agreed. He asked, 'Before that, right now, I need to know how you came by this number.'

Lynda gave a laugh of delight. 'How do you think?' she said.


It was late morning and the lunch time crowd hadn't arrived. Joe and Lynda Lomas sat on a small wooden deck overlooking a broad reach of the river. An eight-scull went by with a long hiss, the glare on the water so intense that the prow and its rowers seemed to evaporate as those in the stern gave chase.

Lynda was drinking Campari-soda, something Joe hadn't seen in ten years. Joe's prejudice had gone before him to create an identikit – bottle blonde, hard faced, tough, over-made-up, almost overweight, designer suit, heavy smoker. In fact, Lynda was slight and had light brown hair parted in the middle and cut to a fringe; she was wearing an embroidered shirt and a long, wrap-round skirt in Indian fabric with a pattern of birds.

'He called this morning: ten minutes before I called you.'

'Did you tape the call?'

'No. I'll tape the next.'

'Will there be a next?'

'What do you think?'

'Did he *tell* you he'd call again?'

'Yes – well, hinted at it.'

'How was it that you came to take the call?'

'He asked for me.'

'Do you know why?'

'I'm a crime reporter. He was reporting a crime.'

'What was your last assignment?'

'The Asian boy in Streatham.'

She was talking about a racist attack. A group of whites had done their best to kick his head off his shoulders and the boy had died after three days in ITC.

'There are a lot of no-go areas down there.'

'I found that out.'

Not hard faced, Joe thought. But tough.

She said, 'I also reported the Sarah Greencroft case; and I did a piece on London's disappeared.'

'When was that?'

'Six months ago.'

'Why do you mention it?'

'Because he mentioned it. In fact he mentioned both.'

'But not the Asian boy?'

'No, not that.'

'What else did he say?'

'He told me about Danny McMahon – that he'd killed him. He told me about Serena Matthews. He also told me about a copper called Joe Morgan. He said, "Joe knows all of it." '

'Said what?"

Lynda didn't repeat the remark; she asked, 'What did he mean by that?'

'It doesn't make any kind of sense. Listen, this isn't you interviewing me, all right? It's the other way round. Everything's off the record. Here's another thing: if I think it's necessary to talk to you in an interview room with a WPC and a tape recorder, then that's what'll happen.'

Lynda laughed and shook her head vaguely as if Joe had said something foolish. 'I know the rules.'

'Sure. That's what worries me. Tell me what he said.'

'He started off by asking me if I was Lynda Lomas. Then he asked about Sarah Greencroft.'

'What did he want to know?'

'Had I seen the body?'

'You told him no.'

'I didn't say no and I didn't say yes. I mean, he *wanted* me to have seen it. I just kept him going. He began to ask me questions that assumed I'd seen her. What did she look like? I thought at first he wanted to get off on it – you know? I thought he'd ask did I see her naked, what had they done to her, things like that.'

Sarah Greencroft had been found on farmland alongside the M40. Two days and three nights of predator damage hadn't been enough to conceal the fact that she had been multiply raped, suffered numerous cigarette burns, been unsuccessfully throttled with a ligature and finally stabbed more than forty times. When the police went to interview her husband, he was falling-down drunk. The knife was in his garage, swaddled in black masking tape and his bloody clothes were in a bin-liner standing by the washing machine. When he sobered up, he implicated two other men: friends of the family for ten years. The faces of their wives and children swam up from the front pages of the tabloids, looking as good as dead themselves.

'That wasn't it, though,' Lynda said. 'He just asked about death.' She paused, looking for a different way of describing it. 'Her state of deadness. What it meant.'

'And you said?'

'I didn't have the slightest idea what he was talking about. Still don't. I just wanted to keep him on the boil.'

'What else?'

'He talked a little about Danny McMahon and Serena Matthews, though not much. Mostly he said, "Ask Joe Morgan. He knows".'

'You don't have a trace on your lines?'

'I dialled 1471. He was calling from a pay phone close to Kensington Gardens. One of the things he was eager to talk about was your relationship.'

'I'll ask the MCB to –'

'Already done it. What does he mean when he says "Morgan knows"?'

'I happened to take the first call into Fellgate. Could have been anyone.'

'What do you talk about?'

'You expect to get an answer to that question?'

'Worth a try.'

'Describe him to me,' Joe said.

Lynda squinted into the upriver gleam. There was a faint breeze that lifted her hair and tugged it, very gently, across the nape of her neck. The sun had raised a dash of sandy freckles across the bridge of her nose.

'White, I'm pretty sure of that. He's got a slight accent – Devonshire? Just in a vowel sound or two. Could be any age, really. Not young as in teenager, not old as in grandfather, otherwise … He laughed a couple of times and at first I thought he was coughing. Softly spoken, but he sounds irritated; I mean, there's a touch of anger there; as if he wasn't getting quite what he wanted from the phone call.'

*Impatience*, thought Joe. *I was right. He's growing impatient.*

'The trace you've organised,' he said. 'The source number will come through to Fellgate Cross.'

'Will it? How?'

Joe lifted his hands a moment as if blessing a crowd. 'See these?' he asked. 'Arms of the law. The MCB will fix it for me. I'm afraid they won't fix it for you.'

Lynda was taking a drink. She spluttered, recovered, and gave a long laugh. 'Morgan,' she said, 'you're a delight. What can I say?'

'Nothing. Especially nothing about the link between McMahon and Serena Matthews.'

'He called a national newspaper, I –'

Joe snorted. 'Please don't tell me you have a duty to your readers, because the fact is I don't eat that brand of shit. Nothing about the connection, nothing about the fact that he talks only to me.'

'How would that prejudice things?'

'It might threaten him. You're right – he thinks we have a special relationship: he's decided that. Make it public and there's a fair chance that he'll stop talking to me.'

'But he might start talking to me.'

'That's another thing. I'm going to give you a number. You'll have to work this with a colleague. If he calls you, your friend dials in, okay? So here's the routine: he calls, you put the trace on, someone else calls the number I'll give you.'

Lynda lifted her bag onto the table and took out a pen and notebook. 'Okay ...'

'No, I haven't got the number now. I'll give it to you.' It would be the second dedicated phone on Joe's desk.

'Suppose he phones but I'm not at the office?' As she spoke, the thought behind the question caught up with her. Joe saw her eyes darken and her mouth go slack for an instant. She pulled the expression into a smile. 'But that can't happen, can it?'

'You're ex-directory I expect.'

'Yes.'

'Then you'll be fine,' Joe said, 'won't you?'

Joe and Steve Tranter had decided to go for a stroll.

They went north from Fellgate Cross towards the Hartsmede Estate, then walked towards a little patch of green with a children's play area in one corner. Next to the play area was a fenced dog exercise patch. A heavy fug of dog shit flooded across. Joe and Tranter sat on a bench, attracting one or two heavy glances from mothers helping their kids on and off the swings.

'It's really difficult for me,' Tranter was saying, 'because I can't look at you without wanting to break your fucking teeth.'

'I can see that it's a problem.'

'Once we've caught this bastard …' Tranter jerked a thumb over his shoulder, three short jabs, like someone wanting a ride. 'You're out. Like shit off a shovel.'

'You can live your life any way you like. Corral everyone with a bad reputation and give them a bag of crack to hold while you read the caution. Just don't expect me to be the laughing face in the background.'

'We're fighting a war, Morgan, and you want to talk about what's fair.' Tranter ripped the cellophane off a packet of Marlboro, then snatched out the gold paper and let them flutter away together. The flame from his lighter was invisible.

'We had this discussion a long time ago.' Joe said.

'I got a long way in with Flitney. Almost too far to turn back.'

'That's right. You made your decisions, I made mine.'

'I was close to –'

Joe interrupted. 'And that's really the last I want to hear about it, because you're still working and you're well-thought-of and well-liked, which is a fucking mystery to me, but there's no reason why you shouldn't make it up the ranks as far as a piece of shit like you can go, and the truth is I should have shopped you, and God knows I wish I had.'

Tranter's body gave a tiny lurch: an all-out attack reduced to a gesture. Joe ignored the moment; he spoke as if their reason for leaving the incident room was to take the air, to talk matters over in the sun.

'He's getting impatient. He wants something to happen. I don't know what; but he's being less careful – using the street phone near the park again, then continuing the call from just a couple of streets away. We should ask for mobile units to be seconded and soak the area. We should also put a camera in the park telephone. I'm told Fisher has been given a spot on *Crimewatch*, which'll make his old mother happy, but might well have some other effect because, as we seasoned coppers know, in a case like this it's a fair bet that someone somewhere knows something is going on, and could well have more than a good idea of who our man might be. Now, if there's any other crucial move we should be making that has occurred to you but not to me, I'd be happy to discuss it. Otherwise, I think the best way forward is to work together and get the case solved so that you can fuck off back to OCU headquarters. If you don't want to go before you've given me the chance to kick your ass up between your ears, well, that's okay too. But it's a pleasure I'm willing to postpone.'

Tranter levered himself off the bench and stood up, but didn't walk away. He looked round, like a traveller in rough territory looking for the bush-breaks.

'This fucker's got more than a couple of murders to answer for,' he said.

# Twelve

There was a hot wind like a wind out of hell, and a hollow din as if from some vast forge, and a chaos of voices.

The Caller sat on a bench close to the arrivals board and watched a train slide into the terminus. He'd been there for seven hours, as a raptor will ride a thermal half the day looking for what it wants. Throughout the afternoon and evening he had observed the trains coming in; lines of people had snaked past as he sat out on the concourse with his can of beer and plastic-wrapped sandwich, later his sweet coffee and pastry, later still his flat half-bottle of Bell's. Provisions for a long day. He was wearing chinos, a Lacoste shirt and a light, linen jacket. Not dressy, not sloppy. He had with him a smart, black briefcase that contained a contract and a list of addresses. The contract was meaningless. Only one address on the list actually existed.

He saw businessmen in a hurry, he saw family reunions, he saw lovers parting; he saw the first step in a long journey and also the last. He saw waifs and strays.

They came carrying little, and they looked out from the shadows and stench of the echoing concourse to the blaze of the city. They followed signs to the tube system, looking this way and that, warily, as if their own faces might suddenly appear on posters or under newspaper headlines.

Now it was close to midnight and most of them would have already found a room; those that hadn't – or couldn't afford to – would have staked out a space in a shop doorway or subway, or else climbed into a park. A few late arrivals might get no further than the concourse itself.

High, hot twisters ran under the glass domes of the station, carrying a confetti of garbage; the odour they brought was diesel fume and puke and spilled beer; it could ream your sinuses. Drifters and losers sat in groups on the ground, the cans racked up around them like haphazard ninepins.

She was one of fifty or so people off the last train from the north, and she came bringing almost nothing with her: the few things she owned in a cheap nylon sports grip – clothes, a photograph, bits and pieces of make-up, a cardboard roll containing three wall posters, a small radio-cassette player and a plastic store bag full of tapes. On the train, she had picked up a discarded magazine full of fashion shots and hand-painted kitchen tiles and antique bath tubs. She looked tired and her eyes were wide.

The Caller intercepted her and she feinted away from him then back, like something caught in a slipstream. He said, 'I'm not a pimp.'

She laughed. 'No?'

'Can I explain?'

'No.'

'Are you hungry?'

'No.'

'Look –' They had emerged from the station. He was pointing at a fast food place on the opposite side of the road. 'What's going to happen to you? Look –' he said again, and spread his arms. The midnight streets were loud with traffic noise, laughter, shouts, music. A marked police car cruised past and made a turn.

He remembered Serena's look, just like this girl's as she glanced up and down the street, setting a free meal against the risk. It was good sign, that look, that hesitation.

*Come on. Come on, come on, come on. Why not trust me – not far, not yet, but just a little? Come on. What have you got to lose?*

Her name was Christine and that was as much as she would give. She kept her sports bag and the bag of tapes on the seat beside her and ate a double cheeseburger and fries while he talked. She wondered whether it made him more or less dangerous – the fact that he was good looking. A narrow face with a honey tan, lips a little too full for a man, soft brown hair drawn back into a ponytail.

'You're looking for a new start, right? All the bad behind you, all the good ahead? And I'm sure you're right.' He laughed winningly. 'Don't worry. I've seen thousands like you. I bet I can guess. You waited until they'd gone out, packed your stuff, took the money from – what? – a pot in the kitchen? An envelope in one of her bedroom drawers? So you've gone. Will they have missed you yet? Or will that take a day or so? You might have stayed at a friend's house … stayed with a boy … maybe they won't even notice for a while. Then you become a missing person. Some day soon – maybe even tomorrow – you'll give them a call to let them know that you're all right. Yes?'

*Almost a shrug from Christine. Good. So I got that right, didn't I? More or less.*

She dipped her burger into a pool of ketchup and took a double-handed bite, leaving behind a little crimson moustache.

The Caller smiled at her. 'Well, it's your privilege, you can do whatever the hell you like with your own life.'

'You're not God Squad, are you?' Christine forked some fries. She was thin, about five-two, and had a sharp, pretty little face. Her hair was long, caught up on top of her head and held with a leather clip. There was a starburst scar on her temple that he could have covered with the tip of one finger. He wanted to trace its ridges and declivities.

*Listen to me, Christine. Listen, because I'm convincing you, aren't I? I sound believable. I'm good at this.*

'I wait at mainline stations and sell people jobs. It's what I do. It's been a long day, but then every day's a long day.' He helped himself to one of her fries. 'People like you.'

She took the ketchup off her mouth with the back of her hand and retrieved it with a long lick.

'Do you want a job?' he asked.

'Doing what?'

'Cold calling. You're selling time-share, kitchens, windows, restaurant and theatre vouchers – whatever we've got on. Listen, it's not easy work and you won't want to do it for much more than a couple of months. We have a big staff turnover. People move on.'

'People like me.'

'That's right. We've got a network of rooms all over London. You get a room and a phone.'

'A room?'

*That's right. That's what makes the difference. A room. I've seen that look before, Christine. A job, yes; but also a room.*

'You get a room, yes, and a phone. Everything comes out of your commission. You don't sell? – sorry, you're out. That's what makes it tough.'

'What's the company called?'

'GTS. It doesn't mean anything. Someone's initials. It's a holding company,' he said, 'you know.'

'What's your name?'

'Joe,' the Caller said. 'Joe Morgan.'

'How does the money come?'

He put fingers to his mouth: speak no evil. 'You'll see me every week, Christine. What do you think? It comes in cash. No one stays three months. You're casual labour. Only the guys that work the follow-ups go on the records.'

'Where's the room?'

He took the list of addresses from his briefcase. It was a photocopy, much annotated, and a number of the addresses had been ostentatiously deleted. He took a ball-point from his pocket and made a circle.

'Do you know where this is?'

'No.'

'There's a night bus,' he told her. 'It's easy if you have a map. Have you?'

She looked at him warily. 'You don't have to come?'

*This is the best bit, Christine. This is what makes me convincing. This is what makes me your benefactor and friend.*

'Yes, I am supposed to do that. I'm supposed to show you to the place, give you a pep talk, explain how cold calling works, agree a weekly minimum for orders. But like I said, it's been a fuck of a long day. I'm going home. You're my last contact.' He put a set of keys on the table. 'Look, it's a bed for the night. If you've gone in the morning, I've lost my commission, but I'm not going to make another pitch now. If you want the job, stay in the room. I'll come round and give you the company speech tomorrow at about half past nine. Ten?'

Christine nodded. She was almost there; almost sold.

*And here's the best bit. Here's the clincher.*

'Listen, it's not much of a place. I mean, the people I work for aren't eager to do anyone a favour.' A sigh, a knuckling of the eyes, a glance at the watch. 'I've had enough of this myself. Maybe you'll last a week; maybe a month. Do you want the keys or not?'

Christine looked at the map while riding the night bus, then she stared out at the city. Even now, there were people on the main thoroughfares and lines of traffic snaking up to the Westway. A road repair gang were working under arclights. Only the sidestreets were quiet. It seemed to her that London never slept and the idea made her feel safer.

She felt almost lucky. Enough of that sour life, parents who wanted each other dead, boys whacked out on glue, stolen cars barrelling through the rat-runs each night. Life like a clenched fist. Life like a dry tap. Someone had told her that in London there was always a way. She'd try this room-and-a-phone gig for a few days. Maybe a few weeks. She was looking forward to coming home and finding no one there.

The room was small, but there was a glass door that opened onto a tiny bedraggled garden. There were three keys on the ring he'd given her. One of the Yales fitted the garden door. She opened it and took a step out, but something rustled and ran among the tufts of overgrown grass and she went back in. She tried to snap down the deadlock, but it was jammed and she gave the door a tug to make sure the lock had connected.

Curtains screened the alcoves on either side of the chimney to make closets. The bed was narrow. She opened a second door to find a tiny kitchen: sink, drainer, a one-dish oven, kettle, basic utensils. Someone had left half a jar of instant coffee.

The bathroom was on the landing above; she didn't see anyone, but there was light under one of the doors on the next floor, and the sound of TV laughter. She sat down to pee and went to sleep for a brief while. She looked at herself in the scabbed mirror and laughed, then went back to her room.

Christine pulled the curtain across the glass door and undressed. Her body was thin and sharp: all ribs and hipbones and tight, pointed breasts. Two narrow lines of soft blonde hair ran across her shoulders, then down her backbone to make a little tuft in the small of her back. She got into bed and lay on her back, arms at her sides, feeling the ache of the day in every bone.

She could hear music and the whine of traffic and distant laughter from the TV, but none of it troubled her. She could feel sleep coming on: her limbs loosening, her heart slowing, her thoughts beginning to stray.

Enough of that life like a wound. She felt almost happy.

The Caller sat close to the glass door, amid clumps of coarse grass and tangles of bindweed and a few accidental flowers. Walls separated this garden from others in the street; there were lights in other windows, but he knew he couldn't be seen.

He had glimpsed Christine in the room; had watched her going to and fro, bringing a cup of coffee in from the kitchen, putting her few clothes behind the alcove curtains. She seemed to exist only in the instant; as if she had no history; as if he himself had invented her.

Her light went out: a dark shutter in the corner of his vision. He held the key to the glass door in his hand like a lucky piece.

He decided to give her two hours: two hours was long enough, even for a girl in a strange city sleeping in a strange bed. He didn't mind. There was a lot to think through. A lot to anticipate.

*Joe, this one's for you. Especially for you. To keep us in touch, to keep us active in one another's lives. To help our little game of Q&A.*

*I don't want to get out of touch, Joe. Don't want us to have nothing to talk about.*

Christine, he feared, would have to be rushed, and it was a shame. With Serena, he'd had a couple of weeks – more – to get to know her, to observe her, to listen to her. He'd made love to her, watched her eat, watched her laughing, pouring a beer, cooking a meal, just walking down the road. All this mattered.

Serena putting on her mascara, eye wide against the blink reflex, mouth slack, suddenly finding his reflection in the mirror behind her, as if his face sat on her shoulder; Serena turning with a half laugh to ask him what he could see.

Danny lifting a drink to his lip, feeling the man's gaze on

him, looking up with a quick smile to ask, 'What is it, then?'

Mick with his crystal, his pack of cards, asking, 'What?'

Jan reading a book; the Caller's gaze drawing her eyes from the page: 'What?'

All of them alive; alive in this way, alive in that. Making up, drinking, telling fortunes, reading. Then dead. A moment, just a moment, and it had all gone. The person had gone. A mystery.

What made her dream the dream she was having in that small room as he entered with the second key?

He stood by the bed letting his eyes adjust to the dark, hearing her voice as she spoke in her sleep – a low mutter, an undercurrent, incomprehensible. He had drawn back the curtains to let in the pale orange light the city shed at night, and her face gathered a gleam on one cheek, along the line of her jaw. He lowered his hand in order to catch her breath, a faint flutter on his fingertips. He bent to her, seeking the *dip-dip-dip* of her throat-pulse, and found it there, rapid, because she was taking the first few steps into a dreamscape.

He moved the cover back a little way, a little way further, and she stirred, turning onto her back, but he knew she wouldn't wake; it wasn't time for that encounter.

Because she was lying down, her small breasts had almost disappeared: a smudge of aureole, the nipple tucked in, and the faintest plumpness rising off the thin rib cage; it stirred him; it made him want to fit his hand to that tiny globe and leave a kiss there. Leave a bite. A soft bite.

Her waist seemed a handspan. Her hips flared briefly, then fell to a little swell of belly, to the springy vee of hair between her legs. He gazed at her, looking hard, wanting to know what it was that could so easily be taken away. She spoke two or three words on an indrawn breath, then passed a hand over her own face and turned her back, offering him the dark cleft of her backside, slightly parted.

The Caller watched, entranced. Something in her dream, some twist in the plot, made her cry out briefly and make a sudden movement. He went back behind the curtain, but she was immediately silent, so he returned. Her left arm was raised, now, and thrown across the pillow, her right knee bent. She looked like a runner caught in mid-stride.

A lullaby came to his mind. Not that anyone had ever sung him to sleep; it came from a childhood memory of a radio story, or something on TV. Along with the memory came a recollection of standing over his father's bed, watching the man sleep and hoping he might die. Souls came out of their mouths when they died: he knew that to be true. He had waited patiently in case father's soul might suddenly appear, gently at the lip like an animal nosing the door of its cage, then rush out with a soft, wet rip, and scuttle across the room to the open window trailing a bloody little tether.

It was all he'd wanted. He'd prayed for it each night.

He hummed the lullaby under his breath and drew the cover back across Christine's thin limbs.

*Not long*, he thought. *Not long to get to know her. Something must happen soon. Something fresh for Joe.*

He stepped back to the door and drew the curtains across. He felt powerful; powerful in his hands, like a surgeon.

He opened the door and went out into the knee-high tangle of garden, using the key to ease the door lock into place.

Good night, Christine ... and he sang, softly, the words of the lullaby.

*... does she want the moon to play with, or the stars to run away with ...*

# *Thirteen*

Lynda Lomas set up her tape machine and took out a notebook. The tape was for accuracy and later ratification of exactly what had been said. The notebook was for the hidden stuff: background colour, physical descriptions, her own impressions, general bite and spite.

She wrote: Alison Leigh. Sd to be best psychic in biz. Cd be 40, cd be 50. Big not fat.

Expectd shapeless print frock, but wrs bad trser suit (lime grn). Shoes like canoes.

Make-up by Coco – clown, not Chanel (use this?). Long strt pepper & salt hair almost to waist plus Alice band (sic!!). Slow movements, slow smile.

Mans flat off Baker St. Dark carpet, doesn't show catpiss (3 cats).

Foul L. Ashley paper hidden (TG!) by 1000s snaps of cats & people wringing hand of AL. (Assume grtefl punters).

Lumpy chintz chrs & sofa. Sidebrd with glass doors for display china, etc – ghastly.

AL spks in sort of mannish whisper. Consulting rm generally: quiet, dustless, chiming clocks, v. tidy, no radio, no TV, stufd bird under glass dome (owl) ears up, eyes wide, as if poker shoved up twat.

AL asks: Tea? Me: Yes, wanting gin. AL: Camomile? Mint? Fennel? *Puke!*

Aprt from mogs, many pics of the famous, so AL bit of a starfukr prhps.

Alison Leigh came back with two cups of camomile tea and handed one over. She said, 'You could have had a gin if you'd sooner.'

Lynda almost pitched her cup onto the rug. 'Have what?'

'A gin and tonic, or a Scotch, or – I mean something stronger. If you'd wanted to. It just occurred to me.'

'You read my mind?'

'Did I –?'

'Read my –'

'Oh, I see. No.' Alison looked at Lynda a moment, as if still not quite sure what had been meant, then she let go a big laugh, her shoulders shaking. 'No, I don't do that sort of stuff. Stage-work.'

'People can read minds, can't they?'

'Not really. At least, not at the level you mean; any more than they can predict the future.'

'So what is it that you do?'

Alison settled in a chair across from Lynda. Behind her was the glass cabinet and on top of that the horned owl in its bell-jar. There was a stillness in the room that seemed to stem from the precise order of everything in there, unchanged and unchanging.

She drank some camomile tea and asked, 'Were you thinking about a drink?'

'I was thinking I'd really like a gin.'

Alison laughed. 'Would you?'

'Yes, but I'm not going to have one.'

'Precisely gin?'

'Yes. And you said, "Have a gin if you'd rather". Something like that.'

'Coincidence,' Alison told her.

'Was it?'

'I saw something in your face when I mentioned herb teas. I might just as well have said vodka.'

'But you didn't.'

Alison gave another rib-rolling laugh. 'I sound like the sceptic, you the psychic. It was a coincidence, believe me.'

'What isn't a coincidence? Bobby Danvers?'

'Of course not.'

'You told the police woodland near water; that the water was the sea but somehow not the sea; and – what was it – trees on a hill?'

'A circular spinney on the crown of a hill. I also gave them a house associated with light, which I later came to believe was a pub. I thought all this was in the east of the country … There were other facts and features.'

'Which took them to an estuary just north of Ipswich, where they found the hill and Bobby. Who was dead.'

'The pub was called the Rising Sun.'

'He'd been dead for more than a week.'

'Well, I knew that.'

'How?'

'How did I know any of it?' Alison asked, as if the notion surprised her more than most.

'That's what I'm asking. How does it work?'

Alison sat very still. She had been asked the question many times before, but each time she gave her reply it startled her. She stared at her teacup a moment, then threw the mood off and said briskly, 'It's like having an idea.'

'I'm not with you.'

'Well, what's an idea?'

Lynda took a sip of her tea; it tasted both burnt and mellow. She gave a little shrug. 'Something you didn't have a moment ago.'

'Very good.' Alison smiled and offered a congratulatory nod. 'I could use that.'

'Feel free. Okay – an idea; and –?'

'Take the business of a word-association test ... you know what I —'

'Your shrink says mother, you say bitch. He says fun, you say clitoris.'

Alison smiled. 'If I were your shrink, I'd be a happy woman. But yes, that's it. Okay, so the idea comes — something you didn't have a moment ago. And the idea is probably an image, or it's a name, or a word that's going to lead to an image. You go with your thoughts. I mean, you let the images associate and breed. What you've got then are a number of perhaps disconnected references — a bit like random words that might make part of a sentence if you arrange them in the right order. It's a matter of working out what the right order might be and then finding the missing parts.'

'How?'

'That's where the detective work comes in — not my area of operations. I get hill, spinney, salt water but not sea, building, light-source. They do all the sleuthing.'

'It's odd to think of the police —' Lynda broke off.

'Making use of a crank like me?'

'I don't think you're a crank.' Lynda hoped it sounded convincing. 'Just that I'd've thought the police would be a pretty sceptical bunch.'

'It works. It's worked on quite a number of occasions. The police are pragmatists above all. They don't have to know how or why it's successful — just that it sometimes is.'

Lynda took a small cassette playback machine out of her bag. 'This is the tape.'

'You say this man called your office.'

'We get a lot of oddballs calling in. He's just one of them. I don't know who he is, but he's making a bit of a nuisance of himself. I thought he might be a good test of your ...' She hunted for a word. 'Gift?'

'This isn't something on police files at the moment?

128

Something the police are currently working on?'

'We don't report these idiots to the police. Newspapers get loony calls every day.'

'I ask, because the police often like to hold back anything I give them. It might alert the person they're looking for – warn him to move, or change his appearance in some way, or adopt a different pattern. It can also help eliminate false confessions.'

Lynda shook her head. 'It's just some goon who likes to call me with a net full of red herrings. If I'm not there, he speaks to my answering machine. Which is how I got the tape.'

'Right. Okay.' Alison settled back to listen.

No, Lynda thought, you really can't read minds, can you? She thumbed the play button and gave Alison a few seconds of heavily edited tape.

'*Hello, Lynda. I just need a spot in the paper. A nice big headline to catch Joe's eye. I can't really talk to you. I only talk to Joe. But I can give you something to write about. They were almost like accidents, you know. Like something I stumbled across. I wonder if that makes any sense to you, Lynda. I wonder whether it means anything.*'

There was a brief pause as if the Caller were reflecting on the matter himself; then came a little sigh.

'*Goodbye, Lynda. I'll call again with my news. Front page news.*'

Alison was hunched over her folded arms and gazing at her own toes. Her long hair hung straight down on either side, masking most of her face. Dust motes danced in four squares of sunlight cast onto the dark carpet from a closed window. The air seemed laden. Lynda could hear the faint saw of the other woman's breathing.

'The accidents he speaks of … A man and a woman.' Alison stopped as her thoughts switched direction. 'There's a house surrounded by fields. Animals in the fields. Maybe a farm, or near a farm. Woodland, little streams. Near the sea, I think. The house has a couple of barns attached.' She hadn't broken her pose, but now she gave a little shiver. 'A place in the city, too; here in London it seems to me.'

'Where?'

'Don't know; and another place, very cold.'

'Another place or another country? I mean Greenland, or somewhere like –'

'Don't know; just that it's very cold. You'd better let the police have the tape.'

'Why?' Lynda tried to sound airy and surprised.

'They're both dead. The man and the woman.'

'Are they?'

'Both dead.'

'How do you know?'

Alison didn't lift her head. 'How do you know it's Thursday?'

'You mean to say – he killed them?' The same light tone; an injection of faint scepticism to leaven it.

'You've heard the tape. They're dead. I'm making a deduction from what he said: "Like accidents. Like something I stumbled across".'

'I thought you didn't do the detective work.'

'I can read an implication as well as anyone else.'

'What about the man?'

'Don't know.'

'Nothing?'

'I can't see him, if that's what you mean. It doesn't work like that. If it did, things would be a lot easier, wouldn't they? Mug shots. Identity parades.' Alison was still leaning forward and staring down, her voice husky, and soft as if she were talking to herself. 'You must take the tape to the police. Tell them what I've said. Tell them I'll talk to them directly if they want me to.'

'Okay, I will.' It was easier for Lynda to lie with Alison staring at the floor.

'Joe is unhappy.'

'Joe.'

'Yes, Joe. The guy he mentions. "I'll only talk to Joe". He's troubled.' Alison looked up suddenly. 'Is Joe a policeman?'

'Joe?'

'Is he a policeman or a ... is he ... is it someone in authority?'

'He runs the news desk. Joe Radlett.' Lynda had rechristened Peter Radlett for the occasion, her immediate boss.

'There's an enormous room close to water. It's filled with images.'

'Images of what?'

'Dream images ... I don't know, really.'

'Is this where he lives?'

'Don't know. No, I think not.'

'Who lives there?'

Alison was staring at her toes again. She gave a breathy little laugh. 'You see ... Look, it doesn't work like that. I think I'm still with Joe. The room is more to do with Joe than with this man on the phone. Does Joe live near the river, perhaps?'

'I'll ask him.'

'It's just impressions – do you understand? I don't get meanings and a narrative. Just images that come through. They're not necessarily ... I mean, the connections could be very tenuous. Two people dead, that's positive. You must go to the police.'

'I will. Is there anything else?'

'Dead heroes.'

'What?'

'I thought it a little while ago. It just came to me to say it.'

'You don't know what it means?'

'No.'

'Not the man and the woman – the accidents?'

'No. Dead heroes. The thought came into my mind. Like when you think of someone you haven't seen for years, or remember some moment from the past. Why does that happen?'

Lynda smiled, waiting to be told. Alison looked up, then looked around the room; she stretched her arms and gave a little yawn.

'Why?' Lynda asked.

'I don't know why,' Alison said. 'Dead heroes.'


Christine had put her clothes on hangers and shelves in the alcoves. The photograph she'd brought with her was of herself; in the background were promenade rails, a lopsided horizon, a tractor harrowing the beach. Christine was laughing directly at the camera and the wind was making her hair fly; she looked genuinely happy.

She took a little ball of Blu-tack from her bag and stuck the photo to the back of her door. Then she took the posters from the cardboard canister and found positions for them on the walls: Jim Morrison and Jimi Hendrix on either side, Janis Joplin facing the bed. Kurt Cobain would never make it up there because Christine liked music from the past; she liked the music of these dead heroes; the plastic store bag was crammed with their tapes. Morrison, Hendrix, Joplin, The Grateful Dead, Pink Floyd, Velvet Underground, Captain Beefheart, the Soft Machine, Cream …

The phone stood on a rickety cane-and-rush table. When she picked it up and listened she heard only silence.

Some outfit, she thought. Cold calling's right. Stone cold on this phone.

She didn't own a watch. The rising sun had flooded the thin curtains over the glass door, waking her early; she had no idea of the time. She opened the door into the garden and went out. It was wrecked: couch grass and weeds and builders' rubble. Someone had left a supermarket trolley there. She thought about buying some wildflower seeds and just dropping them all over. It made her laugh that she was thinking that way: as if she really lived there; as if she might stay.

She went through her room and out to the stairwell in the hope of meeting someone from another room: she could ask the time. Maybe it would be a good-looking boy.

She thought the man who called himself Joe Morgan was good-looking, but he must be at least thirty-five; maybe forty. She liked his soft hair and the way he pulled it into a ponytail; she liked his slender, serious face. He was tall – maybe six-two – and she guessed he was quite muscular.

Christine walked all the way up the staircase to the attic room. She passed five doors but heard no sound of music or conversation and there was a stillness about the house that meant 'no one home'.

After he'd given his speech and authorised the phone connection and left, she would go for a walk. Find the park, find the Social Security office, find a supermarket. Find the pub where she could make a little score.

If I make any money at this, she thought, I'm going to buy a linen button-through dress like the model in that magazine, a pair of clear-plastic platforms, and a CD player. And I'm going to build a joint the size of a log.

When she opened her door he was standing in the middle of the room, smiling at her, the sun backlighting his hair so that it seemed to trail wisps of fire.

Joe was sitting across the table from Blake Adams, but he was on the phone to Leonard Ackerman. DC Bishop went past and put a note on Joe's desk. The radio was playing *They Don't Make Cars Like They Useta*, but just audibly. Adams was wearing headphones to listen to the Caller's tapes.

Ackerman said, 'He wants to be caught. I mean, he won't

stroll into Fellgate Cross with his hands out for the cuffs, but capture is the logical end-process of the way he's behaving: taking risks, becoming more public, this business with the journalist to attract your attention.'

'Is that what it's for?'

'I'm pretty sure.'

'We've set up a video unit in the pay phone by the park.'

'Can he see it?'

'Christ, I should hope not. No one can see it. We've already bagged three obscene callers and given the Drugs Squad the time and place of a coke drop.'

'Well, he's getting careless; he wants to be careless. So you might get lucky.'

'What's his motive?'

'Wanting to be caught?'

'Yes.'

'It's a subconscious desire. I know I've said that, but I don't want you to think that it's just a matter of time. You have to catch him – that's still the deal. The difference is that, without fully intending to, he's making it easier for you. Motive ... It's as I said when we met: he wants to confess. He wants to share it with you.'

'Share what?'

'Whatever it is he feels about killing. He wants you to understand. I suspect that, for some reason, he's decided you half understand already.'

'Why would he think that?'

'It's a delusion, Joe. No one's saying it's rational. But because he does believe it, there's a strong impulse in him to talk to you at length, face to face, to hear what you have to say. He's excited by the idea. I'm just guessing – you know.'

'Why do you always say that?'

'Because I'm just guessing.'

'What should I do?'

'What can you do? Sit and wait.'

'No way to box clever?'

'If you cut his calls short in the hope of making the idea of a meeting attractive, you might annoy him – seem less of a potential soul-mate. If you gab on, he'll suspect you're trying to keep him on the phone while an armed response vehicle runs red lights to get to him. I don't know,' Joe could sense Ackerman's shrug, 'act natural.'

Joe laughed. He liked Ackerman more and more. When he'd hung up the phone he said, 'I'm sorry.'

Adams shook his head; he was still listening. Joe picked up the note Bishop had left. It said, *Woman called in response to the* Crimewatch *slot – eight times so far. Asks about the investigation, then hangs up. Payphone. Trying to get her onto the dedicated line.*

Someone somewhere always knows, Joe thought.

Adams took the headphones off. He said, 'This guy's from the West Country all right. Cornwall or Somerset is my best guess. The vowel sounds are too bland for Devon, unless he's been away a long time, but even then you can hear the long "a" and the "i" sound warped to "er".'

Adams was a short man, less than five-six Joe guessed, and had a thatch of thick grey hair that stood up from his forehead in a double wave. A full beard emphasised the pudginess of his face. He had a smile that would charm honey from the bee.

'Not fake then,' Joe said.

'Unless he's a professional. It can be difficult to detect a fake accent if it's broad enough – say lowland Scottish or Geordie or even Ulster – and if the person using it is an expert. West Country accents are different; something to do with the timbre of the voice and the subtlety of changes area to area.'

'So we're looking at everywhere south-west of Bristol.'

'If you want to play safe and include Devon, then yes.' Adams had a thought. 'He's in London, now, you say.'

'That's right.'

'So knowing where he's from only helps if he's got some sort of a criminal record down there.'

'We can give a very loose possible description together with an MO. It's a punt.'

Adams got up. 'Let me know if you catch him. I'd love to know if I'm right. Cornwall,' he said as he left, 'but Somerset's a little more likely.'

Joe called across to DC Andy Bishop: 'This call: tell me about it.'

Bishop came over, rolling a cold can of soda against his forehead. He said, 'You know, my brother works for a direct mail company – office supplies. They have air conditioning, a river view and a VDU on every desk.'

Carol was filing at the lazy Susan: mostly scene of crime details under the heading Serena Matthews – forensic opinions on the weapon and time of death; fingerprint findings – fifty-seven different prints, none of them on record; tests made on fabrics and carpeting; blood typing; Tranter's notes and Joe's and Paddy Godwin's; notes from the post-mortem.

She was listening to Bishop without breaking her rhythm and she spoke without turning round. 'Yes, but how many axe murderers do they catch?'

'Tell me about this woman,' Joe said. 'She called several times?'

'Eight. Sounds genuine.'

'You've spoken to her?'

'No. The front office.'

'What does she say?'

'Okay. First time round she asked for whoever was investigating the murder of Serena Matthews.'

'She used the name?'

'She said something like "Serena-it-was-on-TV". The call never transferred; she was already off the line. That's been the pattern, pretty much, except that the calls are getting shorter.

"It's about Serena". That's as far as we get. The officers give her the incident room number, try to jolly her along, be chatty – you know. Click. She's gone.'

'You think she knows the number down here?'

'They say it to her every time she calls. They think she's been listening long enough to get it.'

'Someone always knows,' Joe said.

Bishop eased back the ring-pull on the can and took a long swig. 'We've had close to fifty crank calls. Could be another.'

'Doesn't sound like it.'

'No,' Bishop agreed, 'it doesn't.' He shrugged. 'Why doesn't she just tell us … whatever she's got to tell?'

'I imagine she's suffering from badly mixed loyalties,' Joe said.

'Even if she knows – suspects, whatever – that she's protecting a killer? If she's right, she could be at risk herself.'

'She could, yes. It's not the pattern, though.'

'How could she live with it?'

Joe shook his head. 'Funny what love can do,' he said. There was nothing in his eyes to make it a joke.

They were waiting for the phone line to be connected. The Caller and Christine, sitting side by side on the bed, a hot scarf of breeze unfurling from the door and bringing into the room a particular smell of the city: bitumen, frying-oil, toxins.

She had signed the fake contract and listened to the fake instructions. As soon as the phone was on, he'd make a couple of calls to teach her the technique. He had arrived with cigarettes, a cheap cigarette lighter, a carton of milk, some bread, six eggs, some bacon.

'Don't suppose you've got anything to smoke?' Christine was leaning back on the points of her elbows, her feet dangling a couple of inches above the floor. She wanted to take the edge off her boredom.

He pointed at the cigarettes. 'Just those.'

'No, okay.'

He got up and listened to the phone. When he returned to the bed he sat close to her and after a moment or two leaned back so that he was beside her, half-lying, just as she was doing. Her eyes flickered across to him, but she didn't move. He brought his face towards hers almost all the way and waited, then kissed her lightly, twice, pulling back to catch her reaction. Her eyes were closed.

She was wearing a cheesecloth shirt with a pattern of flowers across the yoke. The Caller unbuttoned it all the way down and teased it free of the waistband of her skirt. Her breast just filled the palm of his hand.

Her eyes opened. She got up from the bed and took off her clothes, standing in a rhomboid of sunlight from the garden door. She said, 'All right', and gave a slight smile, as if someone had offered to freshen her drink.

His look as he came into her made her close her eyes again. It was a look of scrutiny. He lunged at her twice, then stopped. She spread her knees wider, but he didn't move. A hand over her mouth made her lurch.

'Look at me,' he said.

She watched as he watched her.

She thought he really wanted to be able to fuck her and at the same time stand back and watch as he fucked her. He peered down to where her legs forked, to where his hips rose and fell. He came out of her, slowly, watching, and went slowly back in. Slowly, for a long time, then suddenly faster.

He kept his eyes on her face as he shoved.

He thumbed her breasts. He gave her soft bites there, then bites that were just a little harder.

He didn't need anything back.

There was a small window next to the glass door. Sunlight

struck through, making her flesh dazzle. Her throat and her breasts carried a tracery of blue veins. If he lowered his head to kiss her neck he could see the tug of her blood; could feel her breath dabbing his cheek.

He watched the small movements of pleasure she made, head moving, hand touching him, her lip caught by her teeth, and asked: 'What is it?'

He was talking to himself not to her, and he meant the business of life going on inside her body, but she misunderstood and said, 'Nothing, do that, keep doing it'.

They were slick with sweat.

He held her arms above her head so that he could watch the pulses in her wrists. He fell on her, arms wrapped round, to feel the rise and drop of her ribs when he made her gasp. He put his tongue into her mouth to taste her, put his mouth between her legs. He turned her on all fours and knelt up behind her. When she came, he used his thumbs to open her cleft so he could watch the dark nub of her asshole pucker and throb.

She sank down, glanced over her shoulder at him, then went to sleep.

A daze of calm, the room still building heat, the sound of insects from the patch of wasteland outside the door.

He sat cross-legged, watching her sleep as he had the night before. He felt light, as if he might suddenly levitate, drifting from the bed into a blaze of white light, carried up on thermals to the sun.

The first compartment of his briefcase held the contract that Christine had signed and a few company rules. Devising that plan had been truly exciting – formulating the terms of employment, commission, deductions for rent, making it clear that the phone bill would be itemised so that private calls could be distinguished from the calls made for the company. As he'd worked on the document, images of what it would lead to had made him laugh with delight, made him dizzy. He would shake with excitement when his mind's eye put him at the station, with his equipment in the briefcase.

The second compartment was zippered. It held a long, narrow chef's knife.

A towel.

A plastic sack.

A large pack of Baby Wet Ones.

The Caller picked up his clothes and took them to a corner of the room, where he piled them neatly under the plastic sack, then got onto the bed and knelt astride Christine. He eased the knife under her throat then treadled the bed with his knees to get the position right – thighs in tight to grip her sides, his free hand taking a purchase on her hair.

She stirred and woke.

'What is it?' he whispered, watching her eyes open, watching her head turn towards him, watching the little hop she gave, of puzzlement and fear, when she felt the blade.

'What is it?' as his knife-hand began to move.

# Fourteen

The beach was broad enough to fill most of the bay. If someone had stood atop the tall cliff, just beyond the lighthouse, perhaps, and looked back towards the far point, he would have seen Connie walking the line where the ocean hissed over wet sand. She was barefoot. The water cooled her feet and ankles; a wind off the sea billowed her skirt and rattled the sleeves of her blouse. She was an inch high to the man by the lighthouse; he was invisible to her, but she waved anyway, knowing he was there.

It must have taken her all day to walk half the length of the beach because when it was dark, and the lamp in the lighthouse was pulsing and dying, she was still walking in the foam. On one side of her, keeping pace, was a dog; on the other a horse. The man reached down a hand, though the cliff was a hundred feet high. He stroked her hair.

Connie got on the horse and the dog ran off into the darkness. The man said, 'He'll find the way.' She could hear what he said even though he was still on the cliff-top, even though the wind had risen and the sea was gathering.

The horse started at a dead gallop. Connie rode with complete ease, complete fluency, barely feeling the motion of the horse beneath her. The darkness flowed round her and she could see nothing — not the sky, not the sea, not the cliff, not the horse under her, not her own hands on the bridle; she was soaked by spray off the wavetops and the drub of hooves went in counterpoint to the sound of the sea.

The beach might prove endless, she thought; it was what

she wanted. Speed through the blackness, the drench, the roar of the ocean. She was lost in it, shaking her head with happiness, shouting as if he could hear.

Michael woke her by putting a hand to her cheek. She was laughing and crying.


The headline over Lynda Lomas's byline read *A KILLER CALLS*. The story made much of the fact that Lynda had been singled out by the man responsible for Serena Matthews's murder. Lynda overworked words like 'psycho', 'butcher', 'slaughter' and 'fiend'. Her interview with Alison Leigh made the woman seem sinister and slightly mad. Lynda told her readers how Alison had 'shaken as she concentrated on the killer's voice', how 'her eyes had rolled up to show the whites and she made noises deep in her throat like someone choking'. It was good copy; lies usually are.

Joe had kept his promise: Lynda was sitting in an interview room with a WPC in attendance. He pushed a copy of the newspaper across the table as if Lynda might not have seen it yet.

'There's nothing crucial in it. Nothing you should have known.'

'Except I should have known that he'd called. I should have been given that tape.'

'I sent it to you as soon —'

'Don't fuck me about, Lynda. I'm pissed off with you. I'm thinking of what I might charge you with.'

Lynda could see that Joe's anger was genuine. There was a rawness about him: stubble on his cheeks, and a brightness in his eye that spoke of sleepless nights. She said, 'I've spoken to our legal people —'

'I'll bet you have.'

'— and there's nothing —'

Joe slapped a hand on the table, making Lynda hop in her

chair. 'You took the tape to Alison Leigh; you should have brought it to me.'

'It came round to you by messenger as soon as –'

'You'd already seen the Leigh woman at that point.'

'I left instructions,' Lynda said. 'Someone forgot. I work in a busy office.'

'Sure, okay.' Joe nodded. 'Bullshit. But forgetting the tape for a moment, and what might well amount to concealing evidence, what about the article?'

'You see a problem with the article?' She was wide-eyed, one hand raised in astonishment.

'There's a balance involved – a balance between me and him. You're changing it.' Joe shook his head in anger. 'You know damn well what you're doing.'

'It's what he wanted. It's what he asked for. You heard the tape. "I need a spot in the paper. A nice big headline." ' Lynda lit a cigarette and drew the smoke down, but didn't exhale, as if she were waiting on Joe's response.

'You don't make those decisions.'

' "I can give you something to write about. I want to catch Joe's eye".' The smoke flickered between her lips. 'That's what he said; that's what I did.'

'And in your opinion he was hoping for a piece of half-assed tabloid psychobabble where he stars as a blood-crazed fiend.'

'Sorry?'

' "I can give you something to write about". What do you think that means?'

'That he's good copy. That he's got an ego. That he wants to be famous – like any publicity seeker.' A line of sweatbeads glistened in the fine hairs along Lynda's upper lip; she smudged them when she put the cigarette back to her mouth. 'Also he wanted to give you a dig in the ribs, thumb his nose, isn't that it?'

'No,' Joe said, 'that's not it. And you're a stupid bitch.'

143

The Caller had gone to a place that no one knew about: a room among dowdy, dusty houses, shops boarded up, a pumping station opposite. No one in the street knew anyone else. A red route went past the Caller's window and four lines of traffic boomed through all day; all night heavy trucks passed in a surf of engine noise.

Out in the street there were a few daytime drunks, women trekking to the neighbourhood supermarket, stray dogs. Wherever you were you could hear the sound of a child crying.

The Caller opened the front door of one house among fifty that couldn't be told apart: no street number, a dirty little bay window, paint weathered off. Black grime from the traffic reamed the glass, the door panels, the chipped brickwork. The hallway was in semi-darkness and smelled like a cellar. He went up two short flights of stairs and opened the door with a single key. No one was burgled in that neighbourhood; there was nothing to steal. Only the petty dealers were turned over from time to time and their stash taken; most carried their stuff on them.

There was a kitchen like a phone booth. The Caller made himself a cup of coffee and read Lynda's piece. He sat down, spread it out on the floor, and bent over the paper as if it were easier, that way, to take a balanced view. In addition to misquoting Alison Leigh, and making her seem like something between a sorcerer and a professional hysteric, Lynda had employed the help of a couple of showbiz shrinks who'd offered meaningless and lurid speculations about the Caller's childhood, his sexual preferences, his mental health and his motives.

The Caller read the article several times without lifting his eyes from the page. The room was tiny and intensely hot. He could feel sweatbeads finding a shaky route across his ribs and his hair darkened from soft brown to black around his temples; the strong light from the window brought highlights and shadows to his face, his eyes downcast and dark. Handsome devil, some had said.

He cut out the article and placed it in a box file along with others, folding it so that Lynda's picture and byline were uppermost. He took a final look at Lynda; a mug shot where she was staring straight at the camera with an expression that was supposed to say fearless-but-feminine; seen-it-all-but-strangely-vulnerable.

He liked the way her hair was cut to a fringe, low and ragged on her forehead. He imagined her somewhere, at that very moment, talking or laughing or preoccupied with work, not thinking about the breath she was taking, this breath, now this one, now this; not feeling the drub of her own pulse, the slow siftings in her body, the wet of her eye.

*Lynda ... There are lessons you have to learn.*

The Caller smiled and tapped the paper alongside Lynda's photo, as if trying for her attention.

*I shall teach you.*

One wall of the room was stacked with glass-fronted display cases, floor to ceiling: a tawny owl, a stoat in its white winter pelt, a kestrel arrowed in flight, a fox, a marten, a pair of jays, a badger, in case after case some creature preserved in its feathers or fur.

The Caller went over and browsed among them, the marten's needle teeth, the hawk's lethal eye, just as in life, except for life itself. Their stillness awed him; their fixity. He thought of Christine and the way he'd crouched over her, watching, waiting to tell the difference. Her eye had grown dull and her body had stopped its shaking.

All the time – his thighs and forearms drenched, his arm sawing – all the time, as he worked, he had watched for her last breath.

Margaret Fulton walked into the reception area at Fellgate Cross bringing with her a bag of evidence: a spiral-bound notebook, two white shirts stained with bloodspots, a sheaf of photographs and a bonehandled knife. She turned them out, one by one, onto the table in the interview room.

Steve Tranter looked at the objects without touching. The photograph on top of the pile showed a woman spreadeagled on a bed, her hands and feet tied with rope that ran under the bed-frame; she was naked; a blindfold covered her eyes. Margaret put the knife down last. It lay on the table between them, trembling slightly like a compass needle; the blade bore a dark stain.

Tranter said, 'You've been making phone calls.'

'I thought it simpler just to come in.'

'You took your time.'

Margaret didn't reply. The shirts were neatly folded side by side. Tranter could see bloodspots on the upper sleeve of one, on the other they were a little lower, where the wearer's ribs would be. Margaret saw where his gaze lay and turned the second shirt; a rash of tiny stains stippled the yoke, just below the collar.

When Joe Morgan entered the room, Tranter looked up in annoyance. He shook his head, a gesture that Joe refused to see. Tranter looked away, his gaze flicking round the blank walls, his teeth clenched; his hands made fists and he tapped them on the table, fast, light blows that wanted to become a furious hammering.

For the benefit of the tape cassette he said, 'Eleven hundred hours, DI Morgan has entered the interview room.'

There was a DC in the room called Jane Lawson; Tranter sent her for some evidence bags, then turned his attention back to Margaret Fulton.

'Has anyone handled these except you? Since you found them, I mean.'

'No.'

'What's your husband's name?'

'Peter.'

'His full name.'

'Peter Douglas George.'

'And he's missing.'

To begin with, Margaret Fulton had seemed close to breakdown – over-busy as she unloaded her evidence onto the table, holding her lip between her teeth, shedding tears without sobbing. Now she gazed at the wall behind Tranter as if looking towards a horizon.

'He's missing,' Tranter said again.

'Five days.'

Jane Lawson returned with the evidence bags and put them on the table. Margaret sat utterly still. Tranter had seen this before; he folded his arms and looked into his lap. A silence grew in the room and filled it. The heat seemed to be a physical presence, aggressive, like something barging round the room.

Joe was lounging against the wall behind Margaret; because he was worried that he might draw her attention, he turned away slightly and closed his eyes. Jane Lawson looked everywhere and nowhere. The woman on the bed floated up into Joe's vision. From the view he'd had over Margaret's shoulder it wasn't clear to him whether the spread-eagled figure was alive or dead. There seemed to be a low hum in the room that sometimes came towards Joe, sometimes retreated, but in truth the only sounds were those that came from outside; what Joe could hear was the energy of silence.

'It was on television about Serena Matthews. They gave the date when they thought she'd died. He was away that day – all day and most of the night. He's a teacher – no school till September. He thought I was asleep. I put the light on and asked him where he'd been; I asked him if it was someone else, you know, if he was seeing someone else. He said, "What are you talking about?" He laughed, you know, like someone laughs when they're trying to make you out a liar or a fool. His fishing tackle was in the boot of the car. He used to go out to Maidenhead and Marlow. Well that's what he told me, but I don't know what he ...'

Margaret stopped as if she'd reached the end of the sentence; she shook her head, looking at Tranter for a prompt. He said, 'Has he ever gone missing before, Margaret?'

'No.'

'Okay.' Tranter was looking at paths in a maze, trying to decide which to take. Finally he asked, 'Keen fisherman, was he?'

'Yes.'

'Did he catch much?'

'Sometimes.'

'But sometimes he said he was going fishing and he wasn't. Is that what you think?'

'Yes.'

'Why?'

'It was different. Things were different.'

'Different ...'

'He was coming home later, but that wasn't so strange. It's summer, warm nights, no reason to stop fishing. Night's a good time; they go on the bait more readily.'

She paused again, and closed her eyes. To keep her going, Tranter said, 'I know, yes ...'

'It's just the way he was – I mean the way he'd started to behave. Peter would come home from a fishing trip, this is before, you know, this is the past, and he'd be chatty and hungry and busy, putting his things away and talking about what kind of day he'd had. I'd make some food, or else he would – a cheese sandwich and a beer, or some scrambled eggs, I mean there was a pattern to all that, I recognised it. And I noticed when it stopped.'

'When was that?'

'About six months ago. Maybe eight. Sometimes he'd come home and I'd think, yes, he's been fishing. Other times

148

I'd wonder where he'd been. Even on the occasions when I thought that he had been fishing, he was still different. He was different all the time.'

'In what way?'

'Didn't want to speak. Spent a lot of time in his room. Seemed depressed. At first I thought perhaps he'd been made redundant and wasn't telling me.'

'How was that different from before?'

'What?'

'Before all this – how would you describe him?'

'He was … fine. He was Peter. Like himself, you know.'

'No, Margaret, I don't.'

'Normal. Just like anyone's husband.'

Joe looked past Margaret at the stack of pornographic photos. Not quite, he thought. Not entirely.

'What did you mean when you mentioned "his room"?'

Joe had been expecting that question, though Tranter was asking it a little sooner than Joe would have done. He wanted to hear something more about Peter Fulton's normal life.

'It's the room where he keeps his hi-fi,' Margaret said. 'He listens to music a lot.'

'On his own?'

'Yes.'

'You don't like music …'

'Not really.' Margaret shrugged. 'I do, but –'

Tranter asked, 'Where did you find these things?'

'In his room.'

'Where?'

'There's a bureau, his bureau. The photos were in a drawer – in a box file. The shirts were in another drawer, inside a supermarket bag sealed up with tape. The book was in with the photos.'

'The knife?' Tranter asked.

'In the car – the driver's door pocket.'

'When did you find them?'

'Three days ago.'

'Was the bureau unlocked?'

'No. I broke into it with a hammer.'

'Why do you think Peter killed Serena Matthews, Margaret?'

'It stands to reason.'

'Does it?'

'Look,' she said, spreading her hands to indicate the knife, the stained shirts, the photo of the woman spread and hogtied. 'It stands to reason.'

When Joe had come into the room, he'd been carrying a small cassette player which he'd set down on the floor at his feet. Now he crouched to pick it up and set it on the table close to Margaret. He explained to her, and to the interview tape, what he was doing, then pressed 'play'.

*Joe, Joe, come on Joe, what are you after? This isn't you talking, is it? No ... it's some profiler. Some shrink. Some old shit-eater who wants my cerebral matter on a slide. Some old turd-muncher just dying to get a probe into my brainbox ...*

*I have to go now, Joe, before your lads come beetling up the street. But I do want to share, Joe. I do want us to be able to swap notes ...*

Tranter reached forward and switched off the recorder. He didn't ask the question, because it wasn't necessary. Almost from the first moment, Margaret started to nod her head; then she shook it from side to side; shook her head and cried into her laced fingers.

'It's Peter,' she said, 'that's him, it's him, that's Peter's voice.'

Tranter and Joe and Jane Lawson waited while Margaret wept. She talked without being understood, her words emerging as a long fluctuating wail muffled by hands. She called his name like a drowning woman calling to someone on the shore.

'Did you ever know a man called Daniel McMahon?' Joe asked her. 'Danny McMahon?'

'No.'

'You're sure it's Peter's voice?'

'It's him.'

'Where do you think he's gone?'

'God alone knows.'

'Was there a place he ever went to?'

'He went fishing. He went to his room and played Mozart.' Suddenly, from nowhere, Margaret was fiercely angry. 'Fucking Mozart!'

She got up from the table, rapping the underside with her knees, and started to walk round the room. 'Fucking Mozart, fucking Mozart, fucking Mozart!'

She hit the wall on the far side of the room and bounced off, then hit the wall again as if someone were throwing her; then she made a run at the wall furthest away. Jane Lawson moved to intercept her, wrapping both arms round, and they fell to the floor together.

Margaret was howling. 'Fucking Mozart! Fuck-fuck-fuck-fuck-fucking Mozart!' She crawled to a corner of the room, taking Jane Lawson with her. She crouched on hands and elbows, her face hidden, and cried heart-shaking cries that came to Jane as a series of shocks transmitted from Margaret's body to her own.

Tranter bagged the evidence, taking his time over the task, then walked out of the room smiling. Joe followed.

Tranter's smile became a laugh. Over his shoulder he said, 'I never liked Mozart either. Fucking Mozart.' The laugh meant: *Got the bastard!*

The photographs told a story. By the time Joe got to the woman roped to the bed the story was less than a quarter told. It was a story of pain, delight in pain, the need for pain, a celebration of pain.

The ring-bound notebook was a series of nightmares written in a neat, stylish hand; they were scenes from the charnel-house. Joe wondered whose nightmares they were and whether they had ever come true.

He turned the pages with a pencil until someone from Forensic arrived to take Margaret's little haul away. He realised that Jane Lawson had been looking over his shoulder as he'd slid each photo aside to expose the next, as he'd read the notebook.

'Is it him?' she asked.

'His wife says it is.'

'Jesus Christ.' She shook her head. 'Jesus. What happens in people's minds?'

Joe wrote down the number of his mobile phone and propped it up against the dedicated phone on his desk and switched off the answering machine. He said, 'If he calls, give him this number.' It was something Joe had avoided until now; the mobile had no means of recording the call and the trace system wouldn't operate.

Tranter was already at Margaret Fulton's house along with search and forensic teams. Joe left Fellgate Cross, stepping out into the bang and blare of the city, trucks towing their hot, sour slipstreams along the through-roads, a low, off-white sky. He hit his first traffic jam on the citybound overpass; you could see a petrol-blue haze crackling on both sides of the freeway.

He looked through the windscreen and saw images reflected there from Peter Fulton's collection of photographs: scenes from the abattoir.

He switched on the radio to drown out what he'd read, but words from the notebook were stronger.

He wondered why he seemed to have some of them by heart.

The Caller was a lithe creature going through furze, flowing under his own pelt, belly down and haunches up. He was muscle on tenterhooks.

He could feel the surge of his blood. His mouth, held part-open, was clean and pink; he could taste his saliva, biscuity and hot.

A snaky sprint downhill; a pause; another rush. He hit the rabbit in full stride, bowling it over and getting his teeth to the nape of its neck. He rode it like a wrangler while it bucked and kicked.

He lay still, covering the creature, his teeth fastened on, feeling the last big shudder strike through his prey, the last slow putter of heartbeats. The dying thing lay in a trance, looking further than its eye could see.

He sat in the chair, the bank of display cases before him. The dream made his hands flex and brought a growl to his throat.

Connie asked, 'What do you see when you paint?'

'It's not what, it's how. It's ways of seeing.'

'I like the burnt colours.'

'This unbelievable summer – the heat. Those colours are everywhere.'

They were walking beside the river. The towpath was white with dust.

'What do you see when you look at me?'

They sat down and he leaned over to dab her mouth with kisses. A pulse went through her that made her breasts ache.

'I can't stop,' Connie told him, as if she were explaining her infidelity to a friend.

They went to a riverside pub and took their drinks to a low wall. The water shone like steel where it flowed out of an upstream bend.

'What's going to happen?'

'I don't know. Do you?'

'No.'

Michael watched her as she drank her beer, trying to discover what it was that so compelled him. That she was attractive? Sexy? Intelligent? That she knew how to punch her weight? That he was drawing her away from another man?

It was simpler than that, and more puzzling. He liked everything about her. The way she looked, the way she spoke, the way she sat, the way she drank beer.

She felt his gaze, steady and unsmiling.

'What do you see when you look at me?'

# Fifteen

The video team had been and gone, Forensic had been and gone, now the search team were taking the place apart. Margaret Fulton had gone to her sister's house where she sat hunched over an empty cup like any refugee. Her sister listened while she talked unstoppably about the times she and Peter had spent together; times that were normal – so normal that you would never normally speak of them. Holidays and anniversaries; celebrations and tiny triumphs; things that happened the same way year after year.

Her topic was 'day in, day out', as if Peter could never have found time for another life, or the need, or the imagination. Everything she remembered – day in, day out – was stained, now, by Peter's secret, just as the shirts were stained, and the knife.

'We've found it,' Tranter said. 'We've got it.'

He and Joe were watching five officers driving rods into the flower beds surrounding the lawn. The earth was baked and they were having a tough time. Inside the house everything was being turned over or taken up. Tranter had come out for a smoke.

'They won't find anything else,' he said.

The gold dust had been under the floorboards in Fulton's music room: more photos, videos, notebooks, an audio tape, a mask, bondage chains with ring clips, a cane, a dildo ... Tranter smoked his cigarette to the last gasp, then licked his fingers, snuffed the tip, and put the butt in his pocket. He was being over-cautious because Joe was there.

Together they went into Fulton's room. Tranter removed the cassette from its evidence bag and used matchsticks to drop it into the deck. It still bore faint traces of fingerprint powder. Later, Leonard Ackerman would listen to it.

It was a woman's voice Joe heard. She wanted to take him on a journey – the same journey that had been described in the photographs and the notebook. Sometimes Joe would be the victim, sometimes the victim would be under his hand. She talked about pain as if you could drink it.

Tranter smiled. He spoke over the woman's voice. 'Hearing this gives me real pleasure, you know? It means I won't have to look at your face every morning. Your shit face. Your fuck of a face.'

Joe nodded and smiled; he cocked an ear towards the cassette deck. 'She gives a lovely performance, your mother.'


Tranter got pretty much everything he asked for: officers drafted in from other divisions to help with the house-to-house, extra detectives to cope with the interviewing of Fulton's friends and relatives and colleagues, more officers to help sift and evaluate items the search team had brought away from the Fulton house. He got extra civilian clerks to deal with the paperwork; he got front-of-the-queue basis for forensic services. Someone from the press office was working on the case full-time in anticipation of the moment when Tranter would go public on Fulton's identity.

Joe took a pack of Labatt's Ice and a dupe tape to Leonard Ackerman's mews house. Ackerman had already heard the tape, but Joe waited while he sat through it again.

'I talked to DI Tranter about this.'

'I know that,' Joe said, 'talk to me.'

'You read my report?'

'Yes.'

Joe took a bottle from the pack and passed another to Ackerman. The profiler held it at arm's length like a myopic connoisseur. He said, 'It's ten-thirty in the morning.'

'It's hot, though.'

'You're right.'

'Also,' Joe told him, 'I know people who drink beer for breakfast.'

Ackerman raised a polite eyebrow. 'Do you? I know people who drink vodka for breakfast: they drink the bottle.' He took a sip. 'So if you read the report ...'

'I want to know more about this guy. It was a good report – informative and making some useful guesses, but it didn't give me much on who he is.'

'Well it wasn't really a profile. You know who he is.'

'Sure. I mean *about* him.'

'Psychiatry isn't an exact science. People don't run to type.' Ackerman took another mouthful of beer. 'On the other hand, of course, they do.'

'Let's talk about a puzzle.'

'Go on ...'

'The bodies of Danny McMahon and Serena Matthews didn't show any signs of sadistic or sado-masochistic activity.' Joe was quoting Ackerman's report. 'Something like that.'

'Something like that, yes. Apart from the fact that they were murdered, of course, and for no apparent reason.'

'But you would have expected it ...'

'Given what little I know of Fulton's psycho-sexual history, I wouldn't have been too surprised to find it. I'm not hedging or anything like that.'

Joe laughed. He wondered whether Ackerman made house calls. 'You read the forensic reports on McMahon and Matthews.'

'Sure.'

'Would you have put someone like Fulton in the frame?'

'Possibly not,' Ackerman agreed, 'unless, of course, I'd

played a tape of the killer's voice and got confirmation from the man's wife that it was him. That might have swayed my judgement.' Ackerman was enjoying his beer, now. He finished his first bottle and started another. 'But it doesn't mean much. Here's how it could go: fantasies for years, then a bit of equipment hidden away for use when the wife's not there. By the way,' he asked, 'did she say that he'd ever asked her to join the SM club? Help him out with a lash or two?'

'No.'

'Mention body-piercing at all?'

'No.'

'Maybe she hadn't seen him naked for a long time, marriages being what they sometimes are. Okay, so – fantasies, some SM paraphernalia under the floorboards, then he goes further – a bit of active participation. I mentioned that in the report.'

'Yes. Where? What sort of place would –'

Ackerman smiled and spread his hands as if to indicate the world at large.

'After that?'

'It's interesting that the wife, what's –?'

'Margaret.'

'– yes, Margaret says that he'd become preoccupied and detached over the last six or eight months. Makes me wonder what he was depressed about.'

'Take a guess?'

'Could have been deprivation, could have been anticipation.'

'Meaning what?' Joe leaned forward to lift his beer and Ackerman's cat hopped up from under the chair, ears back, and threw a left hook at the sudden movement. Joe hit the beer bottle backhanded, then juggled with it a moment before getting control. Ackerman watched the performance with interest. Finally he said, 'Good reflexes. Shall I put the rest of these in the fridge?'

Joe wasn't sure whether the question had to do with the temperature of the beer, the possibility of spillage, or the avoidance of temptation.

Ackerman got up and wandered out. A minute or so later he returned, carrying a full six-pack with a cold dew on the necks of the bottles.

'Meaning,' he said, 'that Fulton could have been cut off from his pleasures; or could have been in an extreme emotional state because he was keying himself up to the real thing.'

'Which?'

'Either.'

'But we're working on the theory that Serena wasn't his first. What about the other times – Danny, at least? The wife would have seen it before – same behaviour pattern.'

'Maybe, maybe not. It depends how hard she was looking. It depends even more on what she was prepared to see. Understandings change. She could brush it aside – pretend it wasn't happening – any number of times before things became intolerable.'

'You mean he might have gone missing before; behaved oddly before. There might have been other evidence, like the shirts and the knife.'

'Nothing so obvious, I'd've thought. Finding that stuff was probably what made it unignorable for her. But there might have been something in the past, yes. You ought to ask her.'

'We have. We'll ask again.' Joe drank some beer; he was thinking it through, and Ackerman let him. A bee circled the room, lazy and heavy, then crawled in among a shelf of books.

Ackerman reflected that he'd seen some cops like Tranter, but none quite like Joe. Tranter was easy to read: in simple terms, he was a gunslinger. He was the man to call when a problem had to be solved and the body-count didn't matter.

Joe was more complicated. Ackerman profiled him as if he were a set of clues.

*A loner by inclination, but a passionate man, too – could be a dangerous contradiction. A straight cop (an obvious virtue, of course, though a possible indication of combativeness). A wry sense of humour, therefore unorthodox. Intelligent, therefore likely to feel undervalued.*

And something else … Ackerman felt round for it. Behind the privacy, a sense of loss? Where did that come from? Childhood, perhaps, or more recent history?

'Would he have seemed depressed,' Joe asked, 'if he was getting ready to kill someone?'

'Sure. Quite possibly. Anyway, what some see as depression, others might identify as aggression – hostile withdrawal, tension, mood swings … It depends what you want to see. If Margaret Fulton had wanted to interpret her husband's emotional state as moodiness and misery, then that's what she'd've found. People have needs. God knows what she was masking.'

'You had him down as a collector. When we first spoke.'

'No, I didn't offer that as a positive theory. It was one possibility among many. It seemed to fit with his apparent obsession with you.' Ackerman gave a broad smile. 'I saw the newspaper piece. Lynda Lomas? Bloody funny, though not for you, of course.'

Joe asked, 'Why did he talk to her? Was he trying to draw me on? Annoy me? What do you think?'

'No, I think he was teasing you. Like a girl who's keen on one guy flirting with another to make the first guy jealous. Sorry about the analogy. It might also be a stage in a progressive revealing of himself. My feeling is still that he wants to be caught. Okay, first he hides it from himself – his feelings, I mean; desires. He hides it from the world. He hides it from his wife. Then he owns up to himself. Next – I suspect – his wife finds out. Now the world's getting to hear about it. But the person he really wants to talk to – for some reason or another –' Ackerman raised an eyebrow at Joe and grinned. 'He gave the story to Lynda Lomas because he wants to provide you with little clues, bits of evidence, hints at the truth.'

'Why not talk to me?'

'Well, he does talk to you. And he's continuing to do that. But you keep his little secrets to yourself, don't you? Lynda Lomas is just a tool – a roundabout way of talking to you, but on his terms. She's a go-between, and I'd suspect a temporary one at that. She'll do for the minute. I expect he bought a dozen copies of her paper.'

'You heard the tape,' Joe said, 'you saw the photos and you read his notebook. Anything there that we might have missed?'

Ackerman opened two beers. There was a little pattern of wet rings, now, on the wheel-and-glass table. 'You probably won't be too surprised to learn that I'd heard it all before. It certainly didn't tell me anything specific about the guy. However inventive people are, the permutations are relatively limited – put your fist up this, hang by your nipples from that. You want the psychopathology of pain in a nutshell?'

'I'm asking whether Fulton liked to do it, or have it done to him. Because it seemed to me he comes into the done-unto category.'

'And if that's so, why would he murder?'

'Right.'

'No. It doesn't work like that. First it's your turn, then it's mine.' Ackerman grinned. 'So to speak.'

Joe passed Ackerman a photograph. It showed Peter Fulton sitting by a swimming pool in the Algarve; he'd put a hand up to shield his eyes. Joe passed over three more photos. Fulton walking down a street in shorts and a Panama; Fulton at a barbecue, talking to a friend, his mouth opening on the next word; Fulton by a riverbank holding up a tench, two forefingers hooked into the gill.

Ackerman nodded, then gave Joe a brief smile. He said, 'Well, they all look like someone.'

Joe got into his car and opened all the windows. The beer and the heat were making him dizzy. The side street beyond Ackerman's mews was quiet and still; a black dog padded by, head hung, tail down, its trot rhythmic as a pendulum.

Joe closed his eyes for a moment, opened them, closed them again. He fell straight into a dream where he was talking to a man he couldn't see. The man – and everything round him – was hidden by a hazy fog, so that Joe couldn't tell whether he was indoors or out, whether it was morning or evening. The man was offering advice Joe couldn't understand in a voice he could barely hear.

When the mist cleared, Joe was standing on a bridge and looking down at the river. His toes gripped the edge of the ironwork and his arms were spread, the pose of someone about to dive. The man was standing behind him and because he was fearful of being pushed Joe turned to see who it was.

It was himself.

Joe gave himself a nudge and dropped towards the water in a perfect swoop of a dive, clear and clean against the brittle blue backdrop of sky. The water looked heavy as mercury. He clove it with his fingertips and slid in with exquisite slowness – forearms, shoulders, head and torso, like putting on a fresh, cool, second skin. When he surfaced, Connie was swimming alongside him holding a mobile phone.

Joe came awake with a sudden lurch; his hand flew out and rapped the car door and his knee came up to hit the steering wheel. He pulled out the mobile and thumbed 'receive'.

'There are other people I could tell you about, Joe. There's Mick or Jan or Angie or Tommo.'

'Who are they?'

'People, Joe. Lost people. And now there's another. Didn't you know that, Joe? Hasn't anyone told you?'

'Who is it?'

'It's Christine. Surely you know that by now.'

'Where is she?'

'I want you to see her. I want you to look at her carefully. Then we can compare notes. Okay? Okay, Joe?'

'I need to have more.'

'No you don't.'

'Tell me where she is.'

'You'll come to her, Joe. You'll come to her in time.'

'I want to talk to you. I know you want to talk to me. There are things I can tell you – about Danny, about Serena; the way they looked when I found them.'

That little laugh like a cough. 'Don't talk to me that way, Joe. I'm not stupid. Do you think I'm stupid?'

Joe said, 'No, Peter, I don't think that. Just tell me where she is.'

A silence began that ravelled out into thin air; Joe could feel himself losing contact.

'Peter?'

'You'll find her, Joe. And when you do, pay attention to her. Pay careful attention. I want to talk to you about Christine.'

He sat in the car, hands on the steering wheel, but didn't switch on.

*Peter* ...

Suddenly there were gulls in the sky, for no good reason, wheeling and calling. Joe started the car and took the horseshoe turn towards Holland Park Avenue. When he rounded the corner he saw the rest of the gulls, a dozen or so, swooping and snatching at fresh garbage in a builder's skip.

Suddenly, he remembered the dream; he remembered flying from the bridge like a bird.

Lynda Lomas was lying under the man of her choice, but she was losing concentration.

Lynda and Mike Fleming had been together for a couple of years, with just a little time off for sideshows. There had never been any talk about moving in together, but they spent a good deal of time at each other's apartments, kept bits and pieces in each other's bathrooms, a few clothes in each other's closets.

Lynda lived on the sixteenth floor of a tower block on the Isle of Dogs with a view straight down the Thames. Mike had an apartment in Hampstead. Lynda had begun to wonder whether the long haul wasn't getting too much for both of them. Mike wouldn't stay that night; his company needed him to be in Edinburgh for a meeting at ten the next morning.

Lynda knew how Mike made love but, even worse, she knew how she made love to him. Just now they had reached a familiar moment – a sort of plateau which entailed slow strokes. She lay still, knees cocked, while Mike slid to and fro, breathing out on the forward movement like a gymnast.

There had been two calls to her home number. Silences, just silences but, on each occasion, something behind the silence that had sent a rash of shivers across her scalp. Her first instinct was to wait and see, her second to phone Joe Morgan. The first was the journalist's instinct and she decided to back it.

She noticed that a little appetite had suddenly grown in her. She ran a hand across Mike's shoulder and down his flank, but it wasn't that. She wanted a drink. She had a glass of whisky, its ice almost melted, on her bedside table, but she didn't see how she could reach out for it – then prop herself up on an elbow to drink – without offering a massive insult to Mike.

Her article had been a major triumph – circulation up, praise from the tenth floor but, best of all, an unbreakable exclusivity. Lynda was the only journo with a line on this guy. Her first editor had once said to her, 'Success is not enough, close friends also have to fail'. Lynda understood the feeling.

Mike's eyes were closed; his rhythm hadn't changed. Lynda wondered whether he'd entered some sort of trance state that would allow him to keep fucking for a couple of days while simultaneously playing the nose flute. She grabbed his shoulders and pulled him down, getting a wide-eyed look and a little grunt of surprise, then turned him over.

Now it was her turn to close her eyes. Now it was her turn to hit the spot. It felt ten times better when she was doing the work. She rode the sensation for while, taking herself up and down the scale, then sat back to take a break. Mike looked up at her and waited. She smiled as she reached for her whisky and took a large gulp, letting the burn flow and settle.

*Yes, that's better; that feels a hell of a lot better.*

She swivelled her hips, a little grind, then another, getting him deeper. The whisky-rush made her head swim. She fell forward, aiming a kiss for his mouth, licking his lips, but rocked back again at once, and sat down hard.

*That's it. Dizzy and busy.*

She flexed like a belly dancer and watched his eyes narrow. She picked up the glass and took another drink.

*Good; that's good; now I'm feeling greedy.*


When the phone went Lynda was asleep and Mike had gone home to pack for the redeye shuttle. She struggled upwards from a dream of power and gain that was lost to her in the moment that she woke. She took the call in the dark.

He said, 'What a mind. What a pigsty.'

Lynda felt her mouth pucker nervously, as if she were trying to speak to him face to face. 'It's a game,' she said, 'don't take it to heart.'

'It's okay, Lynda. I know the rules. I don't care what you choose to say about me.'

'Joe Morgan noticed.' Like someone who wanted to earn his favour. 'You were right about that.'

'Was Joe angry with you, Lynda?'

'He wasn't pleased.' She reached out and switched on the light. In her own flat, in her own bed, she had to remind herself that she was talking to a murderer and that he was probably insane. The thought brought a fear forward. 'How did you get my number?'

'You think that's difficult? No. Don't worry, I just wanted a chance to talk to you without any interference. You understand what I mean?'

'Yes.'

'I told you I'd give you something to catch Joe's attention; do you remember?'

'I remember.'

'Tell me something, Lynda. Did you imagine that Danny and Serena were the only ones?'

'The only –'

'The only ones.'

'Ah …'

'Did you?'

'I hadn't thought about it.'

'No? Surely – you must have.'

'I suppose I might have wondered whether –'

'I can give you something to write about. Remember I said that to you, Lynda?'

'Yes.'

'What did you think it meant?'

'I'm not sure.'

'Guess, Lynda. Take a shot in the dark.'

She remembered her conversation with Joe.

*– good copy … he's got an ego … wants to be famous like any –*

No, that's not it … and you're a stupid bitch.

'There are more,' Lynda said, knowing that she'd got it right.

'Yes, there are more. How many more? Well, Lynda, that's for me to know, isn't it? But I'm going to give you something, don't worry. I'll give you something that'll make your name.'

'What's that?'

'Not yet, Lynda. Not yet.'

'When?'

'Listen … Here's a little starter. This lets you know that I'm serious, okay? Lets you know that I'm not bullshitting. Remember the name Christine; and when you hear it again, remember that I told you.'

'What does it mean?'

'It means that I'm going to give you a story, Lynda. Such a story. The full story –'

'When?'

'– but listen. Are you listening?'

A silence fell between them. His voice had become low and intimate, as if he were drawing her on, and Lynda didn't know that she was supposed to respond.

'Lynda …'

'I'm listening, yes.'

'Nothing to the police. Nothing to Joe Morgan. Not yet. Nothing about this phone call. Nothing about Christine.'

'I can't do that,' she said, knowing she could, knowing she would.

'If you say anything to them, I'll never tell. There's your justification, Lynda. Christine, the other names, the places, the times, the dates … None of that ever, *ever*, if you tell before I'm ready.'

'Why?'

'For you, Lynda? Front page headlines, centre page spreads, everyone knocking at your door. For me –'

The Caller smiled, resting his back against the wall of the phone booth; a quiet corner of a fashionable square near private gardens. A thrush, fooled by the streetlights, sang into the blackness beyond. Lynda could hear it where she lay.

'– for me, the recognition I deserve.'

'You want to meet?' Lynda asked.

'Meet?' The Caller laughed, a staccato of dry coughs, *huff-huff-huff-huff*. 'You think you'd like to meet me?'

'Somewhere very public, somewhere out in the open, perhaps.'

'No, I don't think so, Lynda. "Fiend Reveals Other Victims" is a good story, but "I Capture Fiend" is a better one.' He laughed. 'Fiend ... What a mind you have.'

'How then?'

'Maybe I'll send you a letter.'


The thrush was still singing when the Caller hung up. Lynda dialled 1471 and retrieved the number. She got up and poured herself a fist-sized whisky, then rummaged around in the fridge for something to eat. She made a salami sandwich, picked up the whisky bottle, and took them both to bed.

When she called the number, no one answered. Lynda sat cross-legged on the bed and thought through what had happened. She checked her feelings and decided that she felt fine. She checked her motives and decided that she was proposing to do the right thing. If she told Morgan what had happened, the Caller would keep his secret. Feeling good and making the right decision were helped along by the whisky.

Lynda was a crime reporter and she'd met some violent people, some crazy people, people with neither conscience nor scruple. People who had killed for gain, people who had administered punishment beatings, people who had tortured and maimed for possession of a territory or control of a criminal operation. Well, not people, she thought: men. Men who had sent a finger or an ear through the mail; men who liked to smash kneecaps; men who were vain and stupid and messily sentimental.

She called the number again, trying to imagine the ringing phone in a bedroom somewhere, the window open to the night air and the song of the thrush, the Caller taking his ease with a whisky, perhaps, and eating a sandwich, and smiling at her persistence.

She slept until five, when she woke, suddenly, and got up and locked her bedroom door.

She called the number again to no reply. A hangover headache was knocking steadily at her temples and her stomach was a glass bowl of yellow slops.

She lay awake for an hour, then slept for two. On her second waking, the hangover had really taken hold; she felt like hell. She took some Neurofen with a pint of water, threw up instantly, took some more. She knew the phone call had really happened, but she had to concentrate to keep it from feeling like a dream.

When she called the number for the last time the phone was picked up by a boy on his way to school. He treated her to an amateur's barrage of obscenities, then left the receiver hanging. Lynda could hear, around that exclusive square, the voices of passers-by, car engines starting, the distant *tickety-tick* of a traffic helicopter.

All the birds were singing.

Joe was on his way to work. He looked for Connie and finally found her in the bathroom; she had just stepped out of the shower and was standing naked, arms raised to wrap a towel round her wet hair; she held the pose for a moment, looking at him, half smiling.

He said, 'Any decisions?'

'Well … I spoke to Marianne. It's fine for me to stay with her.'

'And will you?'

'I expect so, yes. Maybe.' She walked through to the bedroom, liking the coolness of air on her damp skin, and he went with her, following, watching droplets of water collect in the nape of her neck and drizzle down her spine. He wanted to gather them on his tongue. He seemed to remember an intimacy that had once lain between himself and Connie, a bond that had to do with looks and touch and understanding, and a sudden sensation of loss overwhelmed him.

Connie was selecting clothes from drawers and closets, throwing them onto the bed. She reached up to a top shelf and her body took on the taut line of a diver just leaving the high board.

Joe looked, then looked away. He said, 'He hasn't called here again.'

'No. I feel … It's so late when you get back. I start to feel uneasy.'

'Which is why you go to the movies sometimes; get back late yourself.'

'Which is why, yes. I get scared.'

'I can't help it, Connie – being late; I wish –'

'No, sure; I know, I know that.'

He looked at her, a steady stare, although for some reason he was the one who felt at a disadvantage, burdened with clothes.

Before he could catch himself, he'd said, 'I love you Connie.'

She nodded.

'Still want a divorce?'

She turned to him and, suddenly, her nakedness showed; she picked up her underclothes, but simply held them as if getting dressed would be too awkward a thing, or too revealing.

'Joe ... If I knew exactly what I wanted – if I had a plan, a clear plan, it would be easy. If I felt the same way all the time. If there were no second thoughts.'

'Sounds like a mess. Sounds dangerous.'

'I know. I'm sorry.'

Connie could think of nothing to do but get dressed; she felt ungainly and oddly embarrassed as she covered up. She kept her eyes lowered, though it was clear how close to tears he was, or to anger, or violence.

She waited for the outer door to close, then walked round the flat to make sure he'd left before lifting the phone.

She said, 'I don't know why I called you. I don't know what I want to say.' She spoke with the phone tucked under her chin, tying the laces of her sneakers at the same time, like someone in a hurry.

'It's a lovely morning,' Michael told her.

# Sixteen

Joe turned the car round in mid-town traffic, taking risks to pass trucks and taxis on the Fulham Palace Road. When he found a clean patch of road on the wrong side he used it, headlights full, hand down on the horn.

'Where's DI Tranter?' His mobile was fitted to a hand-bracket.

'Can't find him, Boss.' Andy Bishop's voice wandered in and out of the airwaves as Joe hit patches of bad reception.

'Who's at the scene?'

'The locals, someone from Serious Crimes. A photo-grapher's already up there apparently. DC Harker's on his way with the video team.'

*Not Tranter*, Joe thought, *but Tranter's man*. 'Forensic?'

'They've been told to attend.'

'Any calls?' Joe asked.

'You mean your friend? No more calls. Frank Jenkins gave him the number of your mobile when –'

'I know.' *A mistake*, Joe thought. *It gives him free access, no constraints.* He said, 'Switch the answer-machine back on. If you hear him come through, activate the trace.'

Joe was driving into the sun, the glare coming at him round the sides of the windscreen visor. He passed a glass-and-steel office block that seemed ablaze with white light.

He drove fast and straight and other vehicles got out of his way.

The Caller had woken early. The girl beside him stirred and

said, 'What's wrong?' though most of her was still asleep.

He pulled back the sheet to look at her body, though he didn't want anything from her.

'Things to do.' He got out of bed and started to collect some clothes. 'Go back to sleep.'

She got up on an elbow. 'It's not your shift.'

'Yes. Of course I know that. But there are things to do.'

The girl knew, of course she did, but didn't know what it was that she knew. It was dangerous knowledge, she understood that much. Most important to her was that things shouldn't change. She had found a safe haven; no one could hurt her now.

Sometimes he stayed out all night, then came home agitated, excited, exhausted. She had found some photographs that he'd hidden, taped to the back of a picture. When she'd looked again they were gone and she was glad. She wondered whether he'd bought them; she trembled to think that he might be the photographer.

He would suffer nightmares fierce enough to scorch his skin, then wake mashing the air with his hands, trumpeting words and strange sounds, though nothing she could understand.

She had found videotapes of moments from TV news broadcasts and part of an episode of *Crimewatch*. They had also disappeared. She asked questions of herself, but refused to listen to the answers.

Sometimes she would confront him: 'What's wrong? Is anything wrong?'

After a nightmare she would hold him until he seemed to recover and his voice would come through, bleak and flat, 'It's nothing. I'm all right', and he would pull away from her and sit up in bed, staring hard at the wall as if it bore some inescapable image from the dream.

Now he stood in the doorway of the bedroom, grinning, ready to go and handsome as the day.

'Listen,' he said, 'everything's okay.' And again: 'Everything's okay.'

She smiled a little smile to hide her disbelief.

Out on the streets, the heat and noise, blare and glare, infused him with a rush of energy that threatened to topple him. He felt light and muscular; he felt as if he could leave a bite-mark in iron.

He made directly for Michael Bianchi's studio because he thought it a fair bet that Connie would either be there or at work and it seemed a long time since he'd looked into Connie's life. He had brought his camera with him, a third eye, and he shot quick snaps of a couple of pretty girls before he reached his car; one of them noticed and looked at him sharply until he waved and grinned and shouted, 'Couldn't resist, sorry, sorry, sorry'.

The girl hid her smile, embarrassed now, but looked over her shoulder at him, once, before turning the corner. The Caller was elated, like a man who has just had tremendous news. It was a day where nothing could go wrong.

Even so, he felt bad about what was happening to Connie and Joe. He gave a fond thought for the girl who had sat up in bed that morning, her little breasts hard as apples, her ribs plain to see, and asked, 'What's wrong?'

'Everyone,' he thought with a smile, 'everyone needs someone.'

Paddy Godwin handed Joe a tube of Vick's. Joe squeezed a coil onto the tip of one finger and smeared it under his nose; the fumes reamed his sinus and made him cough.

Christine was lying face down on the bed, looking to one side, eyes open; the gash in her throat was crusty and wide, the flesh puckered. A vast stain had flooded the sheet on both sides of her body, then seeped down to the mattress which held her blood like a black reservoir. Joe stood still, looking hard at everything there was to see; looking hard at Christine.

*I want you to look at her carefully. Then we can compare notes. Okay? Okay, Joe?*

Paddy said, 'She bled a hell of a lot: that'll have delayed decomposition. On the other hand, she's naked and it's hot as hell.'

'How long?' Joe asked him.

'Three days? Four? You'll know when they get her onto the slab.'

DC Harker said, 'The person in the room above moved out three days ago, which helps us a bit. It was the man two floors up who noticed the smell, though that was when he was coming and going through the front door. He called the landlord who called Dyno-rod. They thought she was a blocked drain or a sewage spill.'

'Person in the room above,' Joe said; it was a speculation.

'No, I don't think so. A woman in late middle age. She left a forwarding address; someone's on the way to see her.' Harker shook his head. 'Okay if I get some air, Boss?'

Joe nodded. Paddy was packing his medical bag, his back to Christine now that his job was done. 'Any chance of catching this fucker, Joe?'

There had never been any doubt about who killed Christine. Her killer had left a message on the wall beside the bed, two words sketched in Christine's blood: *LOOK JOE.*

The room was thick with flying insects, in the air, on Christine, on the bloodsoak. They were a black swarm spelling out Joe's name on the wall. His instinct was to move, but he wanted to know what the Caller wanted him to see; what he was supposed to find when he looked at Christine.

He said, 'We'll get him, Paddy,' and heard the hollowness in it.

*LOOK JOE.*

Scrawled up there alongside the dead heroes.

*

Tranter was trying a theory out on Andy Bishop.

'If we go public on Peter Fulton, he knows we know. Not in our favour. On the other hand, once his name's out there, and his mug shot, anything could happen; we might get a call within minutes. Okay? But we might not; and if we don't go public, he still thinks we're in the dark. He doesn't know his wife's spoken to us, doesn't know she's found the shirts and the knife and so on. He's feeling smart. That's in our favour.'

Tranter picked up a pocket file containing the first few details of Christine's murder and walked off towards the stairway outside the incident room. He didn't need Bishop's reply; he'd already had a conversation on the selfsame subject with George Fisher and been told to wait. It wasn't what he wanted to do, but Fisher outranked him and out-talked him, too.

Christine's death made Fisher nervous. It was political bad news. Lynda Lomas's article had set the tone; now the tabloids would be licking their lips. It had already been decided that no journalist would get to hear about the message on the wall.

Joe was waiting in the upstairs room set aside as office space for the DIs. There was a swivel chair behind a desk and Joe had taken that, leaving Tranter a low sofa that gave him nowhere to put his gut.

Joe might have been asleep. He was thinking about Christine, about the way she'd looked, trying to describe it to himself as if he didn't know what 'lifeless' meant, or 'still', or 'gone'.

Tranter sat with him in silence for a while. Finally he said, 'You talked to Fisher.'

'You think I did.' Joe opened his eyes.

'It makes sense to go public.'

'That's not what our man wants.'

'You mean Fulton?'

'Yes. Fulton.'

'How in hell can you know that?'

'He wants it to be between him and me.'

'That's why he phoned Lynda Lomas, right?'

'He did that to annoy me. He didn't actually tell her anything. Lomas's article was shit, start to finish. She conned the psychic – what's her name? – Drage – and roped in a couple of tabloid doctors with more mouth than brain; the rest she made up.'

'He asked her about Sarah Greencroft. He talked about you. He told her about McMahon and Serena Matthews. Jesus, he gave her the article on a plate. Come on, Morgan, don't tell me he really wanted to talk to you but he'd lost his Filofax.'

'He's getting impatient. He's anxious, he wants things to move faster.'

'Anxious to be caught.' Tranter laughed out loud when he said it.

'He doesn't know that, not really. He wants more excitement. He's needling me and at the same time he's taking chances.'

'Make the name public; someone'll come out of the woodwork soon enough.'

'Wrong move,' Joe insisted. 'The murders are public; he's private. At present he's playing a game of tag. It's not a very fair game because I'm playing blindfold, but it's tag sure enough. He's got a way of thinking about this and it's to do with me and him and where the game might take us. Let the world know who he is and it's a manhunt – anyone's game. He'll go underground and you can add it to your unsolved list.'

Tranter sighed and looked away. There was a single window and, on the floor, two hard white oblongs of sunlight so sharply defined that they could have been painted on. Tranter stared at them as if he were saying a silent mantra.

Joe had seen the act before; in fact he'd used it. He waited until Tranter reacted to the smile on his face.

'He told you what her name was; the dead one.'

'Christine. I wrote a report.'

'Christine was it?' Tranter shuffled some papers in the pocket file.

'No cheque book, no credit cards, no driving licence, no envelopes addressed to her ...'

'A runaway.'

'Maybe. Some people simply don't possess those things.'

'So we can't be sure of the name after all.'

'It's Christine,' Joe said. 'Christine-who is another question.'

'What were the other names he gave you?'

'Mick,' Joe said, 'Jan, Angie, Tommo. But this is Christine.'

'What do you want to do?' Tranter asked. 'We're talking to everyone who knew him – relatives, colleagues, the kids in his class.'

He seemed to be containing a rush of anger; his fingers drummed the arm of his chair and he kept glancing away as if not wanting the sight of Joe's face for more than a few seconds at a time.

'I've spoken to his wife again; she's pretty near a basket case – the way she tells it now, her marriage was normal until the moment when she took a claw hammer to her husband's bureau. Normal's a word she uses a fuck of a lot.'

'I'm waiting for a call,' Joe told him. 'Then I'll know more.'

'Jesus!' Tranter shifted on the sofa, trying to get his paunch right. 'We need some movement, we need something to break the pattern. Talk to Fisher – back me up.'

'You're wrong. I'm not saying we should sit still and do nothing, but you're wrong about releasing the name. Listen, he knows I know. I called him by his name. I called him

Peter. If I seem to be keeping it to myself – a secret between him and me – think how close that brings him.'

'Close to you,' Tranter observed.

'Well, he won't talk to you, will he? I didn't ask for the fucking job.'

'Okay.' Tranter sat on the very edge of the sofa and put his face into his hands. Joe knew how much of a struggle it was for the man to reason with him. When he emerged from his own grip, Tranter was showing a red flush along his cheekbones. 'Let's give it four days.'

'Let's give it as long as it takes,' Joe suggested. 'How do I know when he'll call?'

'No, you're right, that's the fucking problem. This bastard's waving his dick at you and you sit there with your mouth open.' Tranter yanked at the door. 'One thing leads to another, you know?'

It was a good gag, but Joe waited until Tranter had gone before he laughed.

Eyes closed again, Joe led himself round the room, the cloud of insects, his own name written there, Christine as the centrepiece, her body marbled red and black.

*I spy with my little eye –*

Paul Harker had been checking unsolved crimes for the other names: Mick, Jan, Angie, Tommo. The only possibility was Angie. Angela Dawes had been found murdered two years earlier in Buckinghamshire. The body had been found in a beech wood; her throat had been cut and there had been an attempt to burn the body. The other names each drew a blank. The Dawes file was on its way to Fellgate Cross.

Andy Bishop came in and stood by the desk. He was holding the audio tape that the search team had found under the floor of Peter Fulton's music room.

'It's called interdepartmental co-operation,' he said. 'A guy called Owen in the Vice Squad listened to this. They know

179

who she is. Mullins says she hasn't changed the spiel in ten years.'

'Name?'

'Lola Lash.'

'Her parents must have had a bleak sense of humour.'

'Or Terri Bennett. Teresa.'

'And is she just in the tape business?'

'She's in the whatever you want business.'

Joe stood up. 'Let's get a warrant and see if that's true.'


The Caller was trying to read the pattern of events. First Connie had gone into Bianchi's apartment. Then came a gap of about fifteen minutes: long enough for kisses and hellos, not long enough for bed. Well, not really ... Then Bianchi had emerged and walked the twenty metres to a double ramp that led down to his garage – a building that might have been a waterside storehouse at some point. He'd driven away in the Mercedes and been gone almost an hour.

The Caller had parked by the wall at the far end of the street. From where he sat, window open, feet up on the passenger seat, he could see river traffic and strollers and gulls drifting on the shreds of a breeze. He could also see Michael Bianchi's door and Michael Bianchi approaching it, having left his car out on the street. The Caller thought Bianchi was a good-looking guy: tall, lithe, blond hair that went straight back from his forehead, a good, strong face, a wide, subtle mouth. He was wearing an outsize white linen shirt over white linen trousers that bagged and flopped as he walked. The clothes were loose, but you got a sense of a hard, long-limbed body beneath.

*Careful, Joe. This guy's trouble. Connie likes this guy. You've got a problem, here, Joe, that you don't know about. It's a big problem.*

Connie and Michael came into the street hand in hand and walked to the Mercedes. The Caller started his engine. He was driving a small Renault, but that wouldn't hinder him. In London, walkers overtook the cars.

*Don't worry, Joe, I'm on the case.* The Caller laughed out loud; he felt light-headed. *I'm invisible, Joe. I'm your eyes and ears. I'll let you know. I'll be calling you soon, Joe.*

When they hit the main street, he fell in a couple of cars behind the Merc and, almost immediately, they slowed for a back-up. Anyone glancing towards the Renault would have seen a man chortling to himself over some remembered incident, some private joke.

*Have you found Christine yet, Joe? Not yet? You will soon.*

The line of cars started to move. Michael and Connie were heading west, taking the line of the river.

*Christ, I feel good, Joe. I feel so good I could kick down walls, I could tear up trees. It's remembering Christine, Joe, that's what's making me feel this way. I looked at her, Joe, I looked at her so closely, and I watched her go, I watched her all the way. I watched her change.*

*Change.*

*Oh, I want to talk to you, Joe. We really need to talk. This is alive, Joe; this is what alive feels like.*

They drove to Richmond Park and walked to a hilly area above the lakes.

Michael was carrying a picnic hamper – the reason he'd left the flat earlier. They walked like lovers, his arm round her shoulders, her hand resting in the small of his back to get a hint, with each stride, of the roll of his ass.

On the crown of the hill was a fringe of trees that gave shade; they were heading for that.

Connie unpacked the hamper like a child hunting surprises. She found champagne in a cooler-compartment, crystal glasses, *gravad lax*, dill and mustard sauce, quails' eggs, beluga caviar in little pastry cups, salad, perfectly ripe Brie, explorateur, strawberries, yoghurt.

As she looked at the feast, a sudden thought came to her and she asked Michael, 'Are you rich?'

'I am,' he said, 'yes. Does it matter?'

'I don't know. I hadn't thought ... hadn't expected it.'

'Family money allowed me to paint – allowed me to serve my apprenticeship without distractions. Now the paintings sell. The family money's still there of course. I know I'm lucky, but it doesn't really register because life's never been any other way.'

'How well do they sell?'

'Pretty well.'

'Are you known for it?'

He smiled. 'Oh, yes.'

'You're famous.'

'Only a bit – and only if you know about contemporary English painters. I don't get mobbed in supermarkets.'

Connie ate and drank without speaking for a while. She looked away towards the activity at the lakes, half a mile downhill: walkers, dogs, kids with radio-controlled boats. Michael left her to think it through.

Without turning her head she said, 'I think it's okay.' Which made him laugh. She looked at him, then, and laughed too, and came across the picnic rug on all fours to kiss him. 'I think it's great.'

She made love to him in the long grass between the trees, half-clothed, the sun hot on her back.

Someone went by. Someone spoke. They didn't stop: not being able to see was the same as not being seen. When Michael was above Connie, she could see fist-sized clouds in a hard blue sky and Michael's face, made rosy by the sun. When Connie sat astride Michael, she peeled off her T-shirt and bent low over him. After a moment she sat back and threw up her arms and laughed out loud.

The Caller was braced in the low branches of a tree. The shutter release sounded like slow applause.

# Seventeen

Joe handed Terri Bennett a cropped and enhanced photo of Peter Fulton and watched her moment by moment collapse.

She said, 'I didn't know what to do.' The accent was raw south London and her voice was shrill. 'I knew I'd have to tell someone. I just didn't –' She sat down and put her elbows on her knees and her face in her hands. Joe was happy to wait.

'I could take a look round,' Bishop offered.

Joe shook his head. 'We'll get there,' he said.

Terri worked in a leather one-piece with nipple holes, a split-crotch, spikes, chains and a mask with a zippered mouthpiece. Her clients didn't notice that she was forty-five, that her complexion was patchy, that her belly had a fold, that she sometimes didn't get all the grey out of her hair; or else they didn't mind.

In denim shorts and a cut-down T-shirt, Terri looked every year of her age. She sat down on a chintzy couch in her sitting room and closed her eyes, as if in the hope that when she opened them Joe and Andy Bishop would be gone.

The house was a big suburban villa, detached and standing in about an acre of garden; a stockbroker's house. There were a couple of bad-taste landscapes on the wall, and a large mirror in a gilt frame tricked out with scrolls and a fat cherub. A bank of framed photographs on a sideboard showed Terri in family groups or with tanned men in foreign towns.

On the way over, Joe had let Bishop drive so that he could call Owen.

'There used to be three of them: the ugly sisters; except they weren't – one was a real looker. We knew about them, and we busted them a couple of times, but generally speaking it wasn't worth the effort. They did funny things to sad men to make them happy. Now Terri works alone.'

'Why?'

'The other girls moved on or gave up the game. Terri took on replacements a couple of times, but each time she found someone who was trouble – rolling the punters or dealing drugs on the side. She came close to getting a serious prison sentence – crack being dealt on the premises by a girl who OD'd on her own stuff and wound up in A & E. Terri said she knew nothing about it and I bet she was telling the truth.'

'The tapes?' Joe had asked.

'Clever merchandising. See the whip, feel the pain, buy the tape.'

'Does she keep files?'

Owen had paused. 'Never thought about it. Maybe. Insurance only though; I don't see Terri putting the black on a punter; she had regulars.' He had laughed. 'Lot of goodwill there if she ever sold up.'

'Minders? Pimps?'

'No. This is strictly suburban sin. Small business. I expect she could get a government development grant if she applied. It's all too far from the centre for any of the real snatch-supply outfits to want some.'

'You like her,' Joe said.

'In her day,' Owen had told him, 'Terri Bennett went off like a belt-fed Bofors.'

The photo of Peter Fulton had slipped to the floor. Joe crouched down to retrieve it and stayed there, at Terri's level, until she opened her eyes. She was shaking; a tic was making her mouth purse, as if she were puckering up for a kiss.

Joe said, 'Come on, Terri.'

'I'm sorry,' she said. 'I'm sorry. I just didn't know what to do.'

'Come on, Terri.'

'I should have said something, shouldn't I?'

'Come on …'

'Has he been missed?' she asked.

The loft space was big, the full floor space of the house except for the mansard roof-slope. There were drawn blinds at every window, though they let through a pale, filtered light, like a false dawn. At a quick glance, you might have thought that it had been converted into a home gym, until you looked more closely at the equipment. Terri stood halfway down the turning stair and let Joe and Andy Bishop overtake her. Bishop seized her arm, but Joe paused and shook his head.

'Don't worry; she doesn't have to come up here.'

There was no door, just an extended bannister that ran along the near edge; the stair took you straight into the room. Joe was at the top and looking directly at the far gable-end under the pitch of the roof.

The crucifix was mounted high on the bare brick, man-sized and bearing the weight of a man, though Fulton seemed half his height, as if death had already shrunk and wasted him. His body had folded at waist and knees, and he hung from arms that reached straight back to the crosspiece. Joe was reminded of medieval sculptures of the Passion, where the ugliness and rack of crucifixion was plain to see.

Fulton was tied, not nailed. He was standing on a support built into the upright and the bonds that held his shanks, his thighs, and both his wrists were thick, soft, red velvet ropes.

His head had fallen to his shoulder like a ripe gourd about to drop. Something had taken his eyes. He was naked apart from a loincloth and you could see where Terri had hit him with the whip by the lines of livid mottling across his torso where the blood had puddled.

Bishop took a couple of steps towards the crucifix, then a couple of steps back, but Joe went close. The insects were working Fulton like a little factory farm; he was bloated, going black at the joints, and it was impossible to know what he'd looked like in life.

Joe heard Bishop going downstairs; he heard the sound of Terri's voice, anguished, apologetic, wretched; he heard Bishop phoning in. He craned his neck at Fulton as figures in paintings gaze up from the foot of the cross. He looked for a long time and saw matter and minerals, skin and a hank of hair; the mechanics of a man.

'What were you doing to him?'

'It was his –' A pause. 'He liked to be hurt. Not like some of them; but he liked ...' Joe waited. 'Liked to feel it.'

'What were you using?'

'A whip.'

'Tell me what happened.'

'It was a – must have been a heart attack.'

'Did you try anything?' Terri looked lost. Joe said, 'Try anything – resuscitation.'

'He was dead. He died up there. I just –'

'How did you know?'

'That he was dead?'

'Yes.'

Terri looked at the floor, then towards the window, then at Joe. 'Of course he was dead.'

'He's dead now.'

'He died.' Another pause while Terri tried to think about what was really being said: not dead; not at first; not immediately. She reached a decision. 'No,' she said, 'he was dead. He died; I saw it happen.'

'What did it look like?'

'Look like ...'

'Tell me how you knew.'

'Everything went out of him.'

They were waiting for police transport, for video and forensic, for Paddy Godwin and Steve Tranter.

'If you'd taken him down, though. Got him down and called an ambulance. Mouth-to-mouth until they got here. Who knows?'

Terri's mood had evolved from shrill to sullen; now that her secret was out most of her nervous energy seemed to have gone with it. She said, 'Well, I don't do mouth-to-mouth,' but didn't even make herself laugh.

They sat in silence for a while. Joe was holding in his mind the picture of Fulton on the cross, his face collapsing under its own weight, his body mottled and waxy. There was an impulse in him, strong as a shove in the back, to go upstairs and take a photo.

'He let out a terrific yell,' Terri said suddenly. 'A great shout. Straining at the ropes, like he wanted to jump down. Then he fell back. He was shaking. I hit him again – I mean, I thought it was all part of the ... you know. Act. He was looking straight at me. Then he died.' She looked thoughtful as if she were running through the sequence of events again. 'Just died. There wasn't anything left. Anything left to do.'

Steve Tranter walked a small circle on the floor of the loft space; he was too angry to stand still. When he'd completed the circle, he started another. While he walked, he muttered to himself. Joe thought the man looked like someone casting a spell.

Tranter's incantation was *Fuck-fuck-fuck-fuck-fuck*, the repetition blending like a mantra. He stopped with his back to the gable-end and stared at Joe with eyes that seemed to have lost their focus.

'Just as well we didn't go public.' Joe had hoped to resist saying it, but no one's perfect.

Tranter said, 'I can't breathe up here,' though he made no move to leave. As if it were an afterthought, he said, 'Don't gloat, Morgan. You called the bastard Peter when he phoned your mobile.'

'I did. On a chance.'

'Bullshit. You didn't –'

'It was a risk.'

'– you didn't think it was Fulton.'

'I wasn't sold on the idea.'

'Smug,' Tranter said. 'You smug gobshite.'

Joe shrugged. He said, 'Whatever you like.'

'She'll go down.' Tranter slapped a roof beam with the meat of his hand. 'Stupid bitch. I'll throw the fucking book at her.' Joe wasn't sure whether Tranter meant Terri Bennet or Margaret Fulton.

Camera flashes lit the gloom like summer lightning. They had put up ladders either side and now were lowering him, slowly, with a care that you might mistake for tenderness, two men above and two below, arms reaching down, arms reaching up, each man aproned and gloved and wearing a toothbrush moustache of gel.

When the corpse was almost grounded, a third man stepped in to help and the weight staggered him slightly. The body slipped and the helper took it under the arms, bending his knees to make a lap.

Paddy Godwin said, 'All right? All right?' though he wasn't asking anyone in particular. As Paddy stepped forward, ready to get down to work, one of the back-up team waved a body-bag like a fan and a cloud of flies rose to the pitch of the roof.

Joe thought he heard Terri crying from somewhere downstairs. Paddy shouted for more light and someone pulled the drawstring on one of the window blinds. The sudden sunlight made everything crude and sad.

Later that day, Joe called on Margaret Fulton. She and her sister, Elizabeth, were sitting side by side on a sofa watching home videos. The videos were like the photos Joe had seen at Margaret's house: high days and holidays. There was a blankness in Margaret's eyes that nothing could replace and she watched the images on the screen like someone watching water.

'This is all she does,' Elizabeth told Joe. 'It's all she can do. Not eat, not sleep, not talk.'

Joe took Elizabeth into the kitchen and told her about her brother-in-law's death. As she listened, Elizabeth's face flushed a bright red; she put a hand to her cheek, leaving white finger-marks. After a moment, she began to shake her head, as if saying 'No' would make a difference, and she was crying, soundlessly, eyes wide.

'What will I tell her?' she asked. 'What will I say?'

'I don't know,' Joe said. 'In your place, I wouldn't know.'

Before he left, Joe went back to the sitting room. Elizabeth glanced at him as if looking to him for a lead, then sat down next to her sister like a movie-goer finding her place in the dark.

Margaret Fulton was intent on her husband's image as he lined up his shot on a seaside putting green. Joe remembered that same intense look as she had stared at the knife and the bloodstained shirts, as she'd listened to the tape and the Caller's soft country burr.

'If you film me I'll miss it,' Fulton said. His voice was slightly masked by wind and the mike on the camcorder wasn't the best; even so, you could hear the broad Scottish accent plainly.

'... I'll miss it,' and his tap-in shot clung to the rim of the hole for a moment, then ran away down the borrow of the green.

# Eighteen

Lynda Lomas sat alone in her office having a cigarette and a spritzer for lunch, wondering whether she was getting good luck or bad. She had written a straightforwardly sensational piece on the bed-sit killing. Police information said victim unknown, perpetrator unknown, but Lynda knew that wasn't so. She hadn't been told about the words *LOOK JOE* written on the wall – none of the press knew; but she was certain that the murdered girl was Christine. That meant another score for the Caller and a very different sort of story – a story in which Lynda could claim to be a major player. It was a story she really wanted to write, but to do so would let Joe Morgan know about her night-time conversation with the Caller. And that might well bitch her chance at the feature of a lifetime.

*Did you imagine that Danny and Serena were the only ones? I'm going to give you a story, Lynda. The full story ... I'll give you something that'll make your name.*

Christine's anonymous death had become 'Runaway's route to evil' and was sharing the front page with a 'Minister slips in sleaze-pool' scandal. Lynda spent some of the afternoon fighting for the lead headline, lost the battle, then took off to avoid the end of day crush.

His message was on her answer-machine. It said *Soon*. It said *Wait-but-not-for-long*. Hearing his voice she felt the excitement of the chase; getting a good story, something that would wipe the opposition and get you a byline in eighteen-point type. But there was something else, something almost completely masked by appetite: a feeling of discomfort, like a toothache starting up or the first flutter of a loose eyelash.

She took a shower as if she couldn't care less, but switched off the machine as soon as she emerged; she walked naked from the living-room to the kitchen area and made herself a long gin and tonic. The temperature was still in the upper eighties and she hadn't bothered to towel off. She stood in front of the big glass doors that opened onto her sixteenth-floor balcony, too far back to be seen but close enough to let the faint breeze off the river cool the droplets of water on her shoulders and flanks.

A tug came upstream, towing eight flatbed containers. There were pleasure-craft and cruisers and a water-taxi with the name of a hotel in gold script along the side. Lynda finished her gin, made another, then went to the bedroom and found a light, cotton sarong and a cross-over halter-top because she was hungry and it would have felt odd to cook while naked.

She made a salad and put a tuna steak under the grill. The phone rang and she walked to it with such calm, such ease, that she could barely feel the floor beneath her feet. Mike Fleming was calling from Brussels; he was watching TV in a room at the Hilton and waiting for two very boring men to pick him up for dinner. They were company clients and had to be indulged. Mike was hoping for a sympathetic ear and five minutes of dirty phone. Lynda pretended she was on the way out and late for the early showing of a movie.

She drank some wine with her supper, telling herself that she'd have just one glass, just two, just this bottle. Her sister phoned with news of children and unpayable bills. A friend called around eleven – the hour of stealthy desperation; the hour of worse-to-come – to tell of a collapsed relationship. No one else called.

Her bedroom was too high to gather water-lights, though

she had set the bed so that she could look down and watch river-traffic and the ragged glow from street lamps sculling the surface.

Wine and the river's reflections sent her to sleep.

She dreamt of him. His face wasn't clear, but his breath stirred wisps of hair as he bent to kiss her neck. Their lips touched, barely touched, and drew apart carrying each other's dampness; his hand rested on her shoulder.

*Soon, not long*, was what she heard him say; and there came a movement inside her, troubling and deep, as if something had touched her lights.

He called at three-thirty, long after the dream had ended and been forgotten. Lynda woke from a mineshaft of sleep, struggling upwards, hearing the sound of the phone a full thirty seconds before she could manage to answer it.

'You were asleep.' His soft accent even softer in the middle of the night.

'Yes.'

'I haven't slept. I've been writing. The full story. I told you I'd give you the full story. It's all written down.'

Lynda said, 'That's great.' She heard her own voice in the quietness and thought it was a stupid thing to have said. The only thing to have said. She was still coming awake and her mind was ahead of the conversation: front page, centre spread, TV commercials, syndication.

'... just as I wrote it.'

She guessed at the rest and said, 'Sure; of course.'

'I'm not saying you can't embellish it. But my statement remains untouched — yes?'

She thought about the word 'embellish'. A good word to use; an accurate word. This guy's had an education; he's read a book. Embellish? You bet I'll embellish. I'll embellish every dollar and Deutschmark out of it. Every franc, every lira.

194

She said, 'It's a deal.'

'I need a promise.'

'Okay, yes, you have it.'

'I need to hear it.'

'I promise.'

'Cross your heart and hope to die.' A piece of foolishness that drew Lynda on then made her hesitate. She heard him laugh his dry cough-laugh.

'I believe you, Lynda. I believe you.'

A little pause settled between them; Lynda caught the low rumble and gear-change of a passing truck.

He said, 'I hope you won't think too badly of me, Lynda. When you read what I've written.'

'I'm not here to judge you.' She smiled at herself: it was like acting a part.

'I've included Christine. I saw your report. I know why you didn't say it was Christine – that you knew it was Christine.'

'Yes.'

'Because Joe Morgan would realise that we'd spoken.'

'Yes.'

'And you want to keep Joe out of things just at present, don't you?'

'It's not like –'

'Or else you wouldn't have got this story. The story of a lifetime.'

'Yes.'

'Do you think of it that way, Lynda? The story of a lifetime?'

'Yes, I –'

'The story of a lifetime. Of course it is.'

'How do I get it?'

'I've arranged for a courier.' He laughed. 'Not from my place, of course. I take it to their office, they bring it on.

Pretty early, Lynda. Pretty early in the morning. A few hours' time. I want you to run it as soon as you can.'

'Do you say who you are?'

'No, I don't say that.' He laughed again, then stopped suddenly. 'You can find a name for me, Lynda. You're good at that. The Fiend.' He laughed. 'Well, I don't mind.'

He hung up, abruptly, before she could really register the fact. There was a silence, then, that carried a weight of things unspoken; things she said to herself.

*Get some protection, Lynda.*

*What? Call Joe Morgan?*

*Why not?*

*Because I'd be handing over an unbelievable story. Whack: straight onto the police spike. They'd kill it to keep back the things he says, things he reveals – a means of identification. Elimination of cranks and weirdos.*

*This guy knows where you live.*

*He's probably known for a while. He's had my ex-D number for a while. Relax. He needs me.*

*The Fiend.*

*That's me, not him. I came up with that one. Listen, he wants the paper, wants publicity, that's me and only me.*

*As soon as the story's in – when it's no turning back – talk to Morgan then.*

*Won't have to.*

Lynda smiled as if she were talking to someone else.

*He'll be talking to me.*

She dialled the trace-code and retrieved the number he'd been calling from. A street phone for sure, so why bother? But she dialled the number anyway.

He lifted the phone. He said, 'Sleep tight, Lynda.'

Darkness still on the water, a blush of light in the sky. First light: pearl and then primrose. Lynda fell out of a doze, fell out of a bright half-waking dream in which a bird came to her window and beat the glass with rapid wings, its face his face, its voice his voice.

She showered, shrugged into a white XL T-shirt with a giant strawberry motif, and switched on the radio. It was just before five a.m. She made coffee and took it to a canvas chair on the balcony, where she sat to watch the city wake up, but went back to sleep herself. When she opened her eyes three hours later, a rush of adrenaline almost toppled her from the chair. She had forgotten where she was – early sunlight dazzling her as she looked out over a sixteen-storey drop. Her door-buzzer wasn't sounding, but she knew the buzzer had woken her.

She looked through the fish-eye, then unlocked the door. The messenger was wearing leathers and a delivery bag with a cross-over strap; he was carrying his motorcycle helmet in one hand, a clipboard and a large manilla envelope in the other. Lynda took the package and signed her name, smiling her thanks. The messenger smiled back, then hit her a clip alongside the head with the boss of his helmet and she imagined for a moment that she was flying.

Her eyes clouded. The side of her head felt numb, but a pain like neuralgia ran in her jaw. She thought someone spoke and considered that it might be important to know exactly what had been said, but a darkness was gathering at the corners of her vision and she could hear only a sound like hammers and anvils which was the sound of her own heart.

' … be disappointed because … Are you with me? Sorry, I wasn't sure whether you could hear me. I'll go back a little. I was saying that you're going to be disappointed, I'm afraid, because I haven't written anything for you. Sorry. I lied about that. In fact, I did consider sending a letter to your editor – or to the Press Council is it? – to complain about the crap you printed about me. Fiend. Monster. All a bit uncalled-for, Lynda. And a couple of pompous bastards to talk about what's inside my head. And a psychic, for God's sake. Although … Although I ought to tell you that she got it right about the fields and the animals; the farmhouse — remember? — with a couple of barns nearby. Spooky, isn't it? It gave me a little jolt, Lynda. Not that anyone could know exactly where, exactly who … but it gave me a little shiver. Near the sea. I wonder how such people do that. Say, near the sea, and get it right. Do you know how? No. No, of course, why would you? You just write it down and twist it round and make lies of it. Psycho. Butcher. Wasn't that it? Let me tell you, Lynda, you don't have the first –'

… *tied can't move oh Christ mouth taped can't speak I'm looking at him this is him really him oh Christ if I …*

' – idea what it means. What it means to be me. I have to get, you see, I have to get Joe's attention. He seems to think I'm someone called Peter. Who the fuck's Peter? He's going, you see, I think he's going –'

… *could speak could speak to him say something get my hands free tell him …*

' – down the wrong track, getting it wrong, getting further away from me. Let me tell you one thing, Lynda, just one thing, about Danny and Serena and the rest, about Christine. One thing I don't –'

… *anything any lie oh Christ I don't know what just anything to make …*

' – understand. It's this. When they've gone, what's left? Do you understand? Do you –'

… *a difference anything what? what difference? I don't know but oh Christ this isn't …*

' – know, Lynda, what it is?'

… *happening he isn't here he is he is I can't bear I don't know what …*

It registered that he was asking her a question and she nodded her head, frantically: *Yes, I know. Take this stuff off my mouth*

*and I'll tell you. I know. Of course I know. I've always known.*
*You want to know? Ask me. Let me speak.*

He leaned towards her, Mr Goodlooking with his lean
face, his even tan and his ponytail; she lost a fleck of skin
from her lip when he pulled the plaster away.

He said, 'If you scream I'll hurt you. Don't scream.'

It would have done little good anyway. The apartment
block was for young professionals; at this time in the morning
they were all in BMWs heading across the river to the banks
and the ad agencies; apart from which, the block was new,
the architects Swedish, and the sound-proofing a sales factor.

Her wrists were taped behind her back, making it
necessary for her to lean back on her elbows. The strawberry
T-shirt had ridden up to the tops of her thighs, but he was
smiling into her face, his eyes holding hers. She wondered if
the thought of sex would help or hinder. The idea fuelled her
panic. She didn't want anything to happen to her, anything at
all, but most of all she didn't want to die.

'Give me your thoughts, then, Lynda. If you think you
know.'

She had forgotten the question. He strolled to the glass
doors, the sun behind him, and cast a shadow that nudged
her foot. He folded his arms and gave her a speculative look.

'If you think you've got the answer.'

Lynda took a deep breath in the hope of controlling her
voice when she spoke. She was shaking so much that the
breath seemed to stutter in and stutter out.

'Look, I know you're angry because —'

'Do you?'

'Yes, I know the things I wrote —'

'Do you know the answer?'

'Listen, listen, please, I'll write, it doesn't matter what,
anything you want, print what you write, or we could write
it together, whatever you want to say, I could help you,

199

please, *please*, I know I can do this, promise this, or else just say –'

He smiled and walked back to where he had left his delivery bag.

' – what I should do, talk to the police, Joe Morgan, whoever, explain things for you, you could go away, I wouldn't –'

He took out a roll of tape and walked towards her, snagging the cut end of the tape with his thumbnail, then pulling it free.

' – tell anyone, I'm sorry if I upset you, please, listen, it was just, half of it I didn't write, subs wrote it, more than half, they changed –'

He tore off some tape and crouched before Lynda, smiling and shaking his head.

' – please, if there's, whatever you wanted from me – you remember, when we spoke on the phone – I can get all the publicity, please, *please*, or whatever you think –'

He held the tape an inch or so from her mouth, as if offering food, and smiled as if to say: Hopeless, give up now; she stopped speaking, but as he laid on the tape he sealed in the first note of a cry.

*He's opening the bag, his messenger's bag, and he'd looked, oh Christ, he'd looked like the real thing through the fish-eye, leathers and helmet and his ponytail.*

She could hardly breathe for fear of him. He took items from the bag and laid them out on her dining-table. He turned and started to undress: boots, leathers, T-shirt, until he stood before her naked. He made a neat pile of his clothes and put them on the far side of the room.

*These noises I'm making, hear me? do you hear me? please hear me! these noises, listen, mean sorry, they mean please, sorry, mean please sorry sorry please sorry please sorry sorry please please please –*

He said, 'You can help me, Lynda. Really. Help me to find the answer. You can help me a lot.'

# Nineteen

Underground was a little cooler than the streets, but airless. Paul Harker was banged up in a windowless room eight feet by ten at the end of a long corridor. To get there he passed five other rooms cluttered with files, cleaning equipment, spare office furniture. One room was locked; it contained rifles and small arms. Harker's room was empty save for a small armchair on coasters facing a TV-VCR setup.

Harker called his room the bunker. He sat with a rotating fan on one side and his notes on the other. He had trapped the notes with a big glass paperweight — a cube with dice spots. He always kept the six uppermost for luck, but he wasn't having much of that.

He was searching three days of tapes from video cameras located in the five pay phones the Caller had used most frequently. Five times seventy-two hours of faces talking down a phone. Sometimes he would hear things that he'd pass on to serious crimes, or the drug squad, or vice. It intrigued him that the most-asked question, when a punter was calling a whore, was 'So can I come round?' as if she were likely to say no, she had a bit of a headache, and why did men think about only one thing?

Before he started the long haul through days and nights of one-sided conversations, though, he would view an edited version of the faces, just the faces and a word or two from each. He was listening for the Caller's accent; he was looking at the faces to see whether he recognised anyone from the interviews he'd conducted.

The edited tape would be screened in the incident room, too, running on a soundless loop. Anyone from the team having a spare moment would sit and watch. Tranter had specified that every officer had to find time to see the tape through. Nothing had come of it, which was what everyone, Tranter included, had secretly expected. People checked the faces when they could: taking a break with a cup of coffee, perhaps; or you'd see two officers talking football scores but both watching the screen.

It was the self same morning. The Caller was at Lynda Lomas's flat. He had just fixed the tape to Lynda's mouth –

*Hopeless, give up now ...*

– just trapped the first plosive moment of a cry as it broke in her throat. Soon he would open the messenger's bag and lay out on the table the items he needed.

Harker had started the dupe tape in the incident room, then gone down to the bunker after stopping to make himself a coffee. Which meant that the incident room tape was five minutes ahead of Harker's.

Enhanced film gave the Caller's face a dead look. The acoustic hollowed his voice as he said, *'Cross your heart and hope to die.'*

There were four or five people in the incident room, talking and watching, laughing and watching, unwrapping a sandwich and watching.

Someone said, 'I've seen that guy before.'

Three cars, ten men all armed. An ARV was diverted for back-up and the siege unit alerted. It was the right thing to do, though Joe was certain of the outcome.

The place was close to where Serena Matthews had been found dead; an end-of-terrace house with a tiny scrub of garden and a front door that opened directly onto the street. Officers covered both sides while others took a power-hammer to the door. The rooms echoed to the sound.

Broken furniture, a smell of rot, a rubble of empty cans and bottles; fast-food cartons in the kitchen; bedding still on the bed.

'We interviewed him here,' Andy Bishop said. 'This is where he lived then.'

'Not for long,' Joe said. 'And it wasn't his place, not really. Is someone speaking to the landlord?'

'It's a lettings agency. Yes.'

'Okay. They won't know much. Whether he paid his rent, that's all.'

'Through a bank?' Bishop wondered. 'A standing order, maybe.'

Joe laughed at the joke. 'Of course. Who would ever think of paying in cash and using a false name?'

Each of the rooms had its own hot stench. Joe turned some detritus with his foot and Bishop reminded him that Forensic hadn't been through.

'Makes no difference,' Joe told him, but he trod carefully as they went back to the door.

In the car, he took a call from Steve Tranter who said, 'She's dead –' Tranter's voice always carried an edge, as if 'Go to hell Morgan' was lurking behind every remark.

'Yes,' Joe said, 'I expect she is.'

'– so much blood, Christ, she must've emptied out.'

'Any message?'

'Yes. He decorated some glass doors that open onto a balcony above the river. He really has got a bee –'

'Saying what?'

'Saying: "Look again Joe." '

'Okay.'

'What?'

'I said, Okay.'

'What did you find?'

'We found an empty house.'

'To think that we had the bastard. Had him within arm's length.'

'No,' Joe said, 'let's not think about that.'

'I'll see you back at —'

'He'd cut her throat, am I right?'

'Like the others. Come and see. Paddy's still working on her and Forensic are everywhere with tweezers and swabs. They won't be bagging her for a while.'

'All right,' Joe said, 'but I know what I'll find.'

There was a pause, then Tranter said, 'Find? Find what?'

'A dead body. Nothing else.'


The waiter brought Connie's third glass of wine to the table, and Marianne Russell looked at it in disgust and envy.

'You're not working this afternoon ... '

'Yes I am.'

'I'd be knock-kneed.'

'It's having no effect.'

'So far.'

They were at a restaurant more or less equidistant from their offices. Connie had insisted on it for its prices, which were close to ruinous, as if doing that were a substitute for true recklessness. 'My treat,' she'd said, and Marianne had responded, as an old friend should, by asking, 'What's up?'

Connie had chosen *gravad lax*; she had cut it into strips one way and was now making squares by cutting it the other.

'I'm sorry,' she said, 'that I made you an alibi.'

'Am I? Or do you really want to stay? You're welcome, you know that.'

Connie nodded. She put down her fork and picked up her wine. 'I might,' she said. 'Neutral ground.'

Marianne had eaten everything on her plate; now she

pushed the plate aside, resentful of her own appetite. Marianne was in love with mirrors.

'Is it serious?'

'Yes,' Connie said and looked up suddenly as if she had surprised herself with the remark.

'There's a theory that says people fall for people when they're unhappy with other people.'

'I've heard that theory.'

'Not so with you.'

'Joe and I aren't right. We haven't been right for a while. The best explanation I can give is: the feeling went. Or it's going; and I don't know how to stop it. Why's another story. Too much time apart? Maybe. Domesticity killing passion? I expect so, because I expect that happens to everyone: doesn't it?'

Marianne shrugged. 'I never had time to find out. It sounds right. Does it matter?'

'I'm not sure. Life-long passion could be pretty wearing I imagine.' Suddenly Connie seemed close to tears.

Marianne offered her a rueful smile. 'Week-long would do for me. Day-long.' She paused. 'If feeling goes, maybe it can come back.'

'Sometimes I sense it there,' Connie said, 'like a ghost-limb. You look back – everyone must do it – and you think: What was it? What did I fall for? And you can't get it clear, because the moment's gone; the excitement's gone – and whatever it was, other things have taken its place. But you have a memory of it, like the memory of a smell.'

Connie drank some of her wine and sat in silence for a moment. 'The way he looked; the way he handled himself …' she shrugged. 'Joe had this knack of looking at the world from an oblique angle. Do you know what I mean?'

Marianne smiled. 'No, of course not.'

'No … He didn't expect things to be straightforward; didn't expect guesses to be easy. It's what made him a good copper, I expect. Anyway, I wanted to get to the bottom of all that. And there was the sex, of course. That can keep the motor running for a good while.'

'It's a snare,' Marianne said, 'but not a delusion.'

Connie's smile came and went, barely visible. 'I don't know … Maybe we just wore each other out – you know, rows and absences; missed connections. Maybe there's a trick to staying married – a way of putting up with some things and pretending others didn't happen.'

'Sounds bleak.'

'Does it? No, I don't think it has to be. I think you have to have a talent for it, though. You have to be prepared to change, to let the first feelings go – things like that sort of hot love where you don't want to be out of each other's sight for a second, magical sex, the fear of loss … you know; and then you look for other things. Other feelings.'

'What would they be?'

'That's the problem,' Connie said, 'that's the place I can't get to. All I know is that if Michael didn't exist, I'd still be thinking, What in hell do I do about Joe? Michael isn't just an escape route. He isn't an excuse.'

'The real thing. Hot love …'

'Looks like it. Feels like it, too.'

'Real for how long?'

'That's another question.'

'Got an answer?'

Connie shrugged and shook her head, which meant, No.

'How long have we known one another?' Marianne asked.

Connie calculated. 'Twenty years almost. Last year of school.'

'And ever since I've known you,' Marianne told her, 'you've liked risk.' She looked for an example. 'There are women who'd never hitch-hike, and those who will, those who like the chance. You'd always do it – remember? You seemed to like the chance.'

'Is that how you see me?'

'Restless, on the look-out.'

'For what?'

'Don't know,' Marianne said, 'something else; something new. It's there in little things: you drink too much, you drive too fast. I don't say you live by it; but it's there in your nature. Truth is, Connie, I never had you down for a quiet life. Joe's great, though. I always thought Joe was good for you.'

'Me too,' Connie said. 'That's what I thought. More importantly, I thought I was good for him. My ambition, his single-mindedness. Sounds right, doesn't it?'

As if she'd happened on a clue, Marianne asked: 'Why did you and Joe never have children?'

'I had a miscarriage.'

'That's not what I asked.'

'I don't know. We never seemed to get round to that discussion: somehow it was never on the agenda. Maybe we never felt secure enough. I've thought about it from time to time.'

Marianne said, 'Don't get me wrong. I'm not saying you're an airbrain.'

Connie smiled. 'No? I was beginning to wonder.'

'It's the opposite,' Marianne told her. 'You think too much.'

'What's too much?'

'Enough to make you unhappy without cause.'

'There's always cause.'

'You see –' Marianne said, '– proves my point,' and she laughed.

They were sitting at a table by the window, and the midday sunlight was at odds with the restaurant's air-conditioning. The glare put a gloss on Connie's hair and a shadow under her eyes. A waiter asked if there was something wrong with the *gravad lax* and Marianne took the opportunity to order her own glass of wine.

'I can't do it,' she said, 'can't sit here and watch. I'll starve tomorrow. What's he like?'

The sudden question took Connie by surprise. 'I don't know. I mean, I don't know how to answer. Good-looking. Blond. A bit younger than me. He's a painter. We met at –'

'What does he paint?'

'They're … They look like abstracts until you really look.' Connie laughed. 'I know fuck-all about painting, really. He doesn't seem to mind. I'd never heard of him; it seems he's famous. A bit famous. And rich.'

'I've never heard of him either. How rich?'

'No, but then art appreciation's not top of your list either, is it?'

'No. *How rich*?'

'I don't know.'

'Jesus Christ, Connie.'

The waiter gave Marianne her wine; she sniffed it and set it down, a little flirtation with calories.

Connie said, 'What should I do?'

'You love him, he's great in bed I hope, he's a bit famous and possibly a lot rich, and this is beginning to look like a foregone conclusion except there's Joe. How right does that sound?'

'Sounds right.' Connie smiled, though the smile was in no way related to laughter. 'Sounds right to me. So what –'

'Is the answer to your question.'

'Yes.'

'Fuck knows.'

'Thanks.'

'It's not the right question is it? "What should I do?" '

'You mean it should be "What will I do?" '

'Yes. And there are other questions …'

'I know.' Connie waved her hand in an almost-forgotten gesture and asked, 'You haven't got a cigarette about you?'

'I wish.' Marianne laughed. 'Those were the days.'

'What other questions?'

'Come on, Connie ...'

'Joe.'

'Yes, Joe.'

'Well ...' Connie looked away as if thinking about something, but the truth was that she couldn't speak. When she looked back, Marianne saw the tears on her face, their tracks whitened by sunlight through the window.

'I'm not sure I can be with him. It's not Joe, not just him. It's not even our life together.'

'What then?'

'The life I've missed.'

'No,' Marianne shook her head, 'no, I don't know what you're –'

'The life I've missed, the life I want, the life I might miss now, if I let Michael go.' Connie wiped her cheek and jawline with the heel of her hand. 'I can't let Michael go.'

'What life?'

'I love Michael, but I love what he can give me, too. The things I can have with him. I can get back some of what I lost.'

'What? Lost what?'

Connie lifted her hands like someone supporting a globe. 'Years – the years I didn't notice as they passed. Everything dull, everything ... I don't know. I can't describe it – it's lost.'

'And Joe?' Marianne persisted.

'I want to protect him from this, but I don't know how.'

'Connie ...' Marianne lifted her wine glass at last and took a long sip. 'You're in trouble.'

*'You were asleep. I haven't slept. I've been writing.'*

Joe was lounging in Paul Harker's armchair as if he'd seen it all before: a late night show and not the critics' choice.

'*I need a promise ... I need to hear it ... Cross your heart and hope to die.*'

Joe cupped his chin. He looked faintly ill-tempered, as if the Caller were proving a disappointment to him, as if he'd hoped for someone shorter, heavier, not so good-looking.

'*I know why you didn't say it was Christine ... Because Joe Morgan would know that we'd spoken.*'

'Silly bitch,' Harker observed.

'Silly dead bitch.'

Joe put the video on pause and picked up the file of interview notes that Bishop had brought to the bunker. He'd read them once already and they didn't tell him much, but he looked at them now as if he were deciphering a code.

A name. An address. An occupation. A few comments. No, he hadn't seen anything or anyone unusual on the night of Serena's death. No, he hadn't heard cries or any similar noise. No, he hadn't been out on the night in question; he'd stayed in and watched television like almost everyone else in the world. No, he hadn't lived in the area long. Where had he been living before?

At another false address, of course.

'He claimed to be a cab driver.'

Bishop laughed. 'Anyone with a car and an *A-Z*, Boss.'

'It's being checked?'

'In the area, in the surrounding areas and, God help us, all over Greater London if we must. He was lying, though.'

'Yeah ... Yes, of course he was. Even so ...'

'It was just part of a routine house-to-house. All the interviews look like this.'

Joe looked at the Caller's face, frozen on the screen. 'He's younger than I thought.'

Bishop peered at the image, the Caller's head tilted to one side, a slight smile on his face as if he were teasing some girl.

'Nice looking,' he said, 'women would like him.'

Joe tapped the pause button again and the Caller went back to fooling Lynda; went back to tickling her vanity.

*The story of a lifetime. Of course it is ... I've arranged for a courier ...*

'That was him,' Bishop said. 'Two people saw him go in, another rode in the lift with him.'

'He had his helmet on.'

'Sure. We think he might have green or brown eyes. Not tall not short, not fat not thin, one person thought he had a ponytail, the others didn't see it, hair dark, well fairly dark, or perhaps not so dark after all. Just as well he made the mistake of becoming a video star.'

*Mistake*, Joe thought. *Who knows?*

He watched the video another five times, then ejected it from the VCR and slipped it back into its box. The box was labelled with a date, place, time, and the interviewee's name.

Henry Parr Olsen.

# Twenty

This is the buzz, Joe. This is the fucking *buzz*. I'm in a cab, Joe, driving along the Bayswater Road and the sun is low in the sky directly behind me and the windows are open and I'm getting a bracing lungful of warm ozone and carbon monoxide. A snort of stale deodorant and sperm. A whiff of drains and disease. All carried on this hot wind, this baking wind, like a wind out of Africa. And I'm laughing, Joe, I can't help it, I'm laughing out loud.

The streets are full of beautiful girls, oh, hundreds of people, yes, sure, but you just notice these *girls*, girls in their summer dresses, hair flying, their breasts moving in that subtle, semi-disguised way, their hips shifting; Christ, I feel so happy for them that they're alive. And I'm headed for the dens, Joe, the sinks of iniquity, where you can see the neon growing stronger as the dusk deepens.

I know this is dangerous for me, Joe, but I can't help it. I love a spree. The cab driver just asked me what I'm laughing at and I told him, 'A joke, it's just a joke', and he laughed too, he laughed too, Joe, even though he hasn't heard the fucking joke. This bastard's talking his face off. He thinks there's going to be a storm and he hates tourists. The pollution gives him asthma. He'd like to live in Florida. Joe, he's talking to me while I'm talking to you.

What did you see when you found Lynda? There, you knew that question was coming, didn't you? What did you see?

*What-see-what-see-what-see?*

Just like Christine, just like all the rest, I watched her go, I watched her as she left, one minute there, one minute between, the next minute gone. It's tough, Joe, to make it last three minutes. You know? Not much between the quick and the dead. What did you see?

Listen, Joe, I think you've got a bad problem. It's with Connie. It's bad. You're in it, Joe. You're up to your neck. I don't think you're going to keep her. I don't see how you can. She's found something she wants very badly, you know? Something she can't avoid. It's a problem, Joe. Could I help you with it? I wonder if I could help you with it.

I'll call you soon, Joe. We need to talk. Not now; later. After I've had some fun. After my spree.

Here I am, Joe, joining the tailback into the forbidden city, heart full of hope, pockets full of money. Sprees don't come free, Joe. No such thing as a free spree. You can see lights coming on all over; you can hear music. Lone men buzzing the streets. Women in their webs.

Know what I'm doing, Joe? I'm taking a night off.

He found a casino and bet the black. He couldn't lose. His luck was like laughter. A girl tagged on; she was over-perfumed, under-dressed and had a sleek helmet of streaked hair; he liked her for that and let her stay.

They moved on, then moved on again. The girl stood at the kerb flagging a taxi.

She said, 'I'm your lucky piece. I'm your rabbit's foot.'

Cab drivers cruised over looking hard; she was wearing a short, low-cut green dress with thin straps and there were all sorts of things about her that you couldn't miss.

He gambled and lost, and it was just the same as gambling and winning. Under other circumstances the girl might have drifted away, but there was something about this guy, she thought, something risky, something wired. He barged through the bad luck and came out the other side.

'I'm your loaded dice,' she said.

At three a.m. the neon was like a flash-fire, but the streets were emptying out. In about an hour's time the city's insomniacs would see the first hint of light sketching the horizon beyond spires and glass stumps and wharves and cranes.

They walked away from the narrow streets and onto the broad pavements alongside a park. He fished out a handful of money and gave it to her; she snapped it into her bag.

'We're going the wrong way,' she told him. 'I live north of here.'

'No,' he shook his head.

'But you live round here?'

'No.'

'Then where are we going?'

He stepped up onto a bench at a bus stop and got a foot between the spikes on the park railings, then dropped down the other side.

She laughed. 'I can't do that.'

'Throw me your shoes.'

She could have taken off with a shake of the head and a wave – the money was safe in her bag – but she did it anyway, hitching her skirt and getting a toehold. He grabbed her wrists and lifted, drawing her towards him so that she toppled into his arms.

They found a place in the dark and he scooped her dress up to her waist. She said, 'You're crazy. You're a crazy man,' and he laughed in her face.

'And you're lucky,' he told her.

She felt the coolness of the grass. He had sweet breath and a winning way.

'I'm your lucky piece.'

A wind shivered the trees one by one.

'Lucky,' he said. 'You'll never know.'

The Registrar General's office records births and deaths by

dividing the year into quarters. If you know the name and the year, you'll be searching four books. Working from his video image, Paddy Godwin had put Henry Parr Olsen at somewhere between a mature thirty and a youthful forty, but common sense told you that much anyway.

To remove all room for doubt, Paul Harker was making that between twenty-five and forty-five, which meant he was making a search through eighty large volumes; and even that was a clear waste of time. This bastard had given a false address and false information, of course he had; why in hell would he give his real name?

Steve Tranter's reasoning was the same; even so, he had told the press they could use the name, along with an enhanced photo taken from the video. Joe agreed. The kind of information they now had made press exposure advisable, but Lynda's murder made it unstoppable. That morning, Lynda's paper carried a banner headline: *THE FACE OF EVIL*. Every other tabloid used a variation on the theme.

The AMIP team was gathered over coffee and carry-in breakfasts and Tranter was giving a pep-talk. Joe sat off to the side, looking at Tranter but thinking his own thoughts.

'Every paper,' Tranter said, 'every nick in the country. Posters, leaflets, the tabloid coverage, every news broadcast from GMTV to the ten o'clock. Someone knows this fucker. Someone's going to see his face and know exactly who he is, exactly where he is. Maybe more than one person.

'We've given a phone number. We asked for seconded officers and we've got them — there are fifty men and women taking calls. We've got four trained counsellors on stand-by in case someone calls in but is too distressed to part with the information.

'The dedicated line in this office stays open and most of the time it'll be manned by DI Morgan. There's a strong chance Olsen, or whatever his name is, will call in. There are observers with back-up teams at all the phone boxes he's used more than once. We can't keep this strength of operation up for long, so it's important that we nail this gobshite sooner rather than later. That means no fuck-ups. *Absolutely* no fuck-ups. Okay?

'Any call that is more than general information will be routed to the incident room. DC Harker's working out a roster. Sorry, but it's day and night. I want as many of you on stand-by as possible. If there's a need to check a call, or to leave the incident room for any outside work when you're on phone duty, check with me if you can, or DI Morgan, or Paul Harker. I know that there are people and incidents still under investigation, and I want those followed up, but don't waste time and don't make unnecessary trips. If we suddenly hear something that will allow us to nail this guy, I want full strength if I can get it.

'DI Morgan and I are working on a basic operations plan for various eventualities. We've alerted passport control points at airports and docks and at the Eurostar terminus. We'll have contingency plans for siege, pursuit, street emergencies, the lot. You'll be able to get all this from Carol Mitchie or one of the other log-and-file clerks by this afternoon. Carol's got a couple more staff for the moment, but they're on loan, so make the best use of them. Everything's on loan. Time's on loan.

'Watch out for cranks and loonies, but don't make hasty assumptions: there'll be hoax calls, there'll be malicious reports, there'll be fuckwits wandering into the front office saying I dunnit. But remember, people who are upset often sound nutty, or don't make sense, or get confused. You might be talking to a schizo, sure, but you might be talking to Olsen's mother.

'Any real leads, anything you think has weight, I want to hear about it right there and then. Or DI Morgan. No delays, yeah? No slackness. We need to collar this guy quickly, before we lose the back-up and before he finds somewhere to hide.

'We've already had him once – nose to fucking nose. That's not general knowledge yet, but it will be soon, and we need to get the rug back under our feet or else we're going to look like assholes. I don't want that for us. Most of all, I don't want it for myself. What I *do* want is this sick bastard in a remand cell and off my mind.'

Joe had the dedicated line switched to the bunker. He watched the video of the Caller talking to Lynda Lomas. He watched the SOC videos of Serena and Christine and Lynda.

He saw *LOOK JOE.*

*LOOK AGAIN JOE.*

He saw that narrow, full-lipped face, that handsome face, and heard the soft voice telling lies that anyone might believe.

He watched the video of Danny McMahon as he came free of the earth, roots ripping under him, being lifted like some leathery vegetable, the last of a crop that had gone to rot.

He waited for the phone to ring.

When the girl woke it was late, almost noon, and half the day's heat was humming behind her closed curtains. She walked dozily to the bathroom and squatted. She pissed for a long time, her gaze fixed on patterns of sunlight decorating the far wall; her eyes were wide open and empty. She could hear the sound of the TV coming from the sitting room and tried to remember whether she had been up earlier that day and watched TV and then gone back to bed. She didn't think she had.

Naked, she looked like the girl who tamed the unicorn: slightly swaybacked, her belly a little hillock, breasts like green apples. Her skin was a lacklustre white. She took a yoghurt from the fridge and went to the living room to eat it. His face was on the screen as she walked through the door.

She said, 'Henry?'

Everything in the room was warm to the touch except the girl. She sat down, slowly, still holding the opened yoghurt and a spoon. She listened to his name being read out, then watched while a fraction of the film was played.

His face, his voice.

*I've been writing. The full story. I told you I'd give you the full story.*

His features froze on the screen, leaving him with his mouth part-open. She said, 'Henry?'

There were photographs of Serena Matthews and of Lynda Lomas. No one had ever come forward to identify Christine, but she was mentioned. Daniel McMahon was mentioned. The girl listened and learned what her lover had done.

She said, 'Henry?' as if he might suddenly appear from the bedroom, smiling, his hands lifted behind his head to fix his ponytail.

The yoghurt ran out onto her leg. She put the pot down on a low table, but let the spillage lie. A policeman called Tranter was being interviewed. She had known without knowing what she knew; she had known something and nothing; but she wouldn't tell Tranter that. When the newscast was over, she walked back to the bedroom and checked the closets and drawers. Everything of his was gone – and she'd slept through that, slept soundly while he'd packed and cleared out.

There was no note. There was no sign of him. She went to the bathroom and turned on the taps and waited as the room clouded with steam, then climbed into the hot water and lay still.

As if she were rehearsing for a play, she ran through the newsreader's words in her head, even saying some of them out loud. On the screen, his face had looked younger than in

218

life. In her mind's eye, she pictured him making coffee or lying full length on the sofa to watch TV, or laughing as he put money on the table for her to take.

Sleeping next to her. Holding her hand as they walked.

An hour later the bath had cooled. She got out and walked to the phone. When they answered she said, 'Henry' and started crying and couldn't stop.


Her name was Donna Rees and hers was the seventeenth call concerning Henry Olsen. Other people had called from local shops, from a pub, from the place where he worked, but no one quite had the edge on Donna.

She sat in an interview room at Fellgate Cross with Joe and Steve Tranter and a WPC borrowed from the back-up pool. To date, the calls they'd received had told them two things: the first that either his name really was Henry Olsen or he'd adopted it; the second that, until recently, he'd worked at Smithfield market: twelve of the seventeen calls were from one-time workmates. No one they'd spoken to could tell them much about the man. He was quiet, affable, liked an occasional drink … you could hear the shrugs coming down the phone line.

They waited for Donna to tell them everything and discovered that she had almost nothing to tell. Tranter put his chin on his fist and stared at the girl as if he might frighten her into knowing more.

'When did you first meet him?'

'About six months ago.'

'Was it?'

'Christmas time.'

'Before or after Christmas?'

'Just before.'

'Where?'

'At the station.'

'Jesus Christ. Which station?'

219

Donna turned to Joe. 'He thinks I'm thick.' She had a Welsh lilt to her voice, musical and fetching.

'There are things we need to know,' Joe told her. 'One of them is why he didn't kill you.'

Her eyes half closed and she went away for a moment. 'He never hurt me. Never did anything bad to me.' She looked at Tranter and said, 'Paddington station. It's difficult for me; can't you see that?'

Tranter said, 'We need to catch —'

'Can't you see?'

'Did you live with him as soon as you met?' Joe asked.

'I had nowhere to stay. He said I could move in for a few nights. He didn't want to put me on the game. Nothing like that.'

'You didn't know anything about him,' Joe said.

'It was cold. I didn't fancy sleeping rough.'

Tranter asked, 'What did you think? He picked you up. What? — you had a few drinks —?'

'Yes.'

'And he says it's okay for you to live at his place for a bit. You'd never met him before. What did you think he wanted?'

Donna gave Tranter a puzzled look. 'I thought he wanted sex.'

'You didn't mind that?'

'Not really.'

'Okay ...' Tranter washed his face with his hands and sighed. 'What happened after that?'

'Nothing.' She paused, trying to find a way to elaborate nothing. 'He looked after me. Brought money.'

'Where did he get it?'

'He worked at the market.'

Tranter said, 'I'm getting bloody bored with you. This shitbag you lived with killed people.' He banged a hand down on the table and Donna shuffled back in her chair. Her face was blank, as if it had been wiped.

'Didn't you know?' Tranter's voice was raised. 'He came home to you after killing people, cutting their throats, he must have been covered in blood, wasn't he? Blood? Ever see any blood, Donna? Blood in the car was there? Upholstery cleaner needed? He'd come in and go straight to the shower, am I right? What about his clothes? You'd see to them, would you? Wash his clothes for him? Am I right?'

He was shouting now. Joe could see Tranter acting, but he could also see the genuine anger that would soon take over.

'What did you know about him?' Joe asked. 'Tell us whatever you knew. Anything.'

'Nothing.'

'Family ... anything about his parents.'

'Nothing.'

'Friends. Places he'd go. What did he talk about? Did he say anything about his past, where he came from, any plans he might have?'

'No,' Donna said. 'Nothing like that.'

'You must have talked about something.'

Donna nodded, then paused. 'Yeah, we talked together. Things that happened, programmes I'd watched. He knew a lot about animals.'

'Did he?'

'We were walking somewhere ... I can't remember ... and there were flocks of pigeons in the sky between the buildings. You couldn't see them clearly because too much was in the way; but he told me about pigeons. People say they're vermin, but they have a very complicated life.'

Tranter was biting the fat of his own cheek. 'About himself, though. Things about himself.'

'No one wants to talk about the past,' Donna told him. 'Who would want to talk about the past?'

Tranter got up and left the room, walking stiff-legged; Joe

logged his departure for the tape. He sat in silence with Donna for five minutes or so. She gazed at her hands, then she began to cry.

'It's important, Donna.' Joe was whispering through her tears.

'I know.'

'Important that we know as much about Henry as possible.'

'Yes.'

'There must be some things, if you think, if you think back, things you can tell us that will help us to find him. We have to find him – you see that, don't you?'

'Yes.' She made a little crippled gesture of helplessness and misery. 'But I don't know anything about him.'

Her tone of voice said, *Can't you see? Don't you understand?*

'I don't know anything about anyone.'

Paul Harker took the photocopy to Tranter and laid it on his desk: a certificate of birth recording that Henry Parr Olsen was born at Cannon Street maternity hospital, Taunton, on 8 March 1960. Father: John Parr Olsen; occupation, small-holder. Mother: Anne Olsen; maiden surname, Witney; occupation not given. Usual address: Lannett's Farm, St Sabbas, Wiveliscombe, W. Somerset.

'He's the only one?'

'Three other Henry Olsens,' Harker said, 'but none of them a Parr.'

'Show it to DI Morgan.'

'Okay, Boss. Where is he?'

'Who knows,' Tranter said. He was already on the phone.

A search team had turned every inch of the flat where Donna had lived with Henry Olsen, every stitch and tile, but there wasn't anything to find. Donna's few clothes hung in the wardrobe-space like ghosts of a former self. She had put posters on the walls and gimcrack ornaments on shelves. In the bathroom, her toothbrush, her make-up, a box of tampons, a bunny-rabbit facecloth.

Joe walked round, but it was just dead echoes.

Connie came into the flat to a smell of cooking and found Joe in the kitchen making roast chicken with onion gravy. He poured her a drink from the bottle of Chardonnay he'd already opened and she sat on a stool to watch him dividing broccoli florets.

'Well,' she said, 'you're home before nine and you're cooking and eventually you'll tell me what it means.'

'You've seen the papers today.'

'Henry Olsen, is that him?'

'Henry Parr Olsen.'

'Will you get him?'

'Listen to Tranter and you'd think so.'

'Someone's come forward ...'

'A lot of people came forward. We found his girlfriend, the guys he worked with, guys he drank with. Makes no difference. We know he came from Somerset, but we also know that the family moved away ten years ago. They used to own a smallholding there. Tranter spoke to the local people. They knew the family and they knew our man Henry, but no one knows where they went next. The people who bought their land never met the Olsens; the farm was sold by solicitors acting for the son.'

'For Henry.'

'That's right. I came home because I couldn't think of where else to be and I'm cooking because I couldn't think of what else to do. I'm early, you're late. Aren't you?'

'I had a drink with Marianne.'

'Girl talk.'

'Mostly.'

'Us talk.'

'Some.'

'Any conclusions?'

Connie walked towards the bedroom to change, taking her wine with her. She said, 'It's not about reaching conclusions.'

'No? What then?'

Connie returned ten minutes later and refilled her glass. 'It's about what we feel.'

'You and Marianne?'

'Joe, look, I'm trying to get this right.'

'Right for you? Right for me? What?'

Connie suddenly felt a rush of anger, swift and completely unreasonable; anger at Joe's edgy questioning and his vulnerability. She knew that the anger proceeded from guilt and for a moment it was on the tip of her tongue to give Joe the truth. To avoid the impulse, she tried changing the subject and wasn't so surprised when it worked; Joe didn't want an answer to his question in case it was the wrong one.

She said, 'Will you go there? To Somerset?'

'No. The locals are talking to people who knew the family, but there's no reason to suppose we'll find anything. It was ten years ago. It's archaeology.'

'You'll hope for a sighting.'

'A sighting?' He nodded, smiling. 'There've been a hundred and eight, to date.' He put a pan of salted water on the stove. 'Eat in fifteen minutes, yes?'

The sun was low in the sky and the glass panels of the conservatory seemed to stream with red light. Their faces were stained by it.

'His girlfriend,' Connie said.

'That's right.'

'What a strange thought.'

'I know.'

'That he killed people – no motive –'

'There's always a motive.'

' – no, I mean, nothing like money or long-term hatred, or sudden anger –'

'Seems that way.'

' – and he has a girlfriend. Goes home to a girlfriend. Lives with her?'

'Lived with her, yes.'

'Difficult to get. Difficult to work out.'

'I know,' Joe said. 'His toothbrush and hers, occasional shopping trips, an evening in front of the TV.'

'And the people who knew him. People who'd have a drink with him, share a joke.'

'It's always like that. They all have ordinary lives. Their friends think they're ordinary. The things that make them monsters are things they do on their own. Denis Neilson decapitated one of his victims, put the head in a pan of boiling water so that he could strip the flesh later, then took his dog for a walk. Dropped in at the pub for a drink.'

'Has he called you?'

'No.'

'You think he will?'

'I think so, yes.'

'Why?'

'Because he could have called from any phone box anywhere, but he chose one he'd used a number of times before. He's been taking risks for a while. Now he's taken one so big that we know who he is and what he looks like. Calling me is part of the risk-taking.'

'Flirting with capture.'

'That's what Ackerman says.'

'Ackerman …?'

'The shrink.'

'This is terrific,' Connie said, 'this is the kind of thing you cook perfectly.'

As soon as she'd spoken, she looked down at her plate,

flustered, a sudden touch of colour clouding her cheek; it was the kind of compliment that might have been made by a friend. Joe leaned across and gave Connie some more wine. She asked, 'What did the girlfriend say? What's she like?'

'A runaway. Not very bright. Didn't say much at all. Tranter treated her like the enemy; he's a fool.'

'Is she pretty?'

Joe thought. 'In a way. Almost. Short blonde hair, I mean dyed that colour, Oxfam clothes, a touch overweight. She's got a crossed tooth, you know? – snaggle tooth. Is this us talking?'

Connie's smile was sad. 'Yes, this is us – talking.'

'Small talk?'

'Yes ... Just small talk.'

'I thought it must be.'

They ate in silence for a while. The sky turned plum and the last of the sun washed the glass.

Joe asked, 'Why did you want to know?'

'Whether she was pretty?'

'Yes.'

'I don't know. I was trying to get a picture of her. A girl who would be with Henry Lawson, is that –'

'Olsen. Henry Parr Olsen.'

' – something must have told her. I wonder why she stayed.'

'Yes,' Joe said, 'I wonder.'

They opened more wine. Joe had bought some cheese and strawberries. Connie wondered if he was thinking: Just like old times. Perhaps he hoped she was thinking the same thing.

The cheese was St Agur and it put her in mind of Joe finding his way round a French menu not long after they first met. They'd been at a restaurant in Eymet, sitting out in the little medieval square; she remembered the half-timbered houses, Joe's shaky French, the purple dusk. She remembered the sound of a two-stroke engine in another street and moths big as wrens in the lamplight.

Joe had ordered confit and tuna and a tomato salad, and she'd asked for the same. Bringing all that to mind, Connie could almost wish that she could live in that safer life; that she could take herself and Joe back to the past and never emerge.

She was half drunk. The bedside lamp threw a scallop pattern high on the wall like a water mark. When Joe kissed her, Connie kissed him back, then drew him up as her legs forked lazily.

After a while, she turned her back to him, got onto elbows and knees, swaybacked, her head cradled on her hands. Joe bumped her, lightly, with long, slow strokes; she could see the hairs on her forearms glistening in the lamplight.

*Who's betrayed here?* she thought. *Is it Michael? Is it Joe? Is it me?* She felt strangely weary and infinitely sad: in the middle of this act of passion, all passion spent.

She closed her eyes and saw treetops. She saw Michael's face, reddened by the sun, swim up at her through clouds.

Connie lay awake until two, then slept until the phone woke her at three-thirty. Joe had answered it and was speaking by the time she had shaken off her dream.

'Hello, Henry, I wondered when you'd call –' His voice light and conversational.

Connie got out of bed and put on a robe. She walked across the bedroom and sat down in a basketweave chair – it would be too strange to sit there beside him in bed while he talked to this man. In the same moment an image came to her of the girl who was almost pretty and not too bright lying next to him – next to Olsen – sleeping soundly right through the night.

Joe had pressed '1' on the dial pad. 'I was talking to Donna earlier. She's okay … I thought you might want to know that.'

Connie listened and watched for a moment – Joe's sweet-talk, his face like a stone, then she went to the kitchen and took some water from the fridge. She was damp with sweat and Joe's smell was strong on her. She drank two glasses and took one back to the bedroom.

Joe said, 'You're famous, Henry; how does it feel?' A touch of laughter in his voice like a friend's chiding.

Connie handed him the water and he took a long sip while he listened. She went back to the chair feeling like someone who slows down to stare at an accident on the motorway. She picked at a loose thread on the belt of her robe.

Joe said, 'I saw her. Yes, I saw her.' After a pause, he added, 'I saw that too but I don't know what it means. You must tell me what it means. "Look Joe" – what does that mean, Henry? What am I looking at?'

Connie could see him working at it – finding a line of talk that he could spin out.

'I don't think I'm getting it right, Henry. Do you see what I mean? I'm puzzled. I want to understand, but I don't think I know enough. I think there are things you need to tell me.'

Connie went to the window and looked out. There were shadows in the sky; shadows inside the room; reflections of shadows in the window panes between.

Joe got out of bed, one swift, urgent movement, as if moving to defend himself, or attack. He stood very still, listening intently. Connie stood up, too, a mirror movement. She said, 'What?'

Joe lifted a hand to silence her. Something was happening that he couldn't get clear and he was struggling to read the signs. After a moment, Connie heard the thin rattle of a voice on the phone, unravelling like thread, then becoming the louder, jerkier sound of laughter.

Joe put the phone down. He said, 'They've got him. That was Tranter talking to me just now. Olsen was at the same phone booth – the one where we videoed him. Stupid bastard. They've got him.'

Connie said, 'Good.'

'Stupid bastard,' Joe said again; he drank the rest of the water Connie had brought him and started to climb into the clothes he'd taken off three hours earlier.

Now that sleep was impossible, Connie took a cup of coffee into the small garden and sat down to wait for the dawn. She wanted to call Michael, but didn't have anything to say. A dawn wind ruffled her hair and turned the flap of her robe.

She thought of the girl who was almost pretty.

Olsen was in an interview room with Paul Harker and a uniformed officer. From time to time Harker said, 'Any time you're ready, Henry', or 'What do you want to tell me, Henry?' Olsen sat in silence.

Joe and Tranter sat in silence. They were in the incident room waiting for a call from George Fisher. When it came, they went together to the superintendent's office and entered to a ragged handclap and an off-centre smile. There was a glass of whisky on the desk.

'Dinner party,' Fisher said. 'Went to bed pissed at half-past one, woke up pissed at ten to four. Thought it best to keep going.' He took a drink and renewed the smile. 'We've got the fucker. You can't imagine how relieved that makes me feel. Questions were being asked – questions I couldn't answer. Very uncomfortable.' He looked from one man to the other. 'Problems?'

'He's sitting in an interview room saying nothing,' Tranter observed.

'Has he spoken at all?'

'He says he'll talk only to DI Morgan.'

Fisher shrugged and turned to Joe. 'Okay, then.'

'Just me,' Joe said. 'No tape, no notes, no one else in the room.'

'He demanded that?'

'Yes.'

'Why?'

'I don't know,' Joe said. 'I spoke to Leonard Ackerman about it. His notion was –'

'Ackerman's the psychiatrist, yes?'

'Yes. It's because – Ackerman thinks it's because – I was the person who first answered the phone to him. First spoke to him.'

'Simple as that.'

'Not simple.' Joe shrugged and said nothing for a short while. Fisher let the silence ride. Finally Joe said, 'He wants me to understand something. Something about the reason why he killed them. He seems to think I might be able to understand. That's why he wrote "Look Joe" up on the wall; that's why he keeps asking me what I see when I look at them – at the bodies. Whatever it is that makes him do it … he's decided I have some sort of insight into that.'

'Have you?'

'No.'

Fisher sighed. 'Steve?'

'Two officers working shifts, coming at him from different directions, different approaches, seeing who makes a friend of him, who scares him, getting to him one way, getting to him another, a third officer there for the purpose of corroboration, tape as further back-up – also as evidence when Olsen comes to court.'

'Yes,' Joe said, 'that's what I'd like too.'

'So what do we do?' Fisher asked.

'Leave him to sweat,' Tranter said. 'He's been charged. He'll want to talk sooner or later.'

'You think so?' Fisher was topping up his drink. He waved

the bottle at the two men, making an offer, then made a second gesture towards a wooden cabinet on the far wall. Tranter opened the cabinet and fetched two glasses.

'Yes, I think so.'

'Fisher looked at Joe as he poured them both a drink.

'Who knows?' Joe said. 'Time's on our side.'

'But what's your guess?' Fisher asked.

'My guess is that he's crazy and therefore likely to do just about anything. Talk to me, talk to anyone, talk to the trees. At the moment, he'll only talk to me. That might last, it might not. He made a point of it during the time he was phoning in. We had a counsellor taking the calls and all he ever got was "Where's Morgan?" My guess is that he'll certainly hold out for a while if he doesn't hold out forever.'

'Steve?' Fisher asked.

'Sweat him.'

Fisher sat back in his chair, moving it on its castors. His eyes looked heavy, suddenly, and his mouth a little loose.

'Look,' he said, 'I don't want any tricky stuff here. I don't want some fucking brief coming in and making a name for himself.' He was looking at Tranter, who gave an irritated little shrug and finished his drink: one gesture and the glass down on the desk with a click. 'If this guy's going to tell us he did it, I mean, if he's going to tell us where the bodies are buried, then sooner rather than later. I don't want to give him time to think it through. I don't want some lawyer helping him to do that. A couple of days in a cell and he might consider there are better places to be. The chances are that right now he's eager for confession – yes? – first flush, still dizzy.' No one spoke. Fisher said, 'Joe?'

'I'm not asking for the job.'

'But do you think I'm right?'

'Yes.'

'Fine. Talk to him. No one in there except you, no tape, no notes.'

'There has to be corroboration,' Joe said. 'Even if he confesses, it won't be enough. We'll need things that only the murderer could know. We'll need forensic evidence, too, if we can get it.'

'Was there any?'

'Impossible to say until we type him. On each occasion the forensic sweep came up with bits and pieces; they always do. Whose bits and pieces are they? – that's the question.'

'So what do we do? Wire you or wire the room?'

'Wire the room,' Joe advised. 'He might want to make sure I'm clean.'

'Taping unauthorised by the defendant – it wouldn't count for much with a good lawyer on the case,' Tranter observed.

'Any lawyer,' Fisher said. 'It's better than nothing. I want two officers listening to what's said as it's said and making their own notes: how Olsen sounded, whether he was under pressure, whether there was any coercion. The whole thing annotated, the notes typed and delivered to me with a dupe tape.' To Joe he said, 'See whether it's possible to get Olsen to sign something at the end of each session.'

'What?'

'Some kind of release. "I wasn't thumped or kicked; I wasn't bribed; no one made any promises". Compile your own notes afterwards and have them typed up – that's in addition to the tape. Then see if Olsen will sign them as a true record of your conversation.'

'I don't think that's the idea,' Joe said. 'It's to be between him and me.'

'Try.' Fisher picked up his whisky and waved Joe off with it. A gobbet splashed onto his hand and he licked his fingers one by one. 'I'll need your personal report in time for a press release later today. Four o'clock. The journos are going to be like ants at a fucking picnic.'

Joe got up and walked to the door. Tranter's stare followed him all the way.

# Twenty-One

Joe stood spraddle-legged with arms outstretched while Olsen patted him down – close enough to kiss as he straightened up and smiled.

'You didn't have to do that,' Joe said.

'Just us,' Olsen said. 'I don't care what happens after that.'

His voice was low, as it had been on the phone, and the soft accent, almost a drawl, was a little more evident. He looked round the room, carefully, as if wanting to take in every detail: the polystyrene ceiling tiles, the green emulsion paint fading on the walls, the office armchairs he and Joe would sit in. He looked closely at Joe, then nodded as if to say, So here we are …

'Why is it so important to talk to me?'

'It has to be someone and it could only happen once. This moment could only come once. And that's why it's you; that's why it's me.'

Joe waited. They sat in silence for five minutes. Olsen was smiling and looking into his lap where his hands lay cupped, as if they were cradling something. He drifted away, then returned. When he started to talk again, he was telling a story. Joe looked away, as if to concentrate better. The room grew still around them as Olsen told the story of Danny McMahon.

He's on the motorway walking up the hard shoulder against the flow of traffic. He's wearing rags; a sort of rag shawl over a ripped-up greatcoat and boots with no socks, and he's filthy. He's so dirty he looks like someone in blackface, isn't that it – where the lips and eyes are whiter than the rest? – and he's shuffling, walking with this jazzy shuffle, hands clasped across his chest, raw ankles, his boots doing a shuffle and tap, like a little walking dance, and he's coming up by the side of a drainage ditch, so he must have crossed the wetland to get there.

The ditch ran on one side, artics slamming by on the other. There was oil spillage on his scarecrow trousers. You'd have to say a bit of a scarecrow ... Crossing the roadside marsh, he must have looked like a scarecrow on the run.

I pull over and he keeps up this little dance in front of the car as if he hadn't got the wit to go round it. I can see his eyes are scarlet round the rim and pink where the white should be. Under the greatcoat, he's got this ragged cardigan pulled across and fastened with a pin. He's talking to himself, and when I get closer I can tell that he's muttering some song, some little ditty; but he can't move unless I move him. The car's in his way and it's too hard to think about.

I say, 'Get in', but he doesn't move.

I say, 'Go on, get in', and he looks at me as if he knows the words but not what they mean.

I take him by the sleeve and lead him round to the passenger door and open it. There's a twist of rain eddying in the slipstreams of lorries and a wind with a cutting edge coming off the Somerset Levels.

I say, 'Get in you daft bastard', and give him a shove and he starts to cry but he gets into the car and I slam the door. He doesn't try to open it.

I'm driving and he's crying and I ask, 'What are you crying for? What are you crying for? What's wrong?' but he doesn't say anything. I put some music on, but he doesn't like that; he starts rocking and smacking his mouth with the back of his hand – smack, smack, smack – all the time getting harder, until I switch the tape deck off.

I tell him what my name is and ask for his, but he doesn't give it. He starts crying again. I say, 'Listen, what is it? What's the problem?'

He says, 'You're going the wrong way'.

We get to London, it's about seven o'clock. I'm not sure what to do with him. I know what I want him for, but I'm not sure what to do with him in the meantime.

I've got this place near Camberwell, I keep some things there, some bits and pieces, it's just a room really with a bit of a kitchen. I drive him down there and take him up to the room. He walks round like a dog turning in its basket, then starts to make himself a cup of tea. He's singing his little song again.

I say my name and ask him for his. 'Danny', he tells me, 'Danny McMahon', and I hear the lilt in his voice, the Irish lilt.

'You can stay here, Danny', I tell him. 'Stay in the room, don't go out'. I show him the kitchen – some tins of food, some saucepans to cook with. I say, 'I'll come back with some bread and milk, Danny. You'll be safe here. Don't trouble anyone and no one'll trouble you. I'll bring you back a bottle'. I show him how the sofa folds out to make a bed.

I feel excited, that's the truth of it. I want to go out, go somewhere to test my luck. I can't take Danny with me. I think about locking him in, but then it occurs to me that he might start hitting the door, or calling out, or might try to get out of the window. I stay with him while he drinks his tea, then go out to a corner shop. When I get back, he's asleep.

I look at him, this old wreck lying half on, half off the sofa, his face seamed with dirt, a line of saliva like a snail-track down the crease alongside his mouth. I think, *No one'll miss you. Who would miss you?*

There's a stink coming off him that's grime and sweat and stale piss. Everything he's wearing is heavy with dirt and grease. I undo the safety-pin that's holding his cardigan and because he's not wearing anything underneath, I can see his chest, white and slack and unhealthy; it looks like dead flesh apart from the rise and fall of his breathing.

I go and get a knife from the kitchen – it's not the right knife, just something for bread – and I touch his throat with it. I lay it across his throat. The flesh is stringy, there, like chicken-neck; the skin makes two folds that fall back from under his chin. It looks easy to cut.

I put my face close to his and I can smell his breath. Dreadful; it's dreadful, like cabbage and sour phlegm. Like illness and swill.

I think: *And if it stopped ...*

I put my hand on his neck and feel the pulse.

I think: *And if it stopped ...*

That's what I've never been able to work out, Joe. That's what makes me so curious. *So curious.* One minute it's alive, the next minute it's dead.

I go out, as planned. I go to a place where I can gamble and pick up a girl. I lose some money which worries me, and I take a girl back to my flat. This is before Donna. Donna doesn't exist yet.

The girl gets straight into bed. Either she's got a need on her or she's in a hurry to get away; anyway, I'm fizzing, I'm electric, and I keep after her for a long time. I'm at her for a very long time and in the end, she says it hurts, I'm hurting her, and could I just get it off. Saying that doesn't help her. In fact, it makes me feel great and I keep on at her for a good while after that and she sees from my face that there's nothing she can do. It's clear that her best bet is to stay still while I go at her – to play dead.

When she's gone I lie on the bed and decide about Danny McMahon. I start to tremble. I always do – I always start to shake when I think about those things. In my mind's eye, I see Danny half on, half off the sofa, just as he was when I left the room in Camberwell. I smell his breath and feel the pulsebeat in his neck. He's alive. He can shuffle and cry and sing his little song. He can see what's about him. He can hear me when I tell him I'll fetch some bread and milk and a bottle. He can taste his tea.

I'm shaking now. I'm really shaking. I have to get off the bed and stand upright to breathe, but my eyes are closed so I can see it plainly: Danny and me, his pulse under my hand, the knife cutting cleanly like the neck was ripe fruit.

I stand there going through it in my mind and wishing the girl hadn't gone.


What do I decide? I decide that I'll keep Danny for a few days. Keep him for observation you might say. I go back the next morning and he's still there; I find him sitting on the sofa eating bread soaked in milk which means he doesn't have to do much work with his teeth. The bottle I brought him was sherry and it's all-but empty now.

He's taken me at my word and stayed in the room. How do I know? Well, first he hasn't got a key to get back in with. Yes, he could have left the door on the latch, but I don't think so because the second piece of evidence is a little pile of hard, black turds on a piece of newspaper laid out in one corner. He follows my look, but doesn't have anything to say.

I've brought him a bag of food and some more drink. I reckon it's the drink that will keep him. I talk to him for a while, but he doesn't answer. I sit with him in silence for a while and he starts to drink. Then he does talk, but I can't understand much of it. I guess that he must be telling me about his life – there are a few key words that make me think that. It doesn't take much to make him drunk. Then he gets up and performs a little dance in the middle of the room, a

237

little jig, and I'm watching him, watching the life still in him, watching him shake his old bones.

I'm watching him, knowing that I'm going to take his life away. Such a strange thing to think, isn't it? – take his life away. It's just this, Joe – just this. That I can watch him being alive, watch him drink, dance, eat, sing, talk. And I can take it away. Danny will still be there – teeth, eyes, lips, hands for holding a bottle, legs for shuffling along, but what's changed?

I can't get over it. There's Danny, eating and drinking and saying things I can't properly understand. Able to walk. Able to shit. Able to sleep and dream a dream perhaps. There's Danny, shuffling along in the rain. Then I pluck him off the hard shoulder. Next I pluck out the life. Gone. It's gone. Danny but no Danny. I can't get over the strangeness of it.

I can't get over the excitement of it.

He says, 'Will I go back? Will I go back now?'

This is the next day, towards evening. I've taken him some things. One is a box with sand in it. 'Go in that Danny', I tell him. 'It's for you to go in', and from the way he looks I think he must understand. I've brought two more bottles, some tea, some milk – stuff like that; and food he can eat from the wrapper.

'Will I go back?' And he starts to talk like ... what? ... like a waterfall, like white water, so I think he'll never be quiet, never stop, and I can't understand a word of it, but that doesn't matter because Danny just sits there with the bottle in one hand, a beef pie in the other, and spools it out, just spools it out. Christ. Maybe half an hour, maybe more, ticking over like a crazy machine.

Then he falls quiet; I don't know why. Maybe he's come to the end of his story. The story of his life. I think that he doesn't need me to understand or to say anything, but perhaps he needs me to be there: a witness. If he knows what he's saying. If any of it makes sense.

I stare at his face. He's looking away to one side and something has switched off behind his eyes. Does he know where he is, or what's happened to him? Does he have a plan for tomorrow or the day after that? He doesn't need one. Not for the day after that.

Suddenly, he gets up and performs a dance. He hops and shuffles and sings to himself, holding the bottle, taking a drink, still dancing, keeping the music going inside his head. I think, *Where does that come from? Were you a champion dancer, Danny? Were you a lad who could turn a foot?*

I want to watch him like this. I want to watch the life in him.

Next day he's morose. I sit there while he gets drunk. He starts to kick things in the room and breaks one of my display cases. I tell him to stop it and he takes a swing at me with the bottle, but it's easy to duck.

I realise that I've got all I need. At first I thought the longer I see him being alive — doing this, doing that — the bigger the buzz, but it's not like that. Time, I think, it's time; and as soon as I know what's coming next, I start to laugh. It's the excitement. Danny laughs too, as if he'd never tried to wreck the room or aimed a blow at me with the bottle.

I go home and get the things I need. When I return, I can see that Danny has been drinking steadily. It's okay, but I know I'll have to keep an eye on him. I think, Drunk is okay, Danny, but not too drunk, please, not out cold. He sleeps for a while, then gets up and takes a piss into the sink. He sits on the sofa and gives me a long stare, like he's trying to work out who I might be.

'Danny McMahon', he says. 'Daniel McMahon', then reclines on the sofa and fishes round for his bottle.

'Henry Parr Olsen', I say, since I doubt he can hear me, and anyway it doesn't matter a damn.

We wait for dark.


There are three fast-food cubby-holes on the street: Chinese, kebab, Indian, all white tile and white Formica and lit with hard white lights like a row of operating theatres. It's raining, which is good. People are in and out of the takeaways but they don't pay us any attention. We walk a quarter of a mile to the car, me in front, Danny following like a dog.

When we get to the first junction and stop for the lights, he says, 'Will I go back now?'

I say, 'Yes'.

What I've brought with me is a torch, a big macintosh, a pair of jeans, a pair of sneakers, some babywipes, a mirror, and a proper knife for the business. They're all in a canvas grip. I know where I'm going because I've been thinking about this for a long time – thinking about someone like Danny – and from time to time I've made little excursions, little reccies. There's a lot of waste land in London; a lot of places where people never go.

I find myself wondering whether Danny has any sense of direction, whether he can understand signposts; if he can he knows that we're heading west – heading back towards the place where I found him. Maybe he's reassured. I get onto a strip of dual carriageway with signs to the airport, make several turns through bleak housing developments, and go further back through a blacked-out industrial estate. Then an access road that passes a row of prefabricated work-units, deserted now; then an old pumping station; then about eighty yards of dirt and gravel road that leads to this patch of land. A patch of urban desert. When I switch off the engine, the silence throbs in my ears. When I switch off the lights, the darkness rushes in and swarms all over us.

I take the bag and the torch and say, 'Come on, Danny, let's go', but he doesn't get out of the car.

I say, 'I'm taking you back'.

Still he doesn't move. I shine the torch on him and he shrinks from the light, which gives me an opportunity to reach in and take the bottle from him.

'Okay, Danny?' I ask, and take a few steps back. 'Okay, it's time to go'.

He gets out and comes at me, wanting the bottle. I lead him on, staying close enough but not too close. It's no joke getting him through the metal-rung gate – not a hope that he'll climb over. I have to wrench and shove, and I can hear grass and bramble tearing as it comes open just a couple of feet.

When we get well into the field, close to a telegraph pole – remember, Joe? – I kick his legs out from under him and he takes a heavy fall; he's winded. I put the torch down on the ground so that it's shining on his face, then I get astride him so that I can control things better.

That's what I always try to do: get astride.

He's making a little yelping noise with a strong wheeze on the indrawn breath and it makes me wonder whether he might have cracked a rib when he fell.

He looks up at me, looking sideways, and I think he probably sees the line of torchlight on the knife blade. I hold on to his hair to steady up his head and wait a moment to watch for the last time – Danny alive, Danny breathing, Danny whole.

A train goes by at speed just fifty yards away: a funnel of noise, a flicker of lighted windows and blurred faces looking out into the dark. A dead silence follows it.

I could get up. I know I could get up and leave him here, and nothing about Danny would have changed. But I kill him and things begin to change.

I kneel astride Danny and it's only a little while, such a

very little while, a minute perhaps. Then everything has changed.

I stay with him a long time. I peer into his face, using the torch. I see the scene as if from afar – a little pool of light in the middle of a black field; and I see Danny in close-up – nothing left, everything stopped or gone. It's so strange. It's so difficult to understand. I'm shaking with excitement and I want to shout; I want to cry and laugh.

Finally, I stand up and take off the mac and my trousers and shoes, then take the replacements from the bag and get dressed. I try to use the babywipes and the mirror, but it's difficult to know whether to shine the torch on the glass or on my face. I'm clean anyway; I'm pretty sure I'm clean.

I stuff the things I was wearing into a plastic bag, then into the grip, and I'm ready to go, I ought to go, but no, I'm stuck there like someone on foreign ground. It's something I've forgotten but don't know what. I run through the pictures I'd already stored of myself doing this – killing Danny or someone like Danny – and it comes to me that I'd intended to bury him, but I haven't brought a spade.

I leave him, Joe, I leave him lying there and go to my car and drive away. It's about midnight, maybe half an hour past, and the roads are as busy as they are at noon. It takes me an hour to get to my flat. When I get in I spread a sheet of polythene over the bedroom floor and dump the clothes from the grip onto it. There's not much blood; I've been careful. A biological wash will do it. I take a drink of brandy, then another. Danny lying on the open ground, I think, Danny for all to see.

I want to think about what happened, about how it was, the stages of his dying, whether I could see the moment when he was more dead than alive, the moment when the balance tipped. That's what I'd planned to do, to recollect it all in tranquillity. But my mind keeps skittering away to Danny-for-all-to-see, so I sit by the window and wait for the dawn to come up, then I wait for the stores to open. It's difficult to wait. It's almost impossible.

I go to a DIY superstore where I can be one of a crowd. I stand in line at a checkout while the girl who scans the bar-code yawns and chats to the girl at the next till and never looks at me. Out in the car park I put the spade in the boot, then sit in the car trying to decide.

It's a risk either way. I drive out along the dual carriageway until I reach the turnoff, drive past, turn a mile or so up the road and drive past again. Next time I take the turnoff and retrace the route I took earlier – houses, light industry, point of no return. There's no activity – no police, no vehicles, no rubberneckers. The housing developments are all cul-de-sacs and avenues, car-ports and fake leaded windows; the industrial estate is noisy but deserted apart from trucks reversing into yards.

I take the access road and just keep going until I get to the metal-rung gate; then, like someone jumping into cold water, I get out of the car bringing the spade with me, shove through the gate, and walk really fast out into the middle of the field.

It's not difficult to see where Danny lies. The ferns are broken down just there, making a hollow. If you knew what you were looking for, you'd find it easily enough. It's almost a shock that Danny's still in place. There isn't much time for it, but I crouch down to look at the differences. And here's Danny ceasing to be Danny now that things have really started to change. Beasts of earth and air have been feeding off him. His lips and eyes have gone, part of one cheek, and the big wound in his throat has drawn little creatures with sharp teeth.

I'm not sure how long it takes me to dig something deep enough. Quite a while. Several trains go through and all I do is turn my back to them and carry on with my work. Imagine all those people with nothing better to do looking out and seeing a man, thigh-deep in bracken, digging a hole. They think nothing of it; they assume everything's all right because that's how their lives run.

I kick the broken ferns about to cover the bare patch. It's not much of a job, but everything will grow back; pretty soon Danny's grave will be under a tangle of leaf and thorn.

When I get home, I stay for a while drinking brandy, but I don't know how to be still – wandering from room to room, looking out of windows, switching the radio on, the TV, switching them off, making food I can't eat.

Finally I go out for a walk and it's odd and powerful to be among people who don't know who I am or what I've done. There's something sad in me, though, like when you know you're unhappy but can't remember why.

I think about Danny's dying and I can't seem to focus on it as I'd like: its stages, its development, and I'm angry with myself, now, because I think I got it wrong – the place too public, the act taking place in darkness, the whole thing too hurried.

As I walk, I start to cry because I'm wishing I had Danny back. Wishing I could start again.


'There are things I want to ask you,' Joe said.

Olsen nodded. He said, 'Okay,' and in the same breath added, 'How's Connie, Joe? Is she all right?'

Joe's attention switched. 'How did you know about Connie? How did you get my number?'

'It's simple, Joe. Think of the simple way. I followed you home, Joe. I kept an eye on you. A few days later I followed Connie to work. And I phoned her office when she wasn't there – I was her cousin – I sounded upset because I was meeting her for lunch and she hadn't arrived; I called her Mrs Morgan, said I needed confirmation of her home number because I'd phoned her flat but no one was answering. I gave the address and guessed at the district code: her colleague kindly gave me the rest. People are easily fooled, Joe. You can tell anyone anything and most of the time they'll believe you. Why wouldn't they? They don't expect people like me to wander into their lives.' Olsen's smile was slight and private, like a whisper.

'Is that how you got Lynda Lomas's address and phone number?'

'More or less … except it was easier.'

'You followed Connie …'

'There was nothing dangerous in it, Joe. I wasn't thinking bad thoughts. It wasn't the only time I followed her … but she never came to harm, did she?'

Joe felt anger rising in him like black blood in the veins; a furious energy shook him and he turned away.

'Joe …' Olsen grinned and wagged his head like someone denying a rumour.

'What was Danny wearing when he died?'

Olsen seemed surprised. 'What he always wore.'

'Tell me what it was.'

'The old coat, the cardigan with the pin, boots but no socks.'

'Did he have a beard?'

'He did.'

'How old would you say he was?'

'Joe … You don't think I'm lying to you?'

'It's Danny I need to identify, not you.'

'Who else would it be?'

'Fifty?' Joe asked. 'Older?'

'Might have been fifty. Might have been sixty.'

Joe said, 'And where …' then stopped. It was going to be a question about Serena Matthews, but in his mind's eye Joe saw Connie walking down the street, dressed for the weather in that sleeveless dress with the full skirt that billowed when the wind took it, so that she would press her palms to her thighs to stop it rising, and behind her Olsen, his eyes on her back, increasing his pace to make sure he didn't lose her at the crossing, getting close, close enough to touch, then stepping onto the crowded train with her as the people behind shoved and pressed, pressing against her, perhaps, because everyone was hip-to-thigh in the early morning crush.

'I'm tired, Joe. I need a rest. I'd like to sleep for a while now.'

Joe nodded. The interview room was anywhere-anytime: windowless and lit by neon strips. A fan buzzed in one corner, but it was only stirring the heat.

Olsen's shirt was patched with sweat. He leaned forward a little as if scrutinising Joe's face. 'What time was it, Joe, when they interrupted our telephone call?'

'About three-thirty, I think.'

'You just got up – got out of bed and came straight here?'

'That's right.'

'I thought that must be it.'

Joe frowned. 'Thought ... what?'

'I can smell it on you, Joe. Smell Connie on you.'

Joe sat very still, his left hand holding his right wrist.

'The thing is, Joe, you never know what another person might be thinking, do you? Even when she's lying under you. She's lying under you and her eyes are closed and you look into her face and she's smiling with it, greedy for it, and she could be thinking anything. Does that ever occur to you?'

Joe got up and walked to the door.

Olsen said, 'You called me Henry – when we spoke earlier, on the phone. I liked that, Joe. It seemed friendly.' He smiled and lifted one hand for a tiny goodbye wave. 'I'll see you later ...'

'Yes, Henry, I'll see you later.'

*

'He knows what McMahon was wearing — a good description; he redescribed the site of the grave. There's no question.'

Fisher and Tranter each held a copy of Joe's report along with a copy of the tape transcript.

Fisher said, 'Send a copy of this to Ackerman — this and all subsequent reports. Send him a transcript, too. Olsen's people will have their expert witness and I want to know what he's likely to say. I also want to know what Ackerman himself thinks. He might be *our* expert witness.'

'Olsen's mad,' Joe said. 'No one's likely to think otherwise.'

'Yes? Except a smart brief and a stupid jury. Let's see what Ackerman has to say.'

'There's already enough for us to charge him,' Tranter observed. 'No one knew the location of the grave. No one knew what McMahon had on when he died.'

'Not yet,' Joe said, 'not if you want the rest.'

'We've got the evidence,' Tranter said, 'we're obliged to lay a charge.'

'In a hurry?' Joe asked. 'Want to go home? Because that's a coincidence — I want you to go home, too.'

'Twenty-four hours?' Fisher asked.

'I doubt it,' Joe said, 'he's enjoying the process; hadn't you noticed.'

'If he takes his time I'll give Superintendent's authority for thirty-six hours,' Fisher said, 'unless you want to go straight to a magistrate for a three-day extension.' To Tranter he said, 'Morgan's right. We could charge him with McMahon and then come back at him with the others, but he might decide to stop talking. I want this squared away; all of it. With this guy, it's likely to be a case of one thing leads to another. Charge him with McMahon and you'll have to stop questioning him about McMahon — you know that, and whoever he gets as a lawyer will know that. The last thing we need is a string of technical objections to the charges.'

Joe said, 'Danny McMahon, Serena Matthews, the girl he called Christine, Lynda Lomas, and he mentioned four others. So – a possible eight that we know of. Work it out for yourself – he gets a sleep period of eight hours in every twenty-four; I need as long as possible.'

Fisher nodded. 'I'll make the application.' As an afterthought, he added, 'He followed you home – that's what he said.'

'Yes.'

'How was he able to know who you were – recognise you, I mean?'

'I know,' Joe said. 'I thought of that.'


Joe heard footsteps clattering downstairs behind him, anxious to catch up but not to overtake.

Tranter said, 'He certainly took an interest in you.' Joe kept walking. 'And Connie.'

They reached the foot of the stair and Joe turned towards the front office; Tranter could have come up alongside him, but chose to stay a pace or so behind. Joe could feel the other man's grin burning his back.

'He's right, you know,' Tranter said, 'I can smell it too.'

Joe stopped dead; he put his hands on his hips and bowed his head. His arms were trembling as if he were holding back something that had broken free on a downhill slope.

Tranter overtook him and half turned without breaking his stride. The brightness in his eye was pure pleasure: a man with a score to settle.

'Just a hint, just a whiff. Lovely. That Connie. What a girl.'


Joe walked to his car and got in, leaving the windows up. It was like sitting in a sauna, the air thick and difficult to breathe.

He watched the life on the street with unblinking eyes. He was trying not to think. Not to think too much.

*You bastard. You sick bastard. Stay out of my head. Get your hands off me.*

He drove home and went into the bedroom where he lay down on Connie's side of the bed and fell asleep at once.

She was taking risks to be with him – faking migraines, leaving early for appointments with a non-existent specialist. Initially her boss had been irritated and a little suspicious; more recently he had started to look at her as if he were wondering whether 'migraine' might soon reveal itself to be 'brain tumour', and it made Connie feel unlucky to be thought of that way.

*If the wind changes, you'll stay like that …*

Michael told her, 'It's easy: leave the job; leave Joe; come and live with me.'

Connie shook her head, but wouldn't look at him. 'No, it's – no, I've thought of it – I think of it a lot –'

'It's … What?' He was painting and talking, which was unusual, concentrating on a particular passage of the picture that might have been sky or might have been water carrying a reflection of the sky. He was working the paint onto the canvas in small staccato slabs.

'It's too soon – is that what you were going to say? Because it's not. It's not too soon.'

'Yes, that's what I was going to say.'

A silence fell between them. Connie asked, 'If it's not too soon … What does that mean? What are you saying? That it's almost too late?'

Michael laughed, his back turned to her as he continued to nudge paint onto the canvas. 'No, Connie, it's not too late. What do you think I'm doing – negotiating a deal? Making a takeover bid?' He turned and smiled at her. 'I'm not trying to frighten you.'

249

She went out for a walk, thinking she ought to leave him to his work. It was new to her, the whole business of Michael's way of life – working alone to make something. She loved the smell of the oil paints and the business of stretching canvas; she loved the fact that what he saw or imagined was something he owned – his way of seeing, his dreaming.

She walked a mile up the riverbank and sat on a flight of stone steps to watch sunlight pitch and scamper on the swell. She thought of Joe and wondered what on earth he could do – what he could suddenly become – that would make her feel differently.

On the way back, she turned off the riverside path and found a small delicatessen. She bought ciabatta and kalamata olives, and some rough pâté. A little further down the street, she bought the ingredients for a salad and two salmon steaks. Buying the food meant staying for dinner: every little gain she made she made by stealth.

When she walked into Michael's loft, he was still working and he didn't notice her at first. He stood at his easel with the brush raised as if caught between the reality of some object and the way he would get it onto the canvas.

Connie watched him, how he was poised on the balls of his feet as if caught in mid-stride; how the muscles in his forearm worked as he laid on the paint; how concentration made him part his lips slightly and look without blinking. She saw him as someone apart, someone private, a stranger, and she fell in love with him – the work of a moment.

# Twenty-Two

**D**aytime dreams seem faster and brighter — more of an attack.

Joe dived off the bridge, hands together, fingers pointed, like a man in the act of prayer. The water sleeved him, cool and close, just as when he'd dreamed the dream before, and he swam downwards effortlessly, arrowed like a gannet.

There was no river-bed to touch. Pillars of sunlight that had been white and hard nearer the surface faded now, becoming first aquamarine, then deep emerald. He seemed to sleep as he swam, not needing to breathe, then surfaced in a place fathoms deep under a mirror-image sky that was backed by a pale, dull glow like storm-light. Olsen was waiting for him there.

He said, 'Not far enough yet, Joe. There's further to go,' and Joe could see a river below the river he'd already swum through, and knew there would be another below that, and others beyond.

Olsen dived making a perfect arc and breaking the surface without so much as a whisper. Joe followed into water that was colder and deeper and darker. He could hear Olsen's voice, though the other man was just a dim shape sounding the depths.

'Deeper than this, Joe. Deeper than this.'

He woke and went to the shower where he stood motionless under the jets, and the deluge brought the dream back to him in fragmented images. He shook his head as if trying to fling off the memory.

In the kitchen, he made a sandwich that he could eat while he drove and left a note for Connie saying that he might not be back that night.

He signed it with love.


Olsen was bright-eyed, like a bird. He sat on the edge of his seat, hands on the table-top, and from time to time he beat a jazzy little riff with his fingertips.

'I could have mentioned others,' he said, 'but Danny was someone you'd find easily enough.'

'How many others?' Joe asked.

'Not sure. I'm not sure, Joe, but the thing is, some of them weren't in this country and some others were too old, you know? Too long ago. You wouldn't have found much, Joe. A rag, a bone, a clump of hair.'

'How many?'

'I don't know.'

'You mentioned some names once, when we were talking on the phone.'

'Did I? Who? Who did I tell you about?'

'Tommo?'

'Yes, Tommo ...'

'Jan, Mick.'

'Jan and Mick, yes. Jan. Jan and Mick.'

Olsen seemed excited; with each name his smile grew brighter. His fingers drummed on the table: a fierce beat that backed a tune only he could hear.

'Angie.'

'Yes, Angie, that's right. Angie, yes.'

Joe waited but Olsen said nothing; he stared at Joe, his head wagging to the inaudible tune.

'Tell me about her,' Joe said.

'You see films of them,' Olsen said. 'You know, European

films, films with subtitles. The train comes into the station and among the passengers are these lost people. They arrive with blanket rolls and shabby clothes and they're lost; they look around at the people hurrying here and there, the busy streets; they can't see the sky properly, and they can't hear the birds singing. They haven't got a job, and they haven't any money …

'What's the film about? It's about whether they survive in the big city, isn't it? Have you ever seen a film like this, Joe? It's about how they get along. Some make it and some don't. Some acquire bad habits. Some get rich, some take up a life of crime, some marry a rich man's daughter. Some find friends, some bump into people who plan to kill them.'

Olsen had become breathless, his words falling over each other, his fingers drumming a cavalry charge. He stopped and put his face into his hands; he seemed at first to be gasping, then Joe realised he was stifling laughter.

'I saw her when she was still a long way off. She stood out. She wasn't the only one of her sort to arrive on the train, not the only lost child, but she was still at the other end of the platform when I saw her yellow hair.'

Joe thought: *Not Angie. This isn't Angie. I know who this is.*

'It's difficult,' Olsen said, 'difficult to work out where to do it, how to get the most out of it. Somewhere private, obviously – where you won't be seen or interrupted. Others hadn't been like that. Mick, for example. Yes, he's a good example. Know where I killed him? On a beach in Greece. Just off the beach, in truth. A cave. A shallow cave, with barely enough room to stand, barely enough light to see. No good. Jan was the same; a hurried thing. It's true what they say about holiday romances, Joe – they don't count for much. Jan was in Malta. She was all over me, Joe. Mad for me. This was a few years ago now. After Tommo, though.'

'Tommo was your first …'

'She wanted everything from me; everything I could give.'

253

It was as if Joe hadn't spoken. 'They never found Jan. I buried her deep. It wasn't easy to do. Know where I buried her? In a graveyard. Think of it. I buried her in a graveyard.'

Olsen's voice tailed off; he seemed lost with his memories. Joe said, 'The private place ...'

'I rented a room from a lettings agency: there are lots that don't ask questions; all they need to see is money up front. I sublet it to her.'

'Serena —?'

'Yes, of course, Serena. Later on, when I found Christine, I pretended I was offering a job, too. Money *and* a place to stay: a nice touch; a grace-note I thought. With Christine I felt different; I took her the next day ... took her life. I don't know what it was; she made me hungry, but it wasn't just that. I think I wanted you to see her, Joe. Yes, that was it. I wanted to show her to you — no delay. But it wasn't like that with Serena.'

A line of sweat was trickling down Olsen's face, making a mazy path from temple to chin. He lifted a shoulder and turned his head, blotting it with his shirt.

He said, 'I wouldn't mind a change of clothes, Joe.'

'Okay.'

'Thanks, Joe. You're a pal.'

Joe nodded. He thought: *I'm getting close to the bastard, which is where I want to be. He wants to confess, sure, but on his terms. Now I have to change that. It was 'his terms' when he was killing. My terms now.*

'Listen,' Olsen said, 'I've got something for you.'

'Something ... What?'

'But I don't think I'll give it to you just yet.'

'Okay.'

'You think I'm kidding, don't you?'

'I don't know.'

'I'm not kidding, Joe.'

'Okay.'

Olsen smiled, and the smile became a little coughing laugh. He put his head back and stared at the ceiling as if wondering whether or not he should change his mind and hand over the gift he had for Joe. The gift of knowledge.

'Tell me about Serena,' Joe asked.

I pick her out as soon as she gets off the train. Long blonde hair, heavy and straight. She's wearing the uniform: jeans and trainers, a T-shirt with the name of some band on the front, but she also has a quilted jacket, a Chinese jacket with ties instead of buttons; it's black with a little red motif repeated on every other quilt-square; the motif looks like a mosquito. She tells me later that she got it in a thrift shop.

As she comes towards me, I move into her path. She swerves, I swerve the same way, we do that little dance that people do who can't find a way round each other. She says sorry and pauses to let me pass, but I stand there. I ask her if she needs somewhere to stay.

This is crucial. It's a crucial moment, because it's when I could lose her. Too little persistence and she'll shrug me off; too much and I'll lose her trust. She asks me who I am. I tell her my name. I say, 'Henry'. Then I laugh and say, 'Unless you want to sleep rough'.

This is a while ago. Just before the heat started. It wasn't cold, but there was rain in the wind that night; the pavements were wet.

She says, 'I've got no money'.

I say, 'Housing benefit'.

She says, 'You've got a scam going', and I wag my head at her and smile a big smile. 'Where is it?' she asks, and smiles back at me, because there are people offering deals a lot like this at main line stations all over London.

All over London; the lost children.

It's day three and I call on Serena. She's still there and that makes me feel lucky. I've waited – I've made a point of it – running the risk that I might lose her. She could've moved on; people move on all the time; but here she is, with some little bits and pieces that make the place hers, and a kettle she's bought, and tins on the kitchen shelf along with a packet of tea and some flowers she's stolen from a garden, arranged in a jampot.

That's the bit that makes me uneasy: the possessions, the feeling that she's settled in. It's my first time doing things this way – finding a private place, a room – and I begin to wonder whether I might have made a mistake.

I tell her I was just passing, but she assumes I've come for the rent.

'I can't pay', she says, but then gives me eight pounds. She raised some money begging in the Underground.

I tell her I don't want it: 'Pay me when you get the benefit money'.

'What do you want?' she asks. 'Do you want me?'

So we make love and it's strange because she takes all her clothes off and lies down and starts singing, as if to herself. She sings all the time I'm doing it to her. I can't remember the words and I can't remember the tune, not now, but it was about a sailor coming home from the sea and in one life he has a family on shore and in another he's married to a mermaid who's bewitched him. She's called a silkie – the mermaid. Do you know that song? And it's so sad and so sweetly sung, that I decide she ought to live that day. Live for that day. Because I've brought the gear with me, Joe. Did I mention that? Taken the things I need to do the job.

The thing is, she's started to fascinate me – really puzzle me – and I've begun to think that she's too good to waste; for the present, anyway. She sings and I'm on top of her, and she doesn't help, or even move much, she's strangely placid, doesn't seem excited or affected by what's happening. If I ask her to do something for me, she does it, but it's a bit like asking someone to pass the sugar.

When I finish she gets up and puts her clothes on and waits until I do the same before tidying the bed; then she goes to sit by the window to look out. There's nothing much to see: just some little patches of garden where nothing grows.

She asks me for some money and I give her the eight pounds back. I ask her, 'Is that for the fuck?' and she nods and says it is, yes, but she's not on the game. Not now.

I'm watching her and trying to think what to do next. I've begun to change my mind about killing her – about killing her there and then – because I've also got this strong urge to ask her out. To take her somewhere. It's a stupid idea, but I can't shake it off. In the end I ask her to go for a drink, and she says yes. Not now, I tell her, this evening. And she says yes.

I go home and start to worry. It's not that I like her or think that she's special, but something stopped me killing her.

She has a defence.

She can't live, of course, because she's met me and knows me and, in any case, there's something I want from her. The same thing I wanted from the others. But I worry about her calmness; it's as if she were half in, half out of a dream. I worry about taking her for a drink.

When I'm on my way back, about eight-thirty, I've still got my things: they're in a small rucksack that I hang from one shoulder, and I think that the best thing, altogether the best thing, would be to take her life as soon as I get there. I sit outside the flat in my car with my eyes closed trying to feel killing her, trying to see killing her, because when I know it's going to happen I get feverish, and the sheer energy involved is almost enough to carry me away.

I remember a time I was so hot with it, so strung up with it, that I kept banging things with my fists and my elbows and my knees, without meaning to, without really knowing how it was happening, as if the world were bumping into me. That was with Angie.

I think of how Angie looked when she was alive, how she looked when she was dead. A minute this way, a minute that. What makes the difference? That's what I can't get straight. What is 'dead'? Where has Angie gone?

There was a bruise on her leg the day she died – the moment she died; the world must have been bumping Angie, too. There it was – a bruise, and she was alive; next, it's still there but she's dead. I know what dead is, I know what people would say, what scientists would say, I know all about the medical details; but I can't get it straight.

In the car, outside Serena's room, I feel excited, but it's not enough. Something's wrong. I feel I've got a choice: kill her or take her out for a drink, but that's almost as strange as not-dead-then-dead. I wonder if she might be asleep and hope that she is: that I'll go into the room and find her asleep on the bed, because then I could put the knife up against her throat and watch the breath and feel the pulse. Then there wouldn't be anything to do but kill her; no choice.

She's waiting for me and we go out to a pub. She tells me stories about herself, but they don't really make sense and it seems to me that Serena's a bit of a fantasist – a spinner of webs, a teller of tales.

We sit in the pub for a couple of hours and things get better and better. I can't really describe how or why – but I'd started to worry about knowing her too well, or liking her. I considered that it might be the sex, but sex had made no difference with Angie or Jan or the others. I knew what I wanted from them. When I spoke to them or lay down with them or laughed at some remark, I saw them plain – they were *mine*, they were *for* me.

No – it was the tins of food and the kettle and the flowers. Now I'm looking at her, and listening to her little fables about herself, and everything's fine again; in fact, I'm thinking that maybe I'll keep her for a while.

We leave the pub and walk to a little park: dusty, the trees sprayed with graffiti. She lets me take her photograph – something I like to do, though there's not always the opportunity. It was easy in Greece, of course, with everyone being on holiday. I photographed Mick in the cave, but the light wasn't good.

In the park, the light's perfect. I stand with my back to the sun and Serena smiles for me, but she's looking over my shoulder when I take the picture – detached, sometimes with me, sometimes not. I shoot the whole reel. She laughs, then, and strikes a couple of poses – arms akimbo, arms aloft.

She really comes alive when she's clowning.

I visit her on and off for a couple of weeks. Each time she lies down for me and sings. On one occasion I'm next to her and she drifts off to sleep. By this time it was hot every day, as if summer had come from somewhere else, as if you might look out of the window and see a desert.

It comes to me that what I should do is keep Serena and kill someone else. I don't mean keep her forever and never kill her; but keep her for longer – for the time being. It's just that I seem to have fallen into a routine with her that I'm finding it difficult to break, though I don't believe it makes any difference to Serena because most of the time she looks through me or around me and talks not to me but to herself.

I get off the bed and open my rucksack. All the stuff's in there: everything I need. I take out the knife and go back to the bed. Serena is sleeping as children sleep: like the dead. Her face is very pale and her hair is fanned out on the sheet. She has turned from the sun and the open window, but her hair catches sunlight and glows red and gold.

I lie down facing her and let her breath play over my face. I put the ball of my finger lightly – so lightly – on the thick pulse in her neck; it is heavy and slow. I lay the knife to her throat and the touch of it makes her stir, lifting her chin a little as if offering her throat to the blade.

Does it matter, I wonder, whether she's awake or asleep? Is it possible that fear only confuses things? I wonder whether the moment might have come and a flush starts in me that goes to my head, making my scalp tighten and the hairs prickle. I kneel up and get astride her. I didn't mean to do this but it's too late now, too late, as I get my weight down on her, my fingers still at her pulse, and I watch her, watch her closely, her eyelids fluttering as she comes awake – disturbed by my movements, or else the feel of the knife, or simply by what's on my mind.

Before she knows what's happening, before she's fully awake, she remembers the song she was singing as she went to sleep and she starts it again as if the tune had lain on her lips the whole time.

It's a strange moment, Joe, a perfect moment, a moment I won't want to forget. First the song, her eyes still closed, then the cut of the knife, the first cut, and she turns and sees me; the word she was singing becomes a question, then my name, then she's going to scream but I bear down, and there's that time of transition, the time of passing from one thing to another, and then she's dead.

Nothing rushed, Joe, nothing hurried. No need to clean up immediately or worry about being seen. No need to dig her a grave: someone else will do that. I stay with her a while and it seems to me that I can feel her getting further from me as the minutes go by.

I lean out of the window and watch the passers-by. The house is in a side street and pretty quiet, but I can hear the wash of traffic from the arterial road just beyond and there are people going to and fro: mothers with children, three kids on rollerblades, a girl in a button-through skirt that flows and shows her legs, an old man who has placed a chair on the pavement and is sitting out in the sun with a bottle of beer.

Serena behind me on the bed.

It's great not having to leave at once, not having to make myself scarce, so I keep watch with Serena – a little vigil – and sometimes I go to the window to catch the world going by. In the end, though, there's nothing to stay for. I take a few photographs to set alongside the reel I shot in the park.


'What about Donna?' Joe asked. 'Didn't she ask questions?'

'Donna ...' Olsen nodded as if he'd just managed to place the name. 'Yes, Donna.'

'Didn't she want to know where you were?'

'I expect ... well, nights, she'd think I was at the market – sometimes I was. If I went out during the day ...' he shrugged, 'she never asked me. Mostly, she used to stay at the flat.'

'Why?'

'She liked it there. A lot of the time she was stoned – you know.'

'Henry ... why didn't you kill her?'

'Donna?'

'Yes.'

'I was keeping her.'

'To kill later?'

Olsen looked thoughtful. 'I don't know. Just ... keeping her. Perhaps to kill. I hadn't thought of her that way.'

Joe started to ask a question about Serena: 'Didn't you worry about being –'

Olsen interrupted, a look of surprise on his face, his voice light with astonishment that was almost laughter. 'I hadn't thought of her that way.'


'Didn't you worry about being seen with her?'

Olsen fell silent. He got up and walked round the room,

hands in pockets, his gaze fixed on the floor, his head wagging from side to side like a man grappling with a new idea. Joe let him be until he returned to his chair, then asked his question again.

'Seen with who?'

'Serena. You took her to a pub and went with her to a park where you took photos. You knew you were going to kill her. Weren't you worried about being seen?'

'I didn't think of it. I mean, who would care?'

'Serena is found murdered. The police ask questions locally. Someone saw you in the pub, perhaps, or someone saw you in the park, the old man drinking beer in the street saw you, we get an E-fit …'

'That's not what happened.'

'No. I just wonder why you didn't take more care; didn't mind if people –'

'But Joe,' Olsen said, 'it never happened.'

'Jan and Tommo,' Joe said, 'Angie and Mick.'

'They were just some … I used to go to Greece, to the islands, spend whole summers there. People travelling, going from island to island, from country to country.'

'You killed them there – in Greece …'

'Not Tommo.'

'All in the same year?'

'Five years,' Olsen told him. 'I went every summer for five years.'

'Three people in five years.'

'Seven,' Olsen said, 'seven people it was, but not Tommo.' As if it were part of a train of thought he added, 'I'm a pretty good photographer, I take photographs a lot; there's a photograph that I'd like to give to you.'

'Okay,' Joe said.

'Not yet. I'll tell you where to find it, but not just yet. Do you understand, Joe?'

'Sure. Whenever you feel ready to give –'

'No,' Olsen shook his head impatiently, 'not that. Do you understand what I'm saying about dead and not-dead? Do you see what it is about the moment before and the moment afterwards?'

'I'm trying to,' Joe said. 'I want to.'

'Do you feel curious?'

'I've thought about it.'

Olsen looked at Joe carefully. 'Yes,' he said. 'I believe you. I'm glad to be telling you these things, Joe, because I think you understand. You're beginning to understand. Understand a little better.'

'How many?' Joe asked him. 'How many altogether?'

Olsen spread his hands and let an outgoing breath whistle across his teeth.

'What about Tommo?'

'That was a long time ago.'

'Where will I find him?'

'You won't, Joe. You won't ever find him. Not Tommo. He's gone forever.'

'And the others?'

'Well … Some in Greece, as you know. Some in Spain. One in Goa, I think; not more. Two in Somerset.'

'Where you used to live.'

'Two there, yes. This isn't very interesting.'

'They're questions I have to ask.'

'Yes. Are they? I don't want to listen.'

Joe didn't want to lose his man. He said, 'We can talk about it another time.'

Olsen smiled and nodded, as if to an anxious child, then closed his eyes. He didn't open them, or speak for ten minutes. Finally, he said: 'I think we've lost the point, Joe. I think we're drifting.'

'What is it you see?' Joe asked, 'when you look at them: after they're dead?'

Olsen nodded as if acknowledging the question, but he said, 'No, Joe, I don't think so. Not now. Perhaps later.' He got up and walked to the door, standing with his face to it and asking to be let out.

'They gave me the three days,' Fisher said, 'but no one was happy about it. We've got more than enough to charge him.'

'I thought four more victims,' Joe said, 'but there are others.'

'There might not be time to hear about them. Not unless he suddenly unloads.'

'How many,' Tranter asked, 'in all?' Like Fisher, he was holding a dupe tape of the interview, and a transcript, but there hadn't been time to listen or read.

Joe shook his head. 'Christ knows.'

Fisher's office was on the west side of the building and he had lowered his blinds against the late afternoon sun.

Tranter said, 'I wouldn't mind having some kind of a role in all this.'

'You're still working on a TIE programme aren't you?' Fisher asked.

'It's pointless.'

Trace. Identify. Eliminate. Tranter's team were still ticking off a few of the suspects that had been thrown up by *Crimewatch*. No one really believed that Olsen was a con man, but until he'd been charged the AMIP team would play it by the book.

'So it may be,' Fisher agreed. 'If we get some locations, you can go looking for corpses, but you can't interview him.'

'He's started talking now —'

'He's talking to Joe. I don't want him to stop. He won't talk to anyone else —'

'Says he won't —'

'And I'm not taking the risk. If he decides to go quiet, we could have a problem.'

264

'Olsen maintains that some of the victims are buried on a Greek island,' Joe told Tranter. 'More interested now?'

Tranter walked out of the room, leaving both tape and transcript on the seat of his chair. Fisher said, 'You're a pain in the ass, Joe. So is he.'

'We could try Olsen again in a couple of hours if we wanted to,' Joe said, 'but I'd like to make it four or five. I know we're short of time, but he's been running things so far and it might be interesting if that changed. He talks when he wants to — when he's full of things to say — then he switches off when he's had his say. I need him to be more eager — anxious to talk, anxious to have me listen.'

Fisher nodded. He was leafing through the transcript. 'Is Ackerman getting copies of these?'

'And tapes.'

'Good.' There was a pause while Fisher read. 'He's going to plead diminished responsibility, you know that?'

'Yes.'

'Yes. Well ...' Fisher tossed the transcript down onto his desk and passed a hand over his eyes. 'Keep at him.'


Connie had cut the bread and put out the olives. She had lit the barbecue on the balcony, and made the salad. It all felt indelibly strange. Now she was standing just inside the room by the open glass doors and staring down river, tranced by the light on the water.

She felt Michael standing behind her. He put his arms through hers so that his hands met by her breasts. He was holding a necklace of large, irregular, tawny pieces of amber. Connie took it from him, draping it across her outstretched fingers, letting it run this way and that.

When he placed it round her neck, the sun settled in every stone, and glowed.


She had already grown used to the sound of ship-horns and

the beat of engines. Michael's smell at this time of day was oil paint and the tartness of white spirit; she could smell it on him now. She looked at him busy eating and, without any warning, was struck through with happiness.

'Where are you tonight?' he wanted to know.

'At a movie with Marianne.'

'What are you seeing?'

'I'll look out for billboards on the way home. It won't matter — Joe never goes.'

'So the lies have started,' he said. 'Good.'


The streets were full of people. A full moon in a clear sky made midnight seem like sunrise. Connie drove with all the windows open, battered by the warm slipstream and by music that came at her from cars and restaurants and invisible open-air parties. The world had decided it was too hot to sleep.

Her hair was still damp from the shower.

Michael had said, 'Stay … When will you be able to stay?'

At the door he had ambushed her with a look and she'd kissed him so hard that even now her mouth felt bruised.

She had poured herself a nightcap, taken off her make-up and half undressed before she found Joe's note telling her there was a good chance he wouldn't be back that night. She stood motionless, reading it a second time and feeling as if she had one foot in her own bed and one in Michael's; then she put her dress and shoes back on, gathered her car keys from the kitchen and lifted the phone to call Michael. In the same moment, she heard Joe at the front door.

About-to-go-out looked exactly the same as just-got-back, but Connie couldn't meet Joe's eye. She poured him a whisky instead, which allowed her to turn her back, then topped up her own as if that's why she had gone to the kitchen. He took the drink and drank it and gave himself another. The greyness in his face seemed to be more than skin-deep.

'That kind of day,' she suggested, and thought: *Making conversation, sounding a bit edgy, looking a bit guilty – how could he miss it?*

'I've interviewed men I knew to be guilty of murder. Hard nuts, you know? Doing a job of work – a gangland revenge killing – or else letting go with an automatic weapon when some idiot security guard wouldn't hand over the money. I've seen domestic stuff and race killings and fatal bar-fights, but I've never seen anything like this guy.'

'What's he telling you?'

'Who he killed. Those he can remember, anyway.'

'Not just those you already –'

'No,' Joe shook his head, 'there were others.'

'He's confessing. What was the name of that shrink you –'

'Ackerman.'

'Yes, Ackerman, wasn't that what he said the man wanted to do? Confess to you?'

'Yes.' It was on the tip of Joe's tongue to tell Connie that Olsen had followed her; he knew the information would frighten her and for some reason he wanted that – wanted her to need his protection. Instead, he said: 'He's confessing, but in his own way and at his own speed. I'm getting limited information which, I expect, is the way he wants it.'

'What do you want?'

'I want to pluck out his soul,' Joe said, 'and pick it to bits. I want to see where the rot set in.' Connie stared at him and he laughed loudly like someone covering for a bad joke. 'I don't know what I want.' He bowed his head and massaged his temples with the tips of his fingers; he looked like a man listening intently to something only he could hear. 'To get everything from him – everything he's done. To tally the dead people; to know where they are and how they died and when.'

267

'Is that going to be difficult?'

'He kills runaways and tramps –' Joe remembered what Carol Mitchie had said. '– waifs and strays. No histories and no futures.'

Connie realised that she was still clutching her car keys; she set them down on a nearby work-surface like someone turning aside from temptation. She saw Michael in her mind's eye and found herself blushing.

'Why does he kill them?' she asked.

'Curiosity.'

'I don't understand.'

'No. Nor do I.' Joe paused, stalled on a thought. 'But he expects me to.'

'What's he like?'

'Good-looking, thirty-five-ish, tall, brown hair that he wears in a ponytail.'

'Intelligent?'

'Clever. Not sure about intelligent. I expected –' Joe thought it through for a moment. 'I expected to be able to see it at once – his madness, you know? I can't. But it's there – you sense it: like searching a box with a hidden compartment.'

Connie felt light-headed, not from the whisky but from the effort of keeping her secret. Moments like this one seemed the worst kind of betrayal.

Joe said, 'I'm exhausted. Just talking to him is like running uphill for an hour. I don't know why. He cleans me out.' He stood up and kissed Connie in passing.

She kissed him back with her bruised lip, flinching slightly, though he barely noticed.


The furthest river was the deepest river. Joe swam down, kicking hard and holding his breath for ever. Olsen was a sleek shape in the murk ahead of him and his voice came back on the flow of the tide.

'Stay with me, Joe. Stay close.'

Connie watched Joe's dream as it played on Joe: a fist clenching and unclenching, feet working a treadle, the low murmur of tangled words. She put out a hand and smoothed his hair; he turned towards her touch, but didn't wake.

All at once she saw him as a man alone: parents dead, few friends, family scattered. It hadn't occurred to her before to tot up his assets in this way and it seemed a bleak piece of mathematics.

She could see his eyeballs moving under his eyelids.

At three o'clock she got out of bed, went into the living room and pulled three large polythene bags out of a cupboard. The bags contained photographs: the hundreds of photographs that everyone takes and forgets. She sat on the floor and sifted through them: frozen moments, the scraps and jots of their life together.

Connie and her father, whom she had loved and loathed; she remembered standing at his graveside seized by a fierce desire to laugh – the slippery edge of hysteria.

Joe's self-portrait on his first day of official leave after taking a hammering from some drugs dealers – a bad case of right place, wrong time. She looked at the bruises, the misshapen features, and remembered how carefully they had made love, Joe wincing and yelping, sometimes pleasure, sometimes pain.

It struck Connie how often a photo would be of one of them because it had to be taken by the other. They were a couple only when you put two photos together. She looked at herself taking a winter walk on a deserted beach, collar lifted against the sea wind, a woollen hat pulled down over her ears; and here was Joe on the same walk, grinning and raising a hand as if they had met by chance.

She remembered, in that moment, what it was that had

first drawn her to him: his self-sufficiency and the strength it seemed to imply. He was still a good-looking man, but then he had been striking: the thin nose, the wide mouth, brown hair a little too long, his habit of sweeping it away from his face one-handed. Something else had attracted her, though. He was a private man and along with that went a certain shyness, or so she had thought at first; much later, after they had married, she had come to see that it was melancholy, and she feared it, remembering her father.

The photographs drifted through her fingers. She looked at them all, one by one.

Connie walked to the phone and dialled Michael's number; it rang only three times before he answered.

She said, 'It's impossible. I can't be with you. I'm sorry. I'm sorry for both of us.'

She walked from room to room, too restless to settle, crying openly.

She thought, I'm a refugee; where do I belong?

She returned to the bedroom just before dawn. Joe was spreadeagled and stock-still, as if the bed had broken his fall.

She lay down next to him, eyes wide, her hand pressed to her lips like someone who has spoken out of turn.

# Twenty-Three

I'm at the station; it's just past ten o'clock, cold and dark, with a wind cutting over the concourse. I'm not intending anything or, at least, I don't think I am. It's difficult to tell sometimes: difficult for me to tell, like when I killed Serena without it really being in the forefront of my mind.

What am I doing? I'm window-shopping, I suppose. A boy of about eighteen asks me for money. He's sitting by a waste-bin with a slip of a dog alongside him and he's holding out an empty giant-shake carton from McDonald's, jostling the few coins that lie at the bottom.

I think: *You don't know this, but it could be you.*

The dog's a pretty thing, lop-eared and silky. 'What's your name?' I ask the boy and he tells me 'Colin'. I pat the dog and give Colin some change and all the time I'm chuckling. Colin looks at me; he probably wonders whether I'm crazy.

I mutter it under my breath: 'Colin, Colin, you're so lucky. Lucky you, you lucky fucker'.

Eleven o'clock and I'm thinking maybe I'll turn up at the market. Then I see her. She's carrying a bedroll and looking for a pitch, but she sees Colin and decides to move on. I follow her and she makes for the arches where the night girls work, but I don't think she's on the game: she's not dressed for it. The girls turn her around fast: one of them shows her a knife. When she passes me again there's a gob of spit on the back of her jacket.

I say, 'Are you looking for a place?'

Of course she's suspicious. I tell her I've got a proposition for her and ask her if she's hungry. That works. She thinks I might be a God-botherer, but she doesn't care where the meal's coming from. She asks me if I've got anything to drink, so we go to a pub first. It's crowded and loud and there's a lot of beer-swill on the floor. You'd have to be flat on your face to avoid inhaling cigarette smoke: it's hanging in thick layers; you virtually have to nudge it aside to get to the bar. There's a lot of shouting and arguing – a fight brewing somewhere, perhaps – and it makes me edgy, so I order two rounds of doubles and even though it's cold we take them outside and find a place on the pavement. She sits on her blankets, back to the wall of the pub, and drinks her vodka in two swallows, then starts to make a roll-up.

'Where do you live?' she asks and then, because I've asked for her name, 'Donna'.

I tell her where the flat is and she laughs, like I've told her a joke. When I ask her why she says, 'It doesn't mean anything to me. I've never been to London before'.

She's wearing jeans and a T-shirt and a leather jacket, ankle boots, a tartan scarf. The raw weather makes her shiver: it must be getting down towards zero. Rain fell earlier and it's likely to start again.

'What do you get out of it?' she asked.

'I might want you to make a few little trips for me.'

'Where to?'

'Just around London.'

She laughs and nods her head, fingers pinched round the stub of her cigarette. 'Drugs run', she says.

'It's nothing heavy', I tell her, 'just a little hash. Okay? Just dope.'

She shrugs and says, 'As long as I can get some'.

Of course, it's a lie about the dope, but I guess that she'll be convinced by it. I haven't got any dope and I don't use it. Donna uses it – I find that out fast enough. But the whole time she's with me she never asks about the drug runs or even tries to score off me. Maybe she never believed it in the first place, I don't know.

She reminds me about the food, but I can't see anywhere to eat close by, so I walk a couple of streets and buy a hamburger and fries and bring it back. She's drinking another vodka and the guy who bought it is squatting on his haunches to talk to her; he's eager – laughing and saying, 'Come on, let's go. You ready? Come on …'

I give Donna the food and the guy stands up, trying to decide what to do. I face him down, but I'm shaking and hope he can't see it. He leaves. He calls her a fucking bitch cock-tease gobshite, but he leaves. Donna eats quickly, finishes her drink, then stands up and says, 'We can go now'.

The streetlights make her seem pale and deepen the shadows under her eyes. She's about five feet one or two and her shoulders push sharp points in the thin leather of her coat. We start to walk towards the flat, I'm looking over my shoulder for a taxi – we're like any couple on the way home.

Donna rides in the taxi with me but spends all her time looking out at the Christmas lights and decorations in shop windows. When we get back to my flat she asks me if I've got any more booze, so I give her a bottle of whisky more than half full and she starts to drink it. She watches TV and doesn't speak. There are about three or four drinks in the bottle when she gets up and lies down on the bed.

I say, 'Where do you come from, Donna?' but she's asleep before she can answer.

'I need to hear about the others,' Joe said. 'Where they are. Who they are.'

'I've told you what I can, Joe. It's not who they are that I want to talk about. It's what they become.'

'What can you remember about Tommo?'

'Tommo was a fool.'

'Was he? How?'

'A fool. Simple-minded. No one missed him.'

'Long ago, you said. When was it?'

'Long ago.'

'And the two in Somerset?'

'That was later.'

'What were their names, Henry? These are things I have to know. We can talk about other matters, but I have to know about all these people.'

'No one missed them. Just like Christine. Like the others. Runaways and strays – they'd already been written off.'

'Who were they, Henry? The couple in –'

'No one mourned them, Joe. Why worry? Listen, I don't want to talk about this.'

'All I need –'

'I don't want to talk about this.'

Olsen rested his head on his fist and looked away. His eyes unfocused like a man gazing at horizons and he didn't speak again that day.


Leonard Ackerman said, 'I'm sorry about this.' He meant the restaurant they were in. 'It's convenient for me and I come here a lot, but it isn't cheap.'

'Expenses,' Joe assured him.

'Really?' Ackerman grinned broadly. 'Oh, good.'

He had the transcripts of Joe's interviews with Olsen on the table and was flipping through them, glancing at notes he'd made in the margin.

'You're doing fine Joe,' he said, 'no point in pushing things.'

Joe liked being on first-name terms; he thought Ackerman was one of the good guys at a time of severe good-guy shortage.

'I've got a day left. Then we have to charge him or go back to the magistrate for a renewal.'

'Will you get it?'

'Doubtful. I'm not even sure that we want it.'

'No?'

'Not if we charge him — with Danny McMahon, say, or Serena, or Christine —'

'Which you could do,' Ackerman said, 'on the basis of what he's already said.'

'Maybe, maybe.' Joe waved at the waiter and said, 'You choose the wine, okay?'

'Okay,' Ackerman said. He looked happier than ever.

'Maybe but not for sure,' Joe went on. 'We've got a good deal of corroborating evidence with McMahon — less with the others.'

'Looks conclusive to me.'

'Reading those transcripts, a clever brief would cackle with glee. The other problem is that we can't talk to him once we've charged him: not about the subject of the charges, anyway, and he can't really confess to more killings without talking about McMahon and Serena — they're all part of a single purpose.'

'Yes,' Ackerman nodded, 'they are.'

'And I get the feeling that this is the only chance I've got to hear about all his victims. Once he's charged, I'm more or less out of the picture.'

'Are you? Then I'd guess you're right — you'll get only one chance and this is it. You could push him on Lynda Lomas, I guess, since you must have more reason to want to close that file.'

'Her paper is running a full page a day on the case. I'm not their favourite copper. Yes, I'd quite like it if I could make sure he was eventually charged with Lynda's death.'

The waiter arrived at Ackerman's shoulder and took his order for roast vegetables followed by sea bass. He ordered mineral water and a bottle of Montagny Latour.

Joe said, 'I'll have the same.' When Ackerman looked at

him in surprise he shrugged. 'I don't care much what I eat. Tell me about the transcripts.'

'And the tapes —'

'And the tapes, yes.'

'– which were more revealing, although the transcripts are completely accurate.'

'Why?'

'The way he talks about the killings.'

Joe nodded. 'You mean so matter-of-fact.'

'Partly that – though it's easy to listen between the lines and find excitement there: the excitement that precedes the kill. The interesting thing is what actually excites him – not so much the business of killing as the opportunity to observe the process of dying. The act – the slaughter, if you like – doesn't seem to hold much appeal. He talks about it in terms of its practicability but, more than that, his real concern is whether or not he's going to have enough time to watch the death. It's death he's intrigued by, not the act that causes it.'

'Which tells us what?'

'That his reasons have more to do with power than anything else – than sex, say, or some delusion of revenge. But then we more or less knew that already.'

'He talks about what he does with such calmness,' Joe said, 'such indifference.'

'Indifference towards the victim,' Ackerman observed, 'otherwise he's not indifferent – he's intensely involved. But yes, you're right, his victims don't mean much to him at all – they're a means to an end. They're crucial to the process, and important for that reason, but he doesn't think of them as people with families and friends. It's typically sociopathic behaviour although –'

Ackerman broke off to taste the wine. After the waiter had filled their glasses he took a long sip, then looked at Joe in sudden apprehension. 'Sorry, perhaps you want to wait for the food.'

'We can always order another bottle,' Joe assured him. 'Although what?'

'Although it has occurred to me that one reason for his choice of victims might be that he still possesses a remnant of compassion or projected feeling buried somewhere in his psyche.'

'You mean the fact that they're runaways and vagrants?'

'Sure. No one knows they're dead; no one grieves; no tearful relative appears on television pleading with those who know to come forward. In one sense, they're completely dispensable. Look at Danny McMahon. If I ask you why it matters that a father of three dies, or a mother, or a husband or wife, or someone with many friends, or anyone at all with some apparent purpose in the world, the answers are easy to find. Ask yourself the same question about Danny.'

Joe drank his wine, stalling for time. He said, 'It matters because everyone has a right to –'

'Exactly,' Ackerman cut him short. 'It matters in principle. Otherwise – does it matter?'

'Principle ought to be enough to prevent you from having your throat cut.'

'Sure, of course. I'm just looking at it from Olsen's point of view. He kills people who don't matter to anyone but themselves; of course they shouldn't be killed –'

'You don't know that.'

'What?'

'That they didn't matter to anyone. Angie and Tommo and Mick –'

'No, okay, but it's the way Olsen thinks of them; it's what he believes.'

'What were you going to say?'

'When?'

'... they shouldn't be killed –'

'Oh – they shouldn't be killed *in principle*. How often do we use that construction meaning, It's okay really? *In principle* you shouldn't do this, *in principle* we shouldn't allow that. It's a term that's always followed by the word *but*. But in this case – But on this occasion – Look at it this way: suppose I were to tear five pages out of the London telephone directory and all the people whose names were listed on those pages died tonight. When you got up tomorrow morning – how would you know? How would you know how to care? You see how it works? A plane crashes – three hundred perish. An earthquake and it's a thousand. It's a headline, Joe. How do you manage to feel anything? It's the same for Olsen. It shouldn't be, but it is.'

'How might this help me?'

'You're asking him questions about the victims: trying to find out their full identities, where they're buried, when he killed them.'

'I have to.'

'Yeah, sure. The problem – the reason you're not getting as far as you'd like – is that you're trying to get him to talk about something he's not all that interested in. He wants to talk about his obsession – the whole business of death and what it is and how strange it is that something can be alive and functioning in one moment and meat the next. He comes back to it again and again. That's what he wants you to share – and you're fighting it. He must be getting a bit disappointed in you.'

'And that's dangerous,' Joe said.

'Yes, it is. If he decides you're not the person he thought you were – the one to hear his confession, the one to share his obsession, then he'll stop talking.'

'What do you suggest?'

'Christ knows. You're worried that if you decide to get more time with him you'll be handing ammunition to his defence lawyers.'

'No question about it. It's sufficiently unusual to go beyond Superintendent's authority and ask for a three-day extension; double that and no matter what we say, a lawyer is going to have it that we were unsure of our evidence and delayed charging him for that reason.'

'Then you'd better charge him. It could take weeks to get the rest out of him. Probably will.'

'Or else it'll never come.'

'Perfectly possible,' Ackerman agreed, 'especially since he says he can't remember some of them — or can't remember exactly where he put them. And given the way he thinks about them, that's not too surprising.'

Their first course arrived and Ackerman said, 'I might take the precaution of ordering the second bottle now. I'm not a lunchtime drinker normally, but I do enjoy a treat.'

Joe laughed and nodded at the waiter. 'Maybe I'll try to get more out of him about Serena and Christine and Lynda Lomas — make sure I can tag him with those three — and forget the others for now; try again after he's been sentenced.'

'Probably best,' Ackerman agreed. 'And you could try pressing him on the two in Somerset.'

'Yes? What makes you think they're a good bet?'

'I wonder who they are ... don't you?'

'I wonder who they all are,' Joe said, 'and I wonder how many they are, and whether anyone will ever —'

He broke off and laid down his fork. Ackerman was looking at him with a smile of anticipation.

'His parents,' Joe said. 'You think they're his parents.'

'That's right,' Ackerman said. 'I do.'


Steve Tranter was sitting on a bench by the river, half turned from the man with him and looking away towards a crane rigged with a ball-and-chain tackle. The gantry swung back, then brought the ball round in a slow arc. It smacked into the gable-end of a tall, disused brewery building on the far bank.

The sound of the impact came a beat later. The wall shivered but kept its shape.

Turned from his companion that way, his eyes elsewhere, Tranter looked like a priest hearing confession in God's plain air.

The other man said, 'So when will he be charged?'

'Christ knows,' Tranter said.

'It could go on? You could keep him without –'

'We've had him nearly three days. He's already told us about McMahon.' Tranter was being careful to avoid lies while not choosing to tell the whole truth.

'What's his problem – Morgan?'

'Likes the limelight. Something else though.'

Tranter watched the ball return, dragged across the sky. The wall seemed to slump, like a man who has been struck and stunned but doesn't go down.

The other man was a journalist named Stan Collier. He was writing the story in his mind as Tranter spoke.

'Something else?' Collier asked. 'What?'

'This guy fascinates him, you know? He's got a thing about the guy.'

'Has he?'

'Not just a rapport. That's to be expected, you work for that, gaining someone's confidence – all of that. No, it's more than that.'

Tranter was trying to find a way of formulating the lie without having to speak it.

Collier helped him out a little: 'What would I say if I were trying to describe it to my readers?'

Tranter kept quiet but he shrugged, inviting Collier to try.

'Okay.' Collier said, 'let's see … Fiend still not charged, inexplicable delay, official sources suggest more than enough evidence to connect Olsen to three or more murders including that of Lynda Lomas …'

The tackle swung round a little faster, the chain curving

like a spinnaker, and hit the selfsame spot. The upper part of the wall lost shape, then folded, then fell.

'... DI Joseph Morgan prolonging interview – worries in some circles that he's ... let's see, what? ... using to his own advantage Olsen's refusal to talk to any other police officer – okay? – unhealthy fascination, strange affinity, no, *eerie* affinity, between Morgan and Olsen worrying senior police officers ...'

'Well,' Tranter said, 'you're the journo.'

'Risk of libel?'

'Nah. Risk of pissed-off George Fisher.'

'Morgan a known careerist ... yes?'

'Why not? We all are.'

Collier smiled. 'All right, Steve, it's a nice piece. I owe you one.'

'I nicked him,' Tranter said, 'not Morgan. I nicked the crazy bastard.'

'He's not going to walk, Steve, is he?'

'No.'

'But it's something that police sources could strenuously deny.'

'Fisher would deny it.'

'Good, well, a denial always helps.'

Collier got up. Tranter continued to stare at the gantry as it drew back for another shot at the blank windows and grimy brick of the old brewery.

'Fancy a drink, Steve? It's hot enough to boil water out here. I think the bloody river's on the simmer. Pint of cold lager.'

Tranter shook his head, eyes averted. 'I don't think so, Stan. Not today.'

'What is it with you and him, Steve? What's the story?'

'No story,' Tranter said. 'He's making a bollocks of it. Simple as that. I collared this piece of shit. I want him sent down for ever. No loopholes, no fuck-ups.'

'Good man, Steve.' Collier set off on his own down the towpath. 'Good man.'

# Twenty-Four

'**D**o you see, Joe? Do you see?'

Olsen had told Joe about the time he killed Lynda Lomas but he'd told the story without saying a single thing that couldn't be challenged later.

*I need to fix him there, put him at the scene. I need more detail.*

Earlier, Olsen had said: 'I listen to my dreams, Joe. Do you listen to yours?' He had called a halt to the interview and slept through the late afternoon and on into the evening.

'Do you see, Joe?'

Now Olsen was asking him to understand. Joe tried to see the scene through Olsen's eyes but when he looked he could still see Olsen.

She's not important, Joe — as I look at her I know that. She made me angry, but it isn't the reason why. I'm taking my stuff off, you know, getting ready, and I think it won't be all that I want, all that I'm hoping for. It won't go quite right. At first I'm not sure why, but later I see it plainly — she's frightened. Mostly, I got them before they really had time ... They might have been on the edge of sleep perhaps, or drunk, or drugged; there was fear, of course, but there was never such anticipation.

Lynda's scared, so scared, Christ, she's really *scared*. It takes the edge off, Joe. Can you understand? But even so, it's still there — the moment when she turns the corner. Do you know what I mean? The moment when she actually passes across. There's one thing about Lynda — one thing that startles me. The contrast, you know? Although she's too frightened for what I want, too frightened to really look at closely before I start her off, there's the *contrast* between the way she is now and what she'll be like when I've done.

At first she's shaking, you know, and making these awful noises behind the gag and trying to crawl away from me, roll away. And even when I get down to it she's still bucking and trying to kick.

Then afterwards – so still. So completely still. All that energy and desperation and fear of a moment before – gone. Gone where? Gone into the air on her last breath, Joe, do you think that's it? I'm not sure. But, oh, the difference. The *difference*.

'Do you see? Do you see the difference?'

'No,' Joe said, 'not the way you see it.'

'You're trying.'

'I'm trying – yes.'

'I know you are.' Olsen put his face in his hands, as if Joe's lack of vision were all his fault.

'Can I ask you something?'

'Okay.'

'How did you know it was me? When you followed me home.'

Olsen smiled. 'Joe … Why do you worry about such things?'

'I'm not worried. I'm puzzled.'

Olsen drifted off into his thoughts for a while. Joe stayed silent, admitting the mistake to himself, hearing Ackerman's voice.

*It's not what he wants to talk about.*

Olsen's eyes refocused. He said, 'You were leaving. The officer on the desk was having a bad time with a couple of women arguing in either Greek or Spanish – he asked you if

284

you knew which. My excuse for being there? Well, just to ask a simple question about where I might park in the area.

'Were you going outside to find me, Joe? Did I convince you? Were you expecting to find me waiting at that phone booth just down the street? You must have known I wouldn't be there, but you couldn't resist. Who could?'

Joe remembered the moment and the two women yelling, but he couldn't bring a good-looking brown-haired man to the scene. Olsen was humming a little tune to himself; Joe thought that must mean 'bored' or else 'growing annoyed'.

He asked, 'Suppose it happened to you. Someone puts a knife to your throat. What do you think you'd see?' and could tell at once that it was the right question. Olsen gave a start, then looked at Joe with wide eyes.

'I hadn't thought of it,' he said; then again, 'I hadn't thought ...' He smiled, but he was shaking. He closed his eyes, face lifted, like someone taking the sun, and Joe let him be.

After five minutes or so – but without opening his eyes – Olsen said, 'When I was a child, I went to ask my father a question. I had with me a small dog, but the dog was dead. I took the dog into the kitchen where my father was sitting at the table writing or looking at papers: I don't know what he was doing, really; accounts perhaps. It was late on a summer's day, late for me anyway, getting dark. I think I was six. I might have been seven. I showed him the dog and asked him where it had gone.

'I remember saying that: "Where has it gone?"

'He looked at the dog and didn't speak. This is as well as I can remember it. He said, "What's happened here?" – something like that. He said: "Christ, boy, what's happened here?" He took hold of the dog and looked at it.

'I said, "Where has it gone?" It was all I needed to know.

'I think he started to laugh. He took the dog from me and

went away. When he came back, he didn't have the dog with him.'

'Was it your dog?' Joe asked.

'No. No, I don't really know whose ...' Olsen paused and frowned. 'A neighbour's, I think; I expect.'

'How had it died?'

'I killed it. I cut its throat with a pruning knife. I was playing with it, throwing a stick, you know, it was scampering to and fro. We had a smallholding – a lot of land. I was in a field by the chicken coops. It was a small dog, but I seem to remember that it ran pretty fast. Have you ever seen a chicken killed?'

'What?'

'A chicken: have you –'

'No, I don't think so.'

'It's an odd thing because you can't think of what a chicken would be for if it wasn't eggs and meat. I used to look at them in the coops and they seemed as good as dead already. It wasn't like that with the dog.'

'What happened?'

'He must have buried it. He said it could be our secret. Another of our secrets.'

'What secrets did you have?'

'I saw them. I used to see them. Sometimes ... very late at night it seemed, though I don't suppose it was. Him and my mother and some of his friends. My mother and some of his friends.'

Joe wanted to follow each careful question with another careful question; it was like walking a minefield in a gale.

'Tell me about that. Your mother and your father and your father's friends. Did you ...' He tried to find a way. 'Did you ever help?'

Olsen lifted his chin higher; Joe saw his eyelids clench. A minute passed, then another.

'After the dog,' Joe asked, 'what happened?'

'Animals. You can kill animals; it's encouraged. Rabbits, stoats, foxes, crows, jays. When I was older, he gave me a gun: a two-two. Before that, I used to set traps and get them alive mostly. Mostly alive.'

'That was important ...'

'Of course. You can see why.'

'Yes,' Joe said, 'I see why.'

Olsen's eyes opened and he looked at Joe fondly. 'Tell me, Joe, have you ever been to a slaughterhouse?' His tone was conversational and warm.

'No.'

'You see the beast come in and it's wild-eyed, you know? – smelling everything, the blood and the scent of fear in the air. I could always smell it myself – acrid like something charring. So the creature is pretty panicky, hooves clattering, trying to go this way and that – anywhere but into the crush – and there's a lot of noise, the slaughtermen yelling, the cattle bellowing, the sound of pulleys and motors; and it goes into the crush and it's held hard, and there's a sort of rigidity that affects it, legs stiff and muscles locked – seems that way, even if it's not – and its eyes are wide and bulging.

'Then they bring up the stun and the bolt slams in, and suddenly the beast is all dead weight, everything goes, everything gives way, and it's hooked up by its heels – not dead yet, the heart still pumping so that it can be bled – and a slaughterman cuts the throat with a single sweep of the knife and it goes down the line, just one, one of many, the blood hosing out, and someone cuts it from bottom to top and the guts come heavy and hot, and by the time it reaches the end of the line, ready to be split and hung, it's meat, just meat, waiting to be jointed and parcelled-out and sold.'

Olsen had spoken softly, almost in a monotone, but at some point – Joe had barely noticed it – he had risen to his feet as if to get a better view of the things he'd been describing. Now he sat down again and crossed his knees and put his chin in his hand.

He said, 'The world is full of lonely people, and lonely people will speak to anyone.'

His expression changed and he was suddenly lost in thought; then he seemed to remember something and a thin smile creased his face.

'When I met Christine, I was ravenous. Ravenous, Joe. Ravenous ... I needed her so badly; and she needed me.'

'Mick,' Joe offered, 'and Jan and Angie ...'

'Serena and Christine and Donna,' Olsen joined in, the smile still in place.

'How was it with Tommo?' Joe asked. 'Tell me about the time with Tommo.'

'He was nothing,' Olsen said, 'he was just a scrap, just a jot. But they were angry about Tommo – angrier than they were about the dog.'

Joe sat with Andy Bishop and looked at the faxes that had come up from west Somerset.

The first was a record sheet that gave 'nothing known on Henry Parr Olsen'.

The second was the result of local information-gathering: it stated that in 1970, Thomas Parr Olsen had died an accidental death at the age of three years five months.

The third was garnered from solicitors and land deed records and revealed that Lannett's Farm, St Sabbas, Wivelis-combe, had been sold in the spring of 1981, the contract being between Henry Parr Olsen acting under power of attorney and one James Attwood. A postscript mentioned that Attwood was a local farmer whose land bordered Lannett's Farm, that the smallholding was now down to grazing land, and that the house was occupied by a tenant.

Tranter came in and read over Bishop's shoulder. He said, 'We charge him tomorrow.'

'There are three deaths here,' Joe said. 'Olsen killed his three-year-old brother. Eleven years later he killed his parents. The brother's death was recorded as accidental, which almost certainly means the parents helped cover it up. It's a pretty fair bet that he buried them somewhere on the farm. He's on the brink of telling me about all three, and if he does it'll be a hell of a task to convince a jury that someone else committed the crimes, however sharp his defence lawyer. I need corroborating evidence as much as I need his confession. I need it more. He'll tell me things that only the killer could know. If I get that far with him, then it's possible that he'll agree to show me the grave.'

Tranter nodded. 'We charge him tomorrow,' he repeated, 'that's Fisher's opinion, not mine.'

He handed Joe a broadsheet photocopy of the next morning's paper, that carried Stan Collier's story under a banner headline: 'FIEND TO WALK FREE'. The quotation marks stood between the editor and a libel suit.

The headline was drawn from a quote attributed to 'a spokesman for the Metropolitan police' who had offered the opinion that '... unless Olsen was charged within twenty-four hours, he would have to be released'.

Tranter left as Joe and Andy Bishop stood side by side, reading the piece in silence.

Bishop said, 'They could have got it from anyone. We have our narks and the press have theirs.'

'Sure.'

'And the fact that we've gone for a magistrate's order — that's sufficiently unusual to have them ask their legal people.'

'Sure.'

'The rest is bollocks — a spokesman and so forth. They always say that. Who can disprove it?'

'I know,' Joe said, 'but imagine you're in the dark and you can feel something in there with you. It's big, it has large ears, tusks and a trunk, and it trumpets. What do you expect to find when you turn on the light?'

'DI Tranter?'

'Good guess.'

Connie was waiting up for him: in the conservatory with the doors open to the little garden and the park beyond. The night wind was warm, like a southern wind.

It was her intention to tell him straight away, before he spoke, before he had time for a drink, almost before he was in the room. He foxed her by handing over the front-page photocopy and saying: 'Look at that.'

It's only human nature to look. Joe went through to the kitchen and took an open bottle of white wine from the fridge. Connie was drinking mineral water. When he came back it was almost too late.

*Now*, she said to herself, *now, now, now.*

And she said, 'So what will you do?'

'Charge him tomorrow, what else? Ask for him to be remanded in police custody.'

'You think he'll go on talking to you?'

'After we've charged him? Who knows. I doubt it. He's in a sort of limbo at the moment. He's confessing. It has everything to do with sharing, nothing at all to do with crime, punishment or the process of law. I'm not even sure he's considered what "arrested" means.'

'You think he expects to be released when he's finished talking to you?'

Joe shrugged. 'Who knows what he thinks? He's crazy.'

'Sharing ... Sharing with you,' Connie asked. 'Sharing what?'

'His feelings.'

'What are they?'

'I'm not supposed to talk about it: you know that.'

'Who would I tell?'

Joe finished a glass and filled up again. 'He killed his brother. The boy's name was Thomas. Olsen calls him Tommo. Tommo was three at the time, which would make Olsen about nine. He also killed his parents. That was later.'

'The parents knew how the other boy died?'

'The coroner's verdict was accidental death. I think they knew.'

'Jesus.'

'I'm pretty certain that the parents – the father at least – abused Olsen. And from what Olsen says, it seems that the father shared his wife out among his friends.'

'Happy families,' Connie observed.

'He told me this story – well, gave a description really – of what happens when cattle are slaughtered. It was sort of linked to a pet dog he killed. The first death he ever caused, I'd guess.' Joe was thinking it through. 'He worked at Smithfield meat market ... And there's something about the whole business of meat. Dead meat.'

He paused for so long that Connie said, 'Yes?'

'We're all dead meat in the end. Alive is happy, or sad, or in love, or without love, just doing all the things people do; and without thinking about it, really, without thinking about being alive. And dead is all of that gone away. All of it lost. It's a mystery: that's how he sees it; the difference between the two. A person ... all that complexity, all that energy, all those emotions – can you see? – becomes dead meat. A little dog that chases sticks and yaps becomes dead meat.'

'I see it, yes,' Connie said. 'I understand what you're saying. I can't feel it. Why does it make him kill?'

'He wants to watch it happen. Watch the mystery.'

Joe stood on the bridge and dived. The water was far below him, so far below that it was like a memory of water. The wind whickered past his ears.

He entered the river and the force of his dive carried him

fathoms. He broke the second surface, the under-surface, and Olsen was showing him rack after rack of rich red sides of beef, wax-white pigs split and splayed, hares stripped and bloody and wide-eyed.

On the nearest rack, hooked up by their heels, were the dog and Tommo, Serena and Christine, Danny McMahon, Olsen's parents.

Donna walked towards him, moving between the racks. She was naked, her pale skin showing a map of delicate blue veins. She stood next to Christine and Joe could see that they looked like sisters.

Olsen said, 'Do you see, Joe?'

He sat up, shaking the bed and bringing Connie awake. She said, 'Are you all right, Joe?'

'I'm fine.'

She lay down again, eyes open.

*Tell him now.*

The room was very dark, darker than the dream. The image of Donna standing among the hanging meat burned in front of Joe's eyes.

Donna and the dead. The cattle, dead; the pop-eyed hares, dead; Serena, dead; Christine, dead; Danny and Tommo and the Olsens, dead.

And suddenly Joe did see. Just for a moment, as if a curtain had been drawn back on the mystery, he understood Olsen's terrible need to know, his lethal curiosity. It wasn't something he could have easily explained, but he caught the sense of it, like a sudden pungent smell, the strangeness of things altering; things stopping; things ceasing to be.

Although Connie was lying next to him, he conjured up the image of her swimming – one of the things she liked to do best; he imagined the energy and grace she always showed, the sweep of an arm, her head low in the water, the slight lofting of the shoulder as she took a breath.

Then he imagined her dead, inert. Not shot or knifed or hit by a truck; just dead, as if her life simply ceased. He imagined her arm coming over for the stroke and never completing the action.

There was the moment.

*There!*

Although he could see her body – motionless in the water – nothing of her was left.

*There* was the moment.

Whatever made Connie Connie had left her. Nothing remained; nothing.

*There was the moment!*


He got up and dressed in the dark.

Tell him now! *Now!*

Connie was close to tears. She knew she would cry as soon as she began to speak.

'Joe,' she said, Joe ...' and switched on the light in the same moment that he closed the front door behind him.


The duty sergeant said, 'He's asleep, Boss. The world's asleep.'

'He had a rest period this afternoon,' Joe said. 'It's logged. Wake him up.'

'There's no one to take corroborative notes; no one to type the transcript.'

'The room's still wired?'

'Yes.'

'Wake him up.'

Joe went with the sergeant past empty offices, empty desks, three empty cells. Joe slid back the Judas-window on the fourth. Olsen was sitting on his bunk and looking directly at the door. He smiled a winning smile.

'Is that you, Joe?'

*

They talked for an hour, head to head. After that, Joe left the interview room and switched on the tape. When he returned, Olsen's eyes were bright with knowledge.

Joe said, 'Henry, you killed Danny, we know that. You killed Serena and Christine. You killed others, too, but we don't have to talk about them. You killed your brother, Thomas – Tommo. And I think you killed your mother and father.'

'What do you want?'

'If I asked you to – could you show me where they are?'

'I could show you, yes.'

'Will you show me?'

'When I was arrested, Joe, I had certain items on me. A wallet with credit cards and cash, a wrist-watch, keys on a key ring.'

'Yes.'

'There's a Yale key that doesn't fit the door of my flat. It fits another door.' Olsen was smiling, just holding back laughter; his eyes were green, almost yellow, in the sallow neon light. He gave Joe an address which Joe repeated back to him.

'It's not much of a place, Joe. Not a home to write home about. But I've had good times there. My bits and pieces are there, if you know what I mean. You'll find some photographs. I want you to see them. They're in a little case under the bed.'

'Okay,' Joe said.

Olsen's laughter bubbled through and his face lit up. Joe sat still, fascinated, like a man watching an image on a screen slowly come into focus.

Olsen was nodding at Joe, his mouth wide, almost crowing with laughter now, almost screaming.

*You mad bastard*, Joe thought. *You murderous mad bastard.*

Olsen was breathless, rocking to and fro, his laughter coming in great sawing gasps. Joe waited him out and it suddenly stopped. Olsen sat still for a moment or two, then looked away as if giving an idea some thought.

'They're buried on the farm, Joe.' His tone was level and completely matter-of-fact. 'I'll take you there. I think I could find the place again. But that's all, Joe – okay? Then we can talk some more. I think we're really getting somewhere, don't you? *Really* getting somewhere.'

An hour with the tape switched off ...

Joe had said, 'I think I understand. I think I do.' He had told Olsen about his fantasy of Connie alive and then dead.

Olsen had grinned, showing his teeth, greedy for Joe's insight.

'Little experiments,' he'd said, 'each one was a little experiment. Each time, I knew more than I had before. Oh, but Joe ... The excitement of it, like a charge of electricity, like a flash of heat in my veins. The wonderful business of changing them, watching them change, you just can't know, you'll never know,' and his eyes had been bright as a child's; his hands trembling.

Joe emerged and the duty sergeant asked, 'I'll bang him up then, Boss?' When Joe nodded the sergeant asked, 'Are you all right?'

Joe carried a crust of darkness under his eyes and his face was pale. 'Tired,' he said. 'I'm tired.'

In the parks and along the riverbank you could catch the hint of a dawn breeze, almost cool, almost refreshing. In the through-road by the house where Olsen kept his hideaway room, the only movement of air was a noxious backdraught from the twelve-wheelers as they ramrodded through on their way to the arterial roads and the south-coast docks.

Outside, engine roar and constant movement; inside, a terrible stillness, as if the air in the room had been siphoned off. In the thin dawn light, the animals inside their display cases stared out at him, each seeming poised on the edge of action.

He found the newspaper clippings Olsen had collected. In a drawer in the tiny kitchen, he found Olsen's killing-pack: knife, towel, bin-liner, Baby Wet Ones, all inside a plastic store-bag. The towel had been laundered; two more towels and a spare roll of liners lay at the back of the drawer. The knife was clean and seemed to have been recently whetted.

The silence sang in his ears, a shrill tinnitus. He held his hand over the knife, palm flat, as if testing it for heat; darkness swam up at him like smoke and he thought he would faint. He pitched forward, inadvertently putting his hand into the drawer and the knife edge drew blood from his fingertips.

He ran water from the tap and held his fingers under the flow, then made a fist in an attempt to starve the capillaries, but the bleeding wouldn't stop. He took one of the spare towels from the drawer and wrapped his hand. He couldn't decide whether or not to wash the knife. He went into the main room and sat on the sofa where Danny McMahon had sat. He was bone-weary; he felt sapped.

His eyes closed for a moment, opened once, then he was suddenly asleep, falling at once into a dream where Danny McMahon slept on the sofa beside him, his throat open and livid with clotted blood. The pine marten slipped from its glass case and fed from Danny's throat. It licked the fresh wounds scored across Joe's fingertips.

Joe flung his hand out to ward the creature off and the gesture woke him. He walked through to the kitchen and took a drink directly from the tap, then went back in to the main room and lifted the bed aside, exposing the boards beneath. He stamped on each board until one rose slightly at the far end, then hefted it out and felt around in the floor cavity until he found the attaché case.

There were photographs of people alive and photographs

of the same people dead. Danny was there, and Serena and Christine and Lynda Lomas, but there were others. Joe shook the photos onto the floor then knelt down and laid the pictures of the living out in a row before fanning the pictures of the dead like a hand of cards for a gruesome game of 'snap'.

It was difficult to do because when they were dead the people didn't look much like themselves any more. Some of the time it was possible to tell from clothing, or hair colour; from jewellery or a wrist-watch. By the time he'd finished Joe had used a process of elimination to match the living with the dead. In all, there were thirty-four photographs of seventeen victims.

Joe sat on the floor and looked at the images as they lay there side by side: Danny, blurred and boozy; Danny dead. Christine sleeping sweetly; Christine dead. Lynda, gagged and terrified; Lynda dead. And the others – nameless – though he guessed that Jan and Angie and Mick were somewhere among them.

To one side there was an envelope that had fallen from the case along with the photos; it had Joe's name written on it and he'd seen it as soon as he'd tipped the case up, but had left it untouched. Now his hand strayed towards it but he redirected the gesture to touch, briefly, two photographs that must, Joe realised, be of Olsen's parents. One was a wedding pose, bride and groom on the steps of a registry office aiming their smiles at the camera; in the other, they were still side by side, lying in twisted, blood-spattered sheets and wearing the wild stares of the recently dead.

Joe took out his mobile phone and reported his find; which meant he would either have to open the envelope or leave it for someone else. He took it to the sofa and sat there to slit the flap while the pine marten and the fox and the jays looked beadily on.

Connie and a man, walking in a park, walking like lovers,

his arm round her shoulders, hers resting in the small of his back.

Connie and the man pausing to kiss; he carries a picnic basket.

Connie and the man eating and drinking, the food spread out on a blanket; she looks into his face and laughs at something he has said; her face is lit by adoration.

Connie and the man, making love; he is beneath, she is astride him and bends to kiss.

Connie kneeling up, bare-breasted, the man still inside her, her arms flung wide; she laughs wildly.

Connie. No doubt that it was Connie.

Connie however hard he tried. Connie no matter what. Connie and whoever-he-was, the dead man, the man who would shortly be dead, dead as soon as Joe could identify him and find him.

Connie in love.

Connie looking as she used to look.

Joe sat with the dead people until a forensic team arrived. Steve Tranter arrived a few minutes later and Joe handed him the bloodstained towel.

'My blood,' he said, 'here and on the knife in the kitchen drawer. Also my prints are on the outer and inner doors, on the drawer, and on the photos.'

The envelope and its contents were in his pocket.

'The knife,' Tranter asked. 'Would that be the murder weapon? A simple guess will do.'

Joe was looking out of the window. He said, 'It's in a plastic bag along with another towel, a bin-liner and some babywipes. Think the sequence through and you'll get the answer.'

'Jesus fucking Christ,' Tranter said. 'Jesus *Christ*!'

He walked through to the kitchen and started to give

instructions to the forensic team. Joe could feel heads turning in his direction.

He returned and asked, 'What's your next move, Morgan? Burn the transcripts and bail him?'

Joe shrugged. 'Accidents happen.'

Tranter was standing close to Joe, but having trouble keeping his voice down. 'How come you didn't splash some disinfectant about and take a hose to the place?'

'I was a bit clumsy,' Joe said, 'and I was curious.' He wasn't looking at Tranter when he spoke and his voice was light, detached, almost carrying a hint of laughter. 'I was very, very curious.' He walked towards the door and Tranter had to step aside to let him go.

'You'll find the parents easily enough,' Joe told him, 'because there's a distinct family resemblance between Olsen and his mother.' He paused before leaving. 'Not now, of course. Looking like him – that would have changed almost immediately. Everything starts to change when you die.'

Tranter went to the window and watched Joe walking away from the house; his car was parked three streets back, out of the red-route zone. The sun was up in a clear sky. Joe went slowly, thoughtfully, among the early morning commuters, a man with things on his mind, it seemed, but no real reason to hurry.

'You bastard,' Tranter said, 'I'll nail you.'

Because Connie's note avoided cheap and stupid remarks like 'I'm sorry, I need time to think, I need space', there wasn't much to be said.

*Dearest Joe, I've gone away for a while; I don't know how long, but I'll talk to you as soon as I've talked to myself, if you see what I mean.*

Joe phoned Marianne Russell as she was leaving to go to her office.

'I'm sorry, Joe. If she was here I'd make her talk to you. She's not. She hasn't called. I don't know where she is.'

'Who's the man?' Joe asked.

'What man?'

'Marianne, I'm not guessing, okay? I'm not trying to get you to break a confidence. He's taller than me, not skinny but not overweight, fair hair worn quite long, good-looking. I got this by accident, Marianne; I wasn't spying on her.' He spoke slowly. His voice sounded infinitely tired and infinitely sad.

She said, 'I don't know who he is. I haven't met him.'

'His name,' Joe said.

'She didn't tell me his name. I'm not lying, Joe.'

'His first name.'

'Oh ... yes. Yes. It's Michael.'

'Michael.'

'Listen, if she calls me, or if I see her, I'll tell her we spoke, okay?'

'Okay.'

'Joe ...' There was long silence. Finally, Marianne said, 'Sorry ... I'm sorry, I don't know what I was going to say. There isn't anything to say.'

'No, there isn't.'

Joe put the phone down and said, 'Michael,' then again, 'Michael,' as if he were speaking to someone he knew.

He went to the wardrobe, the chest of drawers, the dressing-table, and found bits of Connie missing. He went into the living room wanting to judge her absence by the holes on the bookshelf, the gaps among the tapes and CDs, but things looked just the same as they ever had.

He toured the flat, marvelling that everything was still in place: you couldn't spot the difference unless you really looked for it. A few clothes, cosmetics, jewellery, toothbrush; enough for a weekend break.

Joe poured himself a whisky, a stiff, top-of-the-morning

whisky, carried it through to the garden, and sat down in a canvas chair. He thought he ought to cry, but didn't know how to start.

'Connie,' he said, 'Connie and Michael; Michael and Connie,' whisky in hand as if he were offering a toast.

'Why did you do it?' Fisher asked.

Joe said, 'It was a mistake.'

'It certainly fucking was.'

'I didn't know I was going to hit treasure trove.'

'Bollocks, Joe. He told you about the place, told you where to find the key, Jesus, what did you expect? You should have gone down there with a full forensic team and you know it. You should have informed DI Tranter, taken a video operative, an SOC officer, you know this, you *know* this.'

'We're charging him anyway.'

'Not the point. Christ, what did you expect to gain?'

'It was a mistake,' Joe said, 'I admit that. Careless.'

Fisher said, 'Tranter's made an official representation to me to have you taken off the case.'

'Will you?'

'I should.'

'Olsen won't talk to anyone else.'

'He doesn't need to. As you mentioned – we're charging him.'

'And asking for police custody.'

'Yes – so he can lead us to his parents' graves. But anyone could take him down there. Tranter could take him.'

'He wouldn't go with Tranter: wouldn't co-operate.'

'What is it you want from this, Morgan?' Fisher used Joe's surname as if hoping to get a 'Sir' in return.

'Nothing. The same as you – Olsen's conviction. When he's got a brief working for him things are going to change, you know that.'

The sudden thought of not seeing Olsen again, of not being able to talk to him, made Joe shaky.

'As soon as possible,' Fisher ordered. 'We have to charge Olsen within the next fifteen hours, so if he decides to lose his memory or thinks it's funny to have half the county dug up, then cut your losses. Arrange transport and advise the locals that you're on your way. It gives them a few hours to set things up their end: to get access to the farm and so forth. Take him in an unmarked car – DI Tranter and one other officer as well as the driver.'

'I know how it's done,' Joe said.

Fisher's voice was a hard whisper. 'I've held on for you, Morgan. I've kept Tranter at bay. I know this sick bastard has decided that you're his father-fucking-confessor, but there's no such thing as an indispensable police officer. The only reason I'm going to forget that you decided to bleed all over a scene of crime is because I don't want someone pointing the finger at me and asking why we bent the rules of interview, or have some shitehawk lawyer with a reputation to make suggesting that his client was denied the due process of law.

'All we really had was his confession, which is worth piss; now we've got the photographs, which is great unless he decides to tell his brief that the room belongs to a friend and he's been going in to water the plants. So, yes, I want him to show us the graves. It's another nail, and I want this fucker nailed. But don't think you own this case, don't think it's yours. It's not. Olsen isn't yours.'

Fisher sighed and knuckled his eyes. He guessed that in the feud between Tranter and Joe it was Joe who had right on his side; he knew Joe to be someone who put in more than the job called for, and Fisher liked him for that. But the Olsen case had somehow taken Joe beyond the rules; there was something disturbing about it, Fisher felt, something half-off the rails.

As if relenting his anger, he said, 'Joe ... Let's just get it out of the way. Get it sorted.'

Joe nodded. He said, 'Yes, sir.'

Olsen's photographs of Connie and Michael were stills from the movie he was running in his head.

# Twenty-Five

'How was it with Tommo? Baby Tom. Little Tommo ... Here's a secret about him, a riddle I never solved: who was Tommo's father? Who was his dad? Could be any one of six or seven. You could see a likeness sometimes to this man or that. One of the fucking plug-uglies, the old man's mates, his muckers.

'How was it with Tommo? He fell into a well, a dry well round by the kitchen garden; it was capped, of course, but no one had ever nailed it down. What a bashing he took – slamming off the walls as he fell, bouncing from one to the other, then hitting bottom fifty feet down. Fifty feet or more. They didn't look closely – who would – because it never occurred to them that he might have been dead before he went down the well.

'I'd used a piece of the hornbeam the old man had felled for firewood: a piece about as long as my arm.

'Tommo dead, Tommo down the well, the hornbeam branch into the stove. And then the hue and cry. It took them seven hours to think of the well.'

They were in Olsen's cell. He had told Joe he wouldn't go until he was ready. Tranter was walking circles in the incident room like an animal measuring its cage.

'You said they knew,' Joe remarked.

'They knew.' Olsen nodded. 'They knew by the way they looked at me. I don't think it mattered to them much. It didn't matter to any of us. We lived in our own thoughts.' Olsen paused. 'He was dead like the dog, that was all I could think. I took him to the well, but I looked at him first. There was egg round his mouth from breakfast. I thought he might speak to me, or get up and walk off — that's how real he looked. But he was dead like the dog. I looked at him for a long time before I put him down there.'

'We have to go,' Joe said, 'are you ready to go?'

Olsen was lost in thought. Finally he said, 'When I killed the other two … Well, that was a long time after and things had changed.'

'The other two?' Joe asked, then realised that Olsen was talking about his parents.

I'm in bed. It's not a dream I'm having, more a memory, but it's so intense that I can see everything behind my eyes, every detail, and hear every noise. Some of the men are laughing. They're all drinking. All laughing and drinking except the mother and the one on top of her. She laughs between times, yes, but now she's too hot for laughing. Someone gives me a drink, beer it was; yes, I think it was beer. Beer or cider.

I'm remembering this — so clear, so intense, you know? The colours bright and the sounds loud. And I want to shake it off, so I get up and walk round the house for a while, but I end up in their bedroom just as I knew I would. They're asleep. I touch her throat with my index finger, like drawing a knife, then his. She stirs, but the father is sleeping like the dead.

I leave them and go back to my room. Now I've decided, I have to make a plan. It's not like Danny or Christine or the rest. You can kill a stranger and just walk away. No motive, no connection, no tracks to cover.

They've decided to sell the farm and they already have a buyer. They're moving to London, they say; they're going to live in a flat. What about me? They don't ask; they don't suggest. It's time for me to go, that's what they think. It's not;

it's time for them to go. Time for the mother to go, time for the father.

I get power of attorney from the father – not that he gives it to me, no, but there's no need for that. It's easy – do you know how easy? I get a form, I write the father's signature, I write a witness's signature. Simple as that. People know we're leaving, and we don't have friends or callers, that sort of thing. In all the time we've lived there only the men come to the house – the secret visitors. Do they expect to have secret visitors in London? The father will collect them from pubs and clubs; the mother will draw them in with her smelly web.

I know that when it's time I can simply say they've already left – the pair of them – and that I'm taking care of the details. For some while now they've been going away on little trips – looking at some place or another. No one notices when they've gone away; no one notices when they've come back. I can transfer the business account to a London bank. It's all so easy, Joe. Anyone could do it. All that comes later, though. First things first.

Each night I lie in bed and think of the moment. You know something, Joe? – in some ways anticipation is stronger than memory. Each day I think of the coming moment and it makes my head spin, makes me fizzy.

The perfect time, the best opportunity, is the day after the father agrees a price for the farm. It's a full moon that night, which makes me laugh. Funny or not, it's easier to dig by; easier to be seen by, too, but I've found a little spot for them, a cosy spot, a sheltered spot – I'll show you, Joe.

Of course I do the digging first; I don't want them lying out in full view for too long. I dig from midnight until about one-thirty; it's a long job and it's thirsty work, so I've taken some cider with me.

I cover their grave with some sacking and some brushwood — not that anyone would find the hole; it's well out of the way and, in any case, I dug it on our property. When I get back, I go upstairs quietly and find the mother and the father asleep. They've been rutting and the mother smells of it.

I go to my room and undress and get into bed. I want to pretend that it's a night like any other, nothing planned, nothing prepared. A night when I'm lying in bed and wondering what it will be like when the moment comes … and then deciding that the moment *has* come, letting the feeling flood me and take me.

Then something wonderful happens, Joe. Something magical.

I go to sleep.

Without meaning to, I go to sleep and I dream about the moment. There are two of me, just as there are two of them. I sit astride the mother and I sit astride the father — both of me trapping them, and I start to cut. The moment lasts for ever, Joe. Seems to last forever; the moment of their changing.

I wake up. An hour has gone by and it's past three o'clock. I'm crying as I wake, crying because it can't be as wonderful as it was in the dream. I go to the bathroom and wash my face and take some deep breaths. It'll be fine, I tell myself. It'll be everything you'd hoped for.

I've set some things aside in my room; they're hidden beneath a floorboard under the bed. Same as where I hid the photos, Joe. Did you find the photos? I'm sure you did.

I take out the things I need and lay them out on the floor: three big plastic grain bags, some baling twine, a knife off the mother's block that she's been asking about for a couple of days. It's got a wooden handle and the blade has been whetted so many times that it curves slightly backwards towards its point.

307

I go into their room and look at them. They're sleeping so heavily that they don't stir even when I part the curtains to let the full moon shine through. The full moon, Joe – so dramatic, so stagy. I ease the sheet back and find that they're sleeping naked, which makes things better somehow; I'm not sure why.

There's already a plan for this, I worked it out days ago: kill the father first, then move to the mother. Of course, I'd thought about killing them separately so that I could have each moment to the full, but the risks seemed too great. And in any case, since that moment when I'd gone into their room and found them sleeping and drew my finger across their throats, that's how I'd wanted it to be – the mother and the father side by side.

I watch him for a long time, his half-open mouth, his hair rumpled, his cheek creased by the weight of sleep in him.

I watch the bowl of his ribs rising and falling, his knee drawn slightly up, his cock lolling on his thigh.

I think how, if I leave him, leave him and go away, he'll wake in the morning with no knowledge of this – of me standing at his bedside and watching him by the light of the moon.

I look at the knife in my hand – the instrument of his changing – and think: *How odd. I can do it, or I can go away; kill him or not; one minute will make all the difference in the world to the father. It's such a little time, such a little thing.*

I get up on the bed and lean over him. I see his eyeballs moving beneath his eyelids and know he's dreaming. What dream? What strange world will I break in on with my knife and my sudden purpose? Eh, Joe?

Even now, sometimes, I wonder what the father's dream was about.

I cut him, bearing down hard, and he's as good as dead when I move over, getting astride the mother. The feel of my body wakes her – that and the father's hand clubbing her shoulder as he throws out an arm, trying to rise. He's halfway up, almost sitting, and gargling; it sounds like someone sucking up the last of a milkshake through a straw.

The mother looks at me, then she looks at the father as he flops back on the pillow, arching his back. His heels are drumming the bed. Then she's yelling: I don't know what, but I know it has to stop. That's when I start on her. She hits me a clout in the face, in the eye, and it hurts, but I get a hand under her chin to hold it up and manage a long, clean cut.

After that, I hold her tight to watch as she comes and goes, one moment more alive than dead, another more dead than alive, until the energy drains off, slowly, and her eyes change.

Want to hear something strange, Joe? In the moonlight the blood looks black. It has a hot smell. There's life in it still. I pull them off the bed onto the floor, then strip the sheets off the bed and turn the mattress. I stay with them for quite a while, sitting close to them on the floor and watching; just watching; then I take myself off and stand in the bath to sluice myself down. It comes off easily; did you know that, Joe? Off skin, off naked flesh – no problem at all.

One by one they go into the sacks, one by one I carry them out to the hole. It's not all that far, but a dead weight's a dead weight. I take the sheets and put them into the third grain bag. Then the lot into the hole, earth on top almost to fill it up but not quite, then over the earth an old door, over the door more earth, over the second lot of earth goes the turf I'd cut and saved, then over the turf a litter of bramble and twig and leaf mould.

I walk away from the grave and back towards the house. Halfway, I stop for a look at the moon, dead white in a deep blue-black sky, all its seas and scars standing plain.

I think: They're gone. An hour ago they were here, they were sleeping, all intact with their rutting smell and their blood going round, pump–pump, and their breathing in and out. But where are they now? What are they now?

Dead like the dog. What a mystery. The mother and the father, dead like the dog.


Joe was sitting on the floor of the cell. He didn't get up when Olsen moved to the door. Speaking softly, he said, 'I found them, Henry.'

'Found what?'

'Can you tell me his name?'

'Whose name?'

'Did you follow them home? Did you ever follow them back to where he lives?'

'Who lives? Who's that, Joe?'

Neither man spoke for a couple of minutes. Then Olsen said, 'Let's go. I'm ready to go now, Joe.'


Tranter was in the passenger seat, Paul Harker was driving, Olsen sat in the back, handcuffed to Joe. They travelled in silence for half an hour. Harker drove skilfully, taking them at exactly twenty miles per hour above the limit.

Olsen was looking out of the window. He said, 'There's always a sign, Joe – isn't there? Always some give-away.'

Tranter half turned and looked at Olsen questioningly, then looked at Joe. 'What's he talking about?'

'I don't know.'

Tranter switched his gaze back to Olsen. 'What do you mean – a sign?'

'Don't you know his name, Joe? Is it Harry, or John, or Stuart, or James, or George? Don't you know where he lives? After all – you're a detective, aren't you?'

'Who are you talking about?' Tranter wanted to know. 'Harry or John who?'

'You didn't recognise him, Joe? I thought you might

know him. It's often the case, isn't it? Not this time, though, eh, Joe? Fred, is it, or Chris, or Steve, or Michael?'

Tranter said, 'Have you got any idea what this fucking idiot's on about?'

'No,' Joe said.

'Shut up,' Tranter told Olsen. 'You're getting on my nerves, so shut the fuck up.'

'Lovely snap, too. Didn't you think so, Joe? A bit intimate perhaps, but so joyful. So full of joy. Didn't you think that, Joe? So full of – what do they call it? – *joie de vivre*.'

Tranter's expression changed to one of wariness and curiosity. 'You know what he means, don't you?'

'No,' Joe said, 'I don't.'

Tranter unsnapped his seat-belt, reached back between the seats, grabbed Olsen's shirtfront, then yanked him forward. 'Talk to me, you bastard. What snap? What fucking snap? Who's this Harry or James or George?'

Olsen looked at Tranter as if seeing him for the first time. To Joe he said, 'Doesn't he know who I am?'

Tranter said, 'You prick.' After a moment he released Olsen's shirtfront, giving the man a shove, then turned and fished round for his seat-belt.

Olsen went back to looking at the view from the nearside window; he didn't speak again.


Beyond the farm, to the west, was a small valley; one side rose to cornfields, the other to a spinney riddled with rabbit holes. Olsen led them along the crease of the valley, walking beside a small, bright stream. Two buzzards were wheeling close to the tree-cover.

Tranter, Harker, a uniformed ranker from the local force, a five-strong search team, two forensic scientists, Olsen handcuffed to Joe Morgan. A blazing blue-and-white day filled with insect-murmur, crow-call, and the distant clank of a tractor going through the lanes. They raised a heron as they went; it hauled up from the stream with big, heavy wing-beats that shovelled air back and away, *whup-whup-whup*.

Olsen had started to speak to Joe again, using a low voice that seemed almost to blend with the insect-noise. Sometimes he looked down as he spoke, sometimes he looked away. Everyone could hear him, but only Joe understood.

*'She looked happy, Joe, wouldn't you say? I thought she looked happy. Her arm round him as they walked ...'*

Up in the spinney it was cooler. Olsen pointed and the search team started to dig. They had brought drinks and sandwiches as if they were on a picnic. They dug for ten minutes then looked up.

Olsen said, 'It was a while ago; things have changed.' He indicated another spot and the digging started again.

*'Did you think they looked good together? Some people do, some people don't. I thought they looked fine ...'*

The search team hit something hard, and grubbed round it cautiously. It was the root of a tree. Olsen looked dubious. He said, 'Well, more to the left then – try here. This looks right.' They were digging amid moss and fungus in cool, crumbly, red soil; already their boots and clothes and hands were stained.

*'What puzzles me, Joe, is why she didn't tell you. If it's over it's over – best to face facts. Connie loves someone else ...'*

Olsen and Joe were standing away from the dig; Tranter and the uniformed officer had formed an alliance; Harker stood on his own. A thin cloud of cigarette smoke rose towards the tree canopy. Olsen's voice was a low buzz in Joe's ear as he turned his back on the others to speak.

*'... but how was it that you didn't know? Weren't you watching, Joe? Weren't you taking care?'*

Olsen showed them another place, then another, then another. Tranter said, 'Forget it.' He was talking to his uniformed colleague. 'Forget it, we've gone far enough.' To Joe he said, 'This cunt's playing games. Enough of this.'

'No, no,' Olsen smiled patiently, 'this is right. I know this is right. I remember it.'

Tranter said, 'We're running into a deadline, remember?' He was still talking to Joe.

'It's here,' Olsen said, pointing at a patch of ground close to the last dig, 'here, they're under here.'

The search team went down a couple of spits and hit the door. They lifted it and dug down another four feet before they exposed a corner of one of the grain bags; after that they used their shovels as scoops, lifting the soil out with a delicate care.

'There they are,' Olsen said in a voice light with accomplishment. 'I told you they would be.'

Olsen's father was still shrouded by the opaque plastic – rotten meat in a bag – though you couldn't see what was what; his mother had slipped part-way out of her sack to show a death's head grin and scraggy tufts of hair. She still wore shreds of flesh that had been dyed red by the West Country soil.

The forensic men went to the lip of the grave and started to work, handling the bodies carefully because they would start to break up as soon as they were moved. Olsen glanced down into the hole, then turned his back; he was still standing very close to Joe.

*'I'll tell you when she looked happiest, Joe. Shall I? She looked happiest when she was sitting on his prong with her tits out. That's what I thought. Did you think the same; did you notice the expression on her face? I thought she looked just about as happy as a woman can be.'*

Joe walked towards Tranter, taking long strides and hauling Olsen after him. He said, 'Your turn. It's enough. Here are the parents; that's all we need. You take him.' Joe was holding the handcuff key, his voice ragged with anger and distress.

Tranter couldn't see where the distress was coming from,

but he was enjoying it nonetheless. 'He only talks to you,' he said, 'he only walks with you. It's like a song from a West End show. Who am I to come between you?' He indicated the local team. 'They'll sort this, now. Let's get this bastard back to London,' and he started downhill, motioning Harker to follow. Joe started after them, Olsen close at his side.

*'What you have to think about, Joe, is not that he fucked her, not that he gave her a seeing-to there in the park, right there in the grass, and her riding him for all the world to see, no, it's how many times he fucked her, and what it was that they did, all the things they did, Joe, and when they did them, and whether they're doing them now, or will be, later tonight, or tomorrow, perhaps in the morning, you know, that wake-up fuck, that fuck-before-anything-else, that sweet and wet first-light fuck, and what she does with her mouth, Joe, and what he does with his, and what it sounds like to him when she comes, what it feels like, what she looks like when she's coming off, Joe, that's what you have to think about, not just the way she looks in the photo, but the way she looks in all the moments you haven't seen, won't ever see, except, surely, Joe, she must look a bit the way she looked when you did it to her yourself — wouldn't that be right? — think of the way she looked when it was you on top, you up between her legs, except that it's him —'*

Joe unlocked the handcuffs from Olsen's wrist and his own and back-handed the man, catching him flush in the mouth. In the same moment he yelled: 'You take him. *You take him,*' but Tranter seemed not to have heard.

Olsen staggered back, the valley slope quickening his pace. He lost his balance, pitched onto his back and rolled, then got up and continued to back-pedal, moving away from Tranter and Harker, who were descending crosswise, against the angle of the hill, and heading towards a five-barred gate at the neck of the valley.

Joe was stock-still. Olsen let the slope take him further and faster, until the distance between him and Joe and Tranter was a shallow triangle with himself at the apex.

'You take him!' Joe's shout was loud enough to put up birds from the hedgerow, and this time Tranter did look back. He saw Joe on the valley-side above him and Olsen sixty feet light of Joe, going backwards, half walking, half running on a long diagonal that was taking him further away from all of them.

Tranter's shout echoed Joe's: *'Jesus Christ Almighty!'* In the same moment, Olsen turned and began to run in earnest.

Harker was the only one likely to come close. Joe wasn't moving, the uniformed men were too far off to know what was happening before it was too late, and Tranter was about as fit as any forty-a-day city man with a belly that hid his belt. He tried, though, running aslant and uphill, arms pumping, head wagging. Olsen was making for the fringe of a wood on the far side of the hill, above the valley-gate. He was moving at a stiff pace even though the going was steep, and Harker was losing ground all the time. Joe started his own run, now, as if he had suddenly come awake to what was happening. He passed Tranter, who was standing stiff-legged on the hillside, back bent, hands on knees, and taking in air as if it hurt.

Joe ran on until he came to the fence that surrounded the wood. He called Harker's name and listened, but there was no answering call. When he looked over his shoulder he saw uniformed men strung out across the valley-side, with Tranter walking behind them and shouting into a mobile phone. He climbed the fence and dropped down into the dry leaf-mould on the other side.

It was cool and dim in the wood, though when Joe looked back he could still see the brilliance of sunlight at the edge of things, like a running tide. Rods of pale light fell from the leaf canopy to the ground, slanting like half-felled trees; like ghost trees. Bird-calls fell into the silence, then faded, then started up again.

One by one the uniformed men crossed the fence and

started to move through the wood. Tranter stayed by the treeline, still using his mobile. Every now and then, they would pause to listen, hoping they might hear a disturbance further on, something to give them direction. There was nothing. Bird-calls and silence; a light plane overhead; the sound of their own feet in the undergrowth.

Joe found Harker. He was on his hands and knees, swaybacked, his head lowered as if he were studying the flora. Joe stood over him and wrapped his arms round the man's chest, but the lift was too much for Harker and he lost consciousness again, slumping in Joe's arms and slithering back to the ground.

A uniformed man appeared off to the left. Joe said, 'Ask for an ambulance. Tell DI Tranter.' Two other men arrived as Joe was hoisting Harker into a fireman's lift; 'I'm fine,' Joe told them, 'I'll get him out. Keep after Olsen.'

As he started back towards the treeline, he could feel dampness spreading on the back of his calf, soaking his trouser-leg, and realised that it was blood from Harker's head wound.

They brought a tractor up for Harker – the only way to get him to the ambulance.

He said, 'I'm okay, I'm fine, I don't need all this,' but his words had a slur to them and he kept swinging his head from side to side like a man unable to focus. Tranter was standing alone, hands in pockets, eyes closed, as if he were hoping to come up with a simple solution. The clatter of helicopters came and went as they searched along a grid ten miles square.

'It's his patch,' Tranter said. 'He knows it back to front.' He was talking to the uniformed officer, whose name was Ian Lowry. From where they stood it was possible to see that the lane beyond the valley was crammed with police vehicles; another had just arrived and was unloading more men. Dog-handlers were already climbing the valley-side.

'We've set up an incident room,' Lowry said. 'Best to work from there. We'll find him, don't worry. They're doing a house-to-house in every village within a ten mile radius, searching barns and outbuildings, and we've already set up road blocks. But he won't have got that far.'

'How long can he stay out here?' Tranter asked.

'Work it out,' Lowry said. 'He needs food. The temperature's in the upper eighties – he needs water. He can't exactly hole up. The helicopters can cover a hell of a lot of ground, we've got men quartering the area and mobile patrols in the lanes. We'll have him by tonight.'

Lowry went down to meet the dog-handlers. Tranter walked over to Joe, who was sitting with his back to a tree and chewing a stem of grass. 'Fisher asked me what happened,' he said.

'Did he?' Joe looked up, shielding his eyes because Tranter had the sun at his back. 'And what did you tell him?'

'I told him you released the prisoner.'

'Yes? Okay, thanks.'

Tranter bent over, as if getting closer to Joe would make his anger more plain. 'What the fuck were you thinking of? What the fuck were you *doing*?'

Joe said, 'I'd had enough of him.' He shook his head, as if ridding himself of Olsen's voice, the unbearable images. 'I was handing him over. I was sending him down to you.'

Tranter straightened up. 'Fisher wants you back in London.'

'Us?'

'You. You and Harker. I'm staying here to bring Olsen back. It's the end of it for you, Morgan; you must be crazy. You must be out of your fucking mind.'

Tranter walked a little way off, then returned like a man with something else on his mind.

'What was he saying to you?'

'Saying?'

317

'On the way down here, in the car. Then afterwards, while we were up there digging. He was whispering to you. Saying things. Saying what?'

Joe shrugged. He spread his hands as if anxious to show them empty. 'It was gibberish. It meant nothing to me. He's mad, hadn't you heard? He talks like mad people talk.'

Fisher had installed two floor-standing fans in his office and they ruffled his hair, giving him a raffish look.

'You uncuffed him,' he said, 'he walked away from you, then he started to run. What do you want me to do?'

'Let me go back down there.'

'Forget it. You know that Steve Tranter's entered a formal complaint.'

'I thought he might.'

'DC Harker saw it, too.'

'Okay.'

'What do you mean: okay?'

'He saw whatever he saw; he's on Tranter's team, you know that. I was transferring the prisoner to DI Tranter. A mistake was made.'

Fisher sighed; he leaned forward and his shirt billowed briefly in the breeze from the fans. 'Joe, listen, there isn't a way out of this. A top —'

'I need to get down there and fetch him back.'

'— top-security prisoner has escaped and it's down to you. Whichever way you look at —'

'So there'll be an inquiry. Let me worry about that when it happens. All I want —'

'Joe, listen to me, whichever way you look at it, you're in the frame —'

'I'll tell it to a board of inquiry, but in the meantime —'

'Tell them what?' Fisher yelled the remark, then yelled it again: 'Tell them what, Morgan?'

Neither man spoke for a while. The fans drew out a high, fluctuating note, like music heard from a long way off.

'You uncuffed him. He escaped. Tell them that, because it's all there is to tell so far as I'm concerned.'

'I'm off it,' Joe said, 'is that right?'

'You're – yes, Jesus, of *course* you're off it. You're off everything. I'm standing you down. You're on suspension, Joe.'

Fisher couldn't make his mind up whether the man sitting across from him was 'Joe' or 'Morgan'. He asked, 'Why did you do it?'

'I was sending him down to DI Tranter. There was a misunderstanding.'

'Tranter says he was talking to you – Olsen. What was all that about?'

'Nothing. Talk – crazy talk; he's crazy. Give me until the inquiry date.'

'No. *No!* For God's sake – I've got a fucking serial killer running round loose, you let the bastard go –'

'No I didn't – that – it wasn't supposed to happen – do you think I wanted that? – It wasn't – No, I was tired of the bastard. I was handing him over to DI –'

'– you uncuffed him, I don't care what you intended – you *uncuffed* him – and you're wondering why I'm taking you off duty? Are you? Really puzzled by that? This is about to hit the fucking press. Can you imagine what the headlines are going to say? Can you imagine the phone calls I've been having since Tranter phoned in from Somerset? I'm not doing this just on my own authority – though I would, Christ, I'd be happy to – but no, there are people in high places who want your balls on a string – of course there are. Are you surprised? The same people have been asking me some pretty hard questions, too. Think I'll get out of this with gold stars in my homework book? Forget it. Okay? Forget it, Joe. You're officially off duty. Go home.'

319

When Joe got to the door, Fisher stopped him. 'He was talking to you. What was he saying?'

'It was garbage. He's got garbage in his head, so that's what comes out of his mouth.'

'Go home, Joe. Spend some time with Connie.'

# Twenty-Six

Olsen was drinking from a stand-pipe close to a trough in a field some eight miles from the spinney where his parents had been buried. He drank as much as he could take on board, then rolled his head and shoulders under the flow of water. He'd come out of a wood and walked the line of the hedgerows for three hundred yards to get to the stand-pipe. Now he took the same route back. His clothing was still damp – he'd waded half a mile upstream in the river that wound down towards the valley. As it happened, the searchers hadn't even taken the dogs in that direction.

The trees were in their summer plush, heavy with leaves. Olsen walked lightly among the litter of brushwood and last year's mulch until he came back to his chosen tree: a chestnut; the leaves made a solid bell from its crown almost to the ground. He climbed two-thirds of its height and wedged himself into the fork between two branches. At that height there was a breeze that moved the branches slightly, and the sway made him feel as if he were aboard ship. He thought he'd stay put until the search was called off, however long that took. Try to get clear too soon and he might stumble across the searchers. They'd be gone soon enough. They were way off-track, miles to the east.

He closed his eyes and started to make plans.

Connie went to work in the usual way, but each morning she woke up with Michael Bianchi, each evening she came home to Michael Bianchi. Now she stood in the bathroom, watching her own face in the mirror and saying his name to herself in a whisper, like something she had to learn by heart.

Her things on his bathroom shelves, her things in his closet. Except she hadn't brought much and, noticing that, Michael had asked, 'Is this keeping a foothold in the past, or is it starting over?'

'The past …' Connie had looked surprised; her life with Joe: was that 'the past'? She said, 'I hadn't thought of it like that.'

She walked towards Michael through the enormous space of his apartment and looked round at the new life: his paintings hanging from wires or propped against the wall, the vast windows with their view downriver, the sofas and dining table and screens arranged to divide the living space. It looked familiar but felt strange. Michael sat at the far end of the room reading by the light of a floor-lamp; he was wearing a pair of tortoiseshell glasses that made him look boyish and studious. She sat on the arm of his chair and he drew her down, folding her into the crook of his arm.

'Look at this,' he said and showed her what he was reading – it was a newspaper report of Olsen's escape.

'I know. Insane killer escapes – police incompetence – national scandal. I read the tabloids and I read the broadsheets. There's a fuzzy picture of Joe in one of them.'

The paper Michael was holding carried a mug-shot of Olsen.

'What will happen to Joe?'

'I'm not sure. It won't be good.'

'Should you call him?'

'Would it help?' Her mouth puckered as if she were about to cry, and she masked the expression with her hand. 'I don't think so. Not really.'

'Do you want to go away?'

'What?'

'Do you want to go away for a while? A holiday. Take a break from things.'

'From what? From Joe? From guilt?'

'From muddle. Why not?'

'Go where?'

'Anywhere you like – France, Greece, America ...'

'What about –? I mean, I have to go to work.'

Michael shrugged. 'No you don't. Not really.'

'I'll never get used to it – being able to do whatever I like.'

'Yes you will,' Michael told her, 'it's easy. Come on, Connie, let's go somewhere.'

Connie laughed, then the laugh faded as she started to think of destinations.


She woke in the small hours of the night and went to stand by the window to look at the river. There was a half-moon and a broad, sinewy reflection of light pushed along with the tide.

*What am I doing here? Is it true my life has changed? Everything strange ... everything becoming familiar.*

She made a cup of tea while Michael slept on, then opened the doors to the balcony and took her drink outside. She sat down, back propped against the wrought-iron work, and watched a darkened barge shove upstream.

*Warm nights, moonlight on the river, the smell of oil paints ... A plane to New York or Athens – wherever I choose. How strange it is. If you have everything you want, what do you want next?*

Connie finished her tea and went back to bed. As she lay down Michael turned and drew her in, kissing her eyes.

As if he'd read her mind he asked, 'Where shall we go, Connie? It's up to you. We can go anywhere.'

She sent him a look like the first waking moment after a deep sleep.

'What could you possibly want with me?' she asked.

*

Olsen spent three days in his tree, more or less, and Joe spent more or less the same time drunk.

In limbo, Olsen travelled within himself, visiting places of shadow; he relived his kills like a hunter browsing among trophies; he looked forward to kills yet to be made, conjuring them up before his mind's eye. From time to time, he went down to the stand-pipe and drank, sometimes seeing searchers in the distance, though after the first day there were fewer and fewer of them, and the person he most often saw was a herdsman driving cattle up to the pasture or home to the milking sheds.

Because he was eating nothing, because of the day-long heat, because the breeze made his bed of branches sway and brought a long whisper from the leaves, Olsen's fancies were strong – fiercely coloured and full of sound; he found it difficult sometimes to tell the difference between his sleeping and his waking dreams.

At the back of his mind, though, lay a plan of escape and he thought it through in moments when his mind was straight. He knew where to go and he knew who to see.

Get to London, get some money, get some help.

Most of the time, Joe stayed indoors with a bottle; the doors and windows were shut and the flat built a terrible heat. It seemed to Joe that he was sweating a dew of whisky. He slept in chairs, or on the floor in the conservatory; sometimes in bed.

On the second evening he went into the streets, already drunk, and found a pub by the river where he drank until he passed out. They brought him round at closing time and he moved to a little unfenced park and lay down between some flower beds, then woke an hour later to find he was under a sprinkler system, his clothes sodden, and a chill on him despite the night-time warmth.

He walked home like a man in chains.

His thoughts turned on Olsen and Connie; each time he woke they jostled in his head, as if he couldn't decide who to think of first.

He was ill from the whisky, and he drank on top of the illness to mask it. On the afternoon of the fourth day he lay in bed, his stomach cramping, his head hurting more than it seemed possible to bear. He got up and swallowed some pills, then took a shower, standing under the flow and turning it slowly to cold, and continuing to stand until his head was numb, his body numb. He took a bottle of mineral water into the garden and fell into a canvas chair.

Joe's last waking thought was that he would find her. *Find her. Find him. Find her. Find him* ...

In his dream, Olsen and Connie embraced. Her face, over Olsen's shoulder, was livid with happiness.

That night, Olsen started a trek that would take him clear out of the county. At last light, he walked to the stand-pipe, drank his fill, then started to navigate a straight line through pasture and cornfields to a wood that covered the better part of three hills. He kept to the treeline for easy walking, though he could have walked in the thick of the wood, had he needed to, and still found the right direction. He knew the wood better than he knew the London streets.

He covered fifteen miles before dawn, finally coming down a long spit of grassland to the sedge and drainage ditches of the Somerset Levels; he was tired and wanted to sleep, but the need to get clear was more urgent. He came up to the motorway after another mile or so and sat in the lee of a hedge to wait for a long gap in the traffic. When it came he scampered across, vaulting the central barrier and taking a run-and-slide down the opposite slope.

After dawn, there was nothing to do but take risks. He walked along lanes and through villages like someone who belonged there, going two hours, taking a break, walking another two, then taking a further break before going two more. The air was heavy and still, and you could hear for miles. By mid-morning, Olsen was very thirsty and was skirting the edge of exhaustion. His hunger had become something rooted in him, something growing, like another mouth in his gut; but here he was, not in a cell, not in the interview room with Joe Morgan, not feeling the chafe of the handcuff on his wristbone.

High on fasting and his own thoughts, he imagined he saw Joe walking ahead of him, beckoning, showing him the way. When the vision faded, Olsen laughed out loud, the sound ringing in the country stillness.


A few cars, a few horses and riders, the sound of insects, cottages with doors and windows open to the weather. He walked until early evening, getting water twice from streams and another time from a garden tap in a cottage where no one was home. He was tempted to break in and find food – money, perhaps – but knew that it would be like leaving a pointer. In a dustbin at the back of the house he found two plastic bottles that had once contained mineral water, and filled them from the tap before leaving.

After another ten miles he crossed a disused railway line and holed up to rest in a linesman's shed. His body had called quits long before; it was his mind that kept pushing him forward. Now his thoughts stalled and he could go no further; he fell into a deep sleep that didn't break until dusk, when he drank the last from one of the water bottles and started walking once more.

He was off his own territory for sure, though his sense of where he was heading was pretty good. The moon gave enough light to let him know what he was doing as long as he kept to the lanes and continued to head east. From time to time he heard the muffled boom of trucks on the motorway and did his best to walk a parallel line to the noise.

At dawn the next day he slept again, this time in a thick copse on the crown of a hill. When he woke it was broad day and he could see to the horizon. Traffic was passing on a length of dual carriageway about two miles off. Olsen walked downhill, making an angle that would bring him to a point where the two-lane strip ended, close to a village. The going had been fairly slow, but he thought he must be fifty miles or more from Lannett's Farm, clear of the searchers, clear of the road-blocks. He walked through the village and stood on the far outskirts with his thumb angled at the passing vehicles.

A truck driver picked him up and listened to a tale of woe: job gone, wife gone, hope gone. When he dropped Olsen off on the outskirts, he fished into his wallet and handed over enough for a meal. Olsen rode the tube back into the heart of London dizzy with starvation and joy and need.

Finding Connie and Michael was an easy enough thing; the question Joe had to ask himself was whether he wanted that or, more precisely, what he would do when he found them, but anger and misery forge a need stronger than good judgement.

Easy because you get in touch with someone who's worked for you, someone who owes you a favour, and you call the favour in. The person who owed Joe was a private investigator called Frank Drage, ex-copper, sometime grass, a man who could serve a writ faster than a card-sharp could fade an ace. Joe called Drage to tell him where Connie worked.

Drage lifted the phone on the second ring: the sign of a man who needs work. He said, 'I don't remember ever meeting your wife, Joe. I'll need a photograph.'

They met at the Park Lane Hilton where Drage was doing a little surveillance for a rich woman with a young husband. The stake-out was in Trader Vic's.

'Why does she bother?' Drage wondered. 'Why does she

care? He's not going to leave her; she counts her money in millions. So he's shafting some bimbo with tight tits and a twat like a bottleneck. How does he pull her? Spends some of the old lady's cash. So what do we have? — useful redistribution of wealth, everyone gets laid, the marriage jogs along fine. But no, she also wants good behaviour. Jealousy's a wasteful thing.'

Joe handed over a photograph of Connie. Drage looked at it a while then said, 'Of course, sometimes it's all you've got.'

'Follow her and let me know where she goes,' Joe said, 'that's all; nothing fancy.'

'A day? Two days?'

'Let's see what we get.'

'Photos of people she meets?'

'Yes.'

'Sure,' Drage said, 'piece of piss.'

'I don't want anyone to hear about this.'

'Comes with the fee.'

'Yeah, I know that. But let me say it again. No one hears about it.'

'Okay, Joe. I understand.' Drage was drinking scotch with a beer chaser and keeping his eye on the door. 'They tell me you're under suspension.'

'It's no secret.'

'What happened, Joe? Why did you take the cuffs off him?'

'Call me as soon as you've got a location.'

'Crazy thing to do, wasn't it?'

'You might have to go two days or three to make sure it's her new address, but let me know anyway: let me know where she goes after work tomorrow night.'

'Where she sleeps.'

'Yes,' Joe said tightly, 'where she sleeps.'

'And who she sleeps with.'

Joe had asked for a beer but the first couple of sips had

seemed to curdle in his stomach. Now he pushed it away and climbed down from his bar stool. 'Just give me what you get,' he said, 'but phone it in. I don't need to see you again.' Immediately, he changed his mind. 'No, better, write it up and bring me the transcript.'

*So I can read it, so I can brood over it, so I can turn the words into pictures and the pictures into torment.*

'I'll see you in here, what? — late tomorrow night?'

Drage said, 'Sit down.'

'What?' Joe thought he'd misheard.

'Sit down, Joe. Please. My mark's just walked in. Okay? Please? I don't want anything to attract his attention. If he sees me now, he might recognise me another time.'

A man of about thirty-five, well built, well dressed, salon hair; a woman in her mid-twenties, beautiful, great figure, fake blonde, wearing too few clothes and too much make-up. They had the set-apart look of people who care much more about themselves than each other.

'Jesus!' Joe got back onto the barstool. 'Am I your cover, Drage?'

'We had to meet anyway. It seemed like a good way of combining business with business.'

Joe shook his head and pulled the beer back. 'You're getting paid for this; I'm not.'

'Am I charging you for watching Connie?'

'You were carrying an unlicensed firearm; I got you off the hook.'

'Sure; and I was following a man who'd done time for attempted murder.'

'Your problem.'

'Just sit tight, okay? Okay, Joe?'

The couple were opposite one another at a small table. The man touched the girl's hair, he touched her cheek, he let his hand slide and rest a moment on the slope of her breast.

Her dress was cut low in front and the hem barely came past her lap.

'Okay, so they've got a room booked upstairs,' Drage said, like a man who knew all there was to know about sexual signals. 'That's fine. They'll have a drink and go. I have to see them go into their room. That'll do. I don't need a snap of her stripped for action with her knees alongside her ears. Couple of minutes, Joe, no more. They're really hot.'

'What's she like?' Joe asked.

'Who like?'

'The client.'

'Rich lady,' Drage shrugged.

'No, what's she like?'

Drage looked at Joe a moment, then away. 'Mid-forties, fading a little, you know. Spends a lot of time at the gym, sunlamp tan, great clothes; could be as much as forty-seven or -eight, now I come to think about it. Sad and anxious and angry. Fuck knows why.'

'Perhaps she loves him,' Joe suggested.

'Yeah?' Drage said. 'Then why does she want to know? It'll just make things shittier for her.' He took a swallow of beer, his eyes fixed on the man with the salon hair and the girl in the tiny dress. 'Maybe I should lie to her. Take her money, leave her happy.'

'Maybe you should.'

Drage shook his head, smiling. 'Wouldn't help. She knows already. She knows inside her head.'

'Then why does she want you?'

'The proof's not for her, it's for him – something he can't deny. She needs to pin him down and make him squirm.'

'What will she do?' Joe asked.

'Forgive him. Forgive the son of a bitch. I'll get another call in six months' time. I've been here before.'

The girl was leaning forward, her hand on the man's thigh. Secret meetings, Joe thought. Exciting secret meetings that heat your blood. Stripped for action with her knees alongside her ears.

Her voice calling him on: *Michael, Michael, Michael ...*

Joe had showered and shaved and washed his hair for the first time in days. He'd put on a cream shirt and a pair of chinos straight from the dry-cleaner's plastic shroud. Drage glanced at him and chuckled. 'You look like shit,' he said. 'Don't take it so hard.'

Joe was watching the girl. She leant across the table to whisper, her skirt pulling almost clear of her rump.

'Jesus,' Drage whispered, 'what would I do for a piece of that?'

'Perhaps it's the real thing,' Joe said, 'perhaps she loves him. Perhaps he loves her.'

Drage laughed a silent laugh. 'Some joke,' he said, 'some chance.'

Men had been posted at Olsen's flat and at his bolt-hole room, though no one really expected him to turn up at either address. The press and TV were co-operating well – there had been twenty-seven sightings of Olsen, three of them genuine. These took place soon after Olsen got back to London, but Tranter discounted them; he stayed in the West Country waiting for Olsen to be found inside the few square miles of the local search.

There were two men watching the room, staked-out in the little park opposite; from behind them came the muffled clang of machinery as the pumping station worked away on its own. Most often, the men used the cover of a row of half-starved plane trees, but they felt pretty stupid doing that. Just now they had walked over to the children's play-area; one of them was going slowly to and fro on a red plastic swing and scuffing the toes of his shoes in the dust. They knew they were wasting their time. In a moment or so, the other guy would vault the park railings and play chicken on the red route in order to get to one of the fast-food places on the other side.

Olsen arrived in a street parallel to the red route. This was familiar ground and he already knew his way in. He went straight to the third house in the row, its walls streaked with black from the fire that had gutted it a year before, and dabbed an elbow at the plywood boarding over the ground-floor window.

He was in and through, noticing the smell of scorch still lingering in the hall. Down-and-outs had used the place and their rats' nest bedding lay in the back room; they would come back when the weather turned. Olsen opened the back door and stepped out into a rubble of cans and boxes and burnt timbers.

He crossed fifteen gardens to get to the right house, then straddled a drainpipe and hauled himself up: the window of his room was less than fifteen feet above the ground. A couple of minutes was all he needed, no more. He eased the sash up one-handed and rolled over the sill into the room, staying low as he crossed to the glass-fronted cages.

The pine marten was standing on almost five thousand pounds in cash. Olsen pocketed the money, restored the marten to its cage, lowered the glass into place, and went back out of the window without a second look.

The watchers were set up with folding canvas chairs, illegal flasks of scotch. They sat side by side on the kids' swings and ate chicken stir-fry and noodles amid the smell of hot dogshit and carbon monoxide. They smoked as they ate and you could see the cherry-red buds of their cigarettes rising and falling in the half-dark.

Lucky. Olsen felt he was a lucky man. In talking to Joe he had put down a burden – the need to tell had gone, for the time being anyway. The need to tell, but not the need to do.

*I can always phone you, Joe, he thought; from wherever I am, I can call and let you know how I feel. Now that you've shared my thoughts with me; now that we understand one another.*

Lucky that it was Joe who first picked up the phone. Lucky to have found him. Lucky to have taken risks and survived them, as if his last call from that same phone booth was part of a plan that would start with capture and end with freedom. Lucky – as if Tranter's smiling face, the ride to Fellgate Cross, his first meeting with Joe, were moments that had already been rehearsed.

Lucky to have been able to show Joe the mother and the father where they lay in the red Somerset soil. Lucky to have found a tree with branches to make a bed. Lucky all the way back to London.

*Lucky all the way.*


Olsen slept among vagrants that night, sharing a concrete warren alongside an underpass; he bought food and water from an Eight-till-Late, his first meal since he'd used the lorry driver's money the previous day. The vagrants fought and argued all night, fuelled on booze, and traffic came downhill to the underpass revving for a gear change at a road junction just overhead. Olsen slept without stirring. The next morning, he bought some clothes and changed in the men's room of a pub, and spent the day watching movies. He found a small salon in a quiet street and had his hair cut to the nape of his neck; it fell softly from a centre parting, sometimes flopping over his eyes now that it was no longer drawn back and tied. He was carrying a heavy growth of stubble which, with his new clothes and haircut, looked merely fashionable.

That evening, he took his luck to a casino.


Half asleep in a chair, Connie heard the siren of a boat going downriver. She put herself and Michael on the boat: they were standing in the prow; then the boat had become a ship under sail, the sun lodged on the masthead, a wind bellying the canvas.

Their journey to the estuary took only minutes and what lay beyond was the sea. They kept going as the water became bluer, the air clearer.

'Connie?' he said, and kissed the top of her head as he passed. She smiled but held on to her waking dream.

It was their second month away, their second year.

'Connie ...'

She looked up to the sound of his voice and saw a white house with red pantiles and above, cypresses, and above those, black-tailed hawks in a southern sky.

Inside the house were all their things: hers and Michael's. Shutters were drawn and the rooms were cool. Michael's paintings were propped up against stanchions of seasoned pine in a big whitewashed studio that opened onto a garden, a swimming pool, a landscape of olive groves and vines.

She had invented her new life. Everyone had forgotten them, herself and Michael, as people forget the dead.

Joe in a new life, too. *Did that sting?* she wondered.

*Yes, it stung.*

She got up and went to the window, but there were no boats to be seen.


Drage was sitting in the same place, drinking the same combination of scotch and a beer to chase it.

He handed Joe a manila envelope and told him, 'There isn't much to report, but I've reported it. She left work at just past six and went straight there – a row of studio-workshops down on the river past Limehouse. An hour later, just before eight, she and the guy went out for a meal at a Thai restaurant. I left them there. Address, pictures, additional physical description of the man: guestimates of height and weight and so forth – all in the envelope. I'll get his other details by tomorrow noon: full name, bit of background. I know some guys who'd be happy to break his legs for you, no problem at all.'

Joe took the envelope. He said, 'There's something else I want you to do for me.'

Drage sighed. 'You called it in, Joe.'

'I stood between you and a firearms charge. An evening's work won't cover it.'

'Well ...' Drage shrugged. 'What?'

'This is something confidential.'

'Something else,' Drage reminded him.

'Yes, something else. I want Henry Parr Olsen.'

'Yes? Who's Henry —' Drage stopped and looked at Joe, then laughed. 'You're kidding me.'

'I want to find him.'

'You're on suspension, there's one objection. Here's another — this guy's a fucking psycho.'

'I don't want you to bring him in on the end of a short lead,' Joe said, 'I want you to ask around.'

'He's not in London, is he?'

'Maybe, maybe not. It's where he'll come if he can. Or else he's here already.'

'I'll ask,' Drage said. 'Has he got any money — I mean, room to manoeuvre, you know?'

'So far as I know he hasn't got anything,' Joe said, 'except the clothes he was wearing. Empty pockets and nowhere to hide.'

'So where is he?'

'Exactly.'


Although it was after ten, Joe called Leonard Ackerman who said, 'Come over'.

When Joe got there he was let in by Ackerman's girlfriend who was long-limbed and pretty; she was wearing a T-shirt and shorts and her hair fell halfway to her waist. She gave Joe a beer then wandered away into the house.

Joe said, 'I've fucked up your evening.'

'It's fine,' Ackerman told him, 'don't worry. Rachel hears more than enough about crazy people.' From somewhere a couple of rooms back came the opening bars of a piano concerto, not loud enough to be aggressive.

'Tell me,' Ackerman said, and Joe told him a long story.

'Tell me why you uncuffed him.'

'I wanted to hurt him so badly that I thought I ought to put him out of arm's reach.'

'Tell me what you thought when you saw the photo of Connie and ... Michael, is it?'

'Michael Bianchi. That was when I wanted to kill him most.'

'Olsen or Bianchi?'

Joe laughed. 'Olsen.'

'Olsen, you think.'

Joe said, 'I didn't come here to see my shrink.'

'Can't help it. Sorry. I was saying my thoughts. Being able to do that is a holiday for me.'

'Definitely Olsen.'

'Because he'd shown you something you didn't want to see.'

'I suppose so. I don't know. I didn't analyse the anger. What will he do?'

'We're not dealing with someone who's beside himself. He can function in the world, hold down a job, be liked by his workmates. What he does he does secretly. He's technically mad, sure – he kills people out of curiosity; but he doesn't wear his madness on his face.'

'And so?'

Rachel came in with some beers; one was for herself. She said, 'I thought it must be about time.' She sat down next to Ackerman and looked at Joe. 'You don't mind?'

'Not if you don't talk about it.'

She smiled and shook her head.

Ackerman said, 'And so ... And so he's not some crazed psycho with a fever of bloodlust on him; he can see he's in a fix and he can probably think of ways out of it. What would you do?' When Joe shrugged, Ackerman added, 'No, I'm asking you because you must know more about it than I do. I can speculate about his behaviour, but I know sod-all about ducking the law.'

'He could try leaving the country,' Joe said.

'Would he make it?'

'People come and go all the time – false passports, or no passports.'

'So he might try that. He'd have to make certain contacts, I imagine. And you'd know who they're likely to be. Could he hide out here?'

'You mean in London?'

'I mean in Britain.'

'Sure. Probably in a city – he'd want to bury himself in people. After the first excitement's over – when the papers and television have stopped showing his face to the world – only people who know him would know him, if you see what I mean. Moving to another postal district will often do the trick.'

'What's his best plan? What would you do?'

'Go abroad if I could. Southern Europe, maybe. Stay away for a couple of years. Or else a major city somewhere else in this country.'

Ackerman smiled; he said, 'You know this already. You didn't come for this.'

Joe took the photograph of Michael and Connie out of his pocket and handed it to Rachel. He said, 'The woman is my wife. The man underneath her is someone whose name I know, though I don't know another thing about him. The photograph was taken by Henry Parr Olsen: you know about –?'

'Yes,' Rachel said.

'– yes, who was following them. As you see. During the time I was interviewing him, he told me where to find this photograph. There were others, though not quite so heartwarming as this particular shot.'

'Consequences,' Ackerman said. 'He followed Connie to be able to phone her office and wheedle your home phone number out of some witless secretary. Then he decides he likes following her – it's a way of being close to you. Then he realises that things are not as they should be. Curiosity takes over. Curiosity is a way of life for this guy. He sees what's going on. He takes photos. That's reasonable enough, given his psychopathology. He likes to photograph people – fix them so that he can examine them later. He photographed all his victims, didn't he?'

'Before and after,' Joe said.

Rachel was still looking at the photo as if something more might be found there than lust and love, misery and betrayal.

'What would you do?' Joe was looking at Ackerman but talking to Rachel.

'I'd burn the photo for a start,' she told him.

'Yes, okay.' Joe took it back. 'But I'll keep it by me for a bit longer, perhaps.'

Rachel smiled at his wryness. 'Are you after her, or after Henry Parr Olsen? Who's got your full attention?'

'When he was talking to me – about killing, why he killed, I began to understand. "The mystery", he called it, or else "the moment", and when he told me how it felt, why he was doing it, this sort of ... *quest* ... I understood. I thought of what he said and it started to make sense. Why should that be?'

'You think there's no logic in madness?' Ackerman asked. 'You're wrong. Kill someone because you have this terrible need to understand the process of death: you're mad; kill someone because of his mother's name: it's warfare.'

Joe got up. 'I'd better go. It's late. I'm sorry.'

Ackerman smiled; he said, 'Sorry for what?'

Rachel took Joe to the door. 'What will they do? That's the question, isn't it?' she said. 'What will Connie do, what will Olsen do? They're both travelling away from you, but in different directions. You need them both, but for different reasons.'

Joe stepped into the street.

She said, 'What do you really want?'


Olsen was holding the lifeline of his luck. The rules were these: don't win too much in one place; leave when you lose, no matter how much you've won; finally – don't let go.

He felt light-headed and far-sighted; he could see his luck coming as if he were trawling deep places for it, the net breaking the surface, crammed with the catch.

The croupiers knew him from somewhere, but didn't know who he was. Now and then a girl would latch on to him and he'd shake her free, gently, regretfully.

Olsen doubled his money in less than an hour, then halved the profit on one big loss, then began a series of steady gains during a carefully judged tour of six casinos. Like many of the gamblers working that night, he made the full trip and started again. By three in the morning he had seventeen thousand pounds for his original five, and his hand was still on the lifeline.

He came away with twenty-three, leaving it at that because two plus one is three and three is lucky; also because his fast during the long walk home had left him in need of sleep, and he could feel his concentration slipping: his hand slipping.

He found a good backstreet hotel in Notting Hill, paid for three nights in advance, signed in as Joseph Morgan and gave Joe's address. It was five a.m. He lifted the phone and dialled Joe's number, then hung up before the ring.

*Joe … I just wanted to say I'm back, Joe. Not for long, I suspect.*

*I'd better pick up somewhere else. That seems like the best thing to do; that's the best idea.*

*I could go anywhere. Killers are freelance, you know.*

Olsen laughed at the thought. He took a shower then lay on the bed wishing he hadn't got rid of those girls.

*I wish I hadn't got rid of those girls, Joe. It would have been a mistake, I know, but I wish, I wish-wish-wish. Well, there'll be time. More time in some other place.*

*I'll miss you, Joe.*

*Don't worry about Connie, by the way. Don't worry about her. I've been thinking about all that. You understand what I mean, don't you?*

*You understand.*

# Twenty-Seven

London was trying to change. There had been hot weather, now, for more than two months: hard, flat, blue skies and a sun that scorched what it touched. Each day the TV told how many minutes an average skin would take to burn. The water companies talked as if they were mining gemstones. There was a permanent smell hanging in the streets, fruity and toxic, stronger always in alleys and basements. By noon, roadside trees seemed stunned and breathless.

London was trying to change, but it didn't really know how. It wanted to become Mediterranean but couldn't get the hang of that sort of ease, that sort of expansiveness. There was always something buttoned-up about the city, something dour, something that expected rain and a chill wind.·

Olsen knew where to go, but he didn't know who to see. He spent most of the next day hanging out in Chinatown, making himself visible, asking shopkeepers where he could make a connection — a sotto voce tone — *You know? Make a connection? Can you help me out?* — pretending to look for the men's room in restaurants but finding other rooms instead where business meetings were in progress. He got picked up just after four o'clock by a young man wearing blue jeans and a black satin blouson over a T-shirt carrying the slogan *How do you feel?*

He smiled and said 'Follow me', as if Olsen were an expected guest who had just that moment arrived.

They went through a restaurant and down a flight of stairs to a large room full of tables each with place-settings, though no one was eating there. As they reached the bottom of the stairs, the young man motioned for Olsen to walk ahead of him, then delivered a little shove to his back: a warning; a statement about power. A man in a dark grey suit was sitting at one of the tables. Nearby were two more young men wearing the uniform of jeans, sneakers, black satin blouson.

The man in the suit waited until Olsen realised he should sit down, then said, 'We knew you weren't police or Customs and Excise but if not them, then who? Now we think we know. What is it?'

'I need a passport.'

'Yes.' The man paused. 'My name is Ho Tak Shing. I tell you so you know you can trust me. Can I trust you?'

'I just need a passport,' Olsen said. 'That's it.'

'Chinatown's doing good deals in passports. Be a seller's market when Beijing takes Hong Kong. Some Hong Kong Chinese are thinking this way now – clever guys, isn't it? Others will think when it is almost too late. Suckers.' Ho shrugged. 'It is an expensive business already.'

'Tell me.'

'Five thousand.'

'Half and half?'

'Sure, half and half. That's the way it's done.'

Olsen put the money down on the table, and Ho smiled delightedly. 'How much of that are you carrying round Chinatown? How much?'

Olsen had brought what he thought he might need, the rest was in the hotel safe.

'Ten grand,' he said, which made Ho laugh: a high-pitched, almost musical *heuk-heuk-heuk-heuk* ...

Ho picked up the money, said something in Cantonese, and handed it to the young man who had brought Olsen to the place. To Olsen, he said: 'Go with him to get the photograph. You will meet someone else who makes the sale, you see? His sale, isn't it? This boy will give him your deposit.'

'What do you get?'

'Nothing,' Ho said. 'I don't sell passports, not me. This other man will have a list of people you can become, and he'll tell you when to come for the passport. Come here, yes? Understand? Come here and we will do the same thing again.'

'Why don't I go to him?'

'He might not be where you left him.'

'What?'

'He might have moved a little bit; not far, but you wouldn't find him. See?'

'Yes, I see.'

'Good.'

They sat in silence for a few minutes until Ho gave a little laugh. 'It's over. That's all, isn't it?'

Olsen went with the young man to an apartment three streets away where he had his photo taken by a man of about forty, wearing shorts and a blue silk shirt with a repeat pattern of yellow pineapples. Pineapple-shirt worked in silence until Olsen's money was handed over, when he said, 'One day'.

'This time tomorrow?' Olsen asked.

'Yeah. One day is what I said.'

Olsen took a bus to Knightsbridge and walked across the park to his hotel. No one spared him a second glance. He sat on the bed in his room and looked out of the window, but his hand tingled for the telephone.

*Before I leave, Joe, and that's a promise. I'll make you happy before I go away.*

His eyes unfocused and the brightness at the window appeared as a white door opening onto a white tunnel. He seemed dazed, then he gave a little laugh like a cough.

343

*Before I depart, before I quit this place, Joe, oh, Joe, I'll cheer you up, I'll force a smile, I'll make you dance and sing.*

*Oh, yes.*

*I'll help you out, I'll be your loving pal.*

He sat on as the day turned towards evening and the horizon gathered tints of aquamarine and pink. The horizon was a place he thought he might visit.

*I'll give you what you want.*


Michael Bianchi sat on his balcony looking towards the same changing sky. There was a glass of gin beside him but it was untouched, the ice almost melted.

He thought she might telephone, or maybe just turn up, and he wanted that to happen so much that he had gone out to the balcony and turned his back on the door: a ruse.

The sky went through shades of blue, and a few tiny islands of cumulus turned lilac and crimson on their undersides. Since the ruse wasn't working, Michael abandoned the balcony and wandered from room to room like a man looking for lost keys. Finally he went out and walked the streets for an hour, winding up at a pizza-pasta place where he ate a plate of spaghetti without wanting it, and drank a carafe of red wine. He called Marianne from the restaurant and called her again when he got home.

'I don't know where she is, Michael.'

'But she'll be with you later.'

'Yes.'

'Is she with Joe?'

'No, I don't think so.'

'Let me speak to her, Marianne. Put her on.'

'Michael, if she was here, I'd tell you.'

'Ask her to call me when she gets to you.'

'I will. I told you I will.'

'Can I come over?'

'Ask Connie when she gets here. I don't know, Michael. It's not my decision.'

'What's the problem, Marianne? Why is she doing this?'

'Ask her.'

'She hasn't talked to you?'

'If she had — Michael, listen, it's not — I haven't really talked to her about this, no. She's not talking at all; I mean, not to me.'

'Or to me.'

'She might be talking to herself — don't you think? She might be asking herself some questions.'

'I'm worried about the answers.'

'Of course you are. I'll make her call you as soon as she arrives, even if — you know — whether she'll talk to you or not. I mean, really talk. But I'll make her call to say goodnight. Will that do?'

'Tell her I'm worried about her.'

'Okay.'

'Tell her I love her.'

'She knows that.'

'Shit,' Michael said, 'shit, shit, shit, shit, *shit*!' There was a pause between them. Michael said, 'Tell her I've killed myself.'

Marianne laughed at the ruefulness in his voice. He sounded like someone who was amazed by his own behaviour, and slightly ashamed.

'I'll send a wreath,' Marianne said, 'hearts and arrows.'

'It's lousy.'

'Yes,' she said, 'I know it is.'

Connie was becoming the artist of the brief note. This one had said: *I'm not going away forever, but I'm going away for now. Being with you makes things too easy. I love you.*

Michael thought about ways of making things tougher.

Take to drink, slap her around, empty the bank account and give it to charity.

He thought, *How can I possibly have lost her so fast? What in hell did I do?* He tried to judge the depth of his misery and found it bottomless. He collected the glass of warm gin from the balcony and drank it, then called Joe's number and picked up the answer-machine. He left a silence after the beep, but only because he didn't know what the hell to say. It was going to have been: 'It's Michael Bianchi', then let Joe Morgan do the talking.

He sat on the floor within arm's reach of the phone, his knees pulled up to his chin. A charcoal sketch he'd made of Connie was thumbtacked to the wall: a standing nude. He had positioned her by one of the big, oak uprights that went from floor to roof-beams, and there she stood now, one knee slightly bent, breasts small and high, her body-hair a smudge. For all her modesty that day, she was looking directly at him.

Nothing but a line here, a line there; a hostage to fortune.

She said, 'Thanks Marianne,' and got a look that could have turned sand to glass.

'There were a number of messages, including he worries about you and –'

'Don't tell me; don't tell me what he said.'

'And I promised you'd call as soon –'

'I heard.'

'I lied for you.'

'I heard that too.'

'Well, listen, it's great to have you here, *mia casa tua casa*; if you're ready, I'll bring you tonight's supper menu.'

'I'm sorry.' Connie started to cry, very gently, as if throttling back on grief.

'Why? Why now?' Marianne asked then, without waiting for an answer, added, 'There's only one thing on the menu –

warm chicken salad, which I'm good at and can just about summon the energy for.'

'Fine.' Connie was wiping her face with the heels of both hands. 'Happiness is a warm chicken,' and she tried to laugh.

Marianne moved towards the kitchen. 'Help me make it.'

'Yes, okay.'

'Why?' It was the same question as before.

'I love it – it's like a holiday – but I'm having trouble making it real.'

'He's good-looking, he's talented, he's rich. He's a good fuck?' Marianne didn't wait for an answer. 'Certainly sounds like a holiday. But why shouldn't it turn into a way of life? Just shred this lettuce. Then it's coriander, salad onions, sesame seeds – all in the cupboard above you.' Marianne was slicing chicken and heating oil in a wok.

I haven't done this in years, Connie thought; making a meal with another woman in this companionable way. Maybe there's a quiet life somewhere: slow and virginal and measured by tasks like this. Maybe I could even live alone. She laughed at the idea, liking it, and Marianne looked up.

'It's not so much what I gain,' Connie said, 'as what I lose.'

'You want two husbands? Good idea. Make it ten. A couple to talk to – intellectual pursuits, gossip, sort of thing – a couple to be seen out with, you know, classy – one good tennis player, one good skier – the others for earning.'

'One for fucking?' Connie wondered.

'Jesus, no, they'd *all* be for fucking.'

Connie spread the sesame seeds onto a sheet of foil and switched on the grill. 'I couldn't do the thinking I wanted to do while I was with him. Being with him made it all theoretical – do you see?'

'Of course I see. You also said that's how it felt with Joe.'

'It did.'

'Okay, how about this –'

Marianne threw the chicken pieces into the wok, stepping

347

away at the same time. There was a little flash-fire and a great hiss; she stepped back and started to stir.

'– you flip a coin and it's heads Michael, tails Joe. It's flipping, now, okay? – flip-flip-flip – and it's landed and you've trapped it on the back of your hand. Tell me what it says.'

Connie was washing the lettuce at the sink, her back to Marianne. She said nothing.

'Come on, Connie; you've had time for a good look. What does it say?'

'It says: Go best of three.'

Steve Tranter said, 'When he comes in, you leave: got it?'

Drage nodded. He had an office on the third floor of a purpose-built block near Shepherd's Bush; an intercom buzzed people in from the street. The design of the whole place was hi-tech brutalism and cruelly dated.

'Just make it clear that it wasn't me who –'

'It *was* you.'

'I mean that it wasn't intentional.'

Tranter shrugged. 'You're a grass. You've worked for him, you've worked for me. I didn't know that; Morgan didn't know that. Happy coincidence.'

'Happy for some. And I'm not a grass.'

'You give me information, I pay you. What the fuck's that?'

'Enquiry agent.'

Tranter was sitting in a low leather chair, side-on to the door and with the wall at his back; he leaned over and took a cigarette from an open pack next to Drage's phone, then wedged his feet against the desk and tilted the chair onto its back legs.

'You might be at the keyhole when some poor sod's getting his bone wet, or sell corporate pillocks a security system that pays you ten per cent of the warehouse price, but to me, Frank, you're a grass.'

Drage smiled. 'Don't think that you can talk to me as if I were crap just because you're the law, Steve. I'm doing this because I don't want a problem with earning a living. But earning a living isn't the same thing as eating shit. That's why I'm an ex-copper.'

The entry-phone buzzer had sounded while Drage was speaking. He picked up a phone and said, 'Okay', then pressed the button to release the door.

Joe walked into the office and saw Tranter first. He said, 'Perfect', then looked at Drage.

'I didn't phone it in, Joe. I work for him too.'

'It came up in conversation,' Joe suggested.

Drage sighed. 'Not exactly. Not quite. I made the mistake of thinking you might be on the same side. Silly.' He shrugged and walked past Joe. 'I have to go now.'

'Yes?' Joe asked. 'Okay, I'll come with you.'

'His word against yours until I saw you here.' Tranter's voice had taken on an edge, as if he stood between Joe and the door. 'Now it's an official breach of your suspension.'

Drage left. He said, 'The door pulls to and then it's locked, okay?'

'I asked him to look for someone,' Joe said.

'Olsen.'

'Someone else.'

'That's not what Drage told me.'

'Yeah,' Joe smiled, 'his word against mine.'

'Fisher knows about this, not just me.'

'I'll bet.'

A little gleam appeared in Tranter's eye: a flicker of joy. 'You sorry bastard; it's Connie, isn't it? He's doing two jobs for you. Olsen and Connie.' He laughed. 'Jesus, they're not together, are they?'

349

Joe lifted a hand, as if shoving Tranter's joke aside. 'You expected to find him in Somerset. How come you're back?'

'I think what you think – he's not there, so he must be here. I also think it would be a good idea if you pissed off home, now, and stayed there. Get in a stack of videos. This isn't just a piece of sound advice, it's an official position. And *your* official position is down on your face with your ass in the air.'

'Tell Fisher, the sooner –'

'Which is probably the position Connie's in, too, except she won't be alone.'

Joe moved in to throw a punch, but Tranter was ready because a punch was what he'd worked for. He sidestepped and hit Joe on the turn, catching him over the ear. When Joe moved back, he walked into Tranter's follow-up, a hard uppercut that took him just under the heart. He sank to a crouch, trying to get his breath. When he looked up, Tranter had gone.

Joe went out into the hallway and heard the crank-and-whine of the lift starting its descent. The stairs were alongside and he took them at a stuttering run, a flow of pain moving under his ribs.

Tranter was halfway down the street, moving at the pace of a man with nothing to run from, nothing to stay for. He turned into a side street and Joe started to run, taking a straight line, letting people get out of his way. He made it to the side street as Tranter thumbed an electronic key and popped the hazard lights on his car from twenty feet back. He had the door open and one leg raised when Joe reached him. He heard something, or half-saw something, and started to look over his shoulder when Joe whacked him: a short, stabbing punch that went into the kidneys, making Tranter stagger and fall back. Joe caught his man by the hair and slammed his face sideways into the bodywork of the car. When Tranter got halfway to his feet, Joe kicked his legs out from under him, and banged him into the car again: two dents, two big smears of blood.

Tranter was all wild violence, trying to get up, but the smacks to his head had done the work and his legs didn't want to take his weight. Joe bent over, holding Tranter by his shirtfront, and punched the man twice in the face, short-arm blows, fast and full-on, then let him drop.

Tranter lay beside his car panting, looking up at Joe. He made a fierce effort to get to his feet – '*You fucking gobshite Morgan!*' – and Joe punched him again to keep him down. Tranter grunted and put up a hand, getting a purchase on the door of the car so that he could pull himself into a sitting position; one of his eyes welled with blood and his nose was a little out of true.

Joe crouched down to get to Tranter's level.

He said, 'I'm looking for something to kill, you understand? I'm deeply bloody unhappy, you know? – Christ, I'm so fucking miserable I can't see round it – and I'm looking for someone to wreck. Someone to rip up. And I'd like it to be you. So keep coming at me, would you? I'm counting on it. I can hardly fucking wait, you piece of shit.' He put his face close to Tranter's – the blood-rimmed eye, the busted nose. 'You piece of *shit!*'

A crowd had gathered. Joe stood up and found himself hemmed in. He said, 'Police officer,' then repeated it, but louder. As he shouldered through Joe added, 'So is he; but I won.'

# Twenty-Eight

Olsen walked through the lobby of his hotel and felt the slow swerve of the desk clerk's eyes. *Means nothing*, he thought. Different hair, now, and a thickening beard ... Even so, he quickened his pace a little and dropped his head.

It happened again at the railway station.

He hadn't intended to go. Safer to stay in the hotel, except that a man who sits in his room all day must have something to hide. Safer to spend the day touring an art gallery, or wandering round a museum, except that people look at each other as well as at the exhibits.

A park, then, or the movies again. There were places to go other than this busy concourse with its baking winds and the incomprehensible quack of the tannoy. Olsen sat in a patch of shadow directly opposite the arrival boards and sipped a beer. He was like a reformed gambler picking winners from the racing pages but never placing a bet.

Except ... there was that girl; a wan face with a lost look, all her worldly goods packed on her back. She needed someone.

There was that boy, on the run from everything, a stranger to everyone. He needed someone.

Olsen finished his drink and walked across the concourse, cutting the boy out with all the deftness of the hunter.

He said, 'First time in London?'

The boy shied, then paused. 'What's up?'

'No,' Olsen said, 'nothing. I thought you might need a room. Do you need a room?'

'Might do. What's the deal?' The boy talked tough; he looked tough, too, but he didn't look mean.

'And a job.'

'Yeah?' He walked a couple of paces off, a couple of paces back. 'On the black is it?'

'Of course it's on the black.' Olsen smiled winningly. 'Cash in hand – that's the point.'

They went to the ouside table Olsen had just left and the boy eased his pack off while Olsen went into the bar and fetched them a drink. When he came back, a woman was looking at him. She was sitting three tables away and had been reading a newspaper; now the paper lay on the table in front of her and though her glance turned from Olsen's and flickered round the concourse, as if she were expecting a friend, it came back to Olsen and the boy. After a moment, she took out a pair of sunglasses and put them on. Olsen tried to judge the direction of her gaze by the angle of her head.

*A picture in the paper? That must have been days ago; old news now. Still possible, though, isn't it?*

The boy drank half his beer in one long swallow. Olsen said, 'My name's Joe Morgan.'

'Marco,' the boy said.

*What is this? Why are you doing this? What's the point? Where would you take him? Where's your safe place?*

'It's Mark, but people call me Marco. Are you queer?'

'No, Marco, I'm not queer. You want a room, I've got a room; you want a job, I've got a job. I make money out of this. That's why I do it.'

*He doesn't know who you are, and neither does she. Stop worrying. I'll find somewhere to take him – some dark spot, some leafy spot. But safe place? There's no safe place.*

'You don't look like a businessman.' Marco was laughing

353

into his drink. 'You don't look like a hotshot to me.'

'You're right. We're all on the black. It's a way of life.'

'Okay,' Marco said. 'I'm interested.'

*Come with me, then. We'll find a place in the dark.*

Olsen was smiling at Marco, getting set to make a move as soon as the boy had finished his beer. He was already fitting together the bits and pieces of a story. Something to eat puts the boy at ease, then comes the job description, after which – a phone call, only to discover that the room will be vacant later, much later, but don't worry, it's yours, and the job's a dead cert. Then an agreement to meet that night near a park or near the river … It's close to here – really close; not worth a cab; let's walk.

They walk: they go to the dark place together.


When Olsen looked again the woman had gone, but when he searched beyond her table there she was, standing at a payphone just inside the bar. He felt a little flurry in his gut, like the first intimation of illness.

'There's something I have to do,' he said.

Marco nudged his beer glass. 'Take it out of my first week's earnings.'

Olsen handed over some money: enough for a beer and a burger. 'I'll be back. Give me fifteen minutes, okay? Half an hour at the longest.'

Marco nodded. 'What kind of job?'

'Cold-calling. You don't have to go anywhere.'

'Chance of a scam?'

Olsen grinned, his eyes elsewhere. The woman was still on the phone – maybe she was having trouble getting connected.

'There's always the chance of a scam, isn't there?'

'I'll be here,' Marco told him.


The whole incident made him edgy: he took a bus to his

hotel rather than use the underground where he felt hemmed-in. He bought a midday paper, but didn't find himself; she could have been reading any old article, any old report; she could have been on the phone to anyone.

He knew what Marco would think: He was a queer all right. Realised he'd picked the wrong guy. Cost him a meal and a couple of drinks. Ha-ha.

On the other hand, she might have been calling Fellgate Cross. So might the desk clerk. He got off the bus early and took a circular route to the hotel. The streets were busy, but didn't seem threatening. He walked through the lobby of the hotel and went to his room. There was nothing in there apart from a toothbrush, a couple of shirts and a leather grip. He packed in five minutes, then went down and asked for his money from the safe.

It was the same clerk. He gave Olsen a key and went with him into the ante-room behind the reception desk; he watched while Olsen removed the money from one of several safety deposit boxes and counted it. Twenty grand going into the grip like lumber. All the time, Olsen was trying to think of a way to open a conversation: he wanted to hear whether the man sounded shaky or excited.

'I'm checking out,' he said. The man nodded. 'I'll pay you in cash – okay? – if you could make up my bill.'

The phone was ringing as they went back to the lobby and Olsen waited while the clerk answered it. Someone was booking a room for that night. Olsen listened hard for any code, then laughed at himself for thinking that.

The clerk hung up the phone and looked at Olsen in surprise. 'Sorry?'

'Nothing.'

'I thought you said something.'

'I was laughing.'

'Right ...' He started to tap Olsen's meagre charges into a

computer. Once or twice, he glanced up, as if expecting Olsen to explain himself or offer an apology.

'I remembered something someone said to me.'

The clerk smiled and nodded as if to say: Who cares? He handed over the bill, then counted out the cash Olsen offered in return, holding the large denomination notes up to the light to find the silver strip. He said, 'Thank you Mr Morgan', and receipted the bill. He seemed to be looking away, looking round the lobby, just as the woman at the station had let her gaze wander away, then back.

Olsen felt the skin on his back pucker and crawl; muscles twitched around his rib-cage as he walked to the door. A woman coming into the hotel smiled at him, as if in response, then looked puzzled, and Olsen realised that he was baring his teeth in anxiety.

*This isn't the same, Joe. I don't feel good about this. Maybe we could talk. I'd like it if we could talk, but I don't think we'll have the opportunity.*

*Just enough time for my going-away present, though.*

*My present to you.*


He sat in the Chinatown restaurant and ate a dish of chow mein with some green tea. Eventually the boy in the black blouson took him downstairs.

'It's done.' There was a pear-shaped flask on the table. Ho Tak Shing was drinking from a milky glass the size of a thimble, which he held upright in the pinch of his fingers, like a stub of candle in a candlestick.

Olsen handed over the second half of the money. He said, 'Not quite done. I need somewhere to stay, and someone to arrange things.'

'Arrange things.'

'I thought I'd go to the airport and find a standby ticket to somewhere.' He paused. 'But now I think there might be a better way.'

'Yes …' Ho nodded as if just the same thought had occurred to him. Then he named a price.

'It's all I have,' Olsen said.

'Surely not. You have life and liberty, isn't it? These don't come cheap.'

'I can't give you everything.'

'Give *me*? No. Mostly to other people. I am the broker. Someone else has the safe house, the boat, the know-how.'

'Take half.'

'Yes, okay.' Ho smiled broadly as if he'd been after a quarter all along, and Olsen had been revealed as a shit negotiator. 'Get your passport now, then this boy will bring you back. Wait just here for me to come.'

'When can I go?'

'To the safe place or out of this country?'

'Out.'

'Day or two, isn't it?'

Ho turned to the boy and spoke in Cantonese for a brief while. The boy tapped Olsen's arm and walked ahead to the stairs.

'Day or two or three.'


On their way to collect the passport, they picked up two minders. Olsen caught them on his nerve-endings, there-but-not-there, like shadows on a radar-scan, and when he turned they were keeping pace half a street back.

'Don't worry,' the boy told him, 'they look out for you. It's paid for, yeah?'

On the way back, Olsen made them all wait while he made a few purchases. He bought a chef's knife, a towel, a roll of plastic refuse sacks, some parcel tape, a pack of Baby Wet Ones and an attaché case to put them in. On each occasion, the boy stood by the door of the shop and watched the transaction, but said nothing. When they got back to the restaurant the minders disappeared.

'There is somewhere,' Ho said. 'A good place. People we know. One-third now, one-third when we fix up for the boat, one-third before you leave. Is that fair to you?' Olsen handed over the first deposit. 'This boy will drive you.'

'Is it far?'

'London, yes. Not Chinatown.'

'Why not?'

Ho spread the fingers of both hands, each like a fan, and joined the tips together. 'Chinatown is a good place for you? No, I don't think it is.'

The underground room was cool and dim. Ho and Olsen sat at one table, the boy at another much closer to the stairs. A waiter came from a side-door bringing two little flasks, two thimbles, two bowls, two pairs of chopsticks.

'You are hungry, I expect,' Ho said. 'And a drink, maybe. There is some time to spare.'

Frank Drage was reading when Joe walked into his office. Drage kept his head down. He said, 'If you hit me, Joe, I shall definitely hit you back.'

'You've got something I've paid for,' Joe said.

'Michael Bianchi, mother English-honourable, father an Italian industrialist, very rich indeed. He's a painter – daubs and dashes with a reputation – shown here, but also in Europe and America. I went to a gallery that handles his stuff – a medium-sized one costs about seven grand, which seemed a fuck of a lot per square inch, but then I don't like art, so what do I know?' Drage looked up. 'I'm sorry. It was my mistake and it was a genuine one. Tranter's a fat fuck. I hear you gave him a smack.'

'What else?'

'No, that's about it.'

'Married, divorced, somewhere in between the –'

'Oh, right. No, sorry; not bisexual, doesn't like dressing in women's clothing, never laid a finger on a little girl. Out of luck, Joe.'

'Okay.'

Joe sat down in the leather chair opposite Drage's desk. Heavy nights showed in his face – booze and little sleep; his eyes were dark and his features seemed ragged, as if he were slightly out of focus.

'I can help you a little better with Olsen.'

'Go on.'

'Tranter will want to know where you got this.'

Joe laughed. 'Up my ass, but not up yours: is that right?'

'I'm trying to make good.'

'I'm not pissed off with you, Frank. You didn't know; I accept that. I've got other things on my mind.'

'They've had reports of Olsen being seen in London: a dozen sightings – four believable, apparently. One, he was getting out of a cab in Notting Hill. Two, he was in the street somewhere about there – west-eight, west-eleven. Three and four, he was at Paddington station – or just outside. He's had a haircut and he's growing a beard – if it's him. The hair and the beard might be a reason for thinking it's not, of course, but apparently the reports were very positive. How in hell do people do that – recognise someone they've never met?'

'The age of television,' Joe said. 'Everyone knows a famous face. How was he dressed?'

'Either blue trousers and a lighter blue shirt, or black trousers and a green shirt. Or not, of course. Carrying a sports bag or suitcase or briefcase. They think he might have tried to pick someone up at the station. A kid – teenager. There's a description of the kid, but he's gone; they'll check people sleeping rough later tonight. Listen, Joe, I'm working a close contact here; I asked for the favour because I'd made things difficult for you.'

'Call it even,' Joe said. 'Forget it.'

*Back there*, he thought. *Are you, Henry? Back among the waifs and strays ...*

Some time between nine and midnight they appear, the dreck, the drifters in London's main-line stations; the flotsam. Commuters are safe indoors, apart from a few swots and stop-outs and adulterers. Late passengers go to and fro, or sit in the fast-food cafés looking edgy and eager to be away.

Then you see them, in ones and twos, in small groups, or lone figures drifting between the bar and the concourse; in the winter, setting up with blankets and bottles and last week's financial supplements. Sometimes they drift out to the street, like scavengers trying farther afield, but they're back within the hour.

Some carry a touch of affluence like brief fame; most of these sit in the bar like shadows, though some get noisy for an hour until they're elbowed through the door. When the police make a tour of the station, everyone fades out then fades back in later, like a time-delay shot in a sepia-tone movie.

The runaways come off the platforms and stand still, staring into the station lights as if they could read their futures there.

Joe sat just inside the bar drinking vodka and a cold beer. A fur of dust was pasted to the condensation on his glass and he could feel the hot soreness of pollution at the back of his throat.

A train came in and a thin crowd flowed into the concourse, then immediately diminished as people found taxis or went down to the tube. Joe watched a girl at the tail end who faltered, looking this way and that before moving towards the bar; it was clear that she couldn't decide what else to do.

A cheap shoulder-bag for clothes and whatever she would have saved from a fire; enough money for a beer. The lighter you travel the further you get. She was wearing jeans and a little flowered blouse that stopped short of her midriff; her navel was pierced and decorated with a thin, silver ring. Joe watched as she settled in at a booth, her face pale and empty and shiny with sweat.

He looked beyond her to the door and saw others: a boy begging, a girl asleep in a doorway, another girl stoned and smiley, barely feeling the ground beneath her feet. How would they be missed? he thought. They were like photographs you find in the loft-space, or bills paid a decade ago. If someone made a bonfire of them, how would you ever know they'd gone?

He wasn't expecting Olsen to show, not now. Earlier, he had roamed the station like a man sent to meet someone he hadn't seen for years, peering into the crowd, weaving between tables in the café. They were everywhere, the lost souls, human chaff, and Joe imagined Olsen doing what he was doing — watching them like a predator under cover, deciding when to move, which one to select.

As if that thought had been the spur, Joe left the bar and went out onto the concourse, walking close to the boy begging, the girl sleeping, the girl stoned and dreamy; close enough to touch. He gave the boy some cash. He touched the stoned girl's arm and she turned a dozy smile on him. How easy to say, 'Want a meal? Want to score? Want a place to stay?'

You take them away and they don't leave a trace.

When Joe returned to the bar, the girl with the navel ring was looking directly at him. He realised that she must have been watching him through the open door. He gave the look back to see what that would do, and it drew her in. She stood at his elbow, dumping her bag on the floor, and waited to be asked.

'Shall I get you something?'

She told him what she wanted, speaking quickly in a low voice. That was all she said. When the drink came, she drank it. When Joe walked out of the bar, she walked out with him. They found a by-the-hour hotel and checked in.

Joe asked her name and she said, 'Katherine', then laughed as if Katherine would be a better name for someone else. She went into the bathroom and came out again, naked, water from the shower still beading on the tips of her hair and trickling across her shoulders. She was like a wraith, the slightest swell to her hips, a neat, dark stripe of hair under her belly, her breasts high and round and giving the slightest sway as she walked towards him.

'Just for tonight,' she said, 'the room. I just need a room for the night.' She lay on the bed and Joe lay beside her; she took his hand and folded it between her legs.

They lay for a while side by side, his hand on her; then she turned her back to him and slept.

For an hour he listened to the faint saw of her breathing and watched her shoulder rise and drop. The light was out, but the curtains were a bad fit and in the glow from the street she showed up pale against the white sheet, like an image fading from an old photograph.

Joe got up and she stirred, turning onto her back to reveal touches of shadow: her eyes, a fall of hair on her cheek, the place where Joe's hand had lain. He stood alongside her and drew a line across her throat with his cocked index finger.

*How easy, Joe.*

He could hear Olsen's voice, the little, dry cough of laughter.

He drew the line again, but longer and slower.

*How easy. And where would she be? Where would she have gone to, Joe? Katherine who got off the train from nowhere, Katherine Nobody who followed where you led, Katherine who was wet from the shower and warm between the legs and slept like a child, dreamless, out like a light? If she were dead ? If your finger had turned to a blade? How strange. How strange.*

He traced the line of the cut once more, making her put up a hand, in her sleep, to brush his hand aside.

*Do you see, Joe? Can you feel it now? Can you see how it would be to take her there, take her all the way, and watch as she changed? Can you tell how deep a mystery it is? This moment, wet from the shower and warm; next moment, dead like the dog.*

*To understand you have to see it happen again and again. Who's there? It's Katherine. What's there now? Something else, something different. Can you say what, Joe? Can you solve the riddle?*

Again, and harder, his fingernail scoring the skin. She woke suddenly, her body shaken by a tiny spasm as she felt the discomfort; she sat up and moved away from him. The ring in her navel caught shreds of light from the window and gleamed like a blind eye.

Joe put a hand in his pocket and brought out some money. He said, 'I meant to give you this.'

'All right.' Katherine took the notes and folded them into her hand.

'I'm going now. The room's paid for.'

'Fine,' she said, 'all right with me.'

He went downstairs and into the street, then walked without bothering to know where he was going. After a while he came down to the river and leaned on the embankment wall to watch lines of light shake out across the water. The brickwork was still warm from the heat of the day.

*Katherine from Nowhere. I'll meet you there.*


It had started out as an even-handed drinking contest, but Paul Harker had given up long since. He was in a club several streets from Fellgate Cross watching Steve Tranter's intake of whisky go from epic to mythical. Tranter could talk, but he couldn't stand.

He said, 'He's a dead man. Morgan's a dead man. Do you know how? Know how he's dead?' His voice was a low sing-song, the syllables blurring into one another.

Harker shook his head. 'Time for a taxi, Boss. Time to go, isn't it?'

'You know how. Firms. There are firms. They've got a price scale.' He had trouble with 'price scale' and had to say it three times. 'Broken leg, broken arm and broken leg, fingers, eyes, teeth …' Tranter paused to laugh, then paused to drink. 'Five grand, last time I heard. Dead man on the ground and five thou in someone's pocket. Not much is it? Five.'

One way and another, Harker had been listening to it all night. He said, 'Morgan's out of it, Steve. There'll be an inquiry. His career's fucked. Let it go.'

A silence followed during which Tranter began to sway to and fro in his seat, staring at the floor; he might have been in a trance, or moving to music in his head. Harker reached for his glass, fumbled it, but managed to get a drink into his mouth. A cigarette haze eddied round the lights and drifted in great floes towards the partly-open door.

'That was a long time ago,' Tranter said; suddenly his eyes were dark with recollection. 'We pulled him out of the car after he rolled it, and he stood up.'

Harker said, 'What? Who rolled it?' He thought that somehow he'd missed the beginning of Tranter's story.

'How did he get out of the car? I don't know. It was just a chase. Pissed, I expect. We were going to pull the bastard over, so I expect he was pissed. Hit the pedal. Didn't want to lose his licence.'

'Who was this, Steve?'

'He rolled it on a bend, doing eighty. Rolled it one complete turn. We pulled him out and he stood up. Denis Mitchel hit him, then I hit him. We were fizzing.'

Tranter's voice tailed off and he seemed to fall asleep for a while. Harker went to the bar and called a cab, then stayed there lodged on a stool until the barman nudged him and nodded at the door.

The cabbie had all his windows open; Tranter came awake in the warm slipstream.

'We hit him and we couldn't stop. He fell down and we started kicking. Couldn't stop. Couldn't. We were laughing. Would've been all right if he hadn't got out of the car. Hadn't stood up.'

He said something Harker couldn't understand, his voice falling to a rumble.

'I don't need to hear this, Steve.'

'It looked like –'

The cab radio was tuned to an easy listening station. Harker said, 'Switch this shit off, okay?'

'What?' the cabbie half turned in his seat; he looked worried.

'This shit.'

'Okay.'

'– it looked like he died in the car.'

'Don't tell me this, Steve.'

The cabbie found a music station playing songs from the sixties.

'They thought he died in the car.'

Tranter laughed and let his head fall back against the seat. He went to sleep instantly, his mouth wide open, breathing like someone sucking up mud. After a while he toppled sideways, his head falling into Harker's lap. Harker put his hands flat on Tranter's back and shoved, tipping him into the well between the seats.

The cabbie looked back, worried. 'He all right?'

'He's asleep. He's fine. Let's hear the music.'

Harker lifted his foot and stamped down on Tranter's head; after a moment he did it again.

'Bastard!' he said, and stamped a third time.

Get that drunk, you're likely to fall; you're likely to fall and not remember.

The cab driver said, 'You like this group? You like loud music, right?'

Harker put his head out of the window into the slipstream, eyes closed, hair flowing, a man swimming underwater.

Like Joe, Olsen was watching the river. The boy in the blouson had taken him to an apartment in Chelsea Harbour and introduced him to Ken and Tony. They both had south London accents with a larding of something smoother, something learned, on top. Their uniform was short hair, a tattoo apiece, and an earring for the right lobe. Tony had a girlfriend called Susan and they seemed to live there like a little family – posters on the walls, a kitchen full of equipment, tweed armchairs and sofa; except that it was really a little business.

Ken had taken Olsen to the third bedroom and stood at the door like a hall porter.

'We mind you,' he'd said, 'we take care of you until you ship out, so there are a few house rules. You can't leave the flat. Not that you'd want to. But you can't. Anything you need, just ask. Almost anything. We don't bring whores in. This is your last stop before wherever it is you're going and it's too much of a risk. Whores talk to policemen. Your sake and ours, okay? There's no phone in this room, but you can make calls through us. That's it. That's all. You'll be here a couple of days. Do what you like – TV, music, whatever. You don't have to stay in your room. One of us will always be around. Susan's with Tony. She's Tony's. You'll find she's not here all the time – does a bit of fetching and carrying, errands, stuff like that. If you want special food she'll bring it in for you. Okay. Got everything you want, now?'

Olsen had slept, like a man with nothing better to do. Now he was watching the night pass. At about four a.m. he

366

went into the kitchen to get a drink and found Tony sitting at the table watching American football on a counter-top TV with the sound turned off.

'If you're awake,' he said, 'I'm awake.' There wasn't much humour behind the words.

Olsen opened the fridge and took out a bottle of mineral water. He said, 'Bad luck'.

'Where are you going?' Tony asked. 'Where will you end up?'

'Somewhere safe.'

'You know something? You're one of those people that look like themselves. D'you get me? You see a picture, then you see the person, and that's how they look. With most people it's not that way.'

'Where did you see the picture?'

Tony laughed. 'Every-fucking-where.'

'And you're sure it was me?'

'Like I just said.'

'It wasn't me,' Olsen said. 'You're wrong.'

He poured a glass of water and took the bottle with him. In the hallway he passed Tony's bedroom, the door showing a wedge of light. Olsen opened the door a little further and looked in. Susan was lying naked on top of the covers, asleep, with her back towards him; a bedside lamp was still on, the bed littered with magazines.

Susan's knees were drawn up, her backbone tapering down to the dark cleft of her ass. Olsen went into the room, rounded the bed so that he could see her face, and knelt beside her. She had large breasts and a plump belly; her mouth was pursed as if on the edge of laughter. Olsen put his face close to hers on the pillow and felt the waft of her breath.

*Hello, Susan. Hello ... You know something? I lied to Tony. Yes, I lied. Lied about the picture he saw. It was me! I look exactly like myself!*

He put out his tongue, like a rude schoolboy, and licked her lips leaving them wet. He waited a beat, then another, until sleeping-Susan's own tongue came out in response, just the very tip, the pink tip, and collected the moisture.

He got up and left, pushing the door wide and leaving it like that.


Connie's message was the most recent on Joe's machine. He dialled 1471 and collected the number of Marianne's apartment. He dialled and let it ring for a long time. Marianne answered from a thicket of sleep.

'Let me talk to Connie,' Joe said.

'Jesus Christ, Joe.'

'Just let me talk to her, okay? I'm sorry.' There was a long pause. He said, 'I'm sorry, Marianne.'

When Connie picked up Joe said, 'Michael Bianchi, boathouse loft on the river, lots of money, paints pictures. Okay? That's so we don't spend a lot of time with you hedging and me getting angry. Now you talk, because I don't understand anything.'

Connie heard the bleakness in his voice. 'I couldn't tell you until I knew what there was to tell.'

'Yes you could. That's crap. You could have told me you'd met someone and he was rich and you liked sucking his cock. You could have told me that. You could have told me that you were falling in love with someone else. Are you?'

'Why do you think I'm at Marianne's?'

'Don't do that!' Joe yelled. 'Don't be fucking waspish with me. You tell me you want to split up, Christ, you even tell me you want a divorce, you tell me you're moving out, what you *don't* fucking tell me is that you're jumping on some bastard's dick in public parks, so spare me the injured fucking tone before I get angry.'

'You followed me.'

'No I didn't.'

'How do you know?'

'About the park? Someone else followed you.'

'Someone you paid to –'

'Henry Parr Olsen followed you.'

The silence between them drew out in darkness, a held breath, until he heard her say, 'Ohhhh!' – an ugly, wrenched little sound.

'He took a photograph; it was a very good photograph; well, it was good of you, with your legs spread and your tits out, but I couldn't see all that much of Michael. Just a snap, you know, but a great likeness. Later he told me where I could find it.'

'Joe, I'm so –'

'You looked as if you were having loads of fun.'

'Joe, I wanted –'

'You looked really chipper.'

'It wasn't supposed –'

'You looked full of it, if you know what I mean.'

'Stop it, Joe.'

'Why are you at Marianne's?'

'Because I don't know what to do next.'

'There are things I need to know.'

'Yes.'

'Is it serious?'

'It feels serious. I don't know whether it feels permanent.'

'How did it happen?'

'I met him.'

'He picked you up.'

'Yes, that's right. He picked me up.' She paused. 'I must have wanted him to.'

'I suppose you must. So ... I'm returning your call, remember?'

'Joe ... We'd better meet.'

'Is that a good idea?'

'I don't know. What else would we do? Never see one another again?'

'Isn't that a possibility?'

'No ... Is it? It hadn't occurred to me.'

'What do you want, Connie?'

'Let's meet, Joe. I need to see you.'

'What do you want?'

'Can we meet? I think we ought –'

'What do you want?'

'Joe, it isn't –'

'What do you want, Connie? Don't you know? Aren't you sure? Let's meet when you've worked it out, shall we? Because I've still got that photograph and I look at it a lot. I don't want to, but I do. And even if I tore it up, or burned it, it would be a long time before I could look at you without seeing the woman in that photo. Maybe never, Connie. Maybe never. So I'm not up for a cosy chat and I'm not likely to wish you well in your new life. At the moment, I'm much more likely to wish you a fatal accident. You and Bianchi.'

He put the phone down and waited for her to ring back, but she didn't.

# Twenty-Nine

**T**ranter sat still in the incident room while people went round him, talked round him, worked round him. Pain like a needle-track went from his eye to his jawline; his teeth ached; there was a raw patch above his ear where Harker's boot-heel had taken off the hair and a patch of skin. If he stood up to get to the coffee dispenser he felt achy and breathless.

He thought it must be anger that was making him breathless, because there was more anger in him than he could cope with. It was in his face and in his stillness, and that was why people were moving round him with such care. He drank five cups of coffee, then asked Carol Mitchie to bring him the case files. He read them through for an hour, then got up and went towards the door.

'Back later,' he said to Paul Harker.

'Need company, Boss?' Harker's expression was unreadable; empty face, empty eyes.

'No.'

Tranter's voice was barely audible. He walked out of Fellgate Cross and got into his car, then sat there for a while with the driver's door open. He'd never felt so bad, but then epic drinking gives epic hangovers. His body felt leaden and hollow at the same time and he was sitting still in the hope that he wouldn't shortly throw up for the tenth time that morning. Strangely, his face didn't look too damaged, despite the blows he'd taken from Joe, but it hurt like hell. He tried

371

to remember when he'd fallen last night, and where, and what he might have hit.

He switched on the engine. If it wasn't so fucking hot, he thought, I wouldn't feel as lousy as this. If it would rain, I'd feel better. He took a flask from his pocket and gave himself first a sip, then a swallow. It was better and worse. The scotch rose and fell in his gut as if it were registering his temperature.

Out in the traffic, he opened his windows and drove fast when he could. From time to time his head swam and he saw lights dancing at the corners of his eyes.

You bitch, he thought, it's time someone put you through the fucking mill. Let's see what you've got to give.

He hadn't really expected to find Donna at the flat. Harker had taken a statement from her as soon as Olsen had escaped; taken a statement and written her off. It had been clear to Harker that she'd been frightened. She'd told Harker she planned to go away and Harker had believed her. Tranter thought she might have more to offer. He thought she was a tight-mouthed bitch and he wanted the chance to get close to her again: within arm's reach.

When the door opened a girl stood there with a child on one hip. The child was crying and there was a radio playing in the flat, so Tranter had to speak louder than was comfortable.

She said, 'I never knew her. They've gone.'

'I know. Let me come in,' Tranter said.

'I never knew her. There's nothing here that belonged to them.'

Tranter had already shown his warrant card. He asked, 'What's your name?'

'Norma.'

'Full name.'

'Norma Haines.'

'Where's Mr Haines?'

Norma looked at him and laughed.

'Draw any state benefits at all, Norma?'

She sighed and stepped aside and let him in, then waited while he made a cursory search of the flat. Things hadn't changed much since Donna and Olsen had lived there: the same furniture, same carpet, same mirror over the fireplace. Tranter glanced at his reflection: a pale, jowly face carrying brown and yellow bruising just under the skin on one side, the nose a little swollen. Norma watched him watching himself, her image floating up behind his.

'I told you they never left anything.'

Tranter nipped at the flask. 'You know who they were?'

'Not really. I know he killed someone. It wasn't here, though.'

Tranter switched off the radio. It made the child's cries seem louder. 'She left you a forwarding address.'

'No.'

'For letters, stuff from the social.'

'Nothing.'

Tranter sat down. He said, 'I don't want to make things difficult for you, Norma.'

'Yeah? Why not make them easy then?'

Tranter passed a hand over his eyes. He so much wanted to hit her that he thought it was the next thing he would do. Definitely. Instead he took out some money and dropped it onto the floor.

'Is that what you mean?'

She picked it up: two tens. 'Not really. I meant more,' and she laughed as if Tranter might see the joke and join in.

He said, 'Push again. Push one more time.'

Norma heard what was in his voice and her smile stopped. She gave him an address on the Hartsmede Estate.

If you look bad and you feel bad and you don't much care what happens next, you can afford to take a risk.

Tranter walked onto the Hartsmede Estate and climbed two flights of concrete stairs to the first walkway. The footsoldiers had picked him up, but knew this wasn't serious; this wasn't *business*. One on his own: it wasn't a bust and it wasn't an arrest. Soon they stopped watching.

Tranter went up two more flights and onto the second walkway: you're boxed in, there, and it's a long drop. A twinge of cramp took him round the ribs, a stitch, and he put a hand to the place as he knocked on Donna Rees's door, then knocked again. He could hear the TV but no one came to the door. Still holding the place where it hurt, Tranter stepped back to brace himself against the parapet of the walkway, lifted a foot, then shoved forward, kicking out at the same time. He took the door just under the lock and it splintered away from the jamb.

The kick, the splintering, went all the way back, churning in his head and chest like an after-shock. He kicked again, yelling with the effort, and the door flew back, hitting off the inside wall before half-closing once more. Tranter went in, shoving the door back into its frame to shut it.

Donna was lying on a sofa watching TV. The sofa and the TV were the only two items of furniture in the room. She looked up when Tranter walked in, then propped herself on an elbow. She said, 'Shit', in a faint, slurry voice and pulled herself into a sitting position. She was almost too stoned to move.

Tranter gave himself a nip from his flask; it seemed to help with the breathing. He said, 'I need to talk to you, Donna.'

The flat was fiercely hot and airless, windows slammed shut, stale smells hanging like streamers. Donna lolled on one arm of the sofa, then slipped a little way towards the floor, dragging the hem of her short-'n'-low sun-dress up to the hip. Looking down on her, Tranter could see her breasts where the neck of the dress sagged.

'We need to talk.'

Her face was blurry, like a bad snapshot, but she shrugged as if to say: Go ahead. Talk.

'Where is he, Donna? You knew him. Where would he go?'

A moment of lucidity struck her, like a clear patch in fog, but she had trouble making the words make sense. 'You think I knew. Him. If I did. Know. How didn't I. Know. He killed. Some people. How not that?'

'Yeah, I read your statement. Crap. Didn't believe a fucking word. You're lying. I'm here to stop you lying.'

Donna stared at him, but there was dead ground behind the eyes. After a moment, she toppled slightly, her head falling against the arm of the sofa, one arm dropping slackly into her lap. She was asleep in the passing of a second. Tranter slapped her lightly across the cheek, then again, much harder. Her head rolled, but she didn't react.

There was a deep muscular ache in his arm; he thought he must have wrenched it when he kicked the door. His head hurt, and he felt strangely light, as if his feet weren't making proper contact with the ground.

'Fuck this,' he said. He took a pull from the flask and sat next to Donna on the sofa. 'Fuck you'. He leaned over and reached into the front of her dress, holding first one breast then the other, holding them hard, his teeth gritted.

'Fuck *you!*' he said again, as if he might, as if he could, but there was no response in him except anger.

Joe was parked by the low wall at the end of the street; he looked back towards Michael Bianchi's boathouse and wondered what in all hell he was doing and why he thought staking the place out would help. Why staking out Michael Bianchi would help.

*It feels serious. I don't know whether it feels permanent.*

Is that right? Well, to hell with you. What makes you think you've got the choice?

Maybe, he thought, it would be a good idea if I stopped to work out what it is I want. Because that's not easy to know. After seeing the photograph, after thinking back on the lies.

But it was easy. He wanted everything back; he wanted the past rewritten as if neither of them had ever lied, or been hurt, or thought the other a fool.

When Michael emerged from the front door, it was almost an anti-climax. Joe saw how good-looking the guy was, how his clothes managed to be both plain and stylish; but he also saw a raggedness that was clearly unaccustomed: the stubble, the tired walk.

He almost thought, *You poor bastard, I know what you're going through.* Almost.

The thought he actually had was, *Die well.*

Michael was walking directly towards Joe. He stopped a couple of cars away and got into the Mercedes, slamming the door and starting the engine in a series of rapid movements, like someone who'd suddenly grown angry. As the Merc drew away, Joe got out and walked along behind it. By the time it turned the corner at the top of the street, he was standing in front of the boathouse. The lock on Michael's flat wasn't possible, but the door that led to the storage area alongside was a credit card and a shove.

The room smelt musty. It backed onto the river and rows of water-lights skipped on the walls. Joe walked between years of lumber and shafts of dusty sunlight, getting to the far end of the room where a short flight of stairs ended at a large bolted trap like a horizontal door. He hit the bolts with the heels of his hands, collecting rust-stain and bruises, then turned over boxes and cartons until he found a hinge-bracket and slammed at the bolts with that.

They came free. Joe supported the door one-handed and

lowered it slowly, then heaved himself up into the near corner of Michael's studio.

Where Connie lives. Where Connie lives.

He wandered through, looking at the paintings, at the furniture, at the bits and pieces of sculpture, at beachcombings, at photographs, at plates and glasses, at books, at a shallow blue ceramic bowl holding a prism, at CDs, at the view from the balcony, at an enormous, carved blanket box against one wall, at lamps and videos and last week's newspapers. Looking at her life.

At Connie's clothes in the bedroom. Connie's Tampax in the bathroom cabinet. Connie's handwriting on a forgotten note: *I'll be late, let's eat out.*

He went into the living area and sat in all the chairs, sat on all the sofas, sat at the table as if he were expecting a meal. He took some cheese from the fridge and ate it. He lay on the bed.

No one came. The place was airy, full of sunlight, vaulted ceilings crossed by a structure of black beams, walls of whitewashed brick decorated with hangings or with Michael's paintings. It looked like a terrific place to live. He went back to the kitchen area and drew a glass of water from the tap.

When the phone rang he moved to answer it, but the machine cut in after the first ring. It was Connie. Joe stood utterly still, the full glass in his hand.

She said, 'It's me.'

What all lovers say. All husbands and wives.

'Listen, I'll see you later.'

A silence followed. Joe drank some of the water because his mouth was parched.

'I'll see you later, because I promised I would.'

Connie hung up and Joe finished the water. He thought he might stay for that – for Connie's appearance later. He

377

thought he might stick around until Michael Bianchi came back and suggest they wait together. No, not suggest. Insist. He might insist and insist and *insist* until the son of a bitch could hardly draw breath, hardly think, hardly see for the blood.

He rinsed the glass, wiped it with some kitchen towel and restored it to its place. He got down through the trap, then swung it back and bolted it.

It was his – the faint imprint of a body on the bed; but which of them would ever realise that?

The TV was showing the lunch-time news. Tranter had slept for a while, now he came to feeling lousy, needing a nip, needing a piss. When he returned, Donna was sitting on the floor, as if she'd fallen. He nudged her with his toe and said, 'Still with the living?'

She stared, seeing him for the first time, and made a move for the door. He caught her arm.

'I need to know where he is.'

'I don't know.'

She was still groggy, a bit stoned, a lot scared because Tranter looked like hell with his bruises, with his hollow eyes, with the sweat standing up like a poisoned dew on his pallid skin.

'Try to know. Help yourself to know.'

'He went off on his own, time after time. Up west gambling. Or else he'd leave for his shift before midnight and not be back the same day. I don't know where he went.'

Tranter pushed Donna back towards the sofa, putting himself between her and the door. His arm still hurt from when he'd come through the door, or else he'd slept awkwardly; he massaged his bicep and worked his shoulder against the pain.

'He's gone,' Donna said. 'Don't you realise that he's gone?'

Tranter stepped forward and slapped her: a clumsy, off-centre blow that caught her high on the head; she stumbled and stepped back, her hand up to deflect the next one.

Missing his shot made him laugh. He went round the sofa to get at her and noticed how hot and heavy he felt, how his head buzzed. She feinted towards the door and he lurched at her, grabbing the front of her dress, then hit her twice with his bunched fist, though he couldn't feel the blows as they landed.

Donna cried, turning her face away. She said, 'You think I knew him? I didn't fucking know him, did I? Think – if I'd known – *think*. I fucking slept with him. He killed people and I was with him all the fucking time. I didn't know anything, did I? Did I? Leave me alone. Fucking leave me …'

Tranter couldn't tell what she knew or didn't know, not any more. He felt angry and ill and he wanted someone to hit. He swung again and the blow travelled beyond Donna's face out into thin air, because he had somehow lost his balance and his swipe was carrying him on into a moment of airy suspension, of dizzy free-fall, before he struck the floor. He sat up, kneading at his arm and thinking: Tired, tired, too much booze, too much shit, too much of every-fucking-thing, and then the pain sizzled across his chest like a brand and he couldn't really breathe at all.

He got into a crouch but slipped back; he bent slowly forward, wrapped over his own arm, and said, 'Christ-oh-Christ-oh-Jesus-Christ-oh-fuck-this-what's-this-fuck this –' and rested his forehead with infinite care on the floor.

The pain was everything, bigger than everything, and he made a reach for his flask because he felt that might do some good, that might help to –

Donna watched him as he died, though she didn't know that was happening, not at first. When he hadn't moved for several minutes, she went to the bedroom and packed the few things she owned. She didn't know it, but she was panting like a runner.

She went back to the living room to collect her stash from its hiding place. Tranter was still on his knees, though he had tipped forward a little and slid skew-whiff, one shoulder dropped, head resting sideways on the floor, his wide-eyed stare meant for no one.

# Thirty

*Tak* is integrity; *Shing* is sincerity – the name of the old man who sat in an underground room and drank green tea. The boy in the black blouson was Ah Lok, and *Lok* is joy. Integrity and sincerity send forth joy.

Tony and Ken sat at the kitchen table while Susan cooked a meal and listened to Lok telling them what would happen next. Every window in the flat was open, but the air hung heavy and still, unbreathable.

'Tomorrow night he leaves here. Someone will come at nine o'clock with a car: black seven-series BMW.' He gave the registration number and Ken repeated it to him.

'This person will not be Chinese. You will travel with him as far as the coast.' Lok's English was barely accented but bore the prissy formalities of the classroom.

'Not Chinese,' Tony said. It was a question.

'From Scotland.'

'Just him.'

'Yes. And you. By the time you reach the coast it will be dark. You don't drive all the way to the dock, but you take him to the boat. It is a slight walk. The Scotsman goes with you. The Captain has the name Peters. This is the name you can use for him. We require a picture of Peters and our friend on the boat, a polaroid photo. This guarantees you the rest of your money.'

Tony put a hand to his side and shifted his position. He was wearing a holstered gun clipped to his belt; if he forgot and leaned back, it dug him under the ribs.

'Where on the coast?' he asked.

'The driver knows. After you deliver, then your job is over. Peters will catch a tide at midnight or so. You need not wait.'

Lok's mobile phone trilled from the pocket of the black blouson. He listened, spoke two words of Cantonese, then got up.

'I will talk also to our friend, but now I must come back to do this. Perhaps two hours, I am not sure.'

He was leaving fast, almost at the run, speaking over his shoulder. In the hallway, he got back on the phone, sounding urgent; the slammed front door cut his voice off. Tony raised a hand in mock salute and laughed. 'Busy, busy ...'

'It's money for nothing,' Ken said. 'They're good payers, never miss, no trouble, no complications.'

Tony nodded towards the door, meaning Olsen. 'I don't like him; fucking psycho. He gives me a bad feeling.'

'He's merchandise,' Ken said. 'He's cash in hand.'

Susan was making chops, salad, baked potatoes, just like any good *hausfrau* with her men to feed. She was wearing a halter top, her breasts heavy in it, and a cotton skirt that just brushed the backs of her thighs; she made Tony hungry every time he looked at her.

A flicker of light caught the corner of Ken's eye and he glanced towards the window. In a moment it came again: sheet-lightning, far off, like a vast camera-flash against a blue-black evening sky.

Susan said, 'How do you think he likes his meat?'

Olsen was sitting at the window watching the lightning when Susan took his meal in to him. She had opened a bottle of Frascati cold from the fridge. There was no sound and no hint of rain.

She stood there with a tray in her hand while he pretended

not to notice her. 'You're getting a holiday then, are you? Sun and sand, booze and babes.'

'Want to come?' Olsen asked.

'Why not?' She laughed, waiting for his response, but it didn't come. 'What's it like?' she asked.

*What is it like to –? How does it feel when –? Won't you tell me your dark secrets?*

He turned towards her, now, his smile thin and viperish.

'I'm sorry, Susan, I didn't quite catch that.'

A little jolt of excitement hit her: a game; they were playing a game. She looked at his narrow, handsome face shaded by rough stubble, the full lips, the soft brown hair falling forward across his cheek. She remembered what she'd read about him and it frightened her, but there was something about being frightened and feeling safe at the same time; something about playing games with a monster.

'What's it like? I asked you, what's it like?'

Olsen got up and took the plate from her. His hand brushed hers and she felt the shock all the way back to her womb.

Finger cocked, he touched her throat.

'You're asking the wrong person, Susan ...'

Touched her lips, her eyelids.

'... aren't you?'

She ate her own meal in silence while Ken and Tony watched TV. Her lips, her eyelids still bore the graze of his touch.

An hour later she went back, to find Olsen sitting in an armchair facing the door as if he'd been waiting for her. She saw that he had almost finished the wine.

'This time tomorrow,' she said.

'This time tomorrow?'

'You'll be somewhere else. Leaving at nine. Down to the coast. Out on the water by midnight. All your troubles over.'

'I haven't got any troubles.' Olsen was looking thoughtful, his mind elsewhere.

'Good for you.'

Susan crossed to where he sat and crouched down alongside his chair. She peered at him.

'What do you want, Susan?'

'Hair brown, nice mouth, blue eyes.' She put a hand on his chest and drew it down to his belly. 'No flab.'

Scared and safe; the breath caught in her throat and she disguised it as a laugh. 'I wanted to see what you really look like. Up close. You should have read the things they said about you.'

'I did.'

'The Fiend.'

'And what do you see, Susan, now that you've been up close?'

'You look the same as anyone.'

'Of course I do.' He laughed, a cough, *hek-hek-hek*. 'I'm the man in the street, my love. I'm the boy next door.'

He smiled and got up, brushing her aside. Ken and Tony were watching television in the main room. Olsen said, 'I have to go out for a while.'

Ken looked up in surprise, then laughed. 'No go. Sorry. Something you want? I'll get it for you.'

'You didn't tell me I'd be leaving tomorrow night.'

'What difference?'

'There's someone I have to see before I go.'

'No.'

'So I'm going out now. I'll be back later.'

Tony picked up some keys from a low table and left the room. He walked to the front door and deadlocked it; when he got back Olsen was holding out his hand for the keys.

'No,' he said, 'you don't understand. I'm going now and I'll be back later.'

Tony stepped back to Olsen's step forward: a little pavane.

384

Susan was coming into the room behind Tony and stopped dead seeing the look on Olsen's face. Tony reached back and drew the gun, holding it out stiff-armed so that the muzzle was almost brushing Olsen's temple.

Nobody moved, nobody spoke.

Tony bumped the side of Olsen's head with the gun, moving him back, then grabbed his shirt and turned him suddenly, whacking him against the wall. He screwed the gun muzzle into Olsen's neck, just below the jaw.

'You don't get it, do you? Tomorrow night – that's when you go. Until then you're banged up. Okay?' Olsen didn't move a muscle. 'Okay?' Tony asked again.

Ken went to stand alongside Tony. He kept his voice low and reasonable. 'You don't make the choices. How could you? Too many people are taking risks. You can see that, can't you?'

The pressure of the gun against his face had made Olsen turn in profile, his gaze directed at the floor. He didn't offer any comment.

'Ease up,' Ken said.

'I want to be sure this fucker understands what I'm saying.'

'He understands.'

Tony dug the gun in harder. 'Tomorrow. You leave here tomorrow. Yes?' Olsen was silent. The gun jabbed him again. '*Yes?*' Tony yelled. '*Yes? Yes? Yes?*'

'Yes,' Olsen said.

Susan came all the way into the room. Ken glanced at her, then back at Olsen. 'How did you know it would be tomorrow?'

'I heard the Chinaman come and go. He was giving you instructions. What else would it mean? I ate my meal, slept for a while. Then I thought I'd go out.'

'Asshole,' Tony said. He backed off a pace and lowered the gun to his side.

Olsen gave a little laugh. 'Ever kill someone?' he asked.

Ken said, 'You can stay with us – watch some TV, go back to your room, whatever you like. But don't fuck us around, okay? Please don't do that.'

Tony holstered the gun. He looked at Susan and laughed, nodding in Olsen's direction.

The windows wide to the night, the night leaden, the last shreds of daylight showing against ragged red-black clouds on the far horizon.


'I forgot this,' Susan said. She was holding another bottle of wine and a fresh glass.

Olsen laughed gently and shook his head. 'I don't want it.'

'I'll leave it for you.'

'Your boyfriend's quick with a gun.'

'Who did you want to see?'

'A friend of mine. Joe Morgan.'

'I could get a message to him,' Susan said, 'after you've gone. Tomorrow night.'

'No good.'

'Is he a good friend?'

'He's the only friend I've got,' Olsen told her. 'The only real friend. The only one I talk to – do you know what I mean?'

'Yes.'

'Do you have a friend like that?'

Susan shrugged. 'I have friends.'

'Joe and me,' Olsen raised his hand, two fingers twined, 'we're like that.'

Susan poured some wine into the glass and drank it herself. 'Why did you say that to him – "Ever kill someone?"'

'Why do you think?'

'He never has,' she said. 'He never killed anyone, but he hurt a few.'

'What are they doing?'

'Watching television. A film. I don't know … some film.'

386

'And you're standing in front of my cage wondering what would happen if you put your hand through the bars.'

He got up, suddenly, fast enough to be right in close before she thought to move. His hand went from her face to her throat, then down to her breast. She smiled into his face, close enough to kiss but not kissing. After a moment, he slipped his hand under her skirt. She allowed him to linger there for a moment, then pushed him away.

'No,' he said, 'no ... well at least we can have a drink together.'

He walked past her to get the wine, then turned and hit her with it, a long, fluid arc flying from the bottle-neck as he swung.

She said, '*Oh, I –*' a plosive sound that was all breath and pain, then walked a couple of paces like someone going downstairs, then fell sideways, knee, hip, shoulder and head. Olsen picked her up and sat her in the chair facing the door; to heighten the effect he pulled off her halter top and her skirt and her underclothes and threw them across the room.

He knelt in front of her for a moment, nuzzling her face with his own. A thin odour of sweat came off her, stronger and sharper when he put his face into her lap. He liked its pungency, the reek of viscera.

'Oh, Susan,' he whispered, 'I wish I had the time for you. To watch you change. To help you with your mystery.'

The bottle had lost a lot of its wine – a lot of its weight. He looked round the room for another weapon. His attaché case? Too clumsy. The knife inside? Too much risk of blood-splash; he needed to be away fast, no time for a clean-up. There was a desk in the room with a wooden chair tucked under. He broke its struts and pulled one of the legs free from the frame, then went and stood on the blind side of the door.

You could see the heaviness in Susan's body: her chin fallen onto her shoulder, her breasts drooping on the rib-cage. Inertia made her vulnerable; she looked more naked than a naked person usually looks.

The film must have been absorbing because it was a good fifteen minutes before Tony came looking for her. He called her name a couple of times from the hallway, then opened the door, stepping through and half-closing it before her image properly registered.

When he saw what he saw he couldn't believe it, couldn't take it in properly, and because of that he made a basic mistake – he took a pace towards her. Olsen moved in the same moment. Tony's instinct kicked in and he began to turn, began to yell, began to reach for the gun. The chairleg took him behind the ear, staggering him, but he turned anyway, his mouth wide, the sound choked off.

Olsen hit him again, bringing the blow back from a long way like a man splitting logs. The sharp edge of the chairleg took Tony on the forehead, a clean vertical that left a dent in the bone and brought a wide wash of blood to his face. Olsen danced away, like a child on the foreshore teasing the tide. Tony fell backwards, all dead weight, his head striking the arm of Susan's chair, then her thigh, then the floor. He lay still, apart from a fevered twitch that shook his left hand. Olsen eased him up and took the gun.

In the same moment, Ken and Ah Lok entered the room.

It must have happened while Olsen was in the act of hitting Tony – a *blip* on the doorbell, Ken answering it, then both men hearing a sound from Olsen's room and Lok reading the sudden troubled look on Ken's face.

Now they came in together, crowding the door, Lok reaching into the pocket of his blouson. Seeing the gesture, Olsen shot him from where he knelt alongside Tony. The bullet angled up and took Lok in the hip, turning him. Olsen shot again, twice, kidneys and spine, so close that the sounds

388

merged. Lok fell forward against the door-jamb, legs out backwards, torso propped up, like a diver. Ken stood still.

Olsen said, 'Where are the keys?'

'In the kitchen.' Ken sounded uncertain, but not about the keys; his was the voice of a man who didn't know what would happen next.

'Let's fetch them.'

They went together. Ken pointed to the keys – they were lying on the low table – then moved to the other side of the kitchen while Olsen pocketed them.

'No,' Olsen told him, 'I want you back in there with them.'

'Don't kill me,' Ken said. 'What have you got to gain from killing me?'

It was a stupid question. Olsen supplied the answer, 'I get clean away,' he said, 'no complications.'

Ken said, 'You shot someone from Chinatown. No complications?'

Olsen nodded. 'I know.'

They were walking towards Olsen's room, Ken speaking over his shoulder at first, then turning and walking backwards. It hollowed his guts to have Olsen behind him holding the gun.

'How're you going to get out of the country now? How are you going to get to the coast?'

'I know. It's a problem.'

'Yeah it's a problem. Big problem. Maybe I can help out. I could get you to the coast. The guy who's taking you across – his name's Peters. I've got the location.'

Olsen shook his head. 'I don't think so. He's expecting us tomorrow night – yes? – which is too late. I've still got my passport and a little money.'

'You could use some help, though, couldn't you?'

'Shut up,' Olsen said.

Ah Lok had moved a little – he was lying on his back a few

389

feet into the room, his eyes open, a gun in his hand. Olsen side-stepped and aimed, then saw that the man was dead. He looked round. Such stillness in the room, as if the air had grown thicker. A line of blood had run from Susan's nose and dried on her chin.

'Sit down,' he told Ken, then: 'No, lie on the bed.'

'Don't,' Ken said, 'please don't.'

'Nothing's going to happen to you.'

When Ken was full-length on the bed, Olsen stripped Lok and Tony of their belts and tied Ken's hands and feet.

'Nothing's going to happen to you. I don't kill for the sake of it.'

He took Ken's own belt and made the man's hands fast to the bed rail.

'I don't kill for fun.'


People had heard the gunshots, but no one wanted to find out what had happened. Olsen emerged a couple of minutes before the armed response team arrived outside the building. He walked away, briskly, a businessman in a hurry clutching his attaché case.

He got a few streets clear then went into a pub and ordered a drink. The place was crowded. He made a phone call from the bar amid music and raised voices and the electronic whirr of fruit machines.

'Joe? I just wanted to say goodbye. Goodbye, Joe. And to say that everything's for the best.'

He was speaking to Joe's answer-phone.

'I hope you'll remember me, Joe. I hope you'll remember the things we spoke about. You understood, didn't you? I know you did. I saw it in your face. It made all the difference, Joe. I want you to know that. It made all the difference to me that you understood, that you knew what I meant about their changing, about the mystery, about the dead dog.

'Everything's for the best, Joe. You'll find out. Connie will find out. Remember what I said to you once about crying over Danny? About wishing I had Danny back, wishing I could have him back and start again? That's how I feel now, Joe. I wish it had just begun – my first phone call to you, your voice on the line, you and me getting closer and closer every time. I wish I had Serena back, and Christine … all of them. All of them, and you.

'Here's another memory – when I told you about Serena waking up – almost awake, not quite – and me sitting astride and waiting for her with the knife; and she started to sing the song she was singing as she went to sleep? Remember, Joe? *Remember*? Such a moment. Oh, *such* a moment! And I shared it with you, Joe, and I knew you understood. I watched your eyes as you savoured it. *Savoured* it. Joe, I'm so glad to have given you that, so glad I could give you a taste of that, a smell of that.

'All good things must end and everything's for the best. Isn't it, Joe? Everything's for the best. Connie will realise that. All good things must end.'

He put down the phone. A man was sitting at the other end of the bar watching him and reading his expression; just a man with nowhere better to be, nothing better to do. He thought that this guy on the telephone must have been talking to someone he loved; someone he didn't expect to talk to again. The watcher had been in the same position himself and he thought this guy was a poor miserable bastard who deserved a drink … but he didn't want to hear another man's problems. He caught the barman's eye and drained his glass, ready for another. When he looked again, Olsen had gone.

Michael stood on the far side of the studio and spoke to Connie across that enormous space.

'I'd like to say, Do what you really want to do. I'd like to say, Do what's best.'

'I know.' She couldn't keep still – was pacing round the furniture, back and forth between the windows, circling the table, keeping to her side of the room as if getting close to him was more than she could risk.

'Let's go away,' he said. 'Anywhere but London would be good for us.' It was a naked plea; he had no defences left. 'It wouldn't change anything.'

'I'd like that. I can't.'

'Not yet.'

'That's right. Not yet.'

Michael said, 'What then? What shall we do? What will happen?'

'Perhaps I should go away. Just me.' And as she said it, she knew it was the only thing to do.

Joe sat in his car and watched the lightning. There was something to hear, now – a dull, blurry sound like someone ripping fabric.

He dialled a number and, when Michael Bianchi answered, hung up.

He was so restless and angry and sad that he knew he would do something. Get drunk, perhaps: bust in on someone's quiet life.

Olsen stood on the doorstep smiling, attaché case in hand, like a salesman making a late call.

When Michael Bianchi answered the door, Olsen showed him the gun and stepped inside. Michael started to speak, but Olsen shoved the gunbarrel against his mouth, then laid a finger on his own lips like a schoolteacher calling for quiet.

Connie started to speak as Michael walked back upstairs into the studio, then Olsen came into view, and the breath went from her body in a rush.

He said, 'Do you know who I am?' and she nodded because speech was beyond her.

Michael said, 'Let her leave, okay? Let her walk out of here.'

'No, no …' Olsen shook his head, looking half-puzzled, half-amused, as if Michael had missed the point. 'No, she can't go. There's something she has to see.'

Michael felt ill. He asked, 'See what?'

Olsen looked at Connie. He opened his attaché case. 'Everything's for the best,' he said, 'you'll come to understand that in time.'

He took out the parcel tape and tossed to it Connie. 'Round his hands and feet, then over his mouth.' She didn't move, so he put the gun against the back of Michael's head. 'Or I could kill him; that would be another way of keeping him still.'

He walked Michael to the sofa and stood a little way off while Connie bound him. Then he took the tape from her and fetched a wooden chair, placing it opposite the sofa and a few feet back.

'Sit down, Connie,' he said, and ripped off a length of the tape. 'Everything's for the best. You'll see.'

*Bust in on someone's life …*

Because something has to change, something has to move. He and Connie and Michael Bianchi would talk, and out of the talk would come a resolution: a life-change. He drove to within a couple of streets of the studio and stopped the car. He tried to see himself doing that – talking, accepting, then leaving having decided that everything was for the best, and the thought sickened in him. He turned the car round and started for home, feeling anger beginning to replace reason; anger and a sense of waste.

*All good things must end.*

If Joe had collected his messages, he would have heard the

genuine sense of regret in the man's voice: someone who would miss Joe like a friend, like a brother.

A great branch of lightning grew in the sky to the south of the city and thunder rolled over the water.

Joe thought what it would be like to kill Michael Bianchi: to wait for him one night and simply take him out – a mugging that went too far. Would that give him Connie back? He thought that, yes, it probably would; or at least, it would give him a chance.

The storm circled but the rain wouldn't come. The cloud-cover was brown and bruise-yellow; all the cars had their lights on. A sluggish slipstream stirred Joe's hair.

Michael Bianchi dead and Connie mourning him … Joe shoved the thought aside and wondered what the truth of it would be. In a year, what will things look like then? In two years, in ten? What will happen if I do nothing? If I leave them to each other? If I go away?

Because the thought was intolerable, because it made him want to weep, because it sent a shock-wave of anger through him, he turned the car again and drove back to Bianchi's studio.

Anything rather than nothing; the worst news rather than no news.

As he parked in the cul-de-sac and walked back up the street, the edge of the storm brushed the city, a thick blatter of rain that dampened the pavements then suddenly stopped.

He stood in the street outside looking up at the tall windows and, almost as if he'd hoped to, saw Henry Parr Olsen float across the glass like an image on a screen.

# Thirty-One

Olsen had explained to Connie, though she hadn't really seemed to want to listen. Explained that Joe was his friend and that friends should help one another. He explained about changing — about how Michael would change, how she would share in that.

She had made noises behind her taped-off mouth and Olsen had nodded, saying: 'Yes, you're right; it's a mystery. It's like the mystery of the dead dog.'

He had taken his equipment out of the attaché case and laid the things he needed side by side on the table. There was a long mirror on the wall behind Connie, and he had been able to see himself making preparations. He'd paused a moment to glance up as he placed each item.

Now he would undress, putting his clothes out of harm's way, and give Connie back to Joe. Give Connie back to Joe but take Bianchi for himself

He looked at her. He looked at Bianchi. He looked at his own reflection in the long mirror and gave a sudden laugh. There was no denying the fun in this; no pretending that he wasn't excited. Connie's eyes were dark. Her fear was a deep, seismic quake that ran through her body and shook it; all the time she was making sounds: cries, pleas, the only argument in the world that could stop him from doing what he intended, all reduced to a muffle of breath and broken syllables.

A fit of dizziness overtook him and he lost focus for a moment, then he saw that Connie's gaze was not on him, but beyond him. The gun was on the table along with the knife and he turned towards them, turned fast, seeing Joe coming at him out of nowhere. He grabbed the knife as Joe collided with him and swung it up, going for the face.

They both went down. The knife took a nick out of Joe's face between the temple and the corner of his eye, a little triangular gouge, then Joe got a hand to Olsen's wrist and held hard. They rolled once and Joe used the momentum to get to his feet. He was still holding Olsen's wrist, as if he were helping the man up, and he managed to get a couple of kicks in, one high under the armpit, the other flush on the ribs.

Olsen twisted away, bringing Joe down on top of him. His arm doubled and the knife sank into his bicep under Joe's weight, then continued to cut a long slice as they slid on the wooden floor. He gave a tremendous shout and shook Joe off, then leapt up and began to run to and fro, smacking against walls and furniture, sending books flying, screens, small sculptures, vases, photograph frames, adrenaline pouring through him like raw energy.

Joe tried to cut him off, but the man was too erratic to second-guess. Connie's eyes were wide with signals: *There's a gun! Go for the gun!* but Joe could only see Olsen spinning round the room, howling with pain and outrage.

'Why Joe?' His voice was a shriek of indignation. *'Why Joe?'*

He ran towards the door, the knife flying from his arm as he twisted against the pain, the energy in him still boundless. Joe went after him, laying hands on an arm, a shoulder, a fistful of the man's shirt. Olsen flung out a hand, turning at the same time, jumping –

*Why Joe?'*

– a leaping turn like a discus thrower's, and took Joe across the eyes, knocking him backwards over a chair. His head came off the floorboards like a bounced ball and his ears filled with noise: a thundercrash, or else something only he could hear. He sat up slowly while Olsen galloped to the far end of the studio and through the door.

Joe got into a crouch, tilting like a sprinter, and ran a few paces, then pitched onto his face. He got up and ran again, but it was like running in a dream. His legs couldn't find a rhythm; they seemed to tangle beneath him. Finally, he sat on the floor with his head between his knees until he stopped seeing double.

Just one of Michael Bianchi. Just one of Connie. Just one of himself, reflected in the long mirror on the far wall, as he walked over to set them both free.

Olsen went down to the river and walked along the towpath for half a mile. His wound was burning now the numbness had worn off; he held his bicep like a man gripping a staff, squeezing the lips of the cut together. He found a dark place of scrub and trees and took off his shirt so that he could bind the cut with his belt, pulling the leather against the buckle and winding it round twice before tucking in the loose end. Then he put his shirt back on and shoved his hand between the second and fourth buttons as a makeshift sling. The position contracted his bicep, tightening the belt and reducing the bloodflow.

*Why Joe?*

His attaché case was still at Michael Bianchi's studio. It held his passport and his money.

Lines of light from apartment blocks on the far bank fell across the water, breaking and reforming in the swell of a high tide. The storm had circled round and was on the way back: lightning flashes beating against the night sky, the thunder following fast.

Olsen felt light-headed; he felt as though he might throw up. There was nowhere to go, nowhere he could think of, but he kept walking anyway.

397

Joe and Michael and Connie sat in a tight circle, as if too much space between them might let in terrors no one could resist. They sat on the floor just in front of the sofa where Michael had lain. Connie had found a rhythm for crying that might be endless, a massive circular journey of crying that would take her beyond herself, which was where she most wanted to be.

Michael had his eyes closed. His left hand was holding Connie's right. Joe's head was lowered, so that he could look at the floor because looking at anything else was too demanding just at that moment. His right hand was holding Connie's left. He was wearing a little delta of dried blood that started just back of the eye and spread in shaky lines to his neck.

Michael said, 'What are we supposed to do?' He was speaking slowly, his voice just audible.

Joe nodded, as if it were time for that question. 'Make a phone call.'

'Okay.'

Connie broke their grasp and wrapped herself in her own arms. 'Nothing –' she said, or perhaps it was, 'No one –' then abandoned words for tears again.

'Yes,' Joe said, 'you make it.'

'Why not you?'

'I won't be here.'

'What do I tell them?'

'Give a description of what he was wearing. Tell them he was hurt.'

'No, I mean –' Michael paused. 'Where are you going?'

'To look for him.'

'He was going to kill me. He wanted Connie to see it happen.'

'Yes. It's my fault. I'm sorry.'

'Is it?'

'If I'd thought about it,' Joe said, 'I'd've guessed he might come for you.'

'For me and Connie.'

'For you,' Joe said. 'He came for you.' He got to his feet, still feeling the rock and swim of a concussion. His hands came away bloody. 'I need to wash.'

Connie said, 'Don't go.'

'He's mine,' Joe said, 'if I can find him.'

'Don't go.' Her voice was tinny with crying.

Michael got up as well. 'Do I tell them you were here?'

'Whatever you like.'

'He won't come back.' It was more of a question.

'No,' Joe said. 'Anyway – don't stay here.'

Michael laughed and shook his head. 'I'm sorry,' he said, 'I ought to be able to do something about it, but I feel as if I'd touched a live wire. I don't feel safe.'

'It's shock,' Joe said.

'Do you feel it?'

'A little. You'll be all right.'

'Sure,' Michael said. 'Oh, yes, sure.'

Connie said, 'Don't go,' and stood up to take a hold on Joe's arm.

'Well,' he said, 'I don't have a lot of choice. Not really,' and took her fingers off his arm, one by one.


There were people coming out of smart restaurants, leaving theatres, leaving cinemas, looking for taxis. After that first hint of rain the storm had retreated; now it was closing again. Olsen walked through the crowds, his shirtsleeve stiff with blood, and no one looked twice.

On patches of waste ground, under iron bridges, in doorways, the city's derelicts drank themselves as deep as they could get. Deeper. He was a wraith to them, less substantial than their own fevered dreams.

In the backstreets close to King's Cross, the whores

worked the kerbside in spike-heels and lycra tight as bandages. He was nothing to them, with his shambling walk and his dead look. They climbed into the cars as they stopped, ready with their litany of fuck-or-suck for the ten-minute trick.

He was a hundred yards light of the station when the storm finally broke: warm, fat raindrops chasing along the asphalt, coming thicker and faster, the thunder right overhead now, the lightning filling the air with a tang of cordite. The sound of the rain was like engines, and steam came off the streets in great scrolls. Olsen was wet to the bone, clothed in water, breathing water.

He walked onto the concourse and found a place to settle. His usual place. A train came in and he watched the passengers arrive. Waifs and strays. Lost people, like himself. Looking for a way out, like himself.

The rain was hammers and gongs.

Travellers from the last train were joining the crowds of late-nighters: refugees from the weather, people wanting tube trains, people wanting taxis, losers, dossers, boozers – chancers like Joe Morgan, who went against the flow of the crowd, looking always towards the perimeter where little villages of blankets and bedrolls were beginning to be built by those who would dig in for the night.

Faces went past like snapshots. A girl crying. A girl angry. A man laughing. His friend suddenly getting the joke. A woman with a mouth on her like a red machine. A man looking backwards for someone lost.

Joe cut a mazy path between them.

An old man slack with drink. A woman arguing. A woman refusing. And suddenly, like the joker in the deck, Henry Parr Olsen, watching as he was watched. Joe sat down next to him and noticed the way Olsen shied away to avoid contact.

'You need a doctor for that.'

'It's fine,' Olsen told him.

They sat in silence for a while. Joe said, 'Are you looking for a room?'

Olsen laughed. 'A room. Yes, I'm looking for a room. I need somewhere to stay.'

'Are you hungry?'

'What do you want? What's in it for you?'

'I might want you to make a few trips for me. Carry some bits and pieces. You know.'

'Sure. I know.'

Joe had forgotten how it went from there, so Olsen helped him out.

'You get a rake-off, do you? On the deliveries I make?'

'Enough to keep me going,' Joe agreed. 'A job and somewhere for the night – that's my offer.'

'Sounds okay,' Olsen said. 'How do I know you're straight?'

'Look, I'm tired. If you don't want it, plenty of others will.'

'No,' Olsen said, 'I want it. Of course I want it; where else would I go?'

Joe got up. 'It's not far from here.'

'Have you got a car, mister?'

'Yes, I've got a car.'

'Good. Because I'm tired. Tired and my arm hurts and I need somewhere to lie down.'

Joe said, 'What's your name?'

'Henry.'

'Come on, Henry.'

The rain was dead straight; it was falling with such force that it made its own wind. You couldn't see through it to the other side of the street. Joe had left his car at the back of the station close to the whores' parade. He and Olsen walked to it like men drowning. The girls stood under brick archways, grouped like a flock of shy exotics.

Olsen fell into the car, giving a shout of pain. Joe started the engine and drove slowly through the downpour, his wipers going double-time.

'I'm a stranger in a strange city,' Olsen said.

Joe nodded. 'Everyone comes to London in the end.'

In Joe's conservatory the light was murky under the weight of water. Olsen sat in a cane chair close to the glass, side by side with his reflection. From time to time his eyes drooped; his face was waxy yellow, bruise-smudges under each eye, the colours of an orchid. Joe sat with him in silence. The rain on the glass roof was like flywheels and jackhammers and pistons.

'You understood, Joe.'

'Did I?'

'You understood. That was important. That was more important than anything, except the mystery itself.'

Half an hour passed. Olsen said, 'They'll be looking for me.'

'Yes, they will.'

'I thought it would be what you wanted, Joe – me to kill him, kill Bianchi and turn your life around. I thought it was for the best.' He laughed. 'I was clear: passport, money, even a destination. Except for Bianchi, I was away clear.'

The rain slackened for a while, then came round again harder than ever, thunder at ceiling-height, lightning bleaching the sky. Olsen seemed to doze.

He said, 'Me sitting here, you sitting there. Like old times. I ought to say, "Forgive me, Father, for I have sinned". I ought to ask you to absolve me, Joe. Is that the word? Absolve.'

'I'm not a Catholic,' Joe said.

'Neither am I. Not a believer. There's nothing after this, Joe. Dead meat. Dead dog.'

'Help me, Joe. Can you help me out?'

'What do you want?'

'Some help, you stupid fucker.' He sounded weary, now, irritable. 'Help. I need some help. Someone to help me. I need a helping hand.'

Joe went to the bathroom and came back with paracetamol, aspirin, temazepam, all he could find. He put them into Olsen's cupped hands —

'Thank you, Joe.'

— and fetched a glass of water from the kitchen.

Olsen scooped them up three or four at a time, rapidly, mechanically, pills then water then pills, tossing his head back with each swallow. The temazepam bottle was untouched: Connie had filled the prescription but never taken them. Her white nights had become part of the tempo of risk and of change.

Olsen took everything.

He said, 'It's like shutting a door that locks behind you.'

Joe waited with him while he fell asleep.

The rain had stopped; the sky had cleared to show a half-moon and a thin cloud-wrack; the air was cool.

Joe went out to the garden and sat in one of the sodden canvas chairs. He could see Olsen through the glass wall of the conservatory, but dimly: nothing more than a pale image projected onto a screen, the screen lit by a fading light.

He seemed to move, but Joe couldn't be sure; seemed to twist and slump in his chair, but Joe thought it must be the effect of cloud movement; seemed to turn his head to stare at Joe, but of course that was impossible.

Joe sat like a statue. He could barely feel the to and fro of his own breathing.

The phone rang. Two hours later? Three? The answer-machine kicked in and Joe could hear Andy Bishop's voice, though not what he was saying.

It rang again an hour after that, but the caller hung up.

Joe went into the conservatory and looked at Olsen. His head was thrown back and there was a smear of puke going from mouth to shoulder. More was on his clothes and on the floor. He'd been dead for a while.

Joe got close to him and looked harder. A terrible stillness, a terrible silence.

'Dead,' Joe said. 'Dead like the dog. Now you know the difference. Now you *know*.' He nudged Olsen's arm. 'How does it feel?'

# Thirty-Two

'What will happen to you?'
'Nothing. I've been written off. What will happen to you?'

'I'm going away for a bit, Joe. As you see.'

Connie was packing, something she hadn't done for Michael but was prepared to do for herself. Joe touched her face, her hair.

'Going with Michael.'

'Going alone.'

He was just wise enough to not say 'I could come too. Let me come too'. He was wise enough to not say, 'Where are you going?' and 'Will you phone?'

Connie dropped some clothes onto the bed then sat down, looking as if she'd been winded.

'I have nightmares every night. I think about it every day. Most of the day.'

'He's dead.'

'In a way,' she said. 'In a manner of speaking.'

Again she asked, 'What will happen to you? What will you do?' and it chilled him because the question seemed to mean that Connie wouldn't be there to see for herself.

'I'm out. Nothing else. Fisher and I agreed a good story. There's no one to dispute it or care about the truth.'

'You saw him dead?'

'Yes, I did.'

Connie put a hand over her eyes and wept for a brief

while, then suddenly she was all business with her packing, finding hangers and a dressy pair of shoes, and a couple of sweaters in case the evenings were cool. She didn't fool Joe with her brisk efficiency, and she didn't fool herself.

She said, 'I'm sorry I had to come here like this.' She meant to collect her clothes.

'Don't worry.'

'I spent the night at Marianne's.'

'Don't worry.'

She locked the case and Joe carried it to the door. She said, 'You could give me a lift.'

He drove her the first leg of her journey, across London to the station. Train to the airport. Plane to wherever it was.

Three days after Olsen's death, four days after Tranter's. George Fisher had worn an expression of stony regret. 'I'm sorry about this, Joe.'

'No one's sorry,' Joe had told him. He'd walked out of Fellgate Cross for the last time without thinking about it.

The storm had brought in breezes and cooler air for a day or so; now the swelter was back. Joe drove with all the windows open, a soup of pollution swilling in and out of the car. Connie sat beside him, still, silent, expressionless, her hair flying. He put a cassette in the machine, but she switched it off.

'Will you tell me, one day, what it was that he wanted? What he wanted from you.'

'I'll try.'

'I think I need to know.'

Joe liked the sound of 'one day'.

Her train was in and he walked with her to the barrier.

She said, 'There's never been a time when I didn't care for you. That wasn't it.'

Joe shrugged. 'Will it help – going away?' But in the

moment that he asked, he was no longer sure what he wanted or how he felt or what he would do.

*What will happen to you?*

Connie kissed him and started down the platform.

Where will I be, he thought, when you get back? How will you ever find me?

He watched Connie as she wove a path between the passengers who were leaving the train she was about to board.

People in a hurry, people with purpose.

But at the far end of the platform, always later than the rest, always uncertain, always wary, the waifs and strays, their bedrolls and backpacks, their lost looks, their hope against hope.

Getting to her carriage, Connie walked towards them, walked among them.

From that distance, she could have been one of them.